PROLOGUE

Aisling

Four years ago

I pull up in my car outside of the glossy black walls of the condo and stare wide-eyed at the scene in front of me.

My bed is outside of the building.

My *bed* is *outside* of the building.

"Oh no, no, no," I whimper, quickly hopping down from the driver's side, pristine white trainers hitting the blacktop at a fast clip. My car keys dangle loosely from the fingers of my left hand as I slip my phone from my pocket and swipe through a barrage of notifications.

How on earth could I have possibly missed it?

When I finally find the notification that I'm looking for I press the heel of my palm against my forehead, internally squealing.

"They changed the delivery time?" I whisper in defeat to no-one in particular, aghast at the prospect of having to carry a multiple-part queen-sized bed into my condo all on my own.

My twin brother Connell has an apartment on the floor below mine, but right now he's at his first official freshman week of Carter Ridge University's Division I football training, meaning that he's about to be so busy that he might not even be coming back to the condo tonight. As much as I would love to use my baby sister privileges and wrangle him into bringing my bed up to my room for me I don't want to bother him during his first week of college football when it's his dream to play in the NFL – especially when, knowing Carter U's track record, being on the team here is one-hundred percent going to make his dream a reality.

Sniffling, I click the lock button on my cell and hold it limply as I stare at the bed.

It stares back at me, looking way too smug.

So maybe I should have been more on top of tracking the delivery, but how was I to know that they would bump up my slot – and not just by a couple of minutes but by, like, four whole hours?

I fold my arms across my chest, car keys jangling as I drum my fingers against the soft cotton sleeve of my baby pink jumper.

There are no two ways about it. I'm going to have to carry the pieces into my building, solo.

Silently weeping, I pocket my phone and my keys, reassessing the situation in front of me.

I had been exclusively counting on the delivery drivers to help me get my new purchase inside the condo, onto the elevator, and then, ideally, unwrapped and placed exactly where I needed them to be in my currently-bedless bedroom. Carrying multiple extremely large wooden panels on my own was not something that I had anticipated happening after my first morning of cheer practice as a Carter U freshman.

The perks of being the heiress to the real estate family

Wildest Dreams

SAPPHIRE HALE

ALSO BY SAPPHIRE HALE

The Phoenix Falls Series

Where We Left Off
Where It All Began
Where We Go From Here

The Carter Ridge Series

Pinkie Promise
Wildest Dreams

CONTENTS

PLAYLIST

Blank Space (Taylor's Version) – Taylor Swift

Creek Will Rise – Conner Smith

I Had Some Help – Post Malone ft. Morgan Wallen

We Got History – Mitchell Tenpenny

Risk – Gracie Abrams

Boy From Carolina – Ashley Kutcher

You Found Me – The Fray

Close To You – Gracie Abrams

More Surprised Than Me – Morgan Wallen

Sleepy – Ashley Kutcher

Lover – Taylor Swift

To access the official Spotify playlist visit www.sapphireauthor.com

who owns the condo that you're about to spend your four years of college living in? If you want to upgrade your bed from princess sized to queen sized, they'll put that cute little princess bed into storage for you and totally give you free rein to decorate your room to your heart's content.

But the downside of being the heiress to the real estate family who owns the condo that you're about to spend your four years of college living in? Your parents are crazy busy and live nowhere near the beautiful mountainous small town that you chose to move to.

If only they'd been able to stick around for a couple more days so that they could help me shift this thing.

But whatever. I'm a big girl. No time to dwell.

I flip my ponytail, roll up my sleeves, and give a piece of bed-frame its first shove.

Oh my God, did they drop this thing in wet cement? Immediately panting, I move around to a different corner of the frame and wrap my hands around the edge of the headboard.

On one, two—

I release an unintentional squeal. The bed doesn't budge one millimetre.

Okay, so this thing weighs about fifty thousand tonnes. I swipe my wrist across my forehead and crouch into a small squat, but not before glancing up at the dark thunderclouds overhead, ominously warning me to get pushing, pronto.

I just need to get each piece of the bed inside of the building. That's my starting point. Just shove them inside as quickly as I can and then when Connell gets home—

I push against one of the panels with all of my strength, the impossible strain making my whole body tense and burn. I moan, gritting my teeth, and continue pushing as hard as I can, borderline growling with exertion by the time that I hear a deep voice rumbling behind me.

"Need some help with that?"

My palms are already sparkling with perspiration, and

when I glance over my shoulder they become a hundred times slicker. They slip on the plastic wrap encasing a piece of the carved wooden frame and I fall onto the blacktop, dark gravel instantly biting into my palms.

There's a guy standing about ten feet away from me, watching me from under the brim of a worn-in khaki baseball cap. He's wearing a short-sleeved shirt that's stretched wafer thin over his broad chest, and a pair of matching grey running shorts that his swollen thighs are protesting out of. He's got to be at least six-four, but I'm so dizzy right now that he might be taller. His face is tan and strikingly handsome, and it looks as though he hasn't shaved for a couple of days.

And he's got the biggest biceps that I've ever seen.

From the sheer size of him he could honestly be anywhere from the age of eighteen to twenty-five, and with the heavy rise and fall of his chest as we watch each other I can only assume that he's just finished a brutal work-out session.

His eyes do a slow sweep of my body before he averts his gaze, blushing crimson.

Interesting.

With slightly shaking arms I push myself up from my bent over position, wiping my palms on the thighs of my grey leggings as I stand to my feet.

He pulls off his khaki baseball cap and sweeps a large hand back through his hair. It's thick and dark-looking in the pre-thunderstorm light, although the sides are closely shaven in a no-nonsense military cut. His eyes stay trained on the blacktop until he's confident that I'm no longer bent over, and then his eyes flash back to mine, curious and unflinching.

"Looks like it's going to rain. You trying to lift those?"

His voice is deep and rough, with a quiet country intonation. He glances at the bed-frame behind me and takes one tentative step forward.

"Yeah," I admit, my voice light and breathless. His gaze slides back to mine and his chest lifts a little higher.

"Want some help?" he asks, taking another slow step forward. He has a kind of lazy cowboy swagger combined with a quiet, understated confidence. "Name's Tanner, by the way. I live around here."

My eyes widen involuntarily and I stare up at the condo in wonder. *How have I been living here for almost a week and not bumped into this gorgeous guy until now?*

Reading my mind he breathes out a quiet laugh.

"No, not this building," he says. "I live around *here*."

He tips his head to the side, in the direction of the imposing mountainous ridges that Carter Ridge is named after.

"I'm from Carter Ridge, I mean."

My breathing halts and my eyes widen, unblinking.

Because one thing about me?

I *love* small towners.

I mean, in theory at least. Technically, before I visited Carter Ridge I wasn't sure that they even existed. It's my biggest secret, something that maybe even Connell doesn't know, because to me small towns encapsulate everything that I have ever wanted, but could never have.

Tradition. Comfort. Privacy. Intimacy.

And most of all? Beyond the beautiful porches, up through the forest and into the mountains?

Something *wild*.

"You're from Carter Ridge?" I ask breathlessly, resisting the urge to fan myself.

His eyes rake me up and down, and he widens his stance, cheek dimpling lazily. "Yeah. And you're new in town."

I blink, enchanted, and clutch a hand over my chest. "How did you know?" I breathe.

He huffs out a laugh and rumbles quietly, "Trust me, I'd remember you."

In the next second a cloud breaks overhead and a few rogue droplets begin speckling the soft fabric of his shirt.

He glances down at his big barrel chest, swiping his palm over the tiny wet marks. When they don't disappear he sighs quietly, rubbing more firmly.

I perch gently on one of the higher edges of the bed-frame, letting out a shaky exhale as I watch him stroke himself.

"Look, uh…" His voice is so deep that he has to clear his throat, flexing out a large hand before raking it through his hair again. "Don't mean to impose. But if you don't have anyone to help you get those inside, I can take a look at them for you, if you'd like."

As much as I would love to spend my morning watching this gorgeous, small town muscle mountain carrying things for me, I can't help but think that the wooden frames will be too heavy for one guy on his own.

"That's super kind," I tell him honestly, "but I think that this is more of a two-man job."

He watches me for a moment before rumbling, "No such thing."

His eyes hold mine for a couple of seconds, before he tips his chin at the headboard leaning against the wall of the condo.

"Want me to give it a try?"

I don't think that it's possible, but I also kind of want to see if he can do it.

I twist my lips, trying to hide my smile, and I nod. "Yeah, okay."

I can tell that he knows that I don't think he can do it because by the time that he's finally two feet away from me he's subtly rolling his shoulders in preparation. When his gaze catches mine his mouth lifts in amusement.

"Can you, uh…?" He looks down into my eyes, humour and heat sizzling in the air between us. He tentatively holds out his khaki cap, silently asking me if I can hold onto it for him.

"Oh, sure, of course," I breathe out, trying to not burst into flames when our fingers accidentally brush against each other.

It's like a zap of lightning. Coarse against soft.

Tanner grunts, quickly averting his gaze.

I re-cross my legs, swallowing nervously.

Tanner moves over to the headboard, leaning back slightly as if sizing it up, and then he crouches down so that he can get one hand positioned beneath it, the other firmly gripping the top. With one deep guttural sound he suddenly heaves it up, turning it ninety-degrees so that he's holding it vertically. Then, when he's sure that he's holding it steady, he meets my eyes and gives me a jerk of his chin.

"This is fine. Thought it was gonna be heavy."

I try to subtly pick my jaw up off the floor.

He nods his head toward the entrance of the condo and says, "Want me to take these inside? I can drop them in the foyer for you, if you want. I'll do it fast, save them from the rain."

I blink up at him curiously, watching the rain sparkle on his cheekbones.

I mean, having him carry them inside for me would be super helpful...

And it doesn't exactly hurt that he's, like, totally gorgeous...

"I'd love that. And that's so considerate, thank you," I say to him, getting to my feet and jogging to the front door. I swipe my key against the fob, opening it up for him.

Tanner carefully manoeuvres the first large piece of wood into the glossy entrance of the condo and, with an almost smile, he murmurs, "No problem."

He sets the headboard gently against one of the dark ruby walls and briefly surveys the foyer before looking down at me again. He jerks a thumb back toward the entrance.

"Want me to grab the rest for you?"

He's so to-the-point that I can't help but smile. And after searching my eyes, he slowly allows himself to smile back.

And his *smile*?

It's the most handsome smile that I've ever seen.

"Yes, please," I say gently, following him tentatively to the doorway.

I watch from my sheltered spot as he trudges toward the largest piece of bed-frame, braces his muscular thighs, and hauls it upright.

By the time that he's carrying in the final section of wood, the light rain outside has turned into a pretty heavy fall downpour.

He carefully sets the wooden panel beside all of the other pieces and then he stands to his full height, watching me from under his lashes. He wipes his palms against his shorts, staying silent as we watch each other.

I glance down at the pieces of my soon-to-be bed now sitting patiently in the luxury foyer, then outside at the late September rain.

Then I slide my eyes back up to meet his.

He looks down at his cap hanging loosely from my fingers. Under the heat of his stare I dangle it a little more provocatively.

"You got a name?" he asks suddenly.

I swish my ponytail. "I have two, actually."

His mouth curves into a smirk before he gives me another sweeping once-over. "What, a first name and a surname?"

I'm fully smiling now. "Yeah."

Tanner shakes his head but he's smiling too.

"Right," he says. "So this is what I'm thinking, ma'am–"

A surprised laugh escapes me. "Ma'am?" I repeat, my chest all warm and sparkly.

He watches me carefully as a handsome smile lifts the corners of his mouth.

"I don't know your name yet, do I?" he rumbles, before teasingly adding, "What would you rather me call you? Sugar?"

My chest shakes as I laugh, heart racing as he smiles down at me.

"So, look," he says, shoving his fingers through his hair. "I'm gonna assume that you don't wanna sleep on your new bed down here in this foyer tonight. But I also don't wanna step out of line and come across as inappropriate... but I'm gonna offer anyway. Unless you've got a mover coming in here in the next few hours that I don't know about, I'd be more than happy to... if you'd like me to, I can..."

He tugs at the neckline of his shirt, a red flush beginning to spread up his cheekbones.

"What I'm trying to say is, with the bed, if you want... because it's heavy for you... not that you're not strong, because you're in, like, fuckin' beautiful shape–"

Wow, he's adorable.

I breathe out a laugh and decide to put him out of his misery.

"Yes," I tell him, a little dimple popping in my cheek. "That would be really great. I'd love you to help me carry it upstairs."

"Yeah?" he rasps, searching my eyes to make sure.

I nod. "Yeah."

"To your room?"

"Yes, please."

He takes a deep inhale and we watch each other for a few long moments, the gentle patter of the rain the only breach in the rich silence.

And deep down? I'm secretly really excited at the thought of having this unbelievably tall and handsome small town boy – who blushes at the thought of going into a girl's bedroom – *in* my new bedroom.

He wraps his fists around the nearest panel and jerks his chin at me politely. "After you."

Without another word I brush past him, heading toward the condo's glossy elevators.

I hear a grunt as he hauls my bed-frame off the floor and then his heavy footsteps as he follows behind me.

I smile to myself as the elevator doors ding open.

How funny. I'd wanted to spend the day with my brother, hanging out with him and all of his football buddies like I did back in high school. But it's starting to look like something *way* better has just fallen into my lap.

The reason why I picked Carter U as my college in the first place is because there's nothing that I want more than a small town life. Sure, there have been upsides to being a prep school girl but at the end of the day that's never the lifestyle that I wanted – mainly because of the people that I've always been surrounded with.

Because those hotshot prep school boys who got the best athletic training and scholarships?

They're the biggest players that you'll ever meet.

I mean, I would know, seeing as my brother Connell was one of the biggest players of all. But even though I love him, I don't *ever* want to be caught up with someone like that – hence why at school *I* was the biggest player of all.

Never caring, never settling down, and never getting hurt.

Because if you're the heartbreaker? You can't get your heart broken.

I step inside the elevator and smile up at Tanner over my shoulder.

He steps in right behind me, his chest swelling as he returns the smile.

What a cutie, I think to myself as I press the button to my floor. *A total sweetheart too. Definitely not a player.*

I bite into my bottom lip as the doors slide closed.

In twenty-four hours I would wish that I'd never met him.

CHAPTER 1

Aisling

Present day

My fingers tighten around the wheel of my brother Connell's 4x4 and Fallon, my best friend riding shotgun in the passenger seat, lets out a high-pitched yip as we lurch over another uneven patch of off-road terrain.

"Are we there yet?" she squeaks, hand gripping into the safety handle above her window.

I look through the rear view mirror and peek at the emerald green larch trees behind us. They've already completely obscured the road that secretly off-shoots onto the lower forest's dirt track, leading to a magical suntrap and Larch Peak's secluded seven and a half mile lake, right before the land trails up into the sloping mountains that the small town was named after.

My eyes drop back down to the navigation system on the dash and that little red pin indicates that we're almost at our destination.

"It's got to be, like, just through here," I say reassuringly, although admittedly I've never actually visited this Larch Peak property. I chew nervously on my bottom lip as the car lurches over another undulation of crunchy rocks. "I mean, it isn't as if no-one has ever been here before. So why the hell is there no signage on the road?" I lift my right pointer finger off the wheel and my glittery golden polish sparkles in the summer morning sunlight. "First port of call on this renovation? Make a road sign so that people can actually find their way here."

Fallon makes a nervous sound, fingertips tapping agitatedly on the back of her lilac phone case. "Are you sure that we can do this? Like, just the two of us?"

I try to tamper down the nerves tingling in my belly.

"Of course! For one, the house isn't in total disrepair." *According to my parents, who haven't actually visited this site in, like, ten years.* "After I get the plumbing and electric contractors to check the water and the wiring, it's going to be mostly the aesthetic side of things for us to deal with. A lot of wood polishing, maybe brushing a few stray twigs off the porch. Repairing the molding around the windows before I start ordering cute furniture. I don't know the finer details but, seriously, how hard can it be? Plus, there's a hardware store in Larch Peak that we can do our errand runs at, and Connell, Logan and some of the other football guys are going to stop by pretty soon, too."

I feel Fallon's eyes slide my way and notice that her fingers begin tapping more pointedly on her phone.

I roll my eyes. "Yes, Hunter can visit, too."

A sunshine shimmer immediately radiates out of my best friend. "He's actually staying in Larch Peak while we're here," she tells me, beaming. "Him and a whole group of the Carter U hockey boys. I think that they're hanging out at his place by the creek."

My grip turns vise-like around the wheel of the 4x4.

"Him and the Carter U hockey boys?" I ask, my eyes

wide and unblinking.

"Mm-hm," she says nonchalantly, before suddenly flipping over her vibrating phone and squealing. "Ooh, look at that! He's texting me right now."

As Fallon clicks open the message on her cell the bright green canopy overhead breaks, and I let out a sigh of relief as we enter a golden clearing. The head of the large Larch Peak lake is twinkling gently on our right and the whole reason why we're here is waiting patiently on our left.

I breathe out a shaky, excited exhale as I take in the sight of the structure before us.

It's a two story wood-built lakeside house, with a wide set of wooden stairs that lead up to a wrap-around porch. The first floor looks to the lake out front, looping around to a forest-facing patio at the back, with rustic columns creating an overhanging shelter outside and a sturdy base for the second floor balcony. There's a cute dormer window set beside a medium-sized stone chimney, and the giant master suite sits imposingly under a gable roof.

I press a hand over my chest, trying to subdue my welling emotions.

"It's perfect," I whisper, fanning back my happy tears.

Fallon makes an intrigued humming sound as a piece of the porch railing thuds to the ground.

We look at it in silence as we mutually try not to panic.

"Okay, so it *will* be perfect once we're finished with it," I admit casually, manoeuvring the truck into a perfect 4x4 sized space beside the porch.

We both climb out of the truck and move around to the front of the hood, looking up at the large cabin with our hands on our hips.

"So, yeah, we're going to have to fix pretty much everything that's made of wood," I confess as we take in the loose boards and water damage.

Fallon's eyes fly to mine. "The whole house is made of wood," she gasps, the magnitude of this summer project starting to dawn on the both of us.

I breathe out a nervous laugh and begin twiddling with my diamond earrings.

"Okay, technically you're correct," I begin, "but I don't think that it's the body of the build that needs the repairs. It's mainly this outside porch patio bit that might need a little fix-up, because I'm guessing that maybe it wasn't part of the original build? Like, the actual house looks lacquered up and secure – it's the exterior railings and stuff that need redoing."

"And then there's the inside," Fallon says, totally reading my mind.

I wave a hand to try and dispel our entwined fear of failure.

"The building isn't hopeless, it just hasn't been utilised. After we check the plumbing and electric it's going to be solely an aesthetic job. Sanding, painting, and then the final stage will be properly decorating." I twist my lips to the side, a frown creasing my brow. "It's such a perfect small town hideaway, with so much potential. I just can't stand the thought of my parents demolishing it."

"Why would they demolish it?" Fallon asks, although when her eyes roam back to the wilting railing she purses her lips and says, "Uh, never mind."

I give her a teasing roll of my eyes. "Okay, so it's not just the fix-up job that has my parents wanting to quit on it, because fixing up a crappy porch can't be that hard."

I mean, I really freaking hope that it isn't that hard.

"They construct and sell real estate, and most of their profits come from the big-money city states. The huge condo in Carter Ridge? That's one of their smaller projects. But if I'm joining the company then I want to make sure that I love my job. And expanding their small town portfolio is literally everything that I've ever wanted."

Fallon nods. "So this lakeside house…?"

"They didn't buy the house to sell it – they bought the

land so that no-one else could. Because those little cabins across the shore there? They're ours too. And they didn't want anyone else getting their hands on this land and then potentially building something which would disrupt the beautiful view. But as soon as I found out about this property I knew that I didn't want them to demolish it, and then it triggered this light-bulb moment of what I wanted my role in the company to be. To me, Larch Peak is perfection, and I want to use my time to restore builds like this one."

"You mean like house flipping?" Fallon asks.

"Exactly," I tell her. "When my parents acquire land, if there's a build like this one, I want to re-establish it. Repair it. Give it a second chance."

I shield the sun from my eyes as it glitters against the lake.

"I want to do this," I admit, "and I'm going to prove to them that I'm the right girl for the job."

Fallon has an understanding sparkle in her eyes as she says, "This is really important to you."

"Yeah," I admit. "And if I don't complete this reno, then this lake house is going to be rubble when the summer is over. And if I don't convince my parents that house-flipping and expanding into the small town avenue is worthwhile…"

I toe the point of my sandal in the dirt and shake my head.

It was always known that I would join my family's business, but I want my role to be one that I head-over-heels *love*. And as a girl who never got to experience a quiet rural life? There's nothing that I want more than to shower these beautiful small towns in love.

Sensing my spiking fear, Fallon gives her hair a confident swish. "You know what? You're right. We can totally do this. Guys do stuff like this all the time, right? Like, in *Jurassic World*. Wasn't Chris Pratt building a house or something?"

"I think he was fixing a motorbike. Oh, wait! In the second one? Yeah, he was totally building a house."

Fallon nods. "Exactly. The point is, we're more than capable of fixing a few wooden panels and turning this place into the sexy hideaway that it was always meant to be. Besides, Hunter will totally help out whenever we need him to, *and* you've got Connell coming to join us too. Honestly, Ash? By the end of this project, I bet that this house will be so beautiful that you're going to want to keep it."

I breathe out a laugh and say, "Okay, that actually isn't allowed to happen. I need to be professional about this project, even if it is my first one. No getting sentimental and attached." *Even if this looks like it could be my dream house.*

I mean, the second that I saw the photos I was immediately love-struck. And I hadn't fallen that quickly in, like, four whole years.

I brush my thumb over the love-heart freckle that sits just beneath my elbow as Fallon and I begin walking toward the wide porch steps.

"This is going to be amazing," I whisper, looking up with shimmery eyes at the gorgeous lake house.

When we reach the steps I give the first wooden board a tentative nudge, making sure that it's solid and secure. Then we walk up to the wrap-around porch and look out across the lake, sparkling blue in the morning sunshine.

"This has so much potential it's crazy," I say. I'm almost overwhelmed by how much good could possibly come out of this risky summer venture. "Just look at that view."

I gently rest a hand on the wooden railing but in the next second I squeal, because the *entire fence* collapses over the ledge.

Fallon grabs my arm to stop me from falling with it, and we stare wide-eyed at the dust cloud that poufs up around the scattered wood.

"So, step one, rebuild this railing," Fallon whispers, a

nervous tremble in her pretty Colorado accent. "Actually, maybe that's step two. Do we have anywhere to sleep while we're here?"

I blink at her innocently and she presses her palm against her forehead.

"Oh my God," she mumbles. "This is why you packed those sleeping bags."

"I'm sorry!" I squeal as she begins pacing the porch. The wooden slats groan ominously beneath her and she quickly decides that maybe pacing isn't such a good idea.

"I thought that maybe we were going camping," she pouts sadly, her eyes drifting longingly to the larch forest bordering the lake.

"We will, I swear! It's part of our summer bucket list, remember? But I have two months to flip this house before my mom gets here to survey it. We'll simultaneously DIY the house *and* check stuff off our bucket list, okay?"

Fallon thinks about that for a moment and then her eyes trail over to the other side of the lake.

"Yes to the bucket list thing, but I'm still not one-hundred percent sure about sleeping on the floor, sleeping bag or no sleeping bag. I mean, what about those cabins?" she asks, pointing a sparkly lilac nail across the shimmering water. "You said that your parents own those too. Maybe we could stay in those while we do the renovation on this one."

I fold my arms across my chest and let out a sigh. "Believe me, I checked. All of the cabins have been booked up for the summer."

"Darn it," she mumbles. "Okay, so, do you have a tent? Because maybe we could set up a tent, just in case the interior flooring isn't up to scratch, and then we could put our sleeping bags inside the tent for extra comfort."

I look at her in amazement as we head back down to the 4x4.

I squeeze her hand in mine and say, "Fallon, you are

beauty and brains."

She gives me a mischievous smile and then lets out a wild howl as we race to the truck.

"Hammering the lake house into shape, camping in the forest, ticking stuff off our summer bucket list in some sexy small town bar…" My heart pounds with adrenaline as we round the bed of the truck, and Fallon leans against the side panel as I lift up the back. I pass her a sleeping bag before hugging my own tightly against my chest and we share an excited laugh as we make our way to the shore. "Like, seriously," I say, "what could possibly go wrong?"

The sunlight sparkles dazzlingly in Fallon's bright crystalline eyes but just as she's about to say something she suddenly cocks her head to one side. A flash of intrigue flares in her pretty irises.

"Hey, look," she says quickly, tipping her chin subtly across the lake. "Seems as though our campsite buddies are arriving at the same time as us."

My gaze flicks across the lake so that I can see what Fallon's looking at and my eyes instantly widen, too stunned to speak.

Oh no.

Oh no, no, no.

I almost stumble back a step as the large black G-wagon pulls into view, parking directly in front of one of the cosy lakeside cabins.

"You have got to be kidding me," I say, as I watch two more trucks pull up to the shore on the opposite side of the lake.

"Oh my God!" Fallon screams, squealing with delight as she realises what's happening right now. "Is that–?"

A small whimper leaves my throat. "Yes," I whisper, horrified.

"Oh my God, I can't believe they did this! Hunter!" she calls out as her soon-to-be-pro hockey player boyfriend heavily dismounts from the passenger side of his best friend's car.

He's immediately grinning our way, radiating his heady natural confidence, but it's the guy in the drivers' seat who sends my pulse into overtime.

My palms grow slick as my cheeks burn red.

I hear the quiet thud of his boots hitting the dirt as he trudges around the front of the car, drawling about something to Hunter in his deep country accent. But Hunter says something back to him and he immediately stops talking.

He lifts his head in our direction, and his eyes burn straight into mine.

After graduating a couple of weeks ago I never thought that I would see him again.

And of all the places to spend his summer break, he's here, with nothing but the lake between us.

Tanner.

He's here.

My jaw practically hits the floor.

He holds my gaze for what feels like an eternity, his large shoulders rising and falling as we stare at each other over the lake in silence.

But then he breaks the daydream, just like he always has.

He shoves a hand through his hair and jerks his chin at me.

"Howdy neighbour."

CHAPTER 2

Tanner

Present day

I keep my eyes locked in with Aisling's until she defiantly lifts her chin and swishes away, and then I'm turning around to face Hunter, jerking my thumb across the lake.

"Explain."

Hunter blinks. "Explain what?"

"Aisling O'Malley," I say roughly. "What the hell is she doing here?"

"She's on summer break," he says, like *isn't it fucking obvious?* "I told you, I'm staying near Fallon while she's doing her thing here. I mean, look at that place." He tips his chin and I glance reluctantly across the lake. "How secure does that look to you?"

Aisling and Fallon are having a frantic conversation in front of a large wood and stone lake house, with large lower and upper story windows and an expansive wrap-around porch.

The forest stretches behind it, dark and dense.

I shove my tongue in my cheek, understanding Hunter's point.

Two chicks in the middle of nowhere? Of course Hunter wants us to bodyguard them.

I look over to the left as the rest of our guys begin dismounting from their trucks.

We rented four cabins for the summer here in Larch Peak. Partially because a few of us have moved out of the hockey house at Carter U and are about to move permanently to Larch Peak, seeing as Hunter and I will be going pro with their home team this fall. But for me it's also because I want to be close to home, knowing that my mom could be calling me about my dad's deployment schedule any week now.

My dad's been in the army for my entire life, and whenever he's back on home turf it's a fucking privilege for me to be able to see him. We know that he'll be likely coming home this month or the next, and I want to get back to Carter Ridge as soon as that happens.

There are at least ten small wood cabins running along our side of the lake, and then the water curves and leads the shore around the base of the Larch Peak mountains.

Hunter and I are bunking in one, then Austin and Tristan, and then Hughes and Shaw. Plus, somehow we managed to convince Caden to join us, with the idea that staying by the lake with his chick would be, like, romantic or something. They usually spend the whole summer down at his ranch in Kentucky but it looks like she was down for something different this year. Which is why when Caden steps down from his rental truck and rounds to the passenger side door, we hear quiet girlish laughter, drawing our eyes in their direction.

Caden braces his forearms against the roof of the truck, smirking as his girlfriend scooches away from him with another giggle.

When he grips a fist around the ankle of her cowgirl boot and starts quietly murmuring to her, I clear my throat hard and look back across the lake.

Aisling and I could have had that, I think to myself. *That would have been us if I hadn't fucked it up.*

"I'm going over there," I decide suddenly, making Hunter's eyes flash back to mine. I cross my arms over my chest as Aisling looks back at us over her shoulder. Satisfaction spreads through my abdomen as she gives me a sulky little once-over.

Would you look at that.

She might not like who I am but she's sure as fuck into what I look like.

"Bad idea," Hunter says as he opens up the back doors to grab his stuff.

"Yeah," I agree, even though we both know that I'm going to do it anyway.

When my gaze settles on the house behind Aisling and Fallon, I frown in contemplation. The exterior wooden banister looks a little worse for wear, and is that the entire porch railing lying facedown on the rocks?

Jesus Christ. I roll my shoulders, not liking the look of that one bit.

I turn to Hunter. "How long are they staying in there?"

"'Til they're finished."

"Finished what?"

His brow creases. "The renovation," he says slowly, like it's obvious.

I duck my head and scrub my knuckles over my stubble, feeling kind of stupid for knowing so little about her plans. Especially when I've been crushing on her for four years straight.

I clear my throat and ask quietly, "Why, uh, why are they renovating a lake house? Is it, uh, Fallon's or something?"

Hunter's eyes are burning into the side of my face. I decide to fully turn around so that he can't see how red I've gone.

"Christ. You really don't know, do you?" he asks.

I stare down at my boots like they're really fucking interesting.

"Tanner," he says, but I shove a hand in my pocket and change the subject.

"You gonna let Fallon stay over there after we get settled?" I ask, given the fact that, as Hunter mentioned, the lake house doesn't look half as secure as I'd want it to.

Hunter's mouth curves, the answer obvious without him even needing to say anything. "Take a wild guess."

I roll my shoulders and nod, because if I was him, I'd be doing the same. No way would I have my girl sleeping away from me across the lake when she could be safely and securely wrapped up in my arms.

Knowing that I'll want a few minutes alone with Aisling, Hunter signals to Fallon across the lake that he'll be over in three. I leave my stuff in my car and begin walking up to the head of the lake, rounding it so that I can make my way to the girls' side.

When I reach their side of the shore I push my hair back from my forehead, roughing up my fringe and letting my gaze settle on Aisling.

She's fucking beautiful. She's got these big sparkly eyes, soft bouncy hair, and she's wearing a tiny pair of denim shorts that show off her toned cheerleader legs.

She's also narrowing her eyes on me in a bone-chilling kind of way.

My voice comes out deep and husky.

"Aisling," I say, unable to resist giving her another once-over. My eyes pause on the padded bag that she's clutching and I tip my chin at it, holding out a palm. "Pass that to me. I'll help you get your stuff inside."

She clutches it tighter and closes the tiny gap between us.

"What are you doing here?" she snaps, the bag in her

arms now pressing up against my abdomen. My Adam's apple slides heavily in my throat as we search each other's eyes.

"You know," I say levelly, "I was just asking the same question." I stare at the bag for another few moments, and then suddenly I'm frowning. "Wait. Is this a sleeping bag?"

She drops her chin, looking up at me from under her lashes, momentarily making me forget what we're talking about because she's so goddamn pretty.

"Right. So you're saying that we just randomly happen to be vacationing at the exact same lake, in houses that are situated exactly opposite from each other?" she asks in that light raspy voice of hers.

I swipe my tongue over my lower lip. Then I start trudging towards her porch.

"Hey!" I hear the sound of her angry footsteps marching behind me, her voice kind of breathless as she tries to keep up. "Where are you going? Your cabin is over *that* way."

I mount the steps two at a time. When I reach the top I almost put my boot through the porch slats.

"Christ," I murmur. "Who the hell did you rent this place from?"

I look down at her over the swell of my shoulder and she's watching me with an unnerving amount of focus.

She huffs prettily. "That's none of your business."

I grunt and get back to scoping out the front of the property. I move over to one of the large first floor windows and as soon as I look through the glass I'm thrusting my fingers through my hair.

"Jesus. Hunter wasn't kidding."

I turn back around to face Aisling, a little gratified when she has to force her eyes away from my pecs.

"What the hell are you thinking? Staying in a cabin in the middle of nowhere, two small chicks and not one piece of furniture? Is Hunter right?" I ask her. "You're renovating this entire lake house on your own?" I look back down at the bag in her arms. "And you're gonna be sleeping in sleeping bags. For how goddamn long?"

She swishes her ponytail. "What's it to you?"

Fallon sighs beside her and looks longingly across the lake towards our cabins.

I breathe out a laugh but after a sharp glare from Aisling I drop it, because we're all thinking the same thing anyway. I mean, Fallon's got a point. There are some perfectly good beds just over the water there, but I'm hardly going to suggest Aisling dropping the hostility and nuzzling into my chest for the foreseeable future, when it seems like one night in the sheets was all that she wanted from me.

No longer laughing I move around her and start making my way to the front door.

Aisling gapes, incredulous, as she pads quickly behind me.

"Have you lost your mind?" she asks. "There is no way that I'm going to let you—"

I give the handle a twist and the door swings wide open.

Not a single bolt or working lock in sight.

I look down at her dryly. "You were saying?"

She stares wide-eyed at the door handle as I walk cautiously inside.

I hear one little sandal step over the threshold and I shoot her a warning look over my shoulder.

"No," I order. "Wait out there."

Stubborn as hell, she waltzes right in.

"Jesus, woman." I jab a blunt finger at the unlocked potential crime den that we're currently standing in. "Let me check both floors before you come sashayin' in here like that."

Then I quickly turn around and trudge as far away from her as I can.

I can't deny it, this place has potential. The interior seems to be all wood despite some of the stonework outside, and it doesn't look like it's sustained any elemental damage unlike the front porch. The panels have clearly been lacquered good because they're that warm caramel colour, but the floor needs one hell of a cleanup because it's got dust and debris all over it.

I head over to the staircase, give the banister an experimental shake, and then begin ascending the wide wooden steps.

When I reach the top I can't help but glance back down at Aisling, something like relief spreading through my chest as we watch each other. She's actually waiting for me to check out the upper floor and not being a little tyrant for once.

After a good two minutes I make my way back down the stairs.

"Both floors are clear," I mutter, eyes flicking over to the empty fireplace.

"So I'm free to sashay now?" Aisling taunts, and I drop my gaze back down to meet hers.

"Funny." I look over her head toward the doorway, where Fallon is now running down the porch steps into the arms of her boyfriend. My abdomen twists like it's just taken a sucker-punch.

"If your car's unlocked I'll grab your stuff from the back," I tell her, taking the sleeping bag gently from her arms. I see her tiny love heart freckle, just below her elbow, and something clenches tight in my chest.

I swipe a patch of the wooden floor with the toe of my boot, and then I set the bag down on the one area that's no longer dusty.

She stares down at the rolled-up sleeping bag for one long beat. Then she brushes right past me so that she can beat me to the car.

I stroll lazily by her side as she jogs toward the truck.

"It's my brother's car," she pants, "so you're not allowed to touch it."

"Okay," I say, folding my arms over my pecs, waiting in

silence for her to point to her bags. After a moment of pouty indecision she rolls her eyes, reluctantly pointing a dainty finger toward a number of expensive looking carry-ons.

I take a deep inhale, feeling guilty as hell that I'm about to dump maybe ten thousand dollars' worth of fabric into the state's dustiest abandoned cabin.

I look down at her for confirmation but she's just staring at her nails, cheeks a little pink.

That seals the deal. Without another word I grab three bags per fist and begin trudging back up the rocky incline, making my pace a little slower so that maybe she can keep up with me this time. When we're back inside the lake house I stand over the sleeping bag on the floor, warring with myself over whether or not I can actually drop the rest of her bags beside it.

I check over my shoulder and see Aisling leaning against the front doorjamb, watching me with a curious but fiery expression on her face.

I start lowering her bags. Her eyes narrow dangerously.

Damn. I glance around looking for a better spot, and then I realise that I could just prop her bags over on the bare kitchen counter. Without looking back I make my way to the kitchen, swipe my forearm over the wood to clear any dust, and then I heft the bags on the top.

For the briefest of moments, something catches my eye – one of her bags partially unzipped and a flash of faded fabric peeking out. Khaki fabric. Worn-in and familiar.

I have to do a genuine double-take before realising that I'm probably seeing things, so I just shake my head and try to push the notion from my mind.

Get it together, asshole. There's no way that's what you think it is.

I slap the dust off of my forearm and we get back to staring each other out.

It's got to be at least fifteen seconds before I finally clear my throat, breaking the tension.

"That lock's rusted to hell," I tell her. "You need a new one, ASAP."

She glances over her shoulder toward the guys at the other side of the lake and says, "I'm sure that I could acquire a bodyguard or two."

I bet she fucking could.

"Yeah, I don't doubt it. But that's not sufficient."

She turns back to face me. "My brother will be here in a couple of days," she says. As if that makes it okay that she's going to be living in an unlocked cabin. Then her voice turns all tempting and husky when she adds on, "with half of his football team."

I shove my tongue in my cheek and feel my biceps tighten.

Great. More men.

I avert my eyes and nod once, telling her without words that I get the picture.

"Anything else you want to express an opinion on before you step foot out of my lake house for the last time ever?" she asks casually. She's so unapologetically savage that it honestly almost makes me smile. "Besides, you're on a boys' vacation. I wouldn't want to keep you from whatever it is that I'm sure you're going to be doing."

That catches my attention, because what the actual fuck is she talking about now? But to my surprise when I look down at her, her eyes are staring unblinkingly at her sandals.

Whatever it is that I'm sure you're going to be doing? What the hell does that even mean?

I walk over to her, wishing that she'd meet my eyes. Give me some of her fire so I can see she's as strong as I know she is.

When I'm only a foot away from her she lifts her perfect nose high into the air, defiantly meeting my eyes.

For some reason, something like pride courses through my chest.

There she is. That's the girl that I know.

I stand there for one long moment, enjoying the sensation of being close to her after so many years of having to keep my distance. Look, I can take a hint, and I know that what we had was a one-time thing. But I also know that if it was up to me that wouldn't have been the case.

But this isn't the moment for a heartfelt confession. So before I step out of the door I jerk my thumb toward the large fireplace, savouring the way her jaw drops to the floor when I say, "Hearth's empty. I'm gonna get you some wood."

CHAPTER 3

Tanner

Four years ago

We watch each other from opposite sides of the elevator, her leaning against the railing with her hands behind her back, and me gripping into one of the pieces of her bedframe, smiling every time she meets my eyes. She lets out a pretty laugh and moves over to the doors, giving me a couple of seconds to check her out from behind.

I mean, I've got eyes and she's the hottest chick that I've ever seen, so as I reposition the wood in my palms I let my eyes trail over her perky cheeks.

She's wearing leggings.

Grey ones.

I clear my throat.

Goddamn.

I'm almost at the end of my first week as a freshman at Carter U and after the fucking bender that the hockey team has taken us on I've been feeling worse for wear. I haven't had a tonne of classes so it's been mainly ice time and a couple of parties, because the guys on the team are dead-set on meeting every chick in Carter Ridge.

The problem with that for me?

I already *know* every chick in Carter Ridge.

God knows how but even the freshmen girls have caught wind of my reputation, which is not exactly ideal seeing as I was intending to make this year my fresh start.

At high school it was fine to fuck around – we all knew that soon we'd never have to see each other again, going to different colleges or moving halfway across the country. But now I'm *at* college, and I'm going to be here for four more years, so I don't want every girl that I meet thinking that I want to fuck her brains out.

Like, if I met the right girl then, yeah, I'd want to fuck her brains out. But mindlessly hooking up isn't what I'm after anymore.

When my dad met my mom he just knew that she was it for him and, even though I've never told the guys, that's what I've always wanted for myself.

To fall and never get back up.

So it's kind of hard to go along with the heartless player act on week one, when really to my core I'm a hopeless romantic.

The girl in front of me peeks back over her shoulder, and a small smile tugs at the corner of her mouth.

She's fucking beautiful.

And from the innocent, curious way that she's looking at me? I know one thing for certain.

This girl doesn't have a clue who I am.

The elevator doors slide open and she sweeps to the right, cute nose high in the air as she makes her way to her room.

I breathe out a quiet laugh and follow right behind her.

She twizzles her key-ring around her fingers as we approach her door, and I stop behind her, waiting for her next move.

"So would it be okay if you actually… place the bed where I need it in my bedroom for me?" she asks nervously. "'Cause I mean, you obviously do not have to do that – I could always get Connell to help me when he gets home – but it would just be, like, really helpful if you did. But no pressure, obviously! I'll understand if you don't feel comfortable going into my bedroom. If you want to just drop them in the living area or whatever, then that would be totally cool, too."

I stare down at her and try to breathe around the tightening in my chest.

Who the fuck is Connell?

I roll my shoulders, hands gripping harder into the wood. "I'll drop them in your bedroom, as long as your boyfriend is okay with that."

I mean, what kind of jackass leaves his gorgeous girlfriend to carry a fucking queen sized bed-frame up to their bedroom on her own anyway? And, while we're on the topic, why didn't he get her a king size?

"Boyfriend?" she asks, her eyebrows lifted in surprise. She watches me for one long moment before she purses her lips in a secretive smile. "Oh," she breathes, drawing out the word. She unlocks her door and gently pushes it open. "Connell isn't my boyfriend. He's my brother."

Wow, this bed-frame feels really light all of a sudden. I haul it higher in my arms and jerk my chin at her.

"Brother. Good." *Wait, what?* "I mean, it's good for you. To have a brother. Someone to look out for you."

She smiles up at me like she thinks that I'm an idiot. Which I am.

"So he lives here with you?" I ask, watching her hips sway from side to side.

"He lives on the floor below this one," she says casually, before suddenly stilling and giving me a cautious glance. "And there's twenty-four hour surveillance in this building, by the way. Just so you know."

It takes a couple of seconds before understanding dawns on me.

Awesome.

She thinks I'm a serial killer.

Wanting to amend that perception as quickly as fucking possible, I lean the first piece of bed-frame against the wall outside of her bedroom doorway and hastily fumble my wallet from my shorts, before holding it out to her.

She glances at it warily as she sets my cap on top of the wooden panel.

"I've got my driver's licence and cards in here. You can snap a pic on your cell if you want, send it to your brother."

Brother. Goddamn. I don't think that I've ever been so happy to hear that a chick has a brother in my entire life.

"And, like, you can just hang onto this if you want, while I help you bring your stuff up here. I swear, I'm not trying to… my intentions aren't…"

She raises an eyebrow and I breathe out a laugh, dropping my chin so that she hopefully can't see how fucking red I'm turning. I mean, where the hell was I going with that? My *intentions*? Who talks like that?

I do, apparently. Because I'm a fucking idiot.

"Sorry," I rasp, gripping a hand around the back of my neck. I give her a sheepish grin. "I'll just…" I place my wallet tentatively on the floor by her bedroom door and she laughs out loud, shaking her head as if I'm downright hopeless.

But she is still smiling.

"Wow, I thought that I was the crazy one," she says, stepping around me while I'm still crouched by her door. My pulse hammers up to triple-time as she looks back at me from over her shoulder.

She crooks her finger at me to follow.

She doesn't need to ask me twice.

I instantly rise to my full height and we're out of the

door in under six seconds, her petite frame barely an inch in front of mine, sashaying lazily down the corridor like she owns the joint. I can't help but smirk down at her when she glances back at me again because she's so effortlessly confident that it's sexy as hell.

When we're back inside the elevator, watching each other from our respective walls, she asks me, "So you're going to help me bring all of the pieces up to my room? Is that what's happening here?"

"That's right." I think for a moment and an even better idea comes to mind. "If you've got the tools on hand, I'll build it for you."

Her jaw drops open and she blinks up at me. "You'll what?"

"I'll build it for you. It's heavy and it'll need repositioning while it's getting screwed, so I can take care of that for you." I shake my head, my ears turning crimson. "I didn't mean for it to come out like that."

It'll need repositioning while it's getting screwed? What the hell is wrong with me?

I definitely need to *not* say shit like that when I'm standing face to face with the prettiest girl that I've ever seen.

"That would be amazing," she whispers, looking at me like I'm some sort of hero. The elevator drops to the first floor and the doors slide open. "If you really don't mind… then yes, I would love you to help me build it."

I jerk my chin at her and step out, grabbing the next piece of thick wooden panelling.

She watches me from the doors and a feeling that I haven't felt before spreads through my chest.

She smiles up at me, biting her lip as I haul in the next piece.

Then I trudge back inside the elevator, wait for the doors to close, and give her a wink.

"Don't mention it."

CHAPTER 4

Aisling

Present day

It turns out that the reason why there was no signage on our drive toward the lake? That would be because I was driving on the wrong road – as in, I wasn't even driving *on* a road.

So when Fallon and I decide to take our first trip into town, we have to drive over to the guys' side of the lake before we can make our way onto the main road.

Not wanting to do a big haul during our first hour of arriving at Larch Peak, we decide to grab renovation essentials from the hardware store and ice slushies from the diner before heading back toward our summer hideaway.

"Shoot," I say quickly, the second that we pull through into the golden clearing.

Fallon gives me an inquisitive expression, quietly sipping on her slushie.

"I forgot to grab pyjamas," I say quietly, glancing toward

the burly hockey players on our right. Then I pull up to an abrupt stop, because all of the men are now shirtless.

My eyes, the damn traitors, are immediately searching for a certain set of large lumberjack shoulders but, to both my relief and irritation, Tanner is nowhere to be seen.

I realise that his car has also disappeared.

A sudden all-consuming wave of disappointment crashes over me.

Did he leave? I think to myself. *Did he really come to Larch Peak not expecting me to be vacationing on the same lake, realise that I was going to be his 'neighbour', and then immediately decide to haul ass and spend his summer some place else?*

I know that it's for the best but all I can think is *we have unfinished business.*

Hunter, Fallon's boyfriend, grins as he jogs our way, scooping Fallon up from the car before her feet even hit the dirt. She lets him give her a little kiss on the cheek and then he sets her back down, taking her hand in his as we meet at the front of my brother's truck.

"Can we have a tour of *your* cabins?" Fallon asks him with a cheruby smile, looking innocently up at Hunter before giving me a mischievous little wink.

I blink at her, instantly suspicious.

She mouths the words *bucket list*, and then I'm laughing as I suddenly understand.

My eyes flash back over to the guys who are currently setting long logs around an unlit campfire, feeling a warm sensation in my belly when I realise that they're all already watching me.

Item number one on my summer bucket list? Kiss a hot guy.

And it looks like there are four hot single hockey players who are more than up for helping me strike that off my list.

Tristan – a tall, tan, six-foot-something defence-man – drops the make-shift bench that he was holding and offers me a wave, his expression both eager and tentative, because he's testing the waters.

He's actually super cute, and I have to bite back my smile. I give him a pinkie wave and laugh when he almost trips over his own feet jogging over to us.

Tristan and I met a few months ago at Hunter's twenty-second birthday party – and although he's super hot we're definitely just friends.

Friends who like to flirt. A lot.

But I think it's good to have someone who you can harmlessly flirt with. I know he was crazy into me but he also knows where I stand, so that means that we can continue our little flirtationship without worrying that it'll go beyond that.

I try to ignore the fact that I can feel Hunter's eyes burning into the side of my face, telepathically telling me to quit flirting with anyone who isn't Tanner. Like there's some invisible string that has already tied me to his best friend.

I snip right through that string.

"Tour please," I say to Hunter with an innocent smile of my own, as if my parents don't literally own these cabins.

He watches me for a beat before giving me a nod, his hand tightening firmly around Fallon's.

Tristan reaches us in about four seconds flat. His hair and jeans are sparkling with water droplets, as if he went for an early morning dip.

I look back at the other guys, checking to see if they're equally as wet, and I'm puzzled when I realise that Tristan is the only one. Even Hunter is untouched by the water, his skin tan and toasty, glowing in the early morning sunshine.

"Hey," Tristan beams, grinning as he falls into step beside us. "I can't believe that you're here. Seriously, what are the chances?"

"Yes, what *are* the chances?" I say pointedly, before shooting Hunter a murder glare.

He tips his chin at me in a cocky *you're welcome.*

Handsome jerk.

I look back to Tristan.

"Fallon and I are having a girls' summer, just the two of us. We have, like, a bucket list of all the crazy shit we wanna do," I tell him, that excited feeling from earlier already surging back into my chest. Tristan laughs with me, his eyes bright as they rake me up and down.

"What's on your bucket list?" he asks, chest heaving as if he already knows the answer.

From the way that I'm fluttering my lashes at him, I guess that he already does.

"You'll have to wait and see," I whisper, smiling when he drops his eyes, laughing huskily.

I know on the surface he seems adorable but the real reason why we can only be friends is because I know that he's a player.

And the only reason why players like him turn into endearing cinnamon rolls with girls like me is because they seem to think that *I'm* a player too. And, like any hierarchy, there can only be one master player sitting at the top of the pyramid – and because I don't take any crap, they all think that's me.

The problem with that? It *isn't* me. I don't want to be the heartless bad girl but, for some reason, it's the role that I always slip into.

So, for now, like always, I guess that I'm just going to have to run with it.

"This is where Tanner and I are stayin'," Hunter says, shoving the front door of his cabin open with the back of his large tan shoulder. He walks Fallon over to one of the two beds and drops his voice to a murmur. "And this is going to be our bed," he says quietly to her.

My eyes flicker over to Tanner's bed and I notice that there's a small khaki carry-on set at the foot of it.

Hope instantly blooms in my chest.

He hasn't left, I realise, heat rising in my cheeks. *Wherever*

Tanner's gone, he's coming back.

Secretly thrilled, I look back to the bed and imagine Tanner's large muscular body lying on those soft floral sheets. The thought is so endearing that I almost wish I could see it for myself.

Tristan, the human embodiment of golden sunshine, rests against the small wooden kitchen table and grins, "This is also exactly what our cabin looks like."

I cross my arms over my chest and smile up at him as he lazily kicks out his legs, setting a boot on either side of my sandals.

"Who are you staying with?" I ask.

"Austin. I could get him to fuck off though if you wanted me to," he adds, his boots caging me slightly tighter.

I partially notice the sound of crunching gravel outside followed by a repetitive grunt-and-thud that lasts for a couple of minutes. Then again, I'm also distracted by Tristan's eight-pack right now so I don't fully register what those sounds could possibly mean.

"You know what," I say, flashing an excited look over to Fallon, letting her know that I'm having a spontaneous moment, "Fallon and I have, like, a tonne of work to do on the lake house, but seeing as this is our first night maybe we should do something fun to settle in?"

Fallon gives me a super encouraging best friend squeal and nod. Her two-hundred-and-twenty pound boyfriend gives me a subtle *do not do this* shake of his head.

I turn to Tristan with my best captain-of-the-cheer-team smile.

"I want to tick 'visit a dive bar' off of my bucket list. We're going out tonight," I tell him, beaming.

Just as Tristan shoves himself to his feet, grinning down at me so adoringly that I actually think he's about to kiss me right now, heavy footsteps sound from the doorway and the room becomes instantly silent.

A hot shiver runs up my spine as I feel a large presence

step up behind me.

"You're doing what now?" Tanner rumbles quietly.

I give myself a moment to steady my breathing before turning around to face him.

And I see that Tanner, like Tristan, is also dripping wet.

Dark hair, broad chest, and denim jeans all soaked, as if he decided to dip in the lake fully clothed.

My subconscious does a little bit of testosterone arithmetic about why only two of the hockey guys here would be soaked to the bone.

My gaze trails down to his knuckles and I notice that they're a little red and swollen.

Tristan's chest brushes against my back as I stare unblinkingly at Tanner's fist.

Oh, my God. Did Tanner and Tristan… have a fight?

What on earth would they have been fighting over?

Or better yet: who *on earth would they have been fighting over?*

Not to be delusional, but I have a tiny inclination about why these two gorgeous hockey players might have had a casual morning brawl.

My eyes flash up to Tanner's and he immediately knows that I know.

"O-kaaaay," I breathe out on a shaky exhale, side-stepping from between their chests and freeing myself from the testoster-zone.

Tanner stares down at me and I swallow hard. This boy has *kiss me for your bucket list* written all over him.

And apparently he's not done with me yet.

"You're going to a dive bar?" he asks huskily. "And what the hell's this about a bucket list?"

I begin speed-walking at a fast clip out of the suddenly very small cabin.

"A bucket list is a list of things you do before you kick the bucket," I say obstinately, squeaking a little when I see that he's thundering right behind me. "Dive bars, swimming in the lake, and then, when Fallon and I finish rocking the hell out of the reno" – I straighten my spine and swish my hair – "we're going to treat ourselves by going mudding."

"You're gonna *what?*" Tanner bellows, and I race to the other side of his G-wagon, a little *ooh* leaving my lips when I see that his passenger door is wide open.

Snooping time.

I expect to see something incriminating like panties around the stick-shift but what I find instead makes me stumble back a step.

Right into the wet hot chest of the car's surly owner.

I spin around wide-eyed to face him and he reaches around me to shove the door shut. He looks a little bit embarrassed and a whole lot pissed off.

"An *axe?*" I wheeze breathlessly, leaning against his car as he towers over me. "What're you gonna do, murder me?"

He watches me long and hard before finally stepping backwards, eyes flicking to my sparkly toes and then back up to meet my gaze again.

"That's not even funny," he rumbles, "I would never hurt you, Aisling."

I breathe out an incredulous laugh and his gaze instantly sharpens.

"It was never like that. That's not who I am. Not with you."

"Right."

"Aisling–"

I'm about to push right past his big sexy body when I suddenly notice what he had been looking at, red cheeked and self-conscious, only moments ago.

A dry twig crunches under my sandal and I pause my footing, surprised and confused.

Tanner meets my eyes, his irises burning desperately, and then he curses roughly before turning around and trudging away from me.

I wait until he's out of sight and then I step closer to the small tidy pile, quickly done but still heart-wrenchingly neat.

The axe suddenly makes sense and I wince, feeling like a jerk.

He cut all of the lumber that I need for the empty fireplace.

CHAPTER 5

Tanner

Present day

I lock my fists under my chin, elbows on my knees, as I stare unblinkingly across the lake toward where Aisling and Fallon are 'getting ready' for their first night out. The log shifts beneath my quads as Austin settles down beside me but I keep my eyes on the right side of the girls' porch, my concentration unwavering.

They've made a make-shift girl den so that they can put their make-up on in 'natural light'. Only problem is, Hunter's sitting protectively by Fallon's side, casually sipping on a beer and being the human embodiment of a door, meaning that I can't actually get a glimpse of Aisling because she's hidden behind his back.

Austin holds a longneck toward me with his left hand. "Beer?"

I shrug. "Sure."

I accept the bottle while leaning down so that I can

swipe a rock from around the unlit campfire. Then I lift my eyes back to the girl den across the lake while I align the rock beneath the cap. I smash it swiftly upwards and the top pops clean off.

We sip in silence, the rest of the guys a little farther down the water.

Besides my harmless *try anything on with her and I'll break your fucking jaw* morning brawl that I had in the lake with Tristan regarding a certain Irish cheerleader, Caden and Winter are the only ones who have been dipping in the lake.

I flick my eyes over to where they're standing knee-deep in the water, Caden in a pair of shorts and his girl wearing one of his t-shirts. It's now one-hundred percent transparent and showcasing the little bikini that she's got on beneath it.

With her back against his chest and his chin resting on her shoulder, he leans them slightly forward and skims a pebble across the surface. Then he wraps his tattooed forearms around her waist as they watch the rock glide soundlessly across the water, golden and sparkling because of the midsummer sunset.

The whole moment is perfect.

I look away, sipping on my beer.

Austin gives me a light shove with his elbow and gestures the neck of his bottle toward the lake house.

I follow his line of sight, barely catching a glimpse of Aisling's ankle as she swishes through the front door, and Fallon pads in behind her, Hunter hot on her heels.

"They must be ready to go," he says, draining the last of his beer. Then he looks for the smallest rock that he can find and carefully sets his bottle down on top of it. "You gonna grab her before we head? I'll join the guys. We'll meet you in five."

"Yeah," I say, finishing my drink, and then waiting for Austin to kick a rock my way.

He nudges a small, shiny pebble in front of my boot,

making me breathe out a laugh as I slowly place my bottle on top of it.

"You're insane," I tell him as we both get to our feet.

He jerks his thumb towards the two bottles. "Tell me that isn't satisfying as hell."

I shake my head, smirking, and we go our separate ways.

As I round the head of the lake I call out to Caden, "Y'all coming tonight? We're about to head."

Technically Caden and Winter are too young to go to the bars, but Caden is so goddamn built that no-one would ever ask him for ID. His cheruby, pink-haired girlfriend on the other hand, I'm not so sure.

Caden turns to face me as I make my way down the girls' side of the shore and he gives me a subtle shake of his head as he splays his palms protectively over Winter's stomach.

Fair enough.

I keep my head down as I mount the porch steps, eyes glancing briefly toward the railing currently in pieces on the ground in front of it.

I scrub my knuckles over my jaw. They really oughta have that fixed.

Just as I reach the top step, Hunter, holding Fallon's hand, ducks out of the front door, his free hand shoved through his hair and his breathing uneven. There's a lipstick print on his cheek and Fallon is smiling naughtily up at him from under her long black lashes.

He meets my eyes and gives me a shake of his head, which really could mean any number of things.

"Is Aisling ready?" I ask him, crossing my arms over my chest.

Knowing that she's in there, barely ten feet away from me, probably looking like the prettiest thing that I've ever seen, is kind of getting me excited, even though I'm trying not to show it.

"Uh…" Hunter says, his expression conflicted. He looks

down at Fallon and then unthinkingly hauls her up, hitching her around the side of his waist and tightening his hold beneath her behind. "I guess," he rasps finally, completely distracted.

I huff out a laugh and nudge his shoulder with mine. "Right. See you in a minute, man."

I trudge up to the open front door and rap two knuckles against the wood.

"Aisling?" I call inside. "Aisling, are you ready–?"

The second that she steps in front of me, perfect eyebrows arched and delicate hands on her hips, I stumble back a step and then force myself to turn one-eighty.

"Sorry, sorry," I rasp quickly, thrusting one hand through my hair. I roll back my shoulders and fold my arms back over my chest, eyes on Tristan across the lake as I block Aisling's doorway like a bodyguard. "I'll wait until you're dressed."

I can't believe that she just answered the door wearing nothing but a freaking nightdress.

I swallow hard, reeling from the sudden surge of testosterone after seeing her in that outfit. Short, tight, and baby pink, with two sexy straps draped off of her shoulders.

No wonder Hunter looked like he'd just been tortured. Is this what Fallon had gotten ready in too?

Do all girls get ready in their secret, private, definitely-not-to-be-seen-outside-of-the-bedroom pyjamas?

A finger prods roughly between my shoulder blades but I stay obstinately still, not about to risk another glance at her.

"What?" I grit out, my jaw muscles bunched. If she asks me to help her out of that thing I will fucking die on the spot.

"Uh, you're in the way?" she says, before two small palms grip into my back, a squeal leaving her throat as she tries to shove me forward.

I blink, confused, before turning around to face her.

Aisling stares up at me, her judgey little eyebrow arched like I'm insane, but my eyes only hold hers for two seconds before they drop back to her nightdress.

Soft breasts rising and falling fast against the neckline, nipples rasping under the thin fabric, and a tight waist that I could fit both of my palms around. Hot damn.

"What is it?" I rasp, my voice growing deeper. I lift my forearm to the doorjamb, wanting to ensure that no-one across the water will be able to see what she's wearing right now.

Maybe it wouldn't be so bad if she asked me to help her out of this thing.

But before I can sink any further into that dream she shoves her palms into my pecs, making me grunt roughly and stumble back a step. I'm so stunned by the amount of contact we just made that it takes me a full five seconds to register that she's already halfway down the porch steps, walking straight toward my teammates who are now rounding the head of the lake. Wearing that. In front of them.

I slam her front door shut and clear the steps in two strides flat.

"Aisling," I bark out, picking up my pace as she hobbles over the rocks, wearing a pair of sexy five inch heels that she could fucking break her neck in.

She glances back at me over her shoulder, eyes widening when she realises I'm chasing her.

"Woman," I growl, catching her up in three seconds, and then wrapping my palm around her elbow so that I can spin her around. Her nipples brush right up against my pecs and I grow another five fucking inches.

"See something you like?" she teases, giving me that sharp vixen stare.

I step into her space and my cock shoves right up against her belly.

"You're going out in a nightdress?" I ask her. "Tell me

you're joking."

She has the goddamn nerve to look affronted.

"You think I'm wearing pyjamas?" she gasps, grabbing her breasts in both of her hands. Sweet Jesus. "This dress cost almost five thousand dollars."

I tear my eyes away from her trembling cleavage and say, "I'll pay you five thousand dollars to get changed and burn it."

"Oh yeah? And wear what?"

"Something that actually fucking classifies as clothing. Not this kind of…" My eyes trail down her front and I swear her neck starts to blush. That does not fucking help my raging hard-on. "This kind of… private stuff. Indoors stuff. Literal pyjamas would be better than this."

She gives me a vicious smile and whispers, "I didn't bring any pyjamas."

I clear my throat.

Okay then.

"You're not wearing this to a dive bar," I tell her, knowing she's never going to listen.

She looks up at me under those beautiful black eyelashes and purrs, "Oh, but I think I am."

"Over my dead body."

"Sounds good to me."

My nostrils flare as I step backwards, before shaking my head and storming past her. Our fingers accidentally brush as I make my way around her and my chest heaves, my whole body on fire.

I don't bother looking at Tristan as he jogs toward her, saying something to make her giggle and probably sweeping her off her feet.

Austin is already passing me another beer for the road as we begin walking our way up the canopied dirt track.

I murmur a "thanks" and take it without another word.

He clinks his bottle against mine.

It's going to be a long night.

CHAPTER 6

Tanner

Present day

They're playing "Kill Shit Till I Die" at the bar and I could take a good guess who picked it, mainly because she looked me dead in the eyes while she requested it, the little psycho.

"What's the deal?" I ask Fallon as I jerk my chin towards Aisling, where she's currently being twirled on the dance floor by both Tristan and Hughes. They're making her giggle and blush, their bodies way too close for comfort.

Fallon blinks at her friend and then looks up at me. "She's dancing."

I give Fallon a look as she wiggles further into Hunter's lap. His hands quickly shoot to her hips, stilling her ass before he nuts.

"I meant, what's the deal with you and Aisling staying up at the lake house," I clarify. "Hunter said you're renovating it, so I want to know the score. Seems to me as though we're about to be neighbours for the summer."

Fallon thinks for a moment and then she gives me a nervous frown.

"Aisling told me that you bought an axe," she mumbles anxiously.

I turn fully around to face her, smirking at that one. "She told you that, huh?"

Fallon gives me a rough little slap across the pecs.

"Yes, you crazy person! That isn't something to be proud of!"

I turn back around so that I can continue watching Aisling; Fallon doesn't need to know that I bought an axe so that I could chop the wood for Aisling's fireplace.

Fallon hums woefully until I glance down at her again.

I stare into her big eyes. "Yeah? What now?"

Hunter kicks my boot under the table and rumbles, "Dude, change the tone."

My eyes flash to his and he gives me that *watch the attitude with my little woman* death stare.

"Yeah, yeah," I say to him, before dropping my eyes back to Fallon's. "What now, Your Highness?"

"Um, we are renovating the lake house," she admits, eyes on her lilac nail polish. "It's one of Aisling's parents' properties and they wanted to knock it down, but Ash thinks that it has small town charm or something, so she wants to give it a second chance and convince them that it should be kept – for the business, I mean – but then we also have this summer bucket list that she thought would be perfect to do while we're staying in Larch Peak–"

"Whoa, whoa, whoa," I say, taken aback by the amount of information that she's piling into that long-ass sentence. "Slow down a minute. What do you mean it's her parents' lake house?"

My eyes momentarily flash to Hunter's because my parents also have a lake house here in Larch Peak. It's the summer house that Hunter is literally buying off of them.

Even though it's just a coincidence, it feels like another binding of fate, secretly tying me to Aisling.

"Maybe she should be the one to tell you the finer details. But the gist of it is, we're staying in Larch Peak until we've completed the renovation. And, while we do the house flip we're going to have our… wild senior year summer."

I stare down at Fallon, unblinking.

"Wild senior year summer," I repeat.

Fallon glances up at Hunter and he gives her a reassuring squeeze. When she looks back at me she says, "You know, the bucket list…?"

Damn straight I know about the bucket list. I've spent all day imagining exactly what kind of things Aisling O'Malley might have put on there.

I clear my throat hard and stare at my clasped fists on the booth's table.

"Yeah, what about it?" I ask quietly.

"Well… it involves doing stuff, obviously. Going out… having fun…" Her voice drops to an almost inaudible mumble when she quickly adds on, "Kissing boys."

One blink and my vision goes red.

"What did you just say?"

"Oh, come on, Tanner." Fallon rolls her pretty eyes. "She's single and cute and she deserves an amazing boyfriend–"

I can't hear the rest of her sentence over the sound of my blood ringing in my ears.

There's no question in my mind: Aisling O'Malley is drop dead gorgeous. As if her face wasn't perfect enough she had to have a killer body too.

And now, even worse, she's actively looking for a dude to hook up with?

I'm suddenly very interested in the idea of helping Aisling and Fallon renovate the lake house. Screw shooting the shit with the guys – I'm going to ensure that Aisling has everything that she could possibly need for this renovation, anything to keep her distracted from her bucket list of sin, which I'm one-billion percent sure the guys would love to help her fulfil.

I flick my gaze over to the dance floor, raking my eyes over Aisling's outfit.

I brace my forearms on the table and wait for her to look my way, not much caring for how Tristan is whispering in her ear right now, one big hand on her shoulder, the other brushing over her waist.

Aisling's eyes meet mine and my knee begins pounding dangerously under the table.

She laughs at something that Tristan whispers to her and I shove my body up to my feet.

"I'm going over there," I rumble, pushing back my hair as I clear the booth.

I begin slowly making my way through the crowd, neither of us able to tear our eyes off each other. She gives the guys a two minutes signal and satisfaction clenches deep in my abdomen.

But she doesn't start walking my way – she waits until I'm close, and when there's barely two feet between us, she legs it.

I curse like a trucker, using my biceps to clear the path that she's slinking through.

"Aisling," I bark, my tone a clear warning.

The second that she glances around at me over her shoulder I hook my forearm around her belly, bringing her gorgeous body abruptly up against mine.

"Aisling, Jesus Christ," I growl as she spins around in my hold, our fronts mashing together as the crowd heaves all around us. I mean, I was mainly coming to see her so that I could prize Tristan's hands off her body, but I was also coming to see her so that I could offer up some free labour for her reno.

But now that we're chest to chest, her baby pink stiletto

heel stabbing purposefully into my boot, the only thing that I can think of is pulling her in tighter. Maybe ticking off the kissing section on her summer bucket list.

She might still be digging her nails into my chest like she wants to rip me limb from limb but she surprises the hell out of me when she purrs, "Thanks for the wood."

She's talking about the lumber that I chopped for her fireplace, but it sure as shit doesn't feel like that's what she's referring to right now.

I grunt and shift my boots wider, well aware that she can feel what's happening in my jeans.

"Plenty more where that came from," I rumble.

"You spoil me," she teases, using that husky voice to toy with me.

My eyes flash back to hers and I murmur, "I wish."

"Whatever." She rolls her eyes. "Why were you at the booth watching me like a stalker?"

"Good question, Aisling. Why were you grindin' on my teammates?"

She leans up and whispers, "Maybe they're on my bucket list."

I smirk down at her, fired up. "Is watching me murder them also on your bucket list?"

But there's something about the moment – her smiling mischievously up at me and me smirking down at her, my biceps caging around her body so that no-one steps into her space – that makes the air between us change. It's one of those *what could have been* moments, where it's just Aisling and me, hands all over each other, looking into each other's eyes like we're sharing a secret that no-one else is in on.

She's breathing in quick little pants, making her chest pump rapidly against mine, and it's so soft and sexy that I just stand there in silence. Blinking down at her in awe, taking in how beautiful she is.

"Aisling," I murmur, my palm on her back sliding up so that I can hold her more securely.

I swallow hard, refusing to drop her gaze, and I steel my jaw as I build up the nerve to tell her how perfect she looks tonight. And not just because she's wearing a bad-girl dress that I want to rip clean off her body, but because, for the briefest moment, I can see that sweet girl-next-door blush, showing me that she feels this too. This chemical pull that made us reckless from the start.

I look down at her mouth and instinctively pull her closer. Then my eyes flick to one of her baby pink straps, draping down her arm, and I hook my fingers underneath it so that I can tug it back up into place.

"Goddamn," I grunt, frowning down at the strap. "Damn thing won't move."

"It's made that way," she whispers back to me, her eyes flickering with intrigue and panic.

I keep my focus on the strap so that I can't get lost in her beautiful eyes. "Been driving me insane all night."

"The dress or the girl wearing it?"

I breathe out a humourless laugh. "Both."

"Would it help if I took it off?" she breathes quietly and my eyes flash down to hers.

I walk her back a step. "Don't say it if you don't mean it," I rumble. My voice is so deep that I watch her nipples stiffen beneath the baby pink fabric.

I swipe my tongue over my bottom lip, feeling my cock grow even heavier.

"That's also on my bucket list," Aisling pants, her knees knocking against mine.

"What?" I rasp, my eyes raking over her tits.

"That," she breathes, pointing to her right.

I take a quick glance at the stripper pole, grunt, and then look down again.

Then I do a double-take at the stripper pole.

She shoves at the large muscles of my chest, freeing herself from the intimacy of our embrace.

"Hold the fuck on," I say quickly as she squeals and

starts racing back through the bar. "You're not going up there," I tell her, right on her tail as she teeters precariously through the patrons.

She eyes the pole deviously over her shoulder before throwing me a sly little look. "We'll see."

I shove my fingers through my hair, keeping pace with her as I look over my shoulder. I'm not sure if seeing Aisling wrap a leg around that pole would be a dream or a goddamn nightmare.

When I turn back around I see that Aisling has led us to the guys, their arms already open and ready to take her in the centre of the huddle.

We stare at each other in heated silence as she squeezes herself into the middle of the group.

"I'm heading," I say, clasping hands with Austin. I keep my stare locked on Aisling though, a silent invitation for her to come with me – to put the past behind us and show her that I could give her the future that she's always wanted.

Instead she places her hand on her heart and mock-gasps. "Oh no, please stay."

I huff out a laugh and slide my eyes over to Tristan. He looks a little worse for wear now that there's a bruise forming on his jaw, so that perks me up a little. We give each other a quick shove on the shoulder anyway.

Even though we're both pining for the same chick, we're still solid friends. It's just something that we're going to be mature about and deal with.

Unless of course he actually starts dating her, in which case I'm going to have to kill him.

When I finish up with the goodbye punches I drop my gaze back to Aisling.

She leans back against the bar and starts sucking my soul out with her eyes.

I jerk my chin at her. "You coming with me or what?"

She lifts a limp wrist and begins inspecting her nails. "No, thanks."

Heat climbs up my neck, every piece of primal instinct telling me to take her with me.

"Aisling."

She flicks her gaze up to meet mine.

"Let me walk you home."

She wafts that limp little wrist delicately around. "I'm in safe hands, don't you think?"

I inhale, sharp and deep, and finally call it a fucking night.

"Fine," I grunt. Then I tip my head at Austin. "See y'all."

When I get back to the cabins it's fucking beautiful. The air is warm and quiet, and the moonlight reflects off the lake's gentle undulations.

But the moment isn't perfect, because she isn't here.

Caden and his girlfriend are wrapped up on a blanket on the water's edge, and he gives me a subtle nod when he hears my boots breaking through the brush.

I nod back at him, neither of us saying a word, because for Caden and Winter the moment *is* perfect. I trudge quietly up to the cabin I'm sharing with Hunter, open the door, and then stare down at the bed.

My eyes slide down to the carry-on on the floor as I think back on something that Aisling told me earlier.

I glance out of the window toward the lake house and frown. I mean, it's not cold out, but that doesn't mean that the girl shouldn't have a pair of pyjamas.

I place the bag on the bed, unzip the fastening, and start flicking through the shirts that I brought here with me. I find my favourite – the perfect XL fit for my chest, in solid military khaki – and then I stuff the rest of the clothes back inside before heading out the door again.

I trudge quietly around the head of the lake, keeping my eyes on my boots as I mount the porch steps.

When I get to the front door I take a long deep breath. Then I give it a gentle shove, opening it.

Goddammit Aisling. My chest heaves because I'm pissed off that she didn't get around to fixing in a new lock yet, but I push that thought to the back of my mind for now as I walk toward the kitchen counter.

Feeling like an idiot, I stare down at the shirt in my fist, my cheeks turning red even though I'm the only person in here. I gently shake out the shirt, fold it in half, and then place it on top of one of Aisling's bags.

Just in case when she gets home she wishes that she'd brought some pyjamas.

CHAPTER 7

Aisling

Four years ago

Leaning against the doorjamb to my bedroom, I watch Tanner position the headboard at the top of the frame, while using his other hand to carefully slot the bolt into place. After giving it a few rough flicks with his wrist he glances down at the tools on the floor, brow creased as he searches for something.

When he spots it he breathes out a laugh and his eyes meet mine, smiling bashfully.

"Didn't realise that it was over there." He jerks his chin toward the large hand-tool that's lying near the foot of the bed, about three feet in front of me. "Mind grabbing that screw for me?" he asks.

I tuck a curl behind my ear and smile. "Of course."

I quickly set down the mug in my hands and gently pad into the room, kind of excited to be involved in part of the process. I pick up the large hand-tool before making my way over to where Tanner's standing.

"Once we've screwed these bolts into place, the frame will be finished. Then all we need to do is grab that" – he tips his chin toward my queen sized mattress resting against the wall in front of us – "haul it up on here, lay down some bedding, and then…" He shrugs. "All done."

He glances down at the tool in my hand and then his eyes flash back to mine.

"Wanna do the honours?" he asks, in that impossibly deep voice of his.

"Me?" I ask, a little nervous.

I can't help but fear that, if I touch the bed, all of Tanner's hard work will come crashing down around us.

A smile tugs at the corner of his mouth, a beautiful warmth in his cheeks. "Yeah, you."

"But what if I mess it up?" I ask, looking desperately at my gorgeous new bed.

He shakes his head. "You can't go wrong with it, I promise. The drill's not electric so the worst thing that can happen is that the bolt slips out before you've screwed it in tight enough. And that doesn't matter either, because I'm still holding the frame in place."

I cautiously flick my gaze over to his right arm, which is currently gripping firmly into the headboard, keeping it erect. I have to gulp down a little swallow as I watch his biceps flex and ripple.

"Okay," I whisper nervously, sliding my eyes back up to his.

He gives me a small encouraging nod and then repositions his body, so that there's a tiny Aisling-sized space between him and the headboard. He taps the bolt with his left thumb and says, "You're gonna find the ridge in the bolt and slip the drill inside. Then start twisting clockwise until it feels tight enough to you."

"Will you check that it's tight enough after?" I ask breathlessly, not wanting to climb on top of my mattress tonight and then have the headboard smash down on top of me.

Tanner's eyes are practically boring holes into the small bolt, his whole face on fire as he murmurs, "Uh, yeah, I can, uh… check how tight it is."

Taking a steadying breath, I lean down slowly. Then after examining the bolt, I slip the drill into the little ridge.

Step one complete.

I look up at him with a hopeful smile and he breathes out a quiet laugh, returning it.

"Yeah, that's it. Now start twisting it," he says.

I drop my eyes back to the bolt and begin tightening it to the right.

"Keep going," he instructs, and I nod in response. I keep my eyes on the bolt, not wanting to lose my concentration.

"I think it's almost there," I say quietly, as I begin to feel a little resistance in my hand.

"Yeah?" he asks, shifting slightly at my side. He removes his left hand from beneath the bolt so that he can grip it at the top of the headboard and he opens his right palm beside mine, crooking his digits in a silent question. "Want me to check?"

I move my hand up the drill so that he can take control of the handle, and then I back away slightly as he jerks his arm roughly. The screw undoubtedly twists another couple of turns.

But he doesn't mention it. Instead he looks at me with a smile and says, "You did it perfect."

I laugh and shake my head. "Yeah, okay," I say, going along with his little lie.

He grins back at me as he moves to the other side of the headboard, grabbing a second bolt from his shorts and beginning to slot it into the next hole.

Feeling kind of bold I fluff up my ponytail and suggest, "Maybe I could, uh… do the other ones too?"

"Yeah," he rasps immediately, quickly making room so that I can slip back underneath the cage of his biceps. I try to bite back my smile as his chest begins pumping unevenly against my back.

We work our way through every bolt on the back of the headboard, Tanner watching my handiwork carefully and then showering me with praise – even though he has to low-key fix every single bolt when I step back for his assessment. But he doesn't mock me or complain. He just makes the little tweak and then smiles down at me, telling me what a good job I did.

And I enjoy every single second of it.

He screws the final bolt and then he gives the headboard a firm shake, making sure that everything is safe and secure.

I can't contain my excitement any longer.

"Is it finished?" I ask him, clutching my hands in front of my chest.

"All done," he confirms, chuckling quietly when I squeal in delight.

I clap my hands together and run around to the bottom of the bed, tears almost flooding my eyes as I take in the sight of my newly-finished investment.

"Well, almost all done," he says, joining me where I stand. Before I can ask him what he means he's gripping his hands around the bottom of the bed and shoving it forward with a low grunt. Then he turns to the wall behind us, rolls his shoulders, and hauls up the mattress. He drops it heavily onto the bed and smacks the edges into place.

Once it's perfectly aligned he turns toward me with a crooked grin.

"Now it's all done," he rumbles, raking a large hand through his messed-up hair.

"Wow," I breathe, falling back against the wall behind me. I'm pretty sure we both know that I'm not talking about the bed anymore.

He smirks and rubs the back of his neck, the stretch of his arm causing his shirt to slide up over his abs. "Anytime."

I blink away from his big muscles and sexy smile creases and I push off the wall, walking on unsteady legs toward the doorway.

"Is there anything else I can get for you?" I ask without turning around. The sound of his footsteps behind me tells me that he's already following.

When I see his wallet by the doorjamb I lean down to pick it up.

"Fuck, thank you," he says, accepting it as I pass it over to him, but as it leaves my hand something begins to slip out of it.

"Sorry! I'll get it," I say hastily, but he bends at the same time, alarm in his voice when he says, "No, no, I've got it, I've got it–"

By the time that we're both on the floor I realise exactly what just slid out of his wallet.

I blink up at him, alarmed, my cheeks burning pink as I hand it back to him.

A mile-long strip of condoms.

XXL condoms.

"Fuck," he rasps, his chest heaving as he frantically tries to stuff them back inside his wallet. Like that's going to happen, there's about seven million on that strip. "I'm so, so sorry," he says quickly, eyes flicking to mine with apologetic concern.

"It's fine," I breathe out, although my walls instantly go up a little bit. Because Tanner is gorgeous and that is a *lot* of condoms. Which immediately has me thinking, *is this guy a total player?*

But then again all of the guys that I know are proud of their prowess, whereas Tanner looks kind of mortified, so maybe he's not–?

He shakes his head, looking anguished. "No, it's not

fine, I'm sorry. I swear I'm not… I'm not like that. I'm not like this." He swallows hard. "My guys have been pulling this kind of shit on me all week."

I instantly exhale with relief, my lashes fluttering shut for a small moment.

My guys have been pulling this kind of shit on me all week.

It's just a prank from his friends. He isn't that kind of guy.

He's gorgeous, from a small town, and he doesn't fuck around.

Let's be honest – he's kind of perfect.

I gently still his fumbling hands with the tips of my fingers, and his eyes fly up to mine, his chest stilling on a deep inhale.

"It's your personal property, I shouldn't have even seen what was inside there," I tell him quietly, although he still doesn't look convinced. I drop my eyes and whisper, "And, just so you know, I'm eighteen. It's not like I don't know what a condom is."

I mean, I assumed it was pretty obvious that I'm eighteen seeing as I'm living alone in this condo. But I want to make it crystal clear because I know that I've got kind of a baby face.

And as soon as I say the words, I'm really glad that I did.

"You're eighteen?" Tanner asks, sounding low-key excited.

I nod my head, breathing out a little laugh. "Yeah, I'm about to start at Carter U."

His eyes widen even more, and he grips a hand at the back of his neck.

"You're a freshman?" he breathes, and suddenly I think that I just messed up.

Because how old is Tanner? This guy is *huge* – is he too old for a freshman?

He shakes his head fervently as if he can sense exactly what I'm thinking. "I'm eighteen, too. I'm also about to–"

"You are?" I squeal, so relieved that I almost hug him.

Instead I just throw myself on the floor and moan, which causes Tanner to sit back against the wall opposite me and release a chuckle of his own.

"What, you think I look old or something?" he asks, his tone teasing.

I sink my teeth into my smile and cover my eyes, laughing hard.

"No way!" I lie, and I feel his sneaker nudge gently against mine, immediately releasing a new onslaught of giggles.

When I peek up at him from under my arms he's smiling back at me.

My laughter gradually dies down, until the only sound in the corridor is our heavy breathing after the sudden whirlwind of emotions.

I slowly push up onto my elbows, his eyes never leaving mine, until my back is against the wall and I'm mirroring his position.

"Aisling," I say quietly, revealing another tiny part of myself. "That's my name."

He exhales calmly. "That's a beautiful name."

A smile tugs at the corner of my mouth as I slowly rise to my feet. He follows my lead while slipping his wallet back into his shorts.

"Um, I don't really have plans this afternoon, except for putting my bedding on and settling in," I tell him. I gesture toward one of the couches in the living room and explain, "I've been sleeping on the couch so I'm pretty excited to finally have a bed again."

Tanner glances at the couch, frowning.

"Wasn't it too small?"

I point toward the size of my body and he drops his chin, smiling. "Right."

"So anyway," I continue, swiping the floor with the toe of my trainer. "I was thinking… if it's still raining or if you wanted to hang out… you could totally stay here for a little while, if you want to? Like, I'll probably watch some football or–"

"Yes," he says immediately. "I mean, yeah, I'd like that. That sounds really great."

"The football part, you mean?" I say with a teasing smile.

He pokes his tongue in his cheek. "Uh, sure. Football. Yeah."

I breathe out a laugh, trying not to get all shy.

"Okay, great," I giggle, gently biting into my lower lip. "I'll just grab my laptop. We can watch it on my bed."

I hear a choking sound behind me as I pad into the living room to grab my Macbook.

"Your bed?" he asks, and I glance back at him over my shoulder.

"Yeah," I say, like *duh*. "I've been *living* on this couch. I don't plan on leaving that bed for, like, one whole week."

"A week," he pants, his tanned biceps straining.

I grin up at him and then point to the bedding on the couch.

"Wanna help?" I ask, and then I stifle a giggle when he launches into action.

"Yeah," he rasps. "Put me to work."

CHAPTER 8

Aisling

Present day

Warm rays of sunlight streak in through the large A-frame balcony window, and I squint against the brightness as I blink myself awake.

It's early – like, before six a.m. early – and the only sounds in the summer air are the gently lapping waves, and a few birds calling before they flit into the forest.

I push myself up onto my elbows as dust motes sparkle in front of my eyes, and I glance down to my left so that I can take a peek at my roommates. Plural. Because when Hunter walked us back last night and then accidentally learned that there was no lock on our front door he started quietly grumbling until Fallon told him that he could bunk with us.

So now six-foot-four Hunter Wilde is currently lying on his back in an unzipped lilac sleeping bag, his calves on the hardwood flooring because he's about a million inches too tall for it. Fallon is draped gently over his chest as his palms protectively hold her head, and her pink cheek rests softly against his steadily beating heart.

I focus back on the dust motes as I wiggle my thighs out of my sleeping bag.

Picking up my phone and my travel bottle I flick the lid to check that there's still some water inside of it and then I pad over to the large balcony doors, quietly making my way outside.

Summer morning sunlight bursts over the Larch Peak mountains on my left, the glowing rays warming my bare legs as I walk toward the balcony railing. Before I step up to the ledge I suddenly remember yesterday morning with the porch railing – as in, I touched it with my pinkie finger and the whole thing collapsed – so I quickly back up a couple of steps, eyeing the balcony lumber warily. I'll have to give it a wobble at some point to check that it actually is secure, but I decide to wait until my helpers in the bedroom are on-hand and conscious, just in case.

But that reminds me. I set the bottle by my feet and unlock my phone, tapping open the Notes app. Yesterday morning Fallon and I picked up some basic essentials from town, but to get this project underway there's a bunch of other stuff that I'll be needing.

I quickly type out *renovation supplies* on a blank page, start a new paragraph, and then begin to type out every item that I can possibly think of – going methodically in my head, room by room.

I read over my list a few times, checking for anything I could have missed, until a quiet sound across the lake suddenly captures my attention. I lock my phone and place it next to the bottle on the floor, before taking a tentative step forward and looking to the other side of the lake.

My eyes roam across the small undulations, crystal clear ripples that burst into light when the sun catches them, until they finally reach the shore and my breathing halts in my chest.

Wearing shorts and a grey shirt, his tan skin glowing in the morning light, Tanner is quietly and methodically working out on the other side of the lake. I don't know how many push-ups he's done so far but when he reaches his next fifty I hear a low stifled grunt. His large back is strong and straight and his biceps pump relentlessly up and down, not stopping even after his next fifty, instead moving straight into one-armed reps. The thick cords protruding in his forearms are the only giveaway of any strain.

I want to lower myself to the wooden floor so that I can watch him in secret, but I decide that it's better not to move, otherwise I might capture his attention.

I stand silent and still, eyes on the large muscles of his shoulders.

He does another fifty, this time with both palms pressed down, biceps bulging like crazy because his body mass is insane. When he finishes his last push-up he drops down onto his back, his broad chest heaving fast in the warm morning rays.

He throws one forearm over his eyes and drops his other hand to his shorts, giving himself a rough squeeze through the fabric before heavily rising to his feet. He shakes out his wrists as he kicks off his sneakers, stealthily making his way toward the lake's golden edge. He's as quiet as a wolf, his expression hard, deep in thought. The short sleeves of his shirt look as though they're cutting painfully into his pumped biceps.

Realising how obvious my position up here is I begin to carefully move back a step, but Tanner's head snaps up and his eyes lock in on my own.

I pause, eyes wide, as his own steps instantly halt.

He holds my eyes for a good five seconds before checking that there's no-one else about. Then his eyes slide back up to mine and something dangerous flashes through them.

When his gaze slowly burns its way down my front I suddenly realise why.

"Oh no," I breathe, fingers twitching at my sides because there's no undoing what he's looking at right now.

As in, he's looking at me, looking at him, and I'm wearing *his freaking shirt.*

I know that it was Tanner who left it for me, because everyone else walked back at the same time. Plus, it's khaki, which is so Tanner it makes my heart ache.

I swallow hard and try to calm down my little palpitations.

It's okay, I tell myself. *Maybe he'll do the gentlemanly thing and just not say anything.*

"Nice shirt," he calls out, jerking his chin at me.

His loud voice carries so well in the bright morning air.

Refusing to be bested, I walk dangerously close to the edge of the balcony, making him pause his steps, narrowing his eyes.

"Isn't it?" I call back, lifting a shoulder on a dreamy sigh. "I'm guessing it's Tristan's."

A smirk pulls up the corner of his mouth because he knows that I know who left it for me.

"I'll bet," he rumbles, resuming his trudge to the water's edge, eyes on mine even as his feet begin slowly sinking into the water. I watch his face, trying to gauge if the water is cool or already warmed, but he maintains his stoic composure, only looking away from me once so that he can squint into the sun.

When his gaze reaches back for mine we watch each other in silence. His breathing is deep and heavy, large shoulders swelling in rhythmic waves.

After a moment, he reaches back and rips his shirt over his head, balling it in his fist and quickly slugging it to the gravel behind him. With his large body exposed he wades deeper into the water, eyes searching mine as he waits for a reaction.

Now it's my turn to maintain my stoic composure.

On a deep inhale, he lowers his body beneath the lake's surface, staying under for maybe ten seconds before breaking back into the sparkling light.

He shoves a hand through his hair, pushing it back from his handsome face, and then begins to swim silently from his side of the lake to mine.

When he reaches the dead centre he settles into a standing float. He gruffly jerks his chin at me as he resists the push of the waves.

"Join me," he says quietly, keeping his voice low, for my ears only.

I give him a playful roll of my eyes which reads, *Tanner, as if.*

Him in a pair of drenched workout shorts and me wearing – what? – his shirt and a pair of panties?

Being with Tanner is dangerous, especially when it's just the two of us. He's as reckless as I am, and when we're naked we get downright stupid.

I gracefully dip down to collect my phone from the wood and, lifting my nose in the air, I tell him, "Actually, I'm working."

His cheek tics up for the briefest of seconds.

"Baby, all you're doing right now is working that pretty mouth."

He swims slowly closer, strong and silent.

"It's a Saturday, Aisling. Get down here and we can tick something off your bucket list."

I blink quickly, alarmed, and then almost jump out of my skin as a tiny knock sounds behind me.

I whip around and see Fallon, still in her dress from last night, beaming up at me, fresh as a daisy. She's pointing to something on the screen of her phone and when I tiptoe closer to the door I see that it's the hardware store's weekend opening times.

Saturday: 7am – 12pm.

Sunday: CLOSED.

I breathe out a shaky, grateful exhalation, relieved that she's here with me to keep me on the straight and narrow – to keep me focused. If we head out in five we can get pancakes at the Larch Peak diner, and then make our way to the hardware store just as it opens. That gives me the whole day once we get back to start hauling all of the debris from the lake house and potentially give each room it's preliminary clean-down, the perfect time to check for any major issues with the wood panelling and any sockets.

I give her an enthusiastic nod and she blows me a kiss before signalling that she needs two minutes to get changed. Hunter is still laying half-out of Fallon's sleeping bag, palms pressed into his eyes as he lets out a low early morning groan. When he drops his hands he shoves himself to his feet, lazily moving our way so that he can give Fallon a rough squeeze from behind, and he drops a kiss to her cheek before she starts explaining our plan for the morning to him.

While they're momentarily occupied I chance one more look over my shoulder and see that Tanner is still waiting for me silently in the bright morning sunspot, water lapping gently at his broad hockey player shoulders in endless golden swirls.

As reckless as I am, I remind myself.

Then I spin around on my heel and rush back inside the lake house.

*

I wipe the back of my wrist over my forehead as I finally sit myself down, my short denim overalls covered in dust and both of my knees rubbed red raw. I keep my back pressed against the wall beside the front door and take in the sight of my full day's handiwork.

The lake house is shining from the inside out. Every

71

surface that I could reach has been dusted and cleaned, ready to be sanded, painted and polished over in the coming days. Even without any furniture, the wooden walls and floors make the place seem cosy and warm.

It's inviting. Intimate. I tip my head to the side, the last of the day's summer light streaking through the large first floor windows, and I bask in the silence, listening mindfully to nothing but the lapping of the lake.

I breathe deep and even, tired but satisfied for my first day's results.

A tiny vibration buzzes in my dungaree pouch, pulling me from my sunset bathing, and I lazily slip my baby pink phone out of the pocket.

It's a text from Fallon, containing a photo of maybe thirty burgers in the back of someone's car, with the caption *your feast awaits* and, like, ten thousand heart-eyes emojis.

I send her back the emoji of my spirit animal – the crawling baby – and tentatively lift myself from the floor, fluffing the fly-away wisps from my face as I nudge the door open with my sandal. There's instant hollering from the other side of the lake as I begin casually making my way down the porch steps, hands in my hair to reaffix my fluffy bun. I flash a smile to the hockey boys who are whistling at me like they've just seen a Hollywood actress.

"Oh my God, stop!" I call over to them, shimmering with delight when they continue for my whole walk over. I'm blushing and hiding my dimples with my hands by the time that I reach their make-shift log-dining situation, comprised of three big pieces of lumber around a not-yet-lit campfire.

"Embarrassing," I say when the guys wrap me in some sort of group bear hug, even though I haven't stopped smiling for a single second.

Fallon teeters over from the log that she's been sharing with Hunter and she presents a baggie of burgers and fries to me as if it's made of diamonds.

I give my own diamonds a little rub, having totally forgotten that I was even wearing them.

They were a gift from my ex. I really ought to stop wearing them.

"Thank you so so so—" I begin, but then I stop my hand mid-reach as a thought suddenly crosses my mind. I retract my hand like I've just touched a hot flame and my wide eyes immediately dart to hers.

"Hold on. Who bought this?" I ask her, well aware that the early morning dipper is currently nowhere to be seen.

Fallon makes a wishy-washy kind of sound that has me narrowing my eyes on her.

"Fallon."

"Yeah?"

"Who bought everyone's dinner?" I ask again, a sinking feeling in my stomach. I already know that I'm about to take the very low, petty, hungry road.

She mumbles something that sounds suspiciously like *well maybe it was Tanner* and I release a tiny howl.

No way am I eating it if that annoyingly hot big shot bought it. I refuse to be in his debt.

So I sniff and say, "Goodbye burger and fries," before turning around so that I can face the guys again.

Except that when I turn around I fully whack my face into the world's hardest set of chest muscles.

"Ow! What the hell!" I squeal, rubbing quickly at my forehead before glowering up at Tanner's handsome face. "Jesus Christ, were you carved from stone?"

He ignores that and jabs a big blunt finger toward something over my shoulder.

"That's for you," he says, his expression unreadable.

I glance back to see what he's talking about and I roll my eyes. Fallon has placed the burger and fries on a log and made a sad little shrine.

"No thanks," I say, brushing past him so that I can head

back to the lake house.

"Aisling, for Christ's sakes. It's just a goddamn burger."

I spin around, shocked to see that he's actually following me. I try to pick up my pace but he just grips me by my elbow and starts herding me over to his irritatingly sexy G-wagon.

"You are one stubborn woman," he adds on in a quiet growl as he snatches the burger, rounds me to the back of his car, and pushes the food into the palms of my hands.

It really does smell good.

I scowl up at him anyway. "My belly, my prerogative."

He swipes his tongue over his lower lip, momentarily checking me out over my overalls.

When he lifts his gaze back to mine he jerks his chin at me and says, "What, you don't like fries or something?"

Before I can answer he pulls me away from the door of his car, tugging it open and jerking his thumb at the backseat.

"I bought a bunch of stuff, take your pick," he says, his voice gravelly and quiet. His cheeks stain pink when he mumbles, "There's a blackberry cobbler back there that's pretty good, too. Sugar cookie crumble on top. It's… it's my favourite."

I tamper down that little squeeze in my heart. *He's offering me his favourite food.*

I hesitate for a second too long and Tanner gently tugs the burger and fries from my tightly clenched fist, replacing it with a small disposable tinfoil tray containing a freshly-baked blackberry cobbler.

He eases a fork into my hand, giving me the world's cutest peace offering.

Tanner clears his throat, his big warm body close to mine. "Try it," he rumbles. "My mom always gets it when my dad's in town. It's our favourite."

I risk a glance up into his eyes and he's looking down at me with red cheeks, his expression hopeful.

Damn it, Tanner, I think to myself. *Why did you have to be a player?*

I drop my gaze and take the smallest forkful of cobbler that I can, nibbling in silence as he watches me from a foot above. It's warm and sweet. I find it kind of adorable that this is Tanner's favourite food.

I swallow my mouthful and place the fork back in the tray, letting him know that the moment is over.

Tanner stares down at me.

"Keep eating."

Heat floods through my chest as I flash him a dangerous glare.

He watches me in silence.

I pick back up the fork.

He grunts when I shovel in a giant forkful of cobbler, eyes gleaming black when they momentarily capture mine.

"Like it?" he asks.

I frown up at him, not saying anything.

He smirks back down at me. "You love it, huh?"

I practically growl as I shove the dish back into his hands, dissipating the intimacy of Tanner feeding me his cobbler. He smirks, dipping his thumb into the juice, and sucking off the flavour with a molten gleam in his eyes.

"Mm," he murmurs. "Been a while since I tasted anything that sweet."

"Oh my *God*," I explode, humourless and exasperated. "You are so freaking smug, Tanner! How the hell did I miss those signs?"

I roll my eyes at myself as I head back to where everyone else is, on the other less intense side of Tanner's giant car.

"Wait." Tanner drops the cobbler into the backseat, blocking my path as I go to walk around the hood. My eyes momentarily flick to the veins in his biceps and I remember just how capable his body can be. "It wasn't like that, Aisling. You and me? It was never like that."

I shove my way past him, hating how much I love hearing the way he rumbles my name. That deep country drawl. I'll never get over it.

I plonk down beside Fallon, turning my head in the opposite direction when I hear him trudging into the clearing.

He genuinely has the balls to sit down right next to me, his giant shoulder pressing into mine and radiating more heat than a mountain bear.

"You. Are. So. Annoying!" I stamp down on his boot with every word that I grind out.

He snickers and hunches forward, taking a huge bite out of a burger.

I blink down at it in confusion as he manages to swallow a whole half in one go.

He takes another abnormally large bite as he silently shoves a brown paper bag onto my lap, inconspicuously, so that no-one around us will see.

Begrudgingly I look inside. He's offering me his fries.

I scrunch the bag shut, my heart a volcano of conflicting feelings.

Tanner finishes off his burger on bite number three, and then, to my amazement, gets to work on a second one.

"No wonder you're so big," I whisper, reaching into the brown bag and cautiously nibbling on a fry.

He grunts and continues eating. Zero ceremony.

As I passively listen to the hockey talk happening between Austin, Hunter and Tristan, Tanner crumples up his second burger wrapper and slides his eyes over to my legs.

"What happened there?" he asks, his gaze burning onto my scuffed kneecaps.

I swish my hair around. "I told you. I'm working."

"Yeah? What're you working on? Sanding your bones?"

He glances away from me for a good five seconds and then, like an obsessive psycho, looks back at my knees again.

"You got any Band-Aids?" he asks.

"I don't need Band-Aids," I reply.

He exhales hard, biceps flexing. "Aisling, you're bleeding."

I glance down at my knees. I am in fact bleeding.

I re-cross my legs in the opposite direction to him, so that he can't see.

He breathes out a humourless laugh and shoves himself to his feet. Then he hauls me up with him.

"Uh, what the hell do you think that you're doing?" I whisper as he starts pulling me silently towards his cabin. Then I spot a third burger baggie beside where he was sitting and I stare at it with my jaw on the floor. "Were you about to eat a third burger?" I ask. His giant hand grips surprisingly gently around my elbow.

He snickers and flicks his eyes down to mine. "Baby, I was already on burger number two before your little ass came struttin' over here. That's burger number five."

I blink up at him, speechless, and he stares down at me, hungrier than ever.

He shoulder-shoves his cabin door open and stabs a finger toward his bed.

"Sit there. I'll grab the first aid kit."

My eyes almost roll out of my head. "There's not a chance in hell that I'm going anywhere near your bed."

"Yeah?" he asks absently as he yanks open a wooden cupboard in the small back bathroom. "Caught you eyeing it up pretty friendly yesterday morning."

I shuffle a little, resisting the urge to give the soft quilt cover a little scrunch.

"That was because I thought that you'd vacated the premises," I say, swallowing hard to try and choke down the lie.

"You'd miss me," he says, his voice seductively deep.

I shove five French fries in my mouth and mumble, "In

your dreams."

He smirks as he moves in front of me, red first aid kit in his big fist.

"You do more than just miss me in my dreams," he drawls.

Then he drops down to his knees.

"W-what are you doing?" I say nervously, stumbling backwards.

His cheeks are red, eyes refusing to meet mine as he searches quickly for some saline. "Gonna fix up your knees," he mumbles, his breathing a little heavy.

He looks up at me from his position on the wooden floor, haunches spread and shoulders heaving. My heart beats wildly in my chest at the amount of adoration in his eyes.

I shake my head quickly and wheeze out, "N-no, that's okay. I'll do it myself."

"Aisling," he rasps.

"Tanner, we shouldn't–"

"Baby–"

A ringing sound makes me jump, and we quickly glance at his bed in confusion.

His phone vibrates gently on the flowery quilt.

The screen is facedown.

Tanner stands up quickly, grabs the phone, and curses.

"Fuck. I have to take this."

I wince at that all-too-familiar twisting pain in my gut.

"Give me the box," I say as calmly as I can, gesturing with a hand for him to just pass it over already.

He watches me for a moment, a deep frown on his brow. Then, slowly, he passes it to me.

I practically run out of the cabin, my heart pounding in my chest, and as much as I try not to, I can't help but listen out for the quiet rumble of his voice as he talks in a gentle hush to whoever is on the other side of the line.

The last thing that I hear before I decide to call it a night is him chuckling softly and saying, "I love you, too."

CHAPTER 9

Tanner

Present day

I scrub the towel over my face before tossing it over the shower frame, grabbing my shirt and the take-out bag, and making my way out of the cabin.

The morning sunlight reflects off the face of the lake and I naturally chance a look toward the other side of the water, hoping for a glimpse of Aisling.

It's only been a week but the lake house already looks different to when we first arrived. The porch may still be in a state of disrepair but everything else is glowing a rustic caramel brown. She's had contractors coming by all week, checking on the plumbing and electric, and from what Fallon's been saying Aisling's finally got the all-clear.

From here on out she's going to be soloing this house-flip.

After a moment of silently staring I realise that Aisling's truck isn't where it's usually parked, beside their porch.

Plus, Hunter's kicking back with Austin around the fire-pit, meaning that wherever Aisling's gone to, Fallon must have gone too.

A frown settles on my brow as I glance over to the dirt road, thinking about where the hell they could have gone.

I heave myself down onto the last unoccupied log and I pull my shirt over my head as I speak to Hunter.

"Thought we were all going hiking this morning," I rumble, inconspicuous as hell – my subtle way of asking *where did Aisling go?*

I keep my eyes on the dirt as I pretend to be very fucking busy tying my laces.

Hunter hurls a small rock off my boot and gives me a knowing grin when I glance over at him.

"They'll be back any minute. Aisling had something she wanted to do in town."

My frown deepens. "Like what?"

He shrugs a shoulder, then checks his phone to see if Fallon's sent him anything. "I think they were getting coffees."

I scrub roughly at my forehead, well aware that Aisling already saw me leave this morning to grab breakfast for everyone.

I clear my throat and stare down at the brown paper bag resting next to me on the log. "She coulda just asked me."

Aisling has been working tirelessly for the past week on the lake house. I was kind of hoping that with today being Friday – with the whole weekend ahead of us – we could get back to where we were last Saturday, before she started giving me the silent treatment.

Ideally, we'd get straight back to the part where she's standing in my cabin and I'm on my knees in front of her, but if she needs me to take it slow this time then I'll be down as hell for that.

I'll be down as hell for anything that Aisling wants of me.

I wrap my fist around the top of the takeout bag and glance back toward the dirt track, knee bouncing up and down as I wait for her to get back here.

A cabin door creaks gently open behind us and we twist around to watch Caden hold the door open for his girlfriend, quickly locking up after them and then sliding two big tattooed forearms around the small waist of her flower-dotted sundress.

Winter gives us a smiley "hey y'all" while her boyfriend, who has lived with us for the past two freaking years, doesn't even seem to notice that we're here. Even when he joins us on the logs and sits right goddamn next to me.

I stare at his face in bemused disbelief, but he's one-hundred percent preoccupied with rubbing his palms down Winter's thighs.

I roll my eyes and give his boot a kick.

"Earth to fucking Caden."

He glances at me in confusion and I can't help but huff out a laugh.

Honestly, I don't even blame him – I wish that I was in a loved-up little daydream right now instead of pining from fifty feet away.

I inhale a deep breath and decide to stop being an asshole.

"If y'all want coffees there's some in the back of my car," I begin, and Winter is off like a little pocket rocket, hauling open the backdoor and then exclaiming a literal verse of prayer.

I breathe out a laugh and slide my eyes over to Caden, who's watching her without blinking, hearts in his eyes.

I surprise both of us when I say, "You're a lucky guy."

Caden's eyes meet mine and he watches me carefully before nodding.

"I know," he says quietly, before turning his attention back to his girlfriend, widening his sitting position so that she can perch on one of his tattooed thighs. I can't help but notice that she only took one coffee, which she hands to Caden, before wrapping her arms around his neck.

"Thanks for the coffee," she says to me in her twangy Kentucky accent, all giggles and smiles like this is the best day of her life.

I have never in my life met anyone as happy as Caden's girlfriend.

I glance at him again, wondering what the hell he did to secure a chick like Winter.

He takes a sip of the coffee and then places it firmly back into Winter's hands.

"Y'all coming hiking?" Hunter asks, jerking his chin at Caden, just as we hear Aisling's truck crunching its way over the track that leads to the head of the lake.

My eyes flash over to her car and I can see that she's talking animatedly to Fallon. Her hair's in a curly bun and she's wearing those cute denim overalls.

Caden looks down at his girlfriend and she twists her lips as if contemplating Hunter's question.

"Wanna hike?" Caden asks her quietly, bouncing her on his quad to make her giggle.

Then Caden brushes the soft pink hair away from her ear and murmurs something against her cheek in a low reverberating rumble. Winter's eyes go wide for a second and then she turns to blink at him with blushing cheeks.

She clears her throat and whispers a tiny, "Okay."

Caden smirks, squeezes her waist, and then slides his eyes over to mine. "Yeah, we're coming."

I give him a grimace that reads *way too much information, man*, before shoving his shoulder with mine and hauling myself up off the bench.

I glance across the lake, one hand quickly shoving my hair back as I clutch the breakfast muffin bag in a death grip. "I'm gonna, uh, head over there for a minute," I mumble. "Meet y'all in a few."

Hunter gets to his feet too, eyes on Fallon as she

dismounts from the truck across the water. "I'll join."

We begin trudging around the head of the lake in silence, both entranced by the squeals and laughter coming from the girls as they make their way up the porch steps.

I glance down at the fallen wooden railing that still hasn't been remade, not much caring for the fact that their fenceless porch is an accident waiting to happen. I scratch roughly at my stubble, wondering if Aisling has made any calls about getting that fixed up yet.

"What's in the bag?" Hunter asks, eyes sliding down to the brown paper in my fist.

"Breakfast muffin," I grunt. "And my pride."

He half-smiles and looks back up at his girlfriend, jerking his chin at her when she turns her full-watt smile down on him.

He jumps the steps two at a time and tugs her roughly against his chest, pressing a hard smug kiss against her happy dimpled cheek.

"Hey baby," he murmurs, hauling her up as she melts against him.

I turn my attention to Aisling's perky little butt as she struts purposefully into the lake house.

She doesn't slam the door in my face so I decide to follow in after her.

While she's busy acting like I don't exist I give myself a couple of seconds to check her out, raking my eyes up the backs of her bare legs until I reach the shorts of her denim overalls. I tug at the neckline of my shirt, roll my shoulders back, and bite the bullet.

"Aisling," I say gruffly, widening my stance as I wait for her to turn around.

I glance briefly down at the take-out bag in my hand and my forearms flex in nervous anticipation.

I got her a breakfast muffin – strawberry, her favourite.

I hope that the butter-cream icing hasn't smudged too bad.

When I return my stare to the back of her curly bun she's still completely preoccupied, placing things out on the kitchen counter.

I frown, a muscle rolling in my jaw, suddenly realising that a breakfast muffin is nowhere near a good enough peace offering. Not when I want her to walk with me on our hike today. Not when I want to fully put my past behind us.

The back of my neck starts to get hot as I realise how stupid this was – me thinking that I could win her back when I haven't done anything to prove my intentions yet.

I rub roughly at my forehead.

Who buys their crush a breakfast muffin? I should have bought her roses.

When she turns around she actually jumps as if she didn't know that I was here, the three take-out coffees that she's holding over-spilling a little beneath their caps.

"Oh my God," she breathes, shaking her head and squeezing her eyes shut. "Sorry, I didn't realise that you were there. I was totally busy trying to–"

She suddenly stops herself when she finally notices my taken aback expression. I mean, besides the fact that she didn't hear me say her name out loud like a normal human being, she's talking to me right now like I'm a guy who she doesn't hate.

She swallows the rest of her sentence and looks up at me with a slightly embarrassed blush.

It's fucking beautiful.

"How are your knees?" I ask, briefly checking that they aren't still bleeding. There's still one Band-Aid in place, which makes me suspicious that she reopened one of her cuts with more floor-scrubbing, but other than that they seem to be back to their perfect selves.

I get a flashback of sliding my hands beneath those knees and I quickly avert my eyes, shuffling my feet and grunting.

"They're fine," she says breathlessly, bouncing agitatedly in her sandals. As if maybe she's just had the exact same flashback as I have.

I swipe my tongue over my bottom lip, psyching myself up to ask her to hike with me, when the coffees in her hands finally register in my brain. As in, there are *three* coffees in her hands.

Aisling and Fallon make two. So who the hell is the third one for?

I shove my tongue in my cheek and jerk my chin towards the cup-holder.

"Who's the coffee for?" I ask, my chest tense and expanding. Because even though I'm a positive guy, I can't help but wonder if it's for Tristan.

My cheeks go damn near crimson as I think about the strawberry muffin in my fist, while Aisling's out here moving onto other men. I mean, as she fucking should. It's not as though we were ever even together.

Goddamn it. I have to avert my eyes for a couple of seconds, staring blankly over toward her fireplace as I try to alleviate the acidic sensation currently burning up my sternum.

But she puts me out of my misery when she looks up at me and quietly says, "The coffee's for Connell. Connell and his guys are coming for the summer."

I almost sigh with relief. *It's not for Tristan. It's for her brother.*

I nod my head, exhaling deeply, and I hold out the breakfast bag containing her muffin.

She frowns up at me, clutching her coffees tighter against her chest.

"What is it?" she asks, dropping her gaze to the bag suspiciously.

"Nothing. Just breakfast." For the sake of her pride I say, "I grabbed some stuff in town for everyone. This one's for you."

She purses her lips, unaware of how distracting that is.

When she doesn't take it I decide to take matters into my own hands. Her little rucksack is on the counter behind her so I close the gap between us, flick the zip, and shove the muffin inside.

"Look, just take it. You don't even have to eat it. Or if you want, you can eat it and then get back to pretending that you don't like me after."

Something like a smile tugs at her lips. "Who's pretending?" she teases.

My eyes flash down to hers and I can't help but smirk, my chest swelling to twice its size at her fiery little quip.

And in the next second she's smiling up at me, as if she can't hold it in any longer. She bites shyly into her bottom lip and tries to suppress the raspy laughter in her throat.

I duck my head, grinning just as hard as she is, well aware that this is the first real smile that she's given me in four years.

Chest heaving in erratic pumps, I grip at the back of my neck with one hand and carefully lift the other just in front of her collarbone, capturing her eyes with mine as I tuck two fingers into her dungaree strap. Slowly I tug it back into place, careful not to brush her bare skin with mine but knowing that she can feel my heat regardless.

She stands totally still and silent, watching me with sparkly wide eyes, her hands gripped tight around the coffee holder.

I give her a little smirk. "Clothes just do not want to stay on you."

She wheezes out a tiny laugh. "Tell that to the pyjamas I left behind in Carter Ridge. Some clothes don't even want to be in the same county as me."

I breathe fast and deep, thinking about Aisling secretly wearing the shirt that I gave her for bed. About Aisling standing on her balcony each morning, watching me in wide-eyed silence as I work out across the lake while she wears *my clothes*.

Now's your chance, man. Ask her to hike with you. Tell her that you want to carry her bags and take her to the top of that mountain.

I swallow hard, reluctantly prizing my fingers from her denim strap.

"Aisling, I–"

In the next second I'm cut off by the sound of wheels crunching over the dirt outside, a door slamming open and the deep bellow of, "Yo, Ash! You in there?"

I curse and glance over my shoulder, pressing slightly closer up to Aisling as we both watch her brother stepping around the hood of a giant Ford, sunlight streaming endlessly through the large lake house windows.

"Fuck," I grunt, pissed off at having this moment interrupted. I turn back to look down at Aisling, all but pinned to the counter, and I grudgingly force myself to pull away from her, already knowing that today can no longer go as I'd planned it.

With her brother, his best friend Logan, and half of his football team arriving there's no way that I'll be able to spend the hike with Aisling because without a doubt he's going to be joining. He's going to be the one guiding her over the steep patches, carrying her bag and keeping her steady.

There's not a chance in hell that he'll be okay with me – the biggest player on campus, let alone out of the Carter Ridge Rangers – swooping in on the little sister duties.

I curse again, heart clenching taut when I see how Ash has neatly stacked my logs beside her fireplace.

My eyes flick back to hers and she glances desperately back and forth, looking between me and the guys outside of the open front door.

"I have to... I've gotta go," she rasps and I nod my head, grateful at least that we're on some non-argumentative talking terms.

"Yeah," I say quietly. "Have a great day with your

brother."

I don't mention his football team. I may be trying to be a gentleman here but Connell's football team can fuck right off.

"Thanks," she breathes, slowly making her way to the front door. Just before she steps outside she smiles and adds on, "Big shot."

She's out of the door before I can say anything but I traipse slowly to the jamb, smirking anyway.

Her brother – Carter U's freshly graduated star quarterback – instantly takes the coffees out of her hands and throws her over his shoulder, talking in a loud happy bellow about how amazing his sister is to his teammates.

I lean a shoulder against the doorframe, watching Aisling giggle with a smile crease in my cheek.

Then my eyes flash down to the broken railing and a different idea comes to my mind.

I take my phone out of my pocket and shoot a quick text to Hunter, telling him that I'm ditching our first hike of the trip. Doesn't matter, I'll join the next one – one where Aisling's brother isn't watching her every move and maybe we can progress on rebuilding our relationship.

Just as Connell and the guys start making their way around to the other side of the lake, Aisling looks up at me from over her brother's shoulder. She's smiling, a little shy and curious, and there's something wild and hopeful burning behind her eyes.

I jerk my chin at her, smirking when she bites her teeth into her lower lip.

Then I give her a wink and watch her breath catch in her throat.

Being hated by this girl feels better than being liked by any other.

CHAPTER 10

Tanner

Four years ago

It's one thing to enter a chick's bedroom to help her construct a piece of furniture, but it's another thing entirely to sit shoulder to shoulder on her bed.

And those sheets that I carried in from where they were cosied up on her couch?

They're softer than sin.

And they're *black*.

I watch, wary as fuck, as she slips her fork into a slice of strawberry, and I have to physically tear my eyes away from her mouth before I get my hundredth hard-on of the afternoon. Her Macbook is positioned on the quilt in front of us, playing a football game that I haven't seen before.

Something nudges gently against my leg and I see that Aisling is silently offering me her little fruit bowl. She slides a second fork my way and I rub my chest, aching for how cute she is.

I give her shoulder a thank-you nudge as I take a piece of strawberry.

"So, do you not like football?" she asks, glancing up at me with those big beautiful eyes.

I didn't have the nerve to tell her earlier that I'm a hockey guy, through and through. If Aisling is into football though for her I can sit back and bear it.

"It's okay, I can tell," she laughs, returning my shoulder nudge. "Actually I… I like that you're not into it. It's really nice to meet a guy with interests that are different from the ones that I'm used to."

A muscle tics involuntarily in my jaw. "What kind of guys are you used to?"

She hums contemplatively as she slides another piece of strawberry into her mouth, sucking at it for a while before shifting her hips and swallowing.

At this rate I could probably grow enough wood to build her another bed.

"I went to a prep school – co-ed, so that Connell and I could be together. I was mainly friends with his friends, so they were all of the football guys, and it just made me super aware of the kind of lifestyle that male athletes lead. Play hard and then *play* hard, if you get what I mean."

I watch her carefully for a moment. "So it's a no to guys who play football?" I clarify, very fucking specifically.

Fingers crossed she doesn't have any preconceived notions about hockey players because, if she does, I'm screwed.

"Kinda," she admits, smiling up at me.

"Then I've never been so happy to not play football in my life."

She breathes out a gorgeous laugh as she leans playfully against my biceps.

"What about you?" I ask her. "What are you studying? You do any sports?"

"I'm a cheerleader," she says, looking up at me from

under her lashes.

I clear my throat hard, unable to formulate a single sentence after that.

She's a cheerleader?

I'm in bed with a fucking cheerleader?

I can't deny it, this is a good moment for me.

"*Anyway*," she says, laughing as she draws out the word, "after I graduate from college there's no doubt about what I'll be doing. I'm going to join my family's business, but I want to see if I can help expand it in a different direction. They construct premium real estate, but I want to go the small town route – house flips and stuff."

I try to focus on what she's saying but I'm starting to get distracted by the way she's leaning into me. The pretty curves of her chest are brushing right up against my biceps.

"And you?" she asks, as if I have a single brain cell left, as if I can remember what the hell we were just talking about.

"Me?" I ask, my voice way too fucking deep. "What about me?"

I swear I hear her tinkle out a laugh but I'm too far gone to risk another glance at her beautiful face.

"Like, what do you do in Carter Ridge? Are you in a family business, too?"

I was about to state the fact that I'm a freshman at Carter U but her second question throws me, and I frown at the game on the screen.

"Uh, no," I say quietly. "We don't exactly have a family business. Like, my best friend Hunter, his dad is a mechanic, so it's a given that some of his sons are going to help him run the joint eventually." I clear my throat and try to rub the tension out of my brow. "My dad's in the army."

A soft whoosh of air caresses my chest, as if Aisling has sucked in a breath, impressed as hell. And I'm proud of that reaction, even if it's reserved for my dad's career, and not my own.

I can feel the moment that understanding dawns on her – the fact that, unlike my dad and both of my brothers, I haven't followed in my father's footsteps and taken the military route. Because I'm here in Carter Ridge, rather than being at a military school.

And I love the path that I've chosen for myself. Partially because I love hockey, but partially because of my mom. Seeing as she was a professional figure skater I love that I've continued her sports legacy, while also giving her one less man to worry about. Because, yeah, hockey's rough but it's nothing like having a loved one in the army – waiting around for months on end, praying that they'll stay safe.

Praying that they'll come home.

So the worrying that she does for my dad and my brothers when they're on deployment? She doesn't need to do that for me.

But even though I love my sport, I respect what my dad and brothers do, and that's the reason why I've sometimes wondered if I made the right decision.

"I'm sorry." Her voice is sweet and sincere. "I didn't mean to pry."

After taking a deep grounding inhale I allow myself to look back down at her.

Those big beautiful eyes knock the air out of my lungs.

"You didn't do anything wrong." I glance down at her lap, seeing her thigh resting against mine. "I respect my dad and my brothers for what they do, but I love what I do too."

"So you have a job, right now?" she asks.

"It's in the pipeline," I admit, thinking about the four years of college hockey that I'm in for. Undeniably, the thought brings a smile to my face. "I have my training years first but technically, yeah, I'm all set."

She prods a finger into my bicep. "Well, as long as you don't play football," she teases.

A deep laugh reverberates through my chest until I

realise that the game we're watching is over. Now we're just two people on a bed, looking at each other with growing hunger.

Noticing that the game has finished Aisling suddenly leans toward her laptop to open a different browser, and my eyes automatically drop to her behind as she bends over right in front of me.

I grunt like a motherfucker and practically throw myself off her bed.

"I should probably take off," I rasp, turning a sharp one-eighty so that she won't see my sudden erection.

And that would have been fine if there wasn't a fucking *mirror* in front of us.

Her startled eyes meet mine in the reflection.

I look heavenward, praying for strength.

"I would love to keep hanging out," I admit, digging my palms into my eyes. "You're funny and beautiful, and I've had a great time with you today. But I think that I've reached the point where I'm… no longer in control of my body."

I drop both of my hands and look at her in the mirror. She's biting nervously into her lower lip, her eyes unblinking on mine. Forcing herself not to look at the situation in my shorts.

I swallow hard.

"I should take off," I rasp, and I expect her to nod and say, *yeah, please leave.*

But instead she scooches a little closer and asks innocently, "Take off what?"

I half-laugh, half-groan as I cover my face with my hands, and the pretty sound of her laughter behind me makes warmth spread through my chest. I know that she's just messing with me, being playful to save me the humiliation of my painfully obvious attraction to her, but even *that* is sexy, the level of compassion in her humour.

"Aisling," I groan, as I turn to face her. My cheekbones

are ruddy and my breathing is way too fast, but we're both smiling at each other with empathy and understanding. "I'm so freaking sorry. Like, I wish I could get a handle on myself. There's nothing I would rather do right now than spend the rest of the night watching stuff with you. Even football," I add, just because I want to hear her beautiful laugh again.

She gives it to me and it's the most incredible sound in the world.

"Well, if you want to go," she begins, stretching her arms in the air and then dropping her body back against her sheets, squealing in delight as her quilt plumps up around her. "Then I'm not going to stop you," she finishes, but her tone is riddled with a dare.

She peeks down at me to where I'm standing like a starved beast at the bottom of her bed, and her thighs squeeze together as I rub a palm down my jaw.

"You should close my door on your way out," she continues, her eyes sparkling now, as she gently taunts me with that naughty smile.

I blink down at her, realisation dawning.

Hold the fuck up.

Am I misreading this situation, or is she daring me to make a move?

I glance toward her partially opened bedroom door and then back to her reclined position in the centre of her bed. She's practically vibrating with amusement, her whole demeanour shimmering with mischief.

It's still piss-pouring outside and the wet sound effects aren't helping my erection. I shove a hand into my hair and rake my gaze over Aisling's body.

"Are you… do you want me to…" I yank roughly on the neckline of my shirt. "Because obviously I would love to… if you would also love to–"

"Tanner."

"Yes?"

"I can tell that you like me."

Her voice is gentle and husky, and it makes my abdomen harden.

"Yeah, I fuckin' do," I say, hoarse with honesty. "I really fuckin' like you. I like you so much, but I can't believe that you would like me too."

Her eyes widen. "Why not?"

"Because you're so beautiful."

She presses a hand to her chest, blinking quickly. "Oh, wow."

I decide to use this moment to state my intentions loud and clear, more grateful than ever that Aisling doesn't know about my reputation off the ice.

"I want to take you to dinner. I want you to know the kind of guy that I am – the kind of guy that I'll be for you. I can tell that you're not a roll-in-the-hay kind of chick and that's fine with me. In fact, I like that."

Aisling picks up her glass of water and begins furiously sipping.

"So, if you'll let me, I'd love to take your number. And if you decide that you wanna see me again, I'll book something real special. Dinner for two, or I could take you horse-riding one town over. Or, hell, if you'd like it, I'm pretty decent in the kitchen so I could show you what I can do–"

"Tanner?"

"Yes?"

"Just kiss me already."

"Yes ma'am."

CHAPTER 11

Aisling

Present day

For the first time since we got here I wake up in the lake house alone.

After our super long hike up the closest of the Larch Peak mountains, which ended with the vastest, sparkliest view of the lake that I'd ever seen, my brother Connell gave me a piggy-back for almost half the return journey, and then we all traipsed lazily for the rest of the trek because after seven hours of working our way through the larches we were all wobbly as hell, which wasn't helped by the fact that we couldn't stop laughing.

The only thing that could have made the hike better had stayed behind at the lake.

I force myself upright in my sleeping bag, refusing to let myself wonder why Tanner didn't join us yesterday. I mean, in the morning I'd definitely thought that he was coming –

in fact, I kind of secretly thought that he'd organised the whole trek.

I frown, unzipping the bag with a violent flourish as I definitely do *not* consider why Tanner didn't want to come.

I love you, too.

His night-time phone call from a week ago, where his voice was hushed and his tone was gentle, makes something clench tight in my chest.

Is he seeing someone? Someone who he literally loves?

I kick the soft quilt off of me and walk over to the doors of the balcony.

The morning light, shimmering all the way to the head of the lake, is so beautiful that it momentarily thaws my temper. But when I realise that Tanner isn't by the shore this morning, doing the workout that I've grown so used to watching, I'm even more emotional than I was ten seconds ago.

Why wouldn't he be out here? I mean, okay, we're kind of the opposite of friends, but I thought that maybe we had some sort of secret understanding that it was okay to feel *something* as long as we didn't get too close. Hence quietly watching each other from afar, a literal lake between us.

I fist my hands into the bottom of his khaki shirt, feeling like an idiot.

There's only one reason why he wouldn't be out here. There's only one reason why he wouldn't care about joining us on yesterday's hike.

There's only one reason why he'd rather stay in bed and put an end to our morning secret.

He's got a new girl in his life.

Trying to push the gut-wrenching disappointment from my mind, I blink rapidly into the golden sunrise and will the stinging sensation away from my eyes.

I mean, this is literally why I pushed him away in the first place. It all happened way too fast and Tanner's lifestyle is dangerous to a girl like me. Someone who just wants a quiet love-filled life, not the drama and stress that comes with falling for the biggest player in the state.

I rub at the crease in my brow, frown in the direction of Tanner's cabin, and then turn back to the balcony doors, determined to finally put the last nail in these unresolved feelings.

I rifle through one of my bags so that I can pick something cute to slip into this morning and, once I've pulled the denim shorts and grey tank top into place, I start to pad quietly down the stairs. I grab the car keys from the kitchen counter, fasten on my sandals, and head outside.

From under the small canopy at the front of the house the lake looks vast and bright, although there's something about the picture that seems a little bit different. I purse my lips and tilt my head, but I'm not able to put my finger on it.

Just as I'm heading toward the edge of the porch I see the door to Tanner's cabin open, and Fallon steps out before Hunter closes the door quietly behind them.

I narrow my eyes.

Closing the door quietly. As if not to awake its sleeping residents.

Fallon instantly spots me and something like a small happy squeal travels across the lake, and she lifts up her free arm, waving excitedly.

Eternally grateful for my best friend, I lift my right hand, waving back.

Beaming, she gestures for me to join them at the logs on the other side of the lake, and just as I step forward I suddenly lose my balance.

My squeal pierces the air, knowing that I'm about to fall over the broken ledge.

But instead of hitting the dirt beneath the porch with a painful thud, I grab quickly onto the wooden railing, steadying myself as it blocks my fall.

My eyes shoot open and I look down at the secure wooden panel.

The railing. It's fixed.

In fact, it's completely redone.

I blink down at it with wide eyes and then teeter a few steps backwards. The debris of the old fence has been cleared away, and a *whole new wooden porch railing* has been carefully cut, nailed together, and erected into place.

The wooden porch is fixed. Falling is no longer a possibility.

I clutch Connell's keys to my chest as I take a tentative step closer to the porch fence, prodding at it with my pointer finger and *oohi*ng when it doesn't wobble an inch. It was so dark by the time that I made my way over here last night, Tristan's body warming my back as he walked me graciously to the front door.

And I was too distracted in the moment to notice the brand new railing.

The night ended with a kiss on the cheek and a dark hunger in Tristan's eyes, but we really are just friends so I'm glad that we didn't do anything stupid.

I turn in a full circle, admiring the wrap-around porch's new fencing.

It's perfect.

I lift my gaze back across the lake, one million percent certain that I know who's behind this huge unspoken act of kindness.

Now I know why he didn't come with us to the mountains – Tanner literally built my entire wrap-around railing. And it's so carefully made that it makes something painful twist in my chest. It's not ostentatious in any way – it's simply the perfect, rustic, *safe* necessity that this lake house needed before I finally got to work on the interior.

I twist my lips in contemplation and then make my way to the other side of the lake.

"Hey," I say to Fallon and Hunter as I jog up to where they're sat around the logs.

Hunter jerks his chin at me, his cell phone next to his

ear, and Fallon pulls away from him momentarily so that she can join me, to Hunter's dismay.

She's wearing flip-flops, pyjama shorts, and one of Hunter's shirts. We both look out across the lake, enjoying the serenity of the blissful summer morning.

"We're heading over to Carter Ridge today, so that Hunter can help out at his dad's garage," Fallon tells me in a hushed tone. "Hence the super early start."

Hunter talks quietly on his cell, his morning voice deep and husky.

"I was thinking I should go with him, if that's okay, and then we'd be back by Monday so that I can help you start up on the lake house's interior." She gives me a nervous hopeful look as she asks me, "What d'you think?"

I roll my eyes playfully and nudge her flip-flop with my sandal.

"Of course you should go and watch your boyfriend do hot mechanic things over the weekend, Fallon. As if I would deprive you of that."

She laughs quietly and smiles, cuddling her arms around her middle. "He does look super hot in his mechanic's vest."

I laugh with her and swipe my sandal through the dirt, wishing that I had a sexy boyfriend of my own – someone who didn't want to play the field, completely head over heels for one girl alone.

Hunter Wilde is the epitome of that. I wonder if I'll ever get my own.

I quietly clear my throat and glance nervously across the lake. The brand new railing seems to sparkle at me in the golden morning sunlight.

"So, um, last night..." I begin, my voice light and cautious.

How on earth do I word this without totally putting my heart out on my sleeve?

"Last night, when you were in... their cabin," I say,

trailing off as I bite into my lower lip.

Fallon slides her eyes over to mine, a mischievous smile on her pretty face. "Yes?"

I swallow and look down at my sparkly toenails. "Was, uh… was Tanner there?"

Fallon looks back out across the lake, smiling as she fluffs her blonde hair around her cheeks.

"Yes," she says, as if she already knows where I'm going with this.

I hum quietly, eyes still on my toes. "Did he happen to mention, uh, what he did while we were on our hike yesterday? Because I couldn't help but notice that—"

"Hey."

Hunter's deep voice rumbles suddenly behind us. Fallon and I both turn around as he leashes his large forearms around Fallon's neck.

To Fallon he asks, "You okay if we set off in half an hour? I can grab us food before we head, and we'll miss the weekend traffic. Journey'll be smooth, I promise," he adds, because Fallon gets pretty bad motion sickness.

Hunter and Fallon are painfully cute together.

After smushing a hard kiss on his girlfriend's cheek, Hunter lifts his head and gives me a smug hockey player smirk.

"Nice fence, huh?" he asks gruffly, eyes flaming with bro-code secrets.

I narrow my eyes on him and he smirks harder. Then I shuffle my feet and slide my eyes toward his cabin.

I clear my throat.

"For… curiosity's sake," I begin, a little nervous to be talking to Hunter about this. "Tanner wouldn't happen to be, like, in there right now would he—?"

Hunter snickers so hard that Fallon gives him a playful slap on one of his giant biceps.

He squeezes her tighter and then glances down at me, giving me a subtle nod.

"Yeah, he's in there. Probably still asleep 'cause he worked like a dog yesterday."

I bite my lip, eyes still on the cabin.

"I'm heading into town this morning," I tell them, anxiously tucking my hair behind my ears. "I'm gonna buy some paint for the house and, uh, probably some pyjamas. But... maybe it'd be polite if I went in there to say thank you–?"

"Yes," Hunter grunts quickly. "He'd like that, yes."

I blink up at him in surprise, mostly shocked by how certain he seems, but then I recompose my expression and give him a little nod of my own. "Okay, yes. I think I will."

I breathe out a shaky exhale and share a *what the fuck am I doing?* look with Fallon. Her pursed little smile makes me think that maybe everything will be alright.

"See you Monday," I say to her, before walking nervously toward Tanner's cabin.

Because, like, what the actual fuck do I think that I'm doing? Tanner and I are *not* friends, no matter how... easy things felt yesterday morning. After what I learned about him four years ago there's no way that I could ever feel settled with a guy like that.

Our 'relationship' is never going to get past the whole *we want completely different things* thing, so why the hell is he acting so darn perfect right now?

And why am I using that as an excuse to get closer to him?

I knock softly on his front door and then press my forehead against the wood, my belly pounding with nerves over how much of a bad idea this is.

Stop trying to fix things. Just move on already.

After twenty seconds pass in silence I tap my knuckles against the door again, frowning at the wood as my anxiety turns to irritation.

I mean, regardless of him potentially being the handyman behind building my railing, that doesn't rule out the possibility of him having a secret girlfriend – who, I quote, he *loves*. I didn't actually get around to asking Fallon if Tanner was inside the cabin *with* someone, even though I'm certain that she would have told me if he was.

Right?

Or should I… see for myself?

I stare down at the door handle, fingers twitching to give it a little shove.

I give it a solid three seconds and then, in the next moment, I'm inside.

My breath catches in my throat as I take in the sight before me, my hands automatically closing the front door, gently so that it doesn't wake him.

Because there on the immediate left Tanner is sleeping on his bed. Totally alone.

And practically naked.

I stumble back against the door, my cheeks burning as I look at him. Tanner is so tall that he's half sprawled off the mattress, thick quads kicked apart, with one large foot hanging over the edge. He has a deep golden tan, biceps swollen from yesterday's manual labour, and he's wearing absolutely nothing except for a pair of stretched grey boxer briefs.

That his big right fist is shoved right into.

I stifle a squeak of fear as his long hard ridge flexes beneath his underwear, and his chest muscles swell, as if he heard the sound through his haze of sleep.

Nervous and panting, I stay completely still, until Tanner finally relaxes again, grunting quietly as he begins stroking his fist.

In his underwear.

Over his erection.

"Oh my God!" I squeal quietly, immediately squeezing my eyes shut.

I slam one palm over my eyes and whip around so that I can't watch what he's doing. But I can still *hear* what he's doing and his rough sound effects are making me lightheaded. Like, he is pumping that thing *hard*. Grunting with every up-thrust, meaty fist slapping against his groin.

Heat whirls low down in my belly as I think *why did we ever stop seeing each other again?*

I crash into a small cabinet, yelping as I stub my toe against the wood, and with shaking hands, I fumble my fingers around the door handle. I squeak a quick *"thank you for the railing"* just in case he can hear me over the sound of his building orgasm, and then I haul ass out of the front door, shutting it as quietly as I can behind me.

I really couldn't have made more noise if I'd tried.

I run the whole way back from Tanner's cabin to Connell's truck.

CHAPTER 12

Tanner

Present day

"Mornin'."

I jerk my chin at Hunter who's currently shoving a couple of Fallon's bags into the back of his truck and he gives me a nod of his head, a smirk playing on his mouth.

I narrow my eyes on him before scoping out the breakfast bags his girlfriend is peeking into, perched on the middle log around the unlit fire-pit.

"What's up with the… smile?" I ask him, slow and suspicious.

"Who's smiling?" he replies, full-on grinning.

I watch him for a moment and then give him a smirk of my own, stepping over the log and dropping down heavily right next to Fallon. Her little thigh against my big quad. Her soft shoulder against my hard one.

Safe to say, he is no longer smiling.

I reach around Fallon's shoulder so that I can grab one

of those breakfast doughnuts and then I push a couple inches away from her, waiting for the information.

"Well?" I ask, hunching forward and ripping into the doughnut.

Strawberry jelly, I think to myself, as I finish off the other half. *Aisling's favourite.*

"Well what?" Hunter asks, shutting the back door of his truck, eyes on the small space between his girlfriend and me as he makes his way over to the fire-pit. When he reaches us he carefully eases Fallon a little further over to her right and then sits squarely between us, subtly pulverising my boot.

I snicker, give him a kick of my own, and move over to the log on their left.

"You're lucky that wasn't the bad ankle," I drawl, thinking back to the injury I got right before the NCAA Championship final earlier this year. I was advised to not play it but no way could I miss our last game. "Otherwise you'd be finding your ass" – I jerk my thumb toward the lake lapping beside us – "in there."

Hunter's cheek tics up with humour, although he winces when he glances down at my other boot.

"It's fine now, right?" he asks, rolling his shoulders in discomfort.

I grunt, not wanting to talk about an injury that should never have happened. It was barely an issue when it did, but I'm not so far up my own ass to know that repetitive sprains are not ideal for a hockey player. Seeing as I'll be starting pro at the end of the summer I'm not exactly on the hunt for too many brawls, and I don't want to exacerbate a dormant injury in the meantime.

"It's fine." I clear my throat. "Y'all heading to your parents' this weekend or something?"

Hunter wraps his forearm around Fallon's neck and says, "Yeah. We'll be back Monday."

Instinctively I glance across the lake, brow creasing when I see that Aisling isn't there. She's not up on her balcony like she has been every other morning, and the 4x4 that she's driving isn't parked up next to her new porch. My knee bounces up and down, wondering where she's gone to.

Today is the first morning that I haven't woken up before six to work out, and my chest tightens with guilt over breaking up our secret routine. I didn't even realise how goddamn tired I was last night until I hit the pillow and went out stone cold.

Although I'll admit, I woke up pretty fucking amazing though.

I shift on the log and jerk a thumb toward the lake house.

"She mention anything last night?" I ask, looking across at Fallon.

She blinks up at me for a moment and then gives me a sparkly smile.

"Aw!" she says. "I bet she was the first thing you thought about this morning, huh?"

I clear my throat and avert my eyes because Aisling definitely *is* what I was thinking about when I woke myself up this morning.

"…Sure," I say awkwardly. Then, "So did she say anything or not?"

Fallon squeals out a happy laugh.

"I need, like, a minute to process this," she says. "I wish that you understood how cute the whole burly cinnamon roll thing is."

I blink at her.

Cinnamon roll?

Then I make a gravelly sound in the back of my throat.

"Fallon."

"Fine," she relents, still laughing. "So, I don't know about her seeing the porch last night because we stayed in this cabin with you, but–"

"Wait, what?"

My head snaps up, suddenly on high alert.

"You slept in the cabin last night? You... you let her sleep over there alone?"

My leg is no longer bouncing.

Fallon's lips part into an *o*, and she glances quickly up at Hunter.

"Well, obviously we said that we'd stay with her... but she said that she was okay staying over there on her own. Like, I think that she wanted to be on her own."

I shove my tongue in my cheek, my breathing turning a little uneven.

She slept over in that un-fucking-locked lake house alone?

"Tanner, I swear, we wouldn't have left her alone if she hadn't asked us to. Besides, Tristan walked her over there because it was dark and—"

My eyes burn into Fallon's and she instantly halts.

"Uh," she says breathlessly, "what I meant to say is that—"

"Tristan walked her home?" I ask, serial killer calm.

Fallon squints into the sunrise and makes a wishy-washy sound, fingers twiddling frantically with her fluffy blonde ponytail.

"You see them go over there?"

She twists her lips to the side and squeaks out a tiny, "Maybe."

"They kiss or what?"

Fallon's eyes fly up to mine and she lets out a nervous hiccup.

Hunter breathes out a laugh, holding Fallon tighter so that she can nuzzle up on his chest.

"No way," he says, his voice confident and gruff. "Connell didn't let 'em out of his sight. Might've pecked her on the cheek but—"

I don't hear the rest of the sentence as my blood rushes around my temples.

Pecked her on the cheek.

I try not to picture one of my former Carter U teammates holding Aisling under the moonlight, probably resting up all cosy against the railing that I'd just goddamn made. But it's right there anyway, ready to haunt me for the rest of my life.

I tug my shirt away from my neck and rasp, "Where is she now?"

"She's gone to town for supplies," Fallon says. "…and some pyjamas."

My eyes flash to Fallon.

"She's doing *what?*"

Fallon blinks at me in surprise. "She needs some clothes to sleep in?"

Seeing red, I shove a hand through my hair and inhale so deep that my chest doubles up.

Aisling already has clothes to sleep in. My clothes. First, she lets Tristan cosy up to her, close enough to *peck her on the cheek.* Then, she's buying herself pyjamas, when there's a solid khaki shirt over there in that lake house for her to snuggle down in. A really good fucking shirt that's been worn in just right.

I roll my shoulders back, and heave myself up off the log.

"I'm going to town," I decide, quickly glancing down at myself – boots, jeans, and a plain grey shirt, hopefully looking presentable enough for Aisling. I tug the cotton away from where it's clinging to my pecs, nodding to Hunter and Fallon as I leave.

The roads are pretty empty even by the time that I reach Main Street, so I go idle on the accelerator, roll down the window, and just bake through the windshield while taking my time checking the shop windows. Just as I'm nearing the end of the block a large 4x4 catches my eye, and I'm instantly pulling back around – doing a U turn and a slack-jawed double take.

I park right up next to Connell's car and stare at the

shop that Aisling's parked outside of. I can see her through the window, swishing her hair and browsing lazily. I rub my palms down my jeans, heart pounding wildly as I watch her.

It's a fucking lingerie shop. And she's in there, right now, brushing her fingers over a table of lace like she has intentions of actually buying that shit.

Who the fuck is she buying lingerie for?

Tristan? One of her brother's football teammates?

I throw myself out of the driver's side and slam the door behind me.

Not on my watch.

I trudge straight ahead to the little white boutique, all but ripping the door off its hinges as I yank the thing open.

Aisling, now casually sashaying around a table a little further back, looks up in surprise, does a double-take, and then flutters her lashes at me innocently as I storm right for her.

"Am I in trouble, Officer?" she breathes, before rolling her eyes and giving me a sexy glare.

"We're leaving," I tell her, not stopping until we're toe to toe.

She swishes deeper into the store, making me curse as I follow after her. "Uh, *you're* leaving, I'm not. How did you even find me, stalker?"

"Your car's parked outside. Anyone with eyes could find you." I clear my throat hard and fold my arms over my chest, standing barely a millimetre away from her as she stops at another table. Her fingers glide tauntingly over wisps of baby pink lace. "Heard you were looking for some pyjamas."

I glance down at the basket in her hands, chest swelling to five times its size when I take in what she's got in there. Nothing but straight up hook-up panties.

I shift my belt buckle to the side and roll back one of my shoulders. "Doesn't look like there's any pyjamas in there."

Aisling gasps as she sees what I'm looking at, and quickly hides her basket behind her little ass. Little does she know, those panties are seared into my brain for life.

"Those are for my eyes only," she says with a dignified frown. Then she lifts her chin and says, "But… technically that is correct. I am looking for pyjamas."

I lower my voice so that the sales assistant can't hear us. "You've already got pyjamas," I remind her, snatching a lacy tank out of her hands when she lifts it off the table, eyes on mine as she holds it tauntingly over her basket.

I slap the top back down onto the counter, watching as she drops another pair of panties into her basket.

Black ones. Fuck.

"You want another shirt or something?" I ask her, voice deep and rough. I'm so turned on that my pecs are twitching. "I'll give you another shirt." *I'll give you anything that you want.* "Let's just get out of here."

"Why?" she asks, suddenly frowning. "So you can come back later and buy something special for your girlfriend?"

I smirk down at her. "Is that what you like to call yourself?"

Growling like a little animal she smacks a pair of panties straight off my chest. I blink down at the pink lace, then cautiously peel them off my pecs.

"Real nice," she says, her bottom lip wobbling dangerously. "I'm sure that she'd love to hear you joking around like that."

I toss the panties aside and grip Aisling's elbow.

"Aisling. What the fuck are you talking about?"

"Let me go, you giant annoying big shot!"

She slaps her palm against my abs and I clench my jaw, trying to calm my breathing.

"First of all," I say quietly, quickly manoeuvring her further away from the sales assistant, "you need to stop calling me 'big shot', unless you want me to remind you of how right you are. And second of all" – I pull her around so that we're face to face – but she keeps her nose in the air, eyes looking anywhere but into mine – "why the fuck would you think that I have a girlfriend?"

She keeps her face turned as far away from me as possible but, after a couple of huffy sighs, she gives me a curious glance.

"Iheardyouonthephone," she mumbles.

A crease forms on my brow, still at a loss to what she's talking about. "You... heard me on the phone? When did you–?"

Suddenly I'm hissing through my teeth as she pinches roughly at my nipple, my hand tightening on her elbow as I try to blink through the sting.

"Goddammit, woman," I say hoarsely, as I try to prise off her murder-grip. Our eyes meet and lock, a heated warning in my blown out pupils. My chest heaves up and down, a ripple of pleasure slicing through my pec.

When I see her fingers in my peripheral twitching to pinch some more, I breathe out a laugh, grab her wrist, and position myself behind her.

"Just so you know, *baby*," I grind out, shoving my chest against her shoulders, "if you're doing that to elicit some kind of negative reaction, you should know that it doesn't have the effect that you seem to think. Now tell me why you think that I'm dating someone so that I can clear this shit up for you, right now."

She uses her free hand to slap another pair of panties off of my chest.

I grunt quietly and toss them aside.

"You done?" I rumble, still holding her wrist.

She shoots a scowl at me over her shoulder before sliding her eyes back down to the panty display.

I huff out a laugh and turn her around to face me.

"Talk to me, Aisling."

There's a wounded look in her sparkling eyes as she finally confesses.

"I just told you," she mumbles. "I heard you on the phone and you said 'I love you'."

I'm momentarily taken aback, shoulders tensing before I realise what she's talking about.

I keep my fist wrapped around her wrist and stroke my thumb over her soft skin.

"Aisling," I sigh, wishing that I could pull her up against my chest. Heat scales my neck as I mumble, "Aisling, I was talking to my mom."

Her eyes widen on mine before slowly trailing down the front of my body. My muscles flex under her heated gaze.

"Your mom," she breathes out, when she's finally looking at our feet – her pretty sandals tucked safely between the wide stance of my boots.

"Yeah."

I can see that she's curious as hell but too proud to ask more questions, so I just stand there, holding her forearms, feeling like I'm dreaming.

After staring at me with those big eyes for a good ten seconds Aisling finally purses her lips and begrudgingly mumbles out a, "Thank you."

I lift an eyebrow in surprise, tugging her instinctively closer. "What's that now?"

Her voice is all sweet and husky when she looks up at me and says, "Thank you."

I'm almost too shocked to speak. "What for?" I rasp.

She frees her wrists from my palms, hypnotising me as she re-ties her ponytail. "The railing," she replies, twisting her hair through the band, tighter and tighter. "Thank you for the railing."

Satisfaction at her approval warms my chest.

I clear my throat, shove a hand through my hair, and give her a quick nod.

That's not the only railing that I wanna give you, baby.

We watch each other in silence for a couple of beats and then, without another word, Aisling resumes her perusal of the tables, this time effortlessly relaxed as I follow right behind her, barely a millimetre standing between us.

It feels as though we've reached a mutual understanding. I'm not seeing anyone else. I want to spend my time proving to Aisling how much I like her. And Aisling will do whatever she wants, while tolerating me trying to win her over.

I place one fist beside her hip as she pauses at another panty table, chest brushing against her shoulders with every breath that I take.

Her little basket catches my eye and I reluctantly glance down at it.

"What're you getting anyway?" I mumble, frowning down at the three strips of lace that I can see in there.

"Nothing for you to worry about," she says, casual as hell.

I huff out a laugh. *Oh I'll worry alright.* "This for your bucket list, huh?"

Ignoring me, she holds a new pair up right in front of her face, pretty ribbons all tangled around her fingers. She makes a questioning *hmmm* sound, then frowns and shoves them back in the pile.

I blink down at the panties, so fucking confused as she picks up another pair that's practically identical.

I grab the ones that she just put back and toss them quickly into her basket.

She looks down at the basket, amusement glinting in her eyes. "What're you doing?" she asks.

A deep sound rumbles up my throat. "Those were a yes," I say quietly.

She cocks a hip and lifts her eyebrow. "What?"

I tug at the neckline of my shirt and rasp, "You, uh… you liked 'em enough to look at them extra close. And they were… nice. So they're a yes."

"A yes?" she asks, moving slightly closer. Close enough for me to feel the warmth radiating out from beneath her tank top. I glance down at her chest, swallow hard, and meet her eyes again.

"Like, a yes pile versus a no pile." If Aisling was my chick, all of this stuff would be on the yes pile. "A yes pile is, like, all of the things that you should get."

She hums in understanding and tilts her head, smiling prettily.

"So those were a yes?" she asks.

"Yeah."

"Okay. They're crotchless."

I hunch forwards, suddenly choking.

"But fine," she continues, brushing right past me. "They're on the yes pile."

"Oh no you don't," I growl, hooking a forearm around her middle, making her squeal as I haul her back to me.

Our eyes meet and my chest swells as something like excitement shimmers in her irises.

"Put them back," I demand, neither of us blinking.

"But I thought you liked them," she says, all wide-eyed and mock-pouting. Her fingers slip into her basket, hook around the panties, and then she holds them right in front of my chin, her eyebrows lifted. A silent question of *you don't want me to keep them?*

I glance down at the panties for a half-second and grunt. With my eyes back on hers I murmur, "You're a tease."

She flutters her eyelashes at me, slowing down my brain.

And then she smacks the panties clean off my jaw.

"That's it."

A deep sound thunders in my chest as I crush Aisling up against my abdomen, squeals of delight tinkling out of her as I slap the crotchless panties back inside her basket. I take the handles and yank them so that I'm the one carrying her very expensive lingerie, and then I cart her back to the middle of the store so that she can grab what she came here for and never step back through those doors again.

I face her in front of a rack of 'pyjamas' and give her a

squeeze.

"Pick one and then we're leaving," I tell her, not much caring for the fact that I can feel her cell phone vibrating in her back pocket. I can take a good guess at who the hell that'll be.

Feeling the same thing that I am she shoots a look at me over her shoulder, pupils all sparkly and dialled out with a naughty smile on her lips.

"That better not be who I think it is," I rumble quietly.

Her eyes twinkle brighter. "What're you gonna do about it, big shot?"

My chest expands as she hits me with that word. She pushes her vibrating cell harder against my thigh.

Refusing to take the bait I tear my gaze away from hers and look blankly at the row of pyjama tops in front of me. I lift the hand clutching the basket and run a knuckle over the fabric.

"This shit's not cotton," I murmur, flicking through the rack to try and search for something that Aisling will actually sleep comfortably in. "All these tops are just gonna make you sweat. As soon as you've got it on you're gonna end up taking it off–"

As the words leave my mouth understanding finally dawns. Heat spreads through my cheekbones as Aisling watches me over her shoulder.

Of course none of this shit is going to be comfortable. We're in a goddamn lingerie shop – these clothes are purposefully designed so that, once you're in them, you end up out of them.

These are hook-up pyjamas.

I swallow hard and step away from the rack.

"I'll give you another shirt," I rumble, dropping my forearm from her belly, grabbing her wrist, and dragging her to the next table. All panties. Of fucking course.

Aisling scoffs. "Uh, I think that I'll be the judge of what I do and do not buy, Tanner," she says, rolling her eyes at me.

"You're not the one doing the buying," I tell her as I finally spot what it is that I was looking for, pulling her toward them with me. I glance at her over my shoulder as she tries to dig her heels in and I pull my wallet out of my pocket. "I am."

Her eyes go stratospherically wide. "Oh no you're not," she whispers, unblinking as I slip my card from the holder and toss it down into the basket with her panties.

She lets out a little gasp.

I shake my head and turn back to the table, so that I can grab the pair of panties that I would die to see Aisling slip up and down her thighs. She watches me in stilled silence as I hesitate above them, then snatch the khaki thong and toss it down with her other items. I don't meet her eyes as I drag her with me to the till.

I drop the basket on the counter, remove my card, and wait for the sales lady to do her thing.

Aisling fumbles in her shorts as she tries to find her card, throwing me these confused, kind of aghast glances every few seconds. I lean casually against the counter, wondering if she realises now that she's the one gripping my hand in a chokehold.

I tap my card, thank the sales assistant, and steer Aisling out of the shop, her hand still in mine.

It isn't until I've brought her to the driver's side of her brother's 4x4, leaning against the back door as I hold her discreet little panty bag between us, that she realises that the big warm thing wrapped around her palm is my giant hockey player fist.

Seeing the sight of her hand enveloped in mine she releases a little squeak and stumbles against her door. She yanks her hand away and looks up at me with wide eyes.

I drop a forearm on the hood of the car and push the bag against her chest.

"Baby, I just spent two hundred dollars on five pairs of

your panties," I drawl. "The last thing you need to be worried about is a little hand holding."

"I didn't… I didn't…" She's blinking fast, a little dazed as she clutches her fingers into the pink bag. "I didn't… mean to. It just… happened."

I watch her carefully, a slight crease on my brow.

"I know," I tell her, my voice quiet and deep. "And that's how it's always going to be with us, Aisling. Inevitable. Meant to be."

She frowns up at me, shaking her head. "You sound crazy right now," she whispers.

My cheek tics up. "Tell that to your blown out pupils."

I give the top of the car a quick slap and motion for her to get inside.

"Hunter and Fallon have gone back to Carter Ridge for the weekend, but the rest of us are heading to the bar tonight," I say as she unlocks the driver's side and pulls the door open. "You're coming with us."

"Oh am I now?" she asks dryly, before leaning forwards. Carefully placing the panty bag on her passenger seat.

I give myself a couple of seconds to enjoy the view of her little ass pressing against my jeans.

She throws me a look over her shoulder that tells me she knows exactly what she's doing.

Little tease.

"And by the way?" I add, gripping the top of the door as she goes to slam it.

She gives me a sexy eye-roll as she sighs and says, "Yes?"

"Next time you wanna spy on someone while they're sleeping, maybe walk into a few less walls."

Her eyes fly up to mine as I step back and close her door.

She pulls out of her parking spot with cheeks more pink than her new panties.

CHAPTER 13

Aisling

Four years ago

"Tanner?" I ask, my eyes wide with disbelief, because I can't believe how cute this small town sweetheart is.

I'd love to take your number. And if you decide that you wanna see me again, I'll book something real special. Dinner for two, or I could take you horse-riding one town over. Or, hell, if you'd like it, I'm pretty decent in the kitchen so I could show you what I can do…

I want to know *everything* that Tanner can do, and I also want to start my college career as I mean to go on. By seizing every beautiful opportunity that comes my way so that, when I finally graduate, I don't have a single regret.

To finally wear my heart on my sleeve.

"Yes?" he rasps, shoving one hand through his hair.

My heart pounds in my chest. "Just kiss me already."

Tanner drops his hand and releases a relieved groan.

"Yes ma'am," he rumbles, immediately reaching

forwards.

I release a squeal of delight as his large palms grip my hips, and he smiles back at me with a quiet chuckle as he hauls me to the foot of the bed. He helps ease me up onto my knees so that I can reach him better, and one of his palms moves to my cheek, stroking me gently.

I go to lift my arms so that I can wrap them around his shoulders but the movement catches his eye and he frowns, gently holding my wrist.

"What's that?" he murmurs, bringing my arm closer to his face.

I peek around his fingers so that I can see what it is that he's looking at.

"Oh, that," I say, breathing out a light laugh, and rolling my eyes at myself as I take in the purple smudge. "Before you came to save me I tried to move the bed on my own, but it wasn't having any of it. It's just a little bruise."

It's actually a really big bruise, which probably occurred somewhere between me trying to shove the fifty-thousand tonne bed-frame solo and me falling onto the gravel when the most attractive guy in the state cowboyed up behind me, but Tanner is so distractingly handsome that I hadn't even noticed it until now.

"Shit, baby," he murmurs, pressing a soft kiss to my skin.

My breathing catches in my throat.

He's kissing it better.

"Oh," I whisper, when he presses another reverent kiss to my wrist. "When I asked you to kiss me, I didn't expect you to kiss me there," I admit.

It's not a complaint though and, from the way that he's smiling, Tanner can tell.

Somehow this is the sweetest kiss of my life.

Tanner eases my arms back around his neck and presses his warm chest down on mine.

"There are a lot of places that I would love to kiss you,"

he murmurs, a dimple appearing in his cheek.

"Oh my," I whisper, dreamily fanning myself. "You have, like, such a way with words."

He laughs at that, his molten eyes sparkling with amusement. "Yeah?" he asks. "I've never been much of a talker."

"Oh?" I ask, my heart pounding wildly. "So you're more of, like… a physical person?"

His smile turns into a full-on grin and he pushes my chest more firmly into his – well and truly answering my question.

"You could say that," he says quietly, the tip of his nose gently brushing over mine.

His hand slides from my hair to the side of my throat.

"You sure that this is okay?"

I nod my head quickly. "Yes, this is—"

His lips meet mine in a warm, gentle kiss, and my arms tighten around his neck, making him groan quietly and hold me closer.

It's soft and sweet, the way that a first kiss should be, and his lips move gently against mine as his hands tenderly squeeze and caress me.

I make a breathless sound as he licks his tongue against mine, and the strong palm holding my lower back roams down to squeeze my behind.

I squish my chest hard against his and suddenly I'm no longer on my knees.

I yelp in surprise as I'm lifted from the bed, my thighs naturally hitching around his abdomen as he uses one forearm to heave my body upwards.

"Where are we going?" I ask breathlessly as he begins carrying me toward the bedroom doorway.

He grunts quietly and shuts me up with another firm kiss.

"The bed will be more comfortable than the couch," I try to explain, but then I hear the sound of the door closing and I pull back in surprise.

Oh.

Oh.

He closed the door with us *inside* of the bedroom.

"Oh boy," I whisper up at him.

Our eyes lock together as he carries me back to the bed.

"Just kissing," he repeats, his voice deep and his cheekbones ruddy. "I meant what I said. I want to wine and dine you first–"

I yank his shirt so roughly in an attempt to drag his face down to mine that he grunts in surprise and in the next second we're both on the bed – me on my back and Tanner pushing two-hundred-and-twenty pounds on top of me.

"Fuck," he rumbles, before cupping my jaw in his hand and meeting my mouth with a hungry kiss. My nails score down his back before sliding quickly under his soft shirt, making him curse loudly as he thrusts his hips between my thighs.

I momentarily lose my breath.

"*Tanner,*" I squeal, the size of his erection making me gasp.

Tanner, on the other hand, seems utterly unfazed by our size difference.

"Yeah?" he murmurs, pulling back a centimetre, just so that he can rub our foreheads together.

"I know that you said just kissing," I whisper, "but your... down there... it's so..."

He shakes his head, a handsome smile teasing the corner of his lips. "I'll deal with it later," he murmurs, and I release a huff, not exactly pleased with that answer.

He notices and grins, right before crushing his mouth back down on mine.

I whimper quietly and dig my nails into him harder.

"Ash," he murmurs. "Let me take you to dinner."

I arch against him and whisper, "But what if I want dessert first?"

On a rough warning growl he shoves himself back onto his haunches, and just as I think that he's about to tell me that he's leaving, he fully rips off his shirt.

"*Holy Mother of muscle mountain*," I whisper, sparkly pink hearts shimmering in my irises. I reach out and run a knuckle down the thick valley of his abdomen, as his beautiful broad chest pumps heavily up and down.

"You like that?" he asks quietly, his own hand hovering beside mine.

After he watches me nod up at him he wraps his hand around my wrist, and I begin to slowly trail my fingers up the thick muscles of his stomach. He watches me from under his long dark lashes, and then his gaze trails up my forearm, stopping just below my elbow, to where my baby pink sleeve is pushed back.

He blinks down at the spot before gently rubbing it with his thumb.

I know exactly what he's looking at before he even says it.

"You've got a love-heart freckle," he murmurs, showing me his dimple when he meets my eyes.

I smile back at him and whisper, "It's a secret. You can't tell anyone."

His dimple deepens as he grins and he dips down to kiss the tiny heart.

"I've never actually worn my heart on my sleeve," I whisper. "It's kind of ironic really."

"I do," he whispers back to me. "If I like something, you're gonna know about it."

I breathe out a laugh at his candidness, my heart shimmering as he moves up to kiss my cheek. Then he grazes his stubble over my skin and murmurs, "Gonna put my heart on my sleeve right now, Aisling. I really fuckin' like you."

I blush with delight, giggling as I squeeze his large pecs.

He half-laughs half-groans and drops his face into the

curve of my neck, and I burst into laughter as he kisses hungrily at my skin. Then he carefully shifts his body upwards so that he's towering over me, and the bed-frame beneath us makes a low creaking sound.

I cover my face with my hands, giggling uncontrollably now, and I hear Tanner huff out an embarrassed laugh as he tries to distribute his weight between my thighs.

"Don't know why the frame's groanin' like that," he says. "Think it's just getting used to taking my weight." Then he murmurs, sounding kind of shy, "I am pretty heavy though – I don't want to break your bed."

I peek up at him from between my fingers and see the innocent look of concern on his face, as if he's worried that the beautiful carved panels might actually not be able to hold up beneath him.

It's so cute that I shrug out of my jumper, pushing it quickly to the floor, and then I hug my arms around his shoulders so that I can squeeze him back down on top of me.

He grunts, eyes blacking out as his pecs slam down on my breasts.

"We'll risk it," I whisper.

His eyes trail down to my chest, his pupils fully dilating, and he carefully brushes two large digits over the black lace beneath my tank top.

"Are you sure that you don't want me to go?" he asks quietly, as his warm hand slides down to my waist.

He gives me a squeeze and I suck in a little gasp.

"Stay," I whisper. "Please."

He grunts quietly, then nods. "Yeah. Okay, I'll stay."

His lips meet mine and my body instantly relaxes, my arms tightening around his neck in the hopes that I don't ever have to let him go. I feel him smile against my mouth before gently slanting me open, his tongue licking me sweetly before sliding inside.

He strokes it slowly against mine, his warm chest

keeping me pinned in place, and he begins rolling his hips between my thighs, his back muscles rippling beneath my fingers.

His solid length rubs heavily over my heat, and my nipples pinch, making me pull back, panting.

"Too much?" he murmurs, his eyes scorching as they search mine.

I shake my head furiously, and he slips his tongue back inside. He groans as he licks us together, his gentle strokes getting faster, and his fingers tighten in my hair as he rubs harder between my thighs.

He pulls back with a curse, looking down at me with a dangerous expression.

"Ash," he rasps, his voice sinfully deep. He moves one of his forearms above my head and he uses his other hand to still my hips. "We need to stop now or I'm… I'm gonna finish," he says quietly.

I try to catch my breath before whispering up to him, "Don't you want to?"

He ducks his head, catching his breath too.

"Yeah, I want to," he murmurs. "But I thought you might wanna take it slow."

That is the cutest thing I've ever heard.

I start tugging my leggings down my hips.

"Aisling," he says warningly, although his gaze stays trained on my fingers.

I slowly roll my pants down my thighs, and as soon as my panties are exposed Tanner is officially done for. He shoves his fist down the front of his shorts, a low groan rumbling through his chest.

I toe off my leggings when they finally reach my ankles and Tanner releases his fist so that he can envelop my hips.

"How the hell are you real, Aisling? You're a goddamn dream."

And with that line right there? Now *I'm* done for.

A giggle bursts out of my chest and I slap a hand over

my eyes, chest shaking as I laugh because he doesn't realise what he's just said.

His big fist gently tugs at my hand, his expression concerned as he searches my gaze.

"What is it?" he murmurs. "I wasn't joking, I'm being serious."

I giggle harder as my cheeks dimple with happiness.

"I know," I laugh, cupping his perfect face. "It's just… that's my name. What you said… about me being a dream?"

My cheeks stain pink but I'm still smiling, overwhelmed with delight.

"That's what 'Aisling' means," I explain. "My name means 'dream'."

Tanner towers over me with a love-struck expression on his face, and I stroke my fingertips over the muscles in his forearms, biting into my smile as we watch each other.

"That's perfect," he whispers. "You… you really are my dream girl."

"If this is anyone's dream, I think it's mine," I whisper back to him.

He kisses me again, sweet and unhurried, and his broad chest rubs heavily against the thin lace of my bra.

"Is this really happening?" he murmurs. "Because if it is, I want to show you all of my cards before we do this. Like, first off, I'm going to need you to give me your number, right the fuck now, so that I know that I can take you out when you're next available. And second of all, this thing right here? I'm not going to let this be a fling–"

I push up onto my knees and kiss him through my unrelenting giggles.

"Thank you," he murmurs roughly, making me laugh even harder.

"You talk so much," I mumble against him, stifling a squeal of delight as he shoves his grey shorts down his quads.

"Sorry," he murmurs back, quickly tugging them off and

tossing them behind us. Then his hand is gripping my wrist and easing my fingers beneath his boxer briefs.

I touch the large domed head and he pants against my neck.

"Tanner," I whisper as he wraps us both around the base of his erection, giving it an experimental tug that's so rough that I whimper for him. "Tanner–"

"On it," he rumbles, misreading my speechlessness for impatience, and he releases a hand so that he can slip it down the front of my panties.

I stare down with wide eyes at the sight of his tan hand in my frilly underwear and with a smirk on his lips he dips down so that he can kiss me again.

"This okay?" he murmurs quietly, pressing two warm fingers against my clit.

"Mm-hm," I whimper quickly, making him grunt and rub me faster. He uses his chest to push me down back onto the quilt and then he drops one large forearm above my head.

His eyes are burning a hole into my tank top, his jaw muscles rolling as his gaze flicks between my panties and my chest.

Breathless, I decide to help him out. "Would you like me to take off my–"

"Yes," he grunts, hard eyes flashing up to mine.

I would breathe out a laugh if he wasn't looking at me with so much need and devotion, so instead I slip my arms through the straps and wriggle the top off of my body. When I'm in nothing but my bra and panties I settle back down on the dark quilt, letting him look at me.

He slowly twists his fingers around the sides of my panties, tightening his fists and making me gasp.

His gaze stares between my thighs for a long unending moment, his breathing loud and heavy as he tries to calm himself down.

When his eyes flash back up to mine I lift my arms,

reaching for him.

His expression softens as he helps me loop my arms around his shoulders, his hands dipping beneath my lower back so that he can hold us together as he lays down on top of me.

"Aisling," he murmurs, "I don't want us to rush this. I don't want you to wake up tomorrow morning and decide that hooking up wasn't a good idea."

His brow creases in a concerned frown.

"I meant what I said. You're my dream girl. Tomorrow morning I want this to be the start of us dating and shit. I don't want this to be a one-time thing. I don't want you to regret me."

Taken aback by his honesty I can't help but gaze into his eyes, awe-struck.

"Wow," I whisper after a small stretch of heated silence, filled with nothing but the sounds of our heavy breathing. "You'd think that *you* were the one who has his heart on their sleeve," I tease.

He drops his eyes, laughing quietly. Then he lifts himself up onto one elbow and strokes his large palm over my cheek.

"I'll always wear my heart on my sleeve with you," he murmurs. His sparkling eyes search mine before he lowers his mouth and kisses me gently.

My hands roam down the large muscles of his back, stopping when I reach the waistband of his boxer briefs. I pull back from the kiss so that he can see the question in my eyes.

He watches me carefully for a moment before he nods his head – and then we're both shoving his underwear down his legs, releasing his heavy erection.

He tosses his boxers across the room as he kisses me deeper, groaning loudly as the lace of my panties rubs his length up and down.

"We're really gonna do this?" he asks quietly, his voice

husky and deep.

I nod, feeling lightheaded, and I giggle as we kiss again. I feel his gorgeous grin against my lips and it makes me laugh harder, which in turn makes *him* laugh, until we're kissing and laughing and panting all at the same time.

"One rule," he murmurs, his heavy chest pushing down on mine.

I nod fiercely, running my fingers through his military fade.

"Tell me," I whisper, my voice hushed beneath the downpour outside.

"We're gonna do it, but I'm… I'm not gonna see you fully naked," he whispers back to me, looking pissed with his own decision but resolute nonetheless. "*Yet*," he adds, after a moment of raking me up and down. "I'm not allowed to see you naked *yet*."

His palms coast up the sides of my body until he's gently cupping my cheeks again.

"What do you mean?" I ask breathlessly, not exactly sure how that will work.

His eyes search mine, hungry and wanting.

"I'm going to keep my underwear on?" I ask, my eyebrows arched. "I don't want anything between us."

"I don't either, baby," he rumbles, "but I don't deserve to see you fully… bared to me, yet. So I want you to hold that back from me for now, until I've proven myself to you."

"Tanner," I laugh, pressing my palms over my face as I giggle at his nonsense.

He reaches for my wrists and tugs them gently down, making me giggle harder.

He grins back at me, his expression unbearably handsome.

A sweet small town guy, I think to myself.

Because when I think about it, Tanner is everything that I've ever wanted. A big, handsome small town guy, without a bad boy reputation that will inevitably break my heart.

He's the opposite of every guy that I've ever known.

Better than that? He's the opposite of *me*.

I mean, he literally respects me so hard that he doesn't think he's worthy of seeing me naked? Who *does* that? How can a guy be so perfect?

How can I be so *lucky* that I have actually been *found* by a guy who is so perfect?

It's almost too perfect to be true.

I smile up at him and he chuckles quietly as he kisses me.

"Okay," I whisper.

"Okay," he whispers back.

CHAPTER 14

Aisling

Present day

For some reason, Tanner insisted on driving us tonight.

We're all heading to the dive bar and Tanner's our DD.

"You aren't drinking?" Austin asks him in that deep rumbling voice of his, as he hunches down his broad shoulders and slides into the shotgun seat of Tanner's G-wagon.

Tanner's eyes slide down to meet mine, before he gives my outfit a prolonged once-over.

He ignores Austin's question seeing as the answer is crystal clear and instead takes a few determined steps in my direction. The heated look in his eyes makes me think that he's been doing a lot of contemplating about our little panty adventure this morning.

When he's a good half millimetre away from me, he gives me a rough jerk of his chin – his silent self-assured caveman version of "hello".

"Aisling."

"Tanner."

His gaze flicks momentarily down to my jeans, a muscle rolling in his jaw, but he doesn't ask the question that's burning in his irises.

Which ones are you wearing under there?

He lifts his right arm so that he can shove his fingers through his hair and a wave of his warmth washes over me.

I try not to wobble on my stilettos.

He clears his throat, eyes lingering on my chest. "You look… good."

I lift an eyebrow. "Wow, you should write poetry."

He grunts, still staring.

"You get what I shoved through your letterbox?" he asks gruffly.

How does he manage to make everything sound like the filthiest euphemism that I've ever heard?

I look innocently down at my nails. I probably shouldn't tell him that I've already folded the soft grey shirt that he quietly slid through the front door of the lake house, and that it's patiently waiting on my sleeping bag for me to snuggle into tonight.

When he told me that he'd give me more of his clothes to wear as pyjamas, he meant it.

"I don't know what you're talking about," I say vaguely, eyes sliding up to his when I feel his molten gaze burning into my cheeks.

His sun-kissed cheekbone twitches. Then he grimaces and nods.

After a couple beats of just watching me I let out a nervous laugh and ask, "Why are you still standing here?"

He frowns. "I'm waiting for you."

I blink. "You're waiting for me to what?"

"To get in the car."

A laugh bubbles out of my throat as I give him a *you're obviously kidding* arch of my eyebrows. "Yeah right, big shot.

Why do you think I'm wearing my walking jeans?"

Tanner glances down at the blue denim on my thighs, jaw hardening as his gaze wanders down the line of my zipper.

"You're ridin' with me," he says, just as the groan of one of the cabin doors behind me creaks open.

"Oh, Tanner," I sigh, "it's so cute that you think you can tell me what to do. I'm walking with Connell," I correct him, turning to look over my shoulder at which of the guys are making their way over here.

I'm startled by a sudden warm press against my front and when my head whips back around Tanner is staring unyieldingly down at me – and his big chest muscles are pushing firmly against my breasts.

"In those shoes you'd be lucky if you could crawl your way to the bar. Get in the damn car."

"Tanner, I would *rather* crawl than get in your 'damn car'."

He lets out a low humourless laugh and drawls, "Baby, that can be arranged. But if you don't wanna cause a scene in front of your brother, walk that pretty ass over to my car and get the hell inside."

In the next second I feel my feet lift straight off the ground as Connell scoops me up from behind, giving me a big brotherly bear hug. His football friends, along with Tristan, Hughes, and Shaw, continue their loud sports-related shooting-the-shit bro talk around him.

When he puts me back down I give Tanner a smug smile and then I turn to Connell with my cutest little sister expression.

"I'm walking with you guys," I tell him, a happy blush spreading up my cheeks when his friends start to cheer.

Connell snickers, shoves one of his friends in a headlock, and then, with a two-hundred-pound teammate tucked under his bicep, he turns back to look down at me with an already-tipsy smile on his mouth.

"Ash, Tanner's driving you."

My smile instantly drops, eyes widening in shock.

"What? *No.* I want to walk with you."

Connell smirks as his friend wrestles free, and then he throws an arm over my shoulder, giving me that intense twin-to-twin eye-contact.

"Ash," he whispers, dropping his voice so that his friends can't hear us, "we did a couple shots while you were over at the lake house getting ready. I don't want to have to fight anyone while we're walking because they can't keep their eyes off of you, okay? Tanner already told me that he's DDing and" – Connell shrugs – "I don't know, I just think he's fuckin' solid. No nonsense. And he's like – what? – six foot four? You're in safe hands, Ash. I trust him to get you there."

I frown up at my brother, a little hurt. I understand his rationale – he doesn't want to be responsible for the one girl in a group that's made up of almost his entire Carter U football team – but it's very freaking unfortunate that instead I'm going to be at the mercy of the one guy who I love to hate.

"Fake brother," I mutter, giving him a shove in his middle.

"Hey, now," he laughs, squeezing me around my shoulders. "I'll see you in there, Ash, and the guys are gonna wanna hang out with you all night, you know that." Then he laughs a little deeper as he says, "And, come on, you don't want to scuff those pretty shoes, right?"

I stab the heel of my stiletto nice and hard into his dirt-road boot.

"Jesus!" he howls, but he's still laughing good-naturedly as I pull away and face him again. He drags me into another hug and says, quieter this time, "I didn't realise that you and Tanner didn't get along, okay? And I'm sorry, Ash, I swear. Next time I'll check with you before I start drinkin'."

I nod against his shoulder because I know that he means

it. Connell has always been my biggest supporter ever since we were in school together. He DD'd for me countless times when we were at Carter U, and I know he would have done the same now if he'd realised that I didn't want to ride with Tanner.

When he pulls back, signalling to his friends to give him one minute, he looks down at me with a tipsy smile, a curious head tilt to the side.

"You know, I actually, uh…" He lifts an arm so that he can scratch at the back of his neck and then looks over my head, jerking his chin at someone in the near distance. "I actually kind of thought that… that maybe Tanner would be, uh…"

My eyebrows rise slowly to my hairline. "Where the hell are you going with that sentence, Connell?"

He drops his gaze and shrugs his shoulders.

"Doesn't matter, I guess. Just thought that he was kinda… not that you should, obviously, 'cause I know that fucker's reputation but… just could've sworn that he was your type. Like, to a fuckin' T." He shakes his head at himself and mumbles, "Must be more drunk than I thought."

After another bone-crushing hug he murmurs, "We'll see you in twenty minutes, tops," and then the guys are disappearing into the trees that border the head of the lake, the deep green canopy cloaking their departure.

I flick my eyes over to Tanner, who's standing about five feet away from me, leaning his large shoulders against his car. His thick arms are folded and flexing over his chest.

I swallow weakly and, maybe possessed by the sheer heat radiating from Tanner's giant biceps, I walk cautiously over to him, not stopping until I'm a couple of inches away from his forearms.

I suppose that sometimes it's okay to just go with it, especially if it's an instance like now – where even Connell thinks that I'd be better off riding with Tanner tonight.

But that doesn't mean that I can't toy with him a little bit first.

Tanner drops his eyes to regard the small inch of air between us, chest expanding deeper on his next inhale and successfully closing that gap.

My eyelashes flutter as his arm brushes over the curves of my breasts.

"I'm actually surprised that you didn't want me to ride shotgun," I tell him quietly – because if *I'm* affected by *him*, then it's only right for him to be even more affected by me.

A smirk briefly tugs at his mouth, half-mast eyes lazily trailing over my breasts.

"I do want you to ride," he rasps quietly, before grunting himself out of his haze and shoving a hand through his hair. "I mean" – he swallows hard – "I do want you to ride, uh, in my passenger seat. But it's not a good idea."

He pushes off the driver's side door, making me stumble back a step as his bulk knocks against me, but he quickly wraps a forearm around my lower back as he steers me to the back door, clicking it open as I turn to face him.

"And why's it not a good idea?" I ask him, the sweet laughter of Winter – his teammate's adorable girlfriend – tinkling inside the car at something that Austin and Caden are murmuring about.

Tanner rakes his hand through his hair, pushing it back off his forehead. I concentrate very hard on not glancing at the large swells of his biceps.

"'Cause you look like trouble, and I need to keep my eyes on the road," he rumbles gruffly, gaze refusing to meet mine as his hand hovers beside my waist. The palm that's slapped on the roof of his car clenches into a fist as he leans barely a millimetre closer.

The heat pumping over me from his chest warms my neck and obliterates my filter.

"Why did Tristan walk with Connell's friends tonight?" I

ask, staring directly into his eyes.

The look he flashes me is smug. "Because he knew that it would be a career-ending move if he didn't."

At my jaw-dropped expression his handsome face actually grins.

"You gonna behave yourself tonight?" he asks, chuckling when I lean up to press the tip of my nose against his.

"You. Wish," I whisper, excitement flaring in my eyes. Because I realise suddenly that, bodyguards aside, I can do whatever the hell I want, with whoever the hell I want, however the hell I want. I made a wild summer bucket list, damn it, and I will give myself a night to remember, so help me God.

Tanner smirks and slips two digits under the buckle of my belt, tugging me towards him until I'm plastered against his heaving chest.

"Actually," he grunts, stubble scraping roughly against the side of my flushed cheek, "I *don't.*"

He gives the buckle another gruff tug and then slides into the driver's seat without a word.

CHAPTER 15

Aisling

Present day

In the absence of Fallon, my best friend in the entire world, Winter and I have spent the past two hours bonding in the bar – sending Fallon cute selfies and excitedly squealing over every country song on the jukebox. Her hockey player boyfriend and high school sweetheart, Caden, is currently sat at the edge of his team's booth, watching her every move.

She slips a coin into the machine and then gives me the happiest smile that I've ever seen as the first chords of another Morgan Wallen song twang from the jukebox.

An uncontrollable giggle bubbles out of me as we run back to the dance floor, her poufy gingham dress bouncing flirtily around her thighs.

I watch as her boyfriend presses a dark bottle to his mouth, draining the last of his drink before purposefully rising to his feet.

"Your boyfriend is, like, way intense," I giggle, my eyes going extra wide to emphasise my point.

Winter bites into her lower lip as she looks at him over her shoulder, and then turns back to face me, cheeks dimpling in delight.

"He's perfect," she sighs, a happy squeal leaving her throat the second that his giant tattooed forearms leash around her neck from behind. In the cutest, most possessive display of ownership that I've ever seen he slides his hand up her throat as he gently kisses her forehead, before hunching lower and sinking his teeth into her neck.

Winter's eyelashes flutter until Caden turns his bite into a nuzzle, burying his face under her soft pink hair, giant shoulders swelling with every inhale.

Smiling at me with a tinge of shyness on her cheeks, Winter drops her eyes for a moment so that she can stroke her fingers up her boyfriend's forearms. He lifts his head only so that he can murmur a secret into her ear.

She tries to shove him away as she giggles uncontrollably but he keeps her in place with his hands, purposefully scraping her up with his stubble.

"Caden!" she laughs, cheeks pink as he kisses her skin. "We need, like, ten more minutes! Twenty tops." She slides her sparkly eyes over to mine, grins, and says, "Maybe thirty! We're doing as much as we can on Aisling's bucket list."

Winter says the words *bucket list* really slowly as if it's something super important, which makes me place a hand over my heart and do a little "aw!"

She gives my hand a happy squeeze and presses a chaste kiss to Caden's cheek.

He inhales deeply, one hand lifting so that he can gently stroke the fine chain around her neck, disappearing under her dress, and then he nods his head, wrapping his arm protectively around her shoulders.

"Are you… doing the list too?" he asks her quietly.

"I mean, why not?!" she says, with her trademark sunshine giggle.

He nods again, clutching her tighter. "So, um… what're y'all gonna do?"

"Well, the first thing was to dance in a dive bar," Winter says, releasing an exhilarated squeak when Caden grips her hips and spins her around. "And we still need to tick off 'make out with a hot guy'–"

Caden's mouth crashes down on Winter's, kissing every thought out of her head. She makes a happy surprised yelp that's quickly swallowed up by her boyfriend, and her delicate hands flutter up to hold onto his broad shoulders.

When he pulls back to stare down at her, stars are sparkling in her eyes.

"O-okay," she whispers, wobbling against him.

He clutches her tighter and rumbles, "Done. Next."

"Um." Winter looks over to me, blinking quickly as she tries to remember the other thing on tonight's agenda, something that we had excitedly texted Fallon about and received fifteen screaming voice-notes as a result of.

I send Winter a girl-to-girl telepathic brainwave and she does a little *oooh* when she finally remembers.

She glances up at her boyfriend's gruff expression, a little smile on her lips.

"Winter." His tone is a gentle warning.

"Well," she laughs, rolling her eyes playfully, "the last thing on Ash's list tonight is… that."

Winter gestures behind us and Caden glances over his girlfriend's shoulder, brow furrowed as he tries to locate what she's pointing at.

Not seeing it, he looks back down at her, a question in his eyes.

"Pole adventures!" she exclaims, before throwing me an adoring look. "Aisling's a competitive cheerleader and she's going to do *amazing*."

I give her a teary smile. "Thank you."

Caden eyes the pole with a murderous expression and then looks back down at his girlfriend, pulling her closer to his chest. His voice is deep and gravelly. "You're… you're not gonna… I mean, you're not–?"

"You have to be twenty-one to get up there, so" – she shrugs and gives him a little shake of her head – "probably no."

Caden releases a low pained groan as he drops his head back to her neck, murmuring an endless stream of rasping *thank God, thank God*'s as he pushes her body up against his chest.

I give Winter a playful roll of my eyes, and decide not to mention the fact that you're supposed to be twenty-one to be here in the first place.

Without Fallon here, my cheerleader bestie, I feel a whole lot less sure about this than I was two weeks ago, when we first saw the silver pole and I instantly added it to our wild summer to-do list.

I feel a warm arm wrap around my collarbones and glance behind me to see Tristan smiling down.

"You getting up there, cowgirl?" he asks, smiling when I let out a little laugh.

I decide to swallow down my nerves and luxuriate in how comforting he feels – uncomplicated, fun, and friendly.

I also refuse to look over to the other side of the bar, where I know that my brother and his football guys are currently being chatted up by a hen party, wearing pink cowgirl hats and matching sashes.

Seeing as Tanner isn't over here, I can take a very solid guess as to where he will definitely be instead.

This is why you don't get attached, I remind myself, hating the idea of Tanner mixing it up with a group of bridesmaids. *Attachment is the root of all longing and loss. Just take life for what it is and enjoy the moment.*

I push the sting away from my heart and lean back against Tristan's warm chest.

"Would you like me to?" I ask, giggling up at him as he squeezes my shoulders.

A low rumble spreads through his chest as he grins back at me.

"Hell yeah, I want to see you up there. You weren't part of the squad that performed for us at the Frozen Four final, and I've been dying to see you do your thing." He leans back so that he can glance down my body and, swiping his tongue over his lower lip, he asks, "You think you'll be able to do those moves wearing this pretty pair of jeans?"

I grin up at him. "Why, you want me to take them off?"

His pupils dial out as he laughs into my hair, hands sliding down to my hips as we walk body-to-body over to the little red stage. It's hidden enough that it's obviously meant to be used amongst friends, without fear of other people leering, and I think that it's pretty perfect for a night of summer fun.

Tristan clutches me tighter as Winter, Caden, and the other Carter U hockey boys join us inside the sexy red nook.

"Should we get a round?" he asks Austin, shoving one hand in his back pocket so that he can pull out some cash.

Austin pulls an amused, curious expression, eyes flickering down to mine, over to the pole, and back again.

He takes Tristan's cash and returns thirty seconds later with a tray of whiskey shots. And in the time it's taken Austin to return from the bar, Tristan, Hughes and Shaw have lavished me with so much undivided attention that my serotonin levels are, like, on the moon.

"You sure about this?" Austin asks, smiling in that kind, big brotherly way of his as he hands me a shot of whiskey.

"I need to have some *fun*," I tell him, my voice a little flirty, and I release a surprised laugh when he boops the apple of my cheek with his finger.

He tips back his own drink, eyes on mine the whole time, then he drops the glass on the tray and gives me an unexpected once-over.

My body shivers at the heat of his gaze and his mouth pulls into a smirk as he notices.

"Aisling," he drawls, "are you sure that you wanna have a little fun *without* your big bad bodyguard?"

I give him a fake-angry pout before lifting up one of my legs and pressing the heel of my stiletto very gently into the centre of his chest. His lips lift into a full grin as he wraps his hands around my ankle, leans down to kiss the top of my foot, and nods his head in acquiescence.

"Okay, cheerleader," he concurs, stepping into me with a naughty smile, pushing me up against Tristan and making all three of us laugh out loud. "Do your thing."

Somehow my thighs end up hitched around Austin's abdomen, Tristan's hands holding me from behind as they help me climb my way up the pole.

I bite into my smile, cheeks pink with whiskey heat.

"I haven't done this before," I whisper to them, "so if I, like, suck at it–"

Austin shakes his head, leaning back against one of the three encasing walls that are equidistantly positioned barely three feet away from the pole. "No matter what you do up there, we'll all be dreaming of you tonight."

I laugh and look down at Tristan, who is still holding onto my waist, a crease of focused concentration on his brow, as if he's worried that when he steps back I'll fall.

Warmth swells in my chest as I realise that, in this moment, these boys – my *friends* – are totally head over heels for me. They would do anything for me, and they support every silly thing that I do.

The song playing through the loud speaker-system changes into a country song that Fallon's obsessed with, and I giggle to myself, closing my eyes and allowing my body to move.

I tip my head backwards, arching my spine, and strengthen my wrists as I grip the pole, lifting my hips higher and kicking my legs into a smooth vertical point. Then I kick my right leg so that it can go from a ninety-degree lift to a full one-eighty split, and I hold the standing split position for a moment, revelling in this use of my flexibility after a full month of no cheer.

I hear a couple of low curses and peek an eye open so that I can see the guys, their jaw-on-the-floor expressions making me flash them my best star cheerleader smile.

When I glance over my shoulder to check on Tristan, he has both of his hands shoved into his hair, his eyes unblinking as he stares hungrily at my ass.

I giggle uncontrollably at his expression, recapturing his attention, and he gives me a breathless, kind of bashful smile, motivating me to show these adorable hot hockey guys exactly what I'm capable of.

"Jesus, Aisling," Austin rasps as I do a pole-holding flip. I lift up my leg so that I can nudge his strong jaw with the sharp point of my stiletto.

A rough sound leaves his throat and he instinctively reaches for my ankle, kissing it again.

The feeling of his stubble on my smooth skin is so unexpectedly sexy that I burst into another round of whiskey giggles, dropping down from the pole and squealing as the guys wrap me up in a team hug.

But as I pull back from the huddle something catches my eyes near the entrance of the booth.

Already knowing what I'm going to see I peek over to my left, my breathing turning raspy as Tanner's eyes meet mine.

His large forearms – even more tan in the low dive bar lighting – are folded heavily over his chest and, despite the murder glare that he flicks over to Tristan when he gives me another squeeze on the shoulder, his expression is quietly awestruck, his breathing unsteady.

Trouble, he mouths to me, a hint of a smirk tugging at his mouth.

Big shot, I mouth back, and this time he full on grins – handsome creases cutting into his cheeks as he keeps his gaze locked with mine. In the next second he pushes off the wall, eyes focused as he makes his way over to me.

Heart pounding with excitement I wiggle out of the group, my eyes closing dreamily with relief when I feel Tanner's forearm wrap around my belly.

In less than three seconds I'm hauled out of the booth, and into the main area of the crowded country bar.

"How much did you see?" I ask him breathlessly, not questioning it when I realise that we're in the middle of the dance floor, the swollen ridges of Tanner's chest pressed possessively into my back.

"Wasn't watching," he murmurs, two digits from each hand tucked tightly through the belt loops on either side of my jeans.

I blink, dazed and confused. "You weren't watching? Then what were you–"

"Guarding the booth," he rumbles. "Had to make sure no-one else would get to see."

Maybe it's the golden hum of whiskey gently warming my veins, but the idea that Tanner felt like it was his duty to guard me during my tipsy pole adventure is so romantic it makes my heart pound wildly.

I breathe out a shaky exhale and whisper, just loud enough for him to hear as his stubbled jaw brushes over the warm curve of my cheek, "I kind of thought that you would've gotten all grumpy and stopped me."

I feel his smirk press into my skin.

"When the hell have I ever been grumpy?" he murmurs, the teasing lilt in his drawl making butterflies flutter in my belly. Then he adds quietly, "You were… having a good time. Yeah, I wasn't loving the sight of my teammates looking like they wanted to be all over you, but I… I liked seeing you laughing." He swallows hard. "I'd never try and stop something that was making you happy."

Without thinking, Tanner's forehead drops down to my throat, a groan rumbling through his chest as he presses his body harder against mine.

My eyes almost flutter closed but then I spot Connell and his teammates, and my chest instantly tightens, remembering the hen party from earlier.

I push away from Tanner's embrace and spin around to look into his eyes.

"We can't do this," I say breathlessly, swiping a hand through the air between us.

I try to put another few steps between us but Tanner grips both of his palms around my hips, yanking me into him with a hunger that I can't resist.

"Why not?" he asks hoarsely, eyes wildly searching mine. "You know how I feel about you, and I can tell that you feel the same way about me. Why aren't you letting us do this? Let us do this, Aisling."

A thought crosses his mind and he pulls me tighter against his chest.

"Is it because you're worried about what Connell will say?" he asks. "Because you don't need to worry about that. Your brother likes me, baby. I'm pretty sure he knows that I'd fucking die for you."

I blink rapidly up at him, overwhelmed and confused.

"If you would *die* for me," I say hoarsely, "then why the hell did you spend tonight getting all flirty with a damn hen party?"

I mean, I don't blame them for wanting to get up close with Tanner, but my own brand of feminism means that I can put my own feelings first sometimes – if other girls are flirting with the guy who I secretly like then that doesn't mean that I have to be okay with it.

Tanner looks up at the dark ceiling, praying for strength. When his eyes drop back down to mine there's fire in his irises.

"What in the hell are you talkin' about, woman?"

"Don't call me that," I whisper, even though I secretly love it. "I saw you over there with the football guys."

"For about five damn seconds. The moment those chicks started climbing up on our table I hauled ass as far away from them as fast as fucking possible. I saw you on the pole, got hard, and then I guarded the booth. I want *you*, Aisling, okay? I want to spend all of my nights with *you*."

I stare up at him in shock, blinking fast as the room sways around me.

Tanner narrows his eyes on me and then they widen, his spine shooting straight.

"Oh," I whisper at his sudden increase in height, "now you're like six-foot-a-billion."

"Aisling," he says urgently, one hand firmly cupping the back of my neck. "Aisling, are you...? No. Aisling, are you *drunk*?"

I frown at his swollen pecs. "You got a problem with that?" I mumble.

"Goddammit Aisling," he rasps, wincing when I peep up at him again. "I didn't... I didn't know. I wouldn't have... hauled you up here like that if I didn't think that you were—"

I roll my eyes so hard they almost fall out of my head. "I had, like, three shots of whiskey, Tanner. I'm a big girl. I can handle a couple of two-hundred pound hockey players."

He blinks down at me, his big chest rubbing against mine.

"The guys... they didn't try anything on with you, right? Before I got there?" he asks quietly, dangerously.

"So what if they did? Everything's just temporary to you, right?"

Wow, I have really got to stop putting my heart on my sleeve like that.

Tanner shoves his tongue in his cheek, his eyes burning as they stare into mine.

"That's what this is about?" he asks. "That's what's had you shit-scared for four years? Seriously?" His jaw tics angrily and then he curses, looking away. "We can't talk about this right now. I need you to be one fucking million percent sober when we talk about this."

I literally never want to have that conversation so I allow myself to tune everything out and bring my fingertips up to explore his beautiful broad shoulders. His muscles tense the second that I touch him but then he allows himself to relax, watching me warily from above.

I glance up at him from under my lashes and then brush my thumbs over his nipples.

"No," he grunts, making me smile naughtily as he turns me around and begins walking us toward the bar's exit.

I look back at him over my shoulder and his palms slide dangerously high up my ribcage. I arch an eyebrow at him and he grunts, stopping himself from reaching what he was hoping for.

"I'm taking you home," he says, more to himself than to me, slipping his phone from his jeans so that he can text to see if Caden and Winter will be joining us.

Another thought twinkles in my mind and suddenly I'm laughing again.

What can I say? I'm a happy drunk!

"Oh *yeah*," I say, biting into my smile as I twist around in his arms. It's so busy in here tonight what with it being a Friday, that there isn't one inch of my body that isn't being bumped into right now.

Tanner notices, frowns, and tugs me closer in the cage of his biceps.

"What?" he rumbles, not seeming to mind the fact that I'm plastered against him.

"Connell told me about our little swap." I give him a sideways glance. "He said that I'm staying in your cabin tonight, because of the no-lock situation and all."

Tanner quickly looks away. "Yeah. Means that your

brother will only be a few doors down, so you'll be safer. I'll stay in the lake house while you're... while you're in my cabin." After a moment he gruffly adds, "And you're sleepin' in my bed."

"After what I caught you doing this morning?" I tease. "Are we trying for the world's first miraculous cabin conception?"

"Jesus Christ," he rasps, avoiding my eyes and flushing crimson.

"Yes, that is His name," I concur, pressing one hand against my forehead as I try to maintain the calibre of my taunting, although it's a little distracting when a six-foot-four hockey player is secreting his warmth directly into your back.

But before Tanner can react one of my stilettos is slipping in a puddle of spilled beer and Tanner's arms become a vise, hoisting me upright against his chest.

And in the next second a crowd of cowboys barge through the front doors.

Two of them knock straight into me, their eyes as wide with surprise as mine, and I feel the heat of Tanner's testosterone as it becomes instantly more possessive – stronger and darker.

"Well, howdy," one of them smiles, looking at me with slightly bloodshot eyes. Then he sees the giant forearm compressed against my chest and his gaze travels over my head so that he can give Tanner an impressed nod.

I glance over my shoulder and find Tanner tipping his chin at me. "You okay?"

An accidental whiskey giggle leaves my throat. "Of course I'm okay, I'm in cowboy heaven," I say teasingly, and something like amusement almost tugs at the corner of his mouth.

Wow, that was almost a smile. From *Tanner*.

The guys in front of us chuckle as we go to move past them, some of them tipping their hats because they are *literally cowboys* but one of the ones at the back – maybe too tipsy to have even realised the hold-up – trips over my stiletto and something drops out of his jacket pocket.

"Oh, here, let me!" I say, leaning over to pick it up while flashing him an apologetic smile. "I think that you dropped your–"

Suddenly my eyes flash down to my hand and I stumble straight back into Tanner.

I hold the heavy object out as far away from my body as possible.

"Oh my God, oh my God, oh my God," I whisper, my eyes wide and unblinking with fear. The cowboy tucks his hands into his jeans and grins like this is all perfectly normal.

I feel Tanner immediately tense behind me, arms locking me tightly against his chest. In a deadly calm voice he instructs, "Aisling, it's okay. Just hand it over to me."

My whole arm is tingling with adrenaline.

Am I having, like, a super country hallucination because of the three shots of whiskey?

"Is that a *gun*?" I squeal as I try to work out where to definitely *not* put my fingers.

"Never held one of those before, huh, Sugar?" one of the cowboys burrs gruffly, a pleased curve to his handsome mouth.

I swallow hard, my hand shaking as I try to slowly angle the weapon toward the ground, away from any patrons.

"Aisling." Tanner's large open palm appears beside my trembling hand. "Pass it over, right now."

"I can't move," I whisper, blinking back tears because I'm tipsy, emotional, and overwhelmed right now. The cowboys don't seem to notice, but Tanner definitely does.

"It's okay. I've got it now, you can let go."

Tanner's hands grip around the handle of the heavy black weapon and it takes me a good ten seconds before I fully pull my arm away from it, worried that any move I make might set it off.

Just another example of a pampered heiress not being right for the small town life.

I tuck my arms against my chest as Tanner quickly empties the gun and shoves it back at its owner. Then he spins me around so that he can tuck my head against his neck.

I'm disoriented and a little scared, but I'm still lucid enough to know that Tanner is pissed the hell off.

"Who in the goddamn *fuck* carries a loaded handgun with them for a chill night in a country dive bar?" he rumbles, his breathing unsteady as he herds us out into the warm summer night.

In less than five seconds we're at the passenger seat of his car, and he's opening the door with a multitude of dangerous emotions flashing over his face.

"Where are Winter and–?" I begin.

"Already left. And I'll text the guys. Get in."

He opens the door wider, gently shoving me down onto the seat.

My legs dangle outside of the G-wagon. He ducks down under the roof so that he can tuck them carefully inside the car.

"That was really scary," I whisper, hands on my chest as it beats up and down, crazy fast.

Tanner stills for a second, eyes on mine as he clicks my strap into the mechanism. "You were really brave in there. That wasn't fair to you."

"How did you know how to–?"

Tanner pulls back and quietly shuts the door. When he heaves down into the drivers' side he rumbles, "There's a man with a handgun in that bar. Cowboy or no cowboy, we don't know him, so I'm not risking keeping you here for another second. We'll talk on the road."

He shoves his seatbelt into the lock, eyes on fire as he kicks the car into drive.

CHAPTER 16

Tanner

Present day

So much happened in the past five minutes that I stay silent for the whole ride, needing the time to just cool off.

Aisling sliding her thighs up and down that pole. The knowledge that every one of my teammates is smitten for her. Having her in my arms again with almost enough nerve to lean down and kiss her – only to find out that she'd gotten tipsy, which means that I had to rule that off the table.

Then there was the matter of her coming face to face with what was very clearly her first ever *gun*, and trying my hardest to keep cool so that she didn't freak out, when all I really wanted to do was bust that guy's jaw for putting her in such an unfair situation in the first place.

I shove the car into park, rip off my seatbelt and throw my head back against the seat. I dig the heels of my palms into my eyes as a long groan shudders through my chest.

When I drop my hands I tilt my head to the right, looking down at Aisling's beautiful face. She's gives me a sulky pout.

I lean over to un-strap her seatbelt, grimacing when her chest brushes gently against my biceps.

"What?" I grunt, not pulling back as far as I should.

"How'd you know how to disengage a gun?" she asks, her chest pumping faster when I lean in to grab some of my stuff from the side in the door.

"We're not talking about this right now," I manage to rasp, turning to open my door.

But then she's brushing her body firmly over mine so that she can halt my progress, her hand gripped around the handle even though I could easily lift it away. I meet her blazing eyes, her body heat radiating straight into my abdomen.

I give her a reluctant glance up and down, before leaning back in my seat, nostrils flaring as she cages me in with her palms on either side of my bouncing quads.

"Aisling," I whisper, "I only wanna talk about this when you're sober."

"Three tiny shots," she reminds me, although her voice is a husky uninhibited purr.

I shake my head, hands clenching into fists on my knees. "Don't care. When I finally get you to listen to me, there is not going to be a fucking chance of you blaming what happens after on a drop of alcohol being in your system. Not to mention the fact that what just happened in that bar was really fucking dangerous."

She pushes up onto her knees so that her face is almost on the same level as mine, and I let our chests brush firmly together.

"You know exactly why I know how to disengage a gun," I tell her. "You know where I come from. You know that I don't take military shit lightly. I don't want you to ever be in a position like that again or, if you have to be, I want you to be prepared. That idiot could have hurt you."

She nudges her nose sweetly against mine. "You wouldn't let anything hurt me. You'd kiss it better."

I shove a hand through my hair as a flashback burns through my mind, and then my eyes are penetrating hers, my palms gripping urgently into her hips.

"You're playing dirty now?" I ask her, eyes on her mouth as she pushes more firmly against me. "You can't outplay a player, Aisling."

She tilts her head and gives me a taunting smile. "Isn't that what I've been doing for the past four years?"

God. Damn.

I smirk and huff out a laugh as she climbs up on me like she's been wanting to, and then I haul her thighs around my middle as I shift us over to my seat. I shove the driver's door open and start carrying her toward the cabin.

"You've got the smartest goddamn mouth," I rumble quietly, stubble scraping over her cheek as I press a hard kiss against the lobe of her ear.

Refusing to behave for one goddamn second, Aisling squeals, "Put me down, put me down!" as if she isn't clinging into the thick muscles of my shoulders like a wriggling baby koala.

Calling her bluff I start to lower her to the sandy dirt path in front of the moonlit cabin, but then she's instantly yelping and clutching her thighs around me tighter.

"No, no, no!" she squeals.

"Come on, tipsy girl," I say gruffly, hauling her higher up my abdomen. It takes balls of fucking steel to tune out the sexy whines she keeps on making as she bounces up and down my chest, panting heavily against my neck.

I pull the cabin keys out of my front pocket, shoving it into the lock so that I can put Aisling to bed as quickly as possible. Then I'm going to put the whole damn lake between me and her horny little ass.

I kick the door shut and drop her to the floor, lacing my fingers at the back of my neck so that I can't cuddle her up.

She jabs her little chin into the warm cavern between my pecs, and looks up at me with those beautiful *did I do something wrong?* eyes.

I grunt and look away from her. "Put the pout away, woman."

She makes a sad little sigh that has me reluctantly glancing back down at her.

"We're talkin' about this as soon as you're sober, Aisling," I promise, my biceps flexing like crazy when she wraps her hands around them.

But then I'm swallowing hard and allowing her to bring my arms gently around her waist. My knuckles brush over her lower back and my eyes close for the briefest moment, chest expanding at how right this feels.

I slowly dip my head as she reaches up on her tip-toes, and I brush my forehead gently over her temple.

"I don't want to talk," she whispers, her warm body heat making me shudder.

I leash my fingers into her ponytail, holding her closer as she clings to me.

"I'm gonna put this shit to rest, Aisling," I rumble quietly. "You're gonna tell me what hurt you so bad and I'm gonna fix it, okay?"

She mumbles something that sounds like *shut up big shot* and I breathe out a laugh, tugging her head back so that I can look down at her.

Prettiest girl in the world.

"Tanner," she whispers, her expression alternating between suspicious and giddy, and suddenly I realise that she's pulling me over to her bed. *My* bed. The bed that I've been sleeping in while thinking about her, wearing my shirt in that lake house.

When we reach the foot of it she squishes her breasts right up against me and I groan quietly as she teases the hell out of me.

"No," I rasp, even as one hand fists her ponytail tighter, and the other grips nice and firm over her hip.

"Can't we just enjoy the moment?" she purrs as she rubs her lower abdomen against my belt buckle. My eyes roll back in my head as she applies the perfect pressure to the thick ridge down there.

"Y-you'll enjoy plenty of moments with me, I swear." I swallow. "Maybe on this bed. Just have to wait 'til you're sober."

Then I grit my teeth and growl as she slowly rakes her nail down one of my nipples.

"Goddamn, Aisling," I pant. "You tryna scratch that thing off or something?"

She presses a gentle apologetic kiss over my erect fucking nipple.

"Sorry," I quickly tell her, instantly backtracking so that she won't have that embarrassed look in her eyes. "Didn't mean to say it like that." I pull her hand back up to my pec, giving her the green light. "Be as rough as you want, I can take it."

It's too dark to make out the finer details, the only light coming from the moon gently streaming in through the side window, but I don't need a light on to feel what she's doing to me. Aisling pushes up the tight cotton of my shirt, letting the bulk of my pecs hold the fabric just beneath my throat, and the next thing that I feel is her warm tongue flicking my nipple.

I gasp and hold her harder, while she looks up at me from under her lashes.

Then she wraps her lips around my nipple and sucks it into her mouth, hard.

My mind goes blank and I involuntarily walk her backwards, until her shoulders hit the wall at the foot of the bed.

"Whaaaat the fuck," I whisper, neck arched back as

Aisling – the fucking Captain of Carter U's elite cheer squad – sucks at my nipple, her nails digging hard into the muscles of my back and making me groan at how good that feels.

I'm confused as hell and turned the fuck on. She looks up at me without blinking and then bites her teeth into it.

A rough sound rumbles up my throat as I leak inside my boxer briefs, leaning a forearm on the wall above Aisling's head and watching through heavy lids as she kisses and sucks at me.

I keep her in place with my palms, not wanting the pain to end.

"Aisling," I pant. "You feel so fucking good. How does that feel so fucking good?"

She bites into me, really fucking hard this time, and I grunt like a beast as she keeps her eyes on mine.

After a painstaking few seconds she finally releases me, and I automatically move my hand to adoringly cup her jaw, bringing her face up to mine as I lean down and tower over her.

She keeps her hands on the large muscles of my chest, feeling how heavily she's got them pumping as I rub our foreheads together.

"Aisling," I murmur, her mouth only a centimetre away from mine. She wraps her arms around my neck, hauling our bodies tighter together, and she nudges the perfect tip of her nose against my own. A silent request – an invitation – for me to give her the kiss that I've been waiting on for four years.

I slide the rough palm of my hand up her jaw, gripping her steady, and she breathes excitedly as my mouth hovers just over hers.

"Ash." She pushes into me more desperately and I inhale deeply, overcome with the warmth and the scent of her. "Ash, baby–"

Four heavy poundings on the cabin's wooden door have our heads whipping toward the sound, eyes wide with shock as a surge of adrenaline shoots through our bodies.

"Aisling! You in there?"

"Fuck," I grunt, gripping Aisling against me tighter as her brother gives the door another rough pounding.

Aisling blinks quickly, trying to pull herself out of the pre-sex haze, and then she turns her head back to my body, eye level right with my chest.

She squeaks as she stares at the giant muscles in front of her and practically tears my shirt clean off as she yanks it back down over my abdomen. Before I can get a single word out she's shoving into me as hard as she can, not moving me an inch but I get the picture and start backing up.

We've been so caught up in each other for the past five minutes that I didn't even hear the crunch of boots on the dirt as Connell and the guys made it back to the cabins. I'm guessing that he's checking in on her to make sure that she's home safe – and alone – so I back-up into the bathroom as she calls out a frantic, "One minute!"

I smirk down at her as she shuts the door to the bathroom, scanning around for a hiding place big enough to fit a six-foot-four hockey player. I tug her sexy little body against me and encase my palms around her hips. She fumbles with something on the wall to my left.

"Not gonna lie, this is kinda hot," I tell her, my voice dropping deeper than usual as she reaches up to twist something. When she doesn't spare me a single word I glance at the wall and blink at it in confusion. "You tryna put me in the cupboard or something?" I ask her teasingly. "Baby, I'll just hide in the shower."

She gives me a withering glare. "Hidden in a lot of showers, have you?"

I clear my throat. Fuck.

She grips my jaw, ripping a primal grumble of satisfaction from my chest, and turns my face so that I'm looking at what she just opened.

Which, it turns out, was not the little cupboard.

"You're not hiding in the shower. You're climbing out of the window."

I stare at the open window, blank and uncomprehending. Then I look back down at her.

"Baby, I don't think I can fit through there." Also, I really don't want to.

"Aisling!" Connell's voice, low and laced with alcohol, sounds from the outside of the cabin.

I shove a hand through my hair, eyes on the delicate golden finger that Aisling is prodding stubbornly into my chest.

"You *will* climb out of the window," she tells me defiantly.

I swipe my tongue over my lower lip, gaze flicking back to the window, which is mounted partway up the wall and only opens on one side, probably so that no-one of normal size can break *into* one of these cabins.

"Fuck. Fine."

Aisling rewards me with a happy pat on the biceps as she frantically checks over her shoulder, but I quickly grab a hand around her jaw, surprising her as I haul her closer. I press a rough kiss to her beautiful cheek and then release her, shoving the window as wide as I can before mounting the ledge. I muscle my shoulders through the frame at a tight sideways angle.

"Fuck," I curse as quietly as possible as I twist my abdomen through the gap, Aisling's warm little hands pushing at me like she's trying to roll a boulder.

"Hurry up!" she whispers, and I have to bite back a groan as she accidently shoves her palm into my fucking nut-sack.

"Jesus Christ," I rasp, reaching for the top of the frame on the outside of the cabin, and using it like a pull-up ledge to haul my hips, quads and feet through the hole.

Aisling laughs excitedly through the window as I drop

heavily to the ground and I lean my palms flat on the bottom of the frame, smirking down at her. She's giggling like I just made her night.

"Wild thing," I murmur, before taking her chin in my palm again and pressing another kiss to her cheek.

Then I push up off the wall and head into the fringe of the forest. No-one sees me as I make my way around the water, and back to the lake house.

CHAPTER 17

Tanner

Four years ago

Our kisses are firm and frantic, the sound of Aisling giggling every time I squeeze her ass enough to have me smirking down at her, my fingers fumbling as I try to tear open one of the condoms.

I rip open the foil and toss the strip to the side, rolling the rubber down my shaft as Aisling giggles underneath me.

Once I've got the condom in place I drop my eyes back to hers, my dimples pulling taut as I look down at her happy face.

"You're perfect, you know that?" I murmur, grinning as she rolls her eyes and gives me a playful shove – just rough enough to make me want to haul her closer, which is exactly what I do.

Then I use two digits to tuck her panties to the side.

My chest swells on a harsh inhale as my knuckles accidentally brush her little heat, but I keep my eyes locked on hers, not allowing myself to glance down and take in the sight of her.

Reading my mind, she bites her teeth into her bottom lip and says, "You can look at me down there you know, if you wanna."

"Ash," I rumble, "trust me, I wanna. But I don't get to do that tonight." I roll my shoulders, trying to calm my heavy breathing. "Haven't earned it yet."

Slowly, I guide the head of my cock between her thighs, nudging at her gently. I keep my eyes on hers to gauge her reaction, before I start to carefully push, my whole body starting to swell and tense.

"Tanner," she whispers, her breathing heavy as she blinks up at me. She peeks down between us and gasps, her arms tightening around my shoulders.

"I'll go slow," I rumble, as the head of my cock finally breaches her entrance. I grunt and push harder, my biceps rippling with restraint.

She whimpers loudly and I drop my face into the warm curve of her neck.

"Th-that's just the tip?" she whispers, squeezing my shoulders as I keep on pushing.

"Yeah," I grunt, my hands shaking as I hold her thighs, keeping them as wide as possible, knowing that otherwise she won't be able to take me. I withdraw gently and then roll back inside, hoping that building a rhythm will help her take it deeper every time.

"Tanner, you're so big," she whispers, moaning as she claws her nails into my back.

"Want me to stop?"

She whimpers quietly and holds me tighter. "Don't you freaking dare."

I huff out a laugh and push slowly until my hips slap between her thighs. The second that we're hit with the smack of skin on skin I roam my palms up to her hips, squeezing roughly.

"Ash," I rumble, my chest pressing heavily on top of hers. "It's in, baby. You tell me when I can move, okay?"

"Now," she whispers immediately, and I brace a palm beside her head, towering over her. "You can… start now. Or whenever you want. Please."

I let my eyes drop down to her bra and then further down to her panties, the black lace already a mess from where it's bunched to the side, making room for me.

I grunt and grip the frilly string at the side, tightening it around my digits.

"You're perfect," I rumble, pressing my forehead down to hers. This time I withdraw the whole thing slowly, loving the way that she keeps those beautiful eyes on mine.

Then I push back inside, right to the hilt, my grip tightening on her panties as she holds my chest down on top of her.

"I'm too heavy for you," I rasp, trying to take some of my own weight, but she shakes her head frantically, eyes wide as she claws me harder.

I grit my teeth through the bite of her nails, loving the deep sting as she scores them down my back.

"No, no, I love it," she whispers, moving one hand down to massage my heavy balls.

"Ash," I grunt, pumping faster, thrusting rougher.

I tangle one hand up in her hair and keep the other wrapped around her hip, kissing at her cheruby cheeks as she holds me tighter.

"You're beautiful," I murmur, moving my hand to her waist, eyes on her breasts as I thrust faster.

She throws her head back on a moan, giggling as I suck at her neck.

I gently lick and bite her as I thrust deeper and deeper inside, the dark quilt plumping up around her as I work my length between her thighs.

She tugs roughly at my hair, regaining my full attention on her face, and I watch her with burning eyes as she whimpers, "Tanner, I'm gonna—"

I shove my cock deeper inside, growling roughly as she screams my name.

I cradle her head against my throat, pumping her hard over the finish line.

"That's it," I pant, massaging her breasts as she falls limp against the sheets. "That's it, I've got you."

"Tanner," she gasps, eyes glassy with disbelief. If anything she looks kind of shy.

"Yeah, baby?" I rumble, still slow-thrusting her against the sheets.

"I didn't mean to, you know… finish so fast," she whispers, her cheeks blushing darker and darker by the second. "I didn't mean to… I'm sorry—"

I shut her up with a kiss, groaning as she strokes her hands down my chest.

"Come as fast as you need to," I tell her, grunting as I pull it out. It's heavy as fuck and ready to blow.

Then I roll her onto her belly and kiss her cheek, positioning myself behind her.

"Think you can come again?" I ask her, using one forearm to lift her hips, keeping her upper body pinned down with my chest.

She moans as I nudge my cock between her thighs, seeking out her perfect little heat.

"Like this?" she whispers, looking up at me from over her shoulder.

I dip down to kiss her mouth, widening the stance of my quads as I gently lick her tongue with mine.

"If you'll let me," I murmur, already using my thumb to hook her thong out of the way.

I suck gently at her throat before moving my mouth up to her ear, my palm caressing her breasts as I scrape my stubble against her cheek.

"This okay?" I ask her quietly, in between the firm kisses I press to her cheek. "You okay with it like this?"

"Um," she whispers, her voice light and sugary sweet. She watches me over her shoulder, her beautiful eyes searching mine. I press our foreheads together, my free hand roaming up to the warm curve of her waist.

"You look kinda nervous," I murmur. "If you don't like it this way, we don't have to–"

"I want to," she whispers quickly, "w-with you. We can… try it. Because you want to."

I give her waist a gentle squeeze while slowly rubbing my length over her pussy.

"It's, uh" – I clear my throat – "it's my favourite position," I rasp, my cheeks warming at the confession.

She sinks her teeth into her lower lip, her eyes still locked in with mine. After a moment she gives me a nod, while one arm reaches behind my neck, pulling me closer.

"Yeah?" I ask her, wanting her verbal confirmation.

"Yeah," she whispers, sucking in a quick breath when she feels the first few inches going in.

"I'll go gently," I pant, my hand tightening around her waist.

My lap smacks loudly against her ass and I push down on her harder, compressing my chest against her back.

"*Tanner*," she whimpers.

I thrust again, grunting hard.

I keep one hand on her waist and sink the other into her hair, tugging it back so that her head is resting against the large curve of my shoulder. Exposing her neck to me while I thrust it in and out.

"You like that?" I ask, my voice breathless, rough.

"Yeah," she whispers back to me, her thighs slipping wider on the dark sheets.

I drop my head against her shoulder, groaning loudly as I start to pound her, my fist tightening in her hair as my other hand roams up to massage her breasts.

She moans against the pillow, and I work her harder and faster, until I'm grunting roughly against her neck.

"I'm there," I rumble, my hand sliding up around her throat.

She moans at the sensation and I squeeze her tighter, my cock ready to unload.

"Can I come?" I rasp, my quads tightening at the impending release.

"Yes," she whimpers, and then she's squealing as I grip her ass, my chest laying heavily on her back as both of my palms squeeze her behind.

I grunt loudly, hips smacking fast, and then I'm dropping on top of her, letting out a ragged curse as I release my spill.

"Tanner," she whimpers, and I grip her tighter.

"Almost done," I murmur, groaning when she looks up at me over her shoulder.

I dip my mouth down to hers, brow creased in pain as I kiss her, keeping it gentle and chaste while I finish pumping my length inside of her.

When I pull back, I drop my forehead to hers, the room quiet except for our shaky breathing and the gentle downpour of the Carter Ridge rain.

I slip out of her, long and slow, my palms stroking her back as I settle down on top of her.

"That was perfect," I murmur, kissing her cheek when she starts to blush. My thumbs rub firmly into her lower back as I ask, "Was that okay for you?"

The apples of her cheeks plump up all cute and rosy, and then she's giggling as she meets my eyes, making my heart thump wildly.

"It was perfect for me too," she whispers, laughing when I dip down to kiss her.

"Dream girl," I murmur.

I really fucking mean it.

CHAPTER 18

Aisling

Present day

I open the door to the cabin as quietly as possible, peeking out around the side of it as I tip-toe onto the dirt.

Not wanting to draw the attention of the two hulking hockey players who are currently sat in front of the unlit campfire, I spend twenty painstaking seconds carefully closing the door without hitting a squeak.

Just as I lift my sandal off the ground, without looking in my direction Tanner takes a huge bite into a breakfast muffin and says a gruff, "Mornin', Aisling."

My arms drop to my sides as I throw my head back. "Aw man."

How did he sense me? Was he raised by wolves or something? He doesn't even bother commenting on my little tantrum. Instead he takes another giant bite out of the muffin and uses his free hand to hold up a brown paper bag.

I wait, like, two seconds before I speed-walk over to where he and Caden are hunched on the logs, devouring breakfast muffins in total silence. When I'm barely a foot away from him Tanner glances up at me mid-chew and gives me a quick once-over before jerking his chin at me.

I ease the bag from his hand and he watches me peep inside of it, lips pursed to the side as I try to work out what the flavours are.

"Two strawberry. One blueberry," he mumbles. Then he finishes off the muffin that he started about two seconds ago and adds, "But if you don't want them, it's fine. I'll have 'em."

I gasp and clutch the bag to my chest. "They're mine."

He breathes out a laugh, unsmiling, and slaps his palm down roughly on the space on the log beside him.

"Sit with me."

Caden, who already has a good two feet of space between him and Tanner, quietly heaves his body off the log and moves over to the empty one on our right.

I give Tanner's big boot a little kick with the toe of my sandal, nudging him to budge up a bit if I'm going to sit beside him.

He watches me impassively for a moment before moving his left quad about one millimetre away from where it originally was.

I pick a strawberry muffin out of the bag, give him a suspicious side-eye, and take a nibble.

He clears his throat as he watches me, shifting his hips agitatedly on the log, and then giving into his base male need to man-spread. A sound rumbles through his chest as he pushes his quad against my thigh.

"Got plans this morning?" he asks, eyes trailing down my outfit.

"All the guys are going hiking – scoping out a spot so that we can camp out in a couple weeks' time." I swallow and swish my hair. "I am obviously invited."

He looks out at the lake, shoulders hunched forwards as he claps his fist into his palm.

I watch him for a beat, the big rise and fall of his shoulders as he wars with himself about whatever is on his mind.

"…Why?" I ask suspiciously.

He clears his throat and rolls his shoulders, psyching himself up.

"I, uh…" He grinds his fist into his palm a couple more times before finally sitting upright, releasing a warm wave of his testosterone. "There's somewhere I wanna take you."

I pause on the muffin mid-bite before narrowing my eyes on him. "Where?"

He glances over at Caden who is looking very pointedly at anywhere but Tanner. He picks up a rock and stares at it intensely.

Tanner looks back out over at the lake for a few beats, before shifting his thighs wider and meeting my gaze again.

"It's… important to me. Maybe just… let's drive there, and if you don't want to, that's fine but…" His sentence trails off as his beautiful irises search mine, glinting in the morning sunshine as the rays illuminate the shimmering lake. "Can I just drive you there, and you can see it for yourself? Please?"

"Now?" I ask, looking meaningfully back down at my unfinished muffins and back at him.

"Doesn't have to be. Or you can eat in my car." He rolls his shoulders as he watches me.

Call it morbid fascination but I really want to know where he wants to take me.

"…Fine," I say, and he quickly shoves himself up to his feet, immediately helping me up with a hand around my elbow, then at the small of my back.

As he begins manoeuvring me with his palms on my hips I twist around and frown up at him.

"This isn't because of… last night, right?" I ask, unsure

if he's thinking that we can just pick up where we left things in the cabin before I shoved him out of the window and then had a fever-dream kind of conversation with my equally tipsy brother.

Tanner's cheeks burn crimson and he removes one of his hands so that he can scrub at the back of his neck.

"N-no," he murmurs quietly, "although, last night was... I really..." He swipes his tongue over his lower lip, eyes staring unseeingly ahead as he opens up the passenger door for me.

I slip inside, watching him curiously, and as if this is something we do all the time he naturally dips beneath the door and teases the belt from its holder, handing it to me and waiting with his forearm on the roof as I buckle myself in.

When the belt is clicked into place he closes my door gently and rounds the hood, the car swaying under his weight as he heaves his body inside.

"You got ID on you?"

I blink at him, thrown by the question. "Uh, yeah?"

He grunts. "Good."

After he doesn't expand on the topic any further I just brush it off for now, although I give him another healthy dose of side-eye.

"So why do you drive a G-wagon?" I ask him as he confidently brings the car to life, his arm hooking around the back of my seat as he checks his back window. His giant biceps are right next to my face and I stare at them without blinking as his other hand lazily swirls the wheel into position.

"It's an off-roader," he replies, total focus on the road.

"So you always come to places like this?"

"Like Larch Peak?" he asks, before a smile flickers briefly across his mouth. "Aisling, I'm from Carter Ridge – aside from the town centre and the Carter U campus, the majority of Carter Ridge *is* off road." He debates with himself for a moment before adding on, "And my parents had a summer house here in Larch Peak."

My eyes flash to his in shock but I bite my tongue, because I think that it's interesting that both of our families own properties here. I mean, that's why I'm here right now in the first place. I'm not sure how much Tanner remembers about my family's business or why I'm here but I decide to stow that information away for now.

I stare at his strong jaw. "Where is their summer house?"

He jerks his thumb in the direction of it. "Thata-way."

I roll my eyes. "No, please. Spare me the details."

His cheek tics up slightly as a smirk tugs at the corner of his mouth.

I work my way through both of my strawberry muffins, Tanner glancing down to watch me whenever we hit a red light.

Ten minutes later we're pulling into a discreet parking lot. It doesn't seem to have any obvious signage. There's a small inconspicuous building right in front of it and a large expanse of rolling hillside at its rear.

Tanner pulls the car into park and then taps his thumbs agitatedly against the steering wheel, his large back muscles rigid as he stares out of the windshield.

After a moment, he un-straps his seatbelt and glances down at me. His eyes drop to the blueberry muffin sitting untouched in the rolled-down baggie.

He swipes his tongue over his lower lip and lifts his eyes back to mine.

"Don't freak out," he starts, unclipping my seatbelt and easing it into its holder.

"Why would you say 'don't freak out' if we weren't about to do something that would make me freak out?" I ask, brow creasing in concern as I fist my fingers into the brown paper.

"Look, we don't have to do it. But I…" He looks away

from me for a second as if to calm himself down. "I just want you safe, okay? I just want you to be as safe as possible, no matter what situation you find yourself in."

I stare up at him, unsure where he's going with this.

After a few beats he leans slightly closer so that he can see out of the passenger window and he points to something beside the door.

I have to squint to read the words but when I do–

"Tanner! What the hell?!" I squeal, whipping around to face him and practically whacking my forehead against his big chest. "You brought me to a *shooting range*?" I ask, completely incredulous.

"Ash, baby, calm down–"

A shiver runs through me and not just because this gorgeous hockey-playing psychopath brought me to a *shooting range*.

"Okay, first of all, you have to stop calling me that," I tell him, my breathing unsteady as I try not to freak out. We are literally in *gun territory* right now.

"What, calling you 'baby'?" he asks, one arm hooked around the back of my headrest. He smells so good it's crazy. "I thought that you liked–"

"I'm talking about when you call me *Ash*," I grit out. "And you called me it last night too, for the first time since–"

I shut myself up because we both know what I'm talking about. Last night Tanner called me Ash for the first time since our wild whirlwind hook up four years ago, when all we knew about each other was that we never wanted to not know each other again.

He had given me the nickname so naturally. It was as if we were meant to be.

I shake my head at myself, a little overwhelmed by the memory.

I may as well roll up my sleeve right now and show him that tiny love heart freckle that I've always got there.

When it comes to Tanner, why do I always wear my heart on my sleeve?

"Just don't call me that," I say breathlessly, swallowing hard as I flick my eyes back over to the shooting range sign.

"Fine," Tanner relents. He kicks back in his seat with all of that hockey player swag. "Look, if you don't want to do it, that's fine, but after the incident last night I'd really like to teach you how to handle a gun. Also, are you gonna eat that muffin? Because if not–"

"Oh. My. *God!*" I smack my palms against his pecs. "You are literally insane. First of all, no way would a civilian without a registered gun licence be allowed to use a shooting range anyway? Like, you did *not* think this through."

"Baby," he drawls, all gruff and country, "it's so cute hearing you talk about this shit as if you think you know something."

When my jaw practically dislocates at the *gall* of the man he reaches his arm back around my headrest, towering over me as he leans closer.

"You're in Larch Peak – mountain territory – where they've got wild things roaming in every patch of land. You don't even need to be a citizen of the *county* to come to this range – all you need is to be over eighteen years old and in the possession of government issued identification. And also? When it comes to you, I think *everything* through. What the fuck do you think I did last night when I was lying on top of *your* sleeping bag in *your* goddamn lake house? All I could think about was what a close call it was at the bar and how it felt like *my goddamn duty* to make sure that you would never be scared in a situation like that again."

"How on earth is it your duty? You're not my boyfriend!"

"About time we changed that don't you think?"

I groan and throw my head back against the seat. "You're *impossible*," I whisper, gripping my hands into the top of the headrest.

He watches me in heated silence, tongue swiping over his lower lip as his eyes rake up my body. When his gaze lands back on mine there's a dark flame flickering in his irises.

"Heard a rumour," he begins, his big fist landing on both of mine at the top of the seat. He gently holds my wrists together in one firm squeeze.

I roll my eyes. He can be so broody.

"Yeah?" I ask.

"Heard you let Tristan give you a peck on the cheek."

At first I'm a little surprised by the sudden subject change, not to mention the fact that I didn't know Tanner knew about that.

I meet his gaze and whisper, "Who said it was on my cheek?"

His fierce eyes are the most penetrative that I've ever seen them. "You better be joking."

"Or what? You gonna put me in the sin bin?" I ask tauntingly, and his hand involuntarily flexes tighter around my wrists.

He grunts and looks at our hands, stroking his thumb gently over my skin.

After a moment he exhales deeply and brings my hands down from the headrest, setting them in my lap. He encases both of his palms around my little fists.

I don't say anything, but his touch is perfect.

"After what happened last night, I want to take some precautions." He keeps his eyes down on my hands as he gently squeezes them. "I'm from a military family, Aisling, so I don't take weapons like that lightly. But I know that, around parts like these, it's not uncommon for a guy to be carrying something that maybe he shouldn't be. But I also know that, if that's the case, I want you to have the belief in yourself that you can handle that situation. If you understand the weapon, it can help dissipate a bit of the fear. Not that you're scared," he says quickly, his eyes sparkling with kindness as they flash up to meet mine, "but a deeper knowledge of it might be beneficial, especially if you're planning on… you know, maybe staying around these parts for some time. I'm not sure what your next move is once you've finished the reno at the lake house but…"

Something warm and hopeful burns in his irises, something that I don't fully understand because I'm more caught up in what he just said – about my potentially staying around these parts. I drop my eyes to our hands, my brow creased and sulky, because I wish I had the nerve to ask Tanner where *he* is planning on staying now that we've graduated.

But that's none of my business.

I peek up at him from under my lashes and he gives our joined hands another squeeze.

"This wasn't on my summer bucket list," I mumble, and his expression softens.

"I know, baby, and we don't have to stay for long. Just seeing you hold that thing the way you did last night…"

He glances away from me for a beat, large shoulders rising and falling as if the memory itself pisses him off.

"I want you to know what's what, and then we can haul ass back to the lake. You're not even gonna shoot it. We're gonna see it, hold it, and then you'll know that – if it's in your hands – you're in complete control."

I purse my lips to the side, secretly loving the feel of Tanner's big hands wrapped around mine.

Even though he doesn't know it yet, he's right – if I *do* want to live somewhere like Larch Peak then I should do everything in my power to familiarise myself with the ways of the place. Ones that I was never exposed to as a sheltered real estate heiress.

Tanner's cheek tics up playfully, sensing my waning anger.

"I mean, it was either this or going into the woods and getting Caden to teach you."

I stare up at him, horrified. "Please tell me that Caden does not have a handgun with him."

Tanner's mouth opens and then he pauses, no sound coming out.

"What the *hell*, Tanner!" I yelp.

"It's not like that," he says, his voice all deep and self-assured.

I mumble *cocky big shot* and he gives me a playful, "What's that now?"

I turn my head away from him, and he drops both of his heavy forearms over my shoulders. I reluctantly glance up at him and see that his face is barely two inches away from mine.

"I want you safe," he tells me, "and it's better for you to be prepared than to wish that you were. I'm good with this stuff, baby. I'll show you the ropes and then we never have to talk about it again, okay?"

I keep frowning up at him until he gently nudges his forehead against mine.

My heart squeezes at the contact, butterflies fluttering gently in my belly.

I nod my head and I feel his large body sigh with relief.

"Okay."

CHAPTER 19

Tanner

Present day

This is simultaneously my best and worst idea of all time.

Hopefully it's about to curb Aisling's understandable fear of armed weaponry, but then again it could end up just freaking her out further.

I keep my breathing steady as I lead us both toward the entrance.

She's actually letting me nestle her under one of my biceps as I stroll us casually to the front door – maybe because she's trying to use me like armour, but still, I'll take it.

I pull open the front door and give her waist a squeeze, encouraging her inside.

It's a rustic ranch-style building, with a couple of cushy seats by the front door, and large wooden cupboards behind the long back-wall counter. The guy standing behind it has got to be at least seventy-five and he looks content as hell watching the sports channel on his iPhone.

"Wanna wait in one of those chairs and I'll grab us the forms?" I ask quietly.

Aisling purses her lips and frowns at the cupboards behind the counter. I'm guessing she knows what's behind there and is feeling a little freaked out.

She shakes her head and, to my immense guilt, clutches at my forearm, dragging it over her collarbones as if she needs the extra protection.

I clutch her as tight as possible, wishing that there was an easier way to help her face her fear. But I think that ripping the Band-Aid is better than mulling over it for months on end, so I lean down to her ear as I walk us to the counter and say, "It's just you and me here this morning, okay? I called ahead and made sure the range would be empty. You're safe, I've got you."

She doesn't say anything, just eyes the form in front of the ranger.

"ID?" he asks, and I slip my ID onto the counter, squeezing Aisling so that she'll do the same.

She releases one of her hands from around my forearm and pulls her phone from the front pocket of her denim shorts.

My head cocks to one side as she pulls the case off the back of her phone, placing her ID carefully on top of mine.

As she clicks the case back into place – a clear Perspex-type thing with little love hearts all over it, holding some cheer photos and vinyl stickers in place – she senses me watching her and glances up at me over her shoulder.

"What?" she asks, lifting an eyebrow as I stare at her phone.

It's a sleek baby pink iPhone, and I'm pretty sure it only came out around a year ago.

I narrow my eyes on it for a moment and then blink myself out of the thought, my eyes flicking down to hers and shaking my head to silently tell her that it doesn't matter.

For now.

She gives me an equally suspicious look as she slides the phone back into her pocket and then swishes her hair dramatically, slapping her ponytail across my jaw. She turns to watch the guy behind the counter input our details into his computer.

I breathe out a laugh and rub my hand over my stubble, savouring the sting of the whip as she tries not to smile at her own naughtiness.

"You been to a range before?"

I collect our IDs as he slides them back across the counter. "Yes, sir," I tell him.

He nods and gestures to the board near the door to his left, which then leads out to the range behind him.

"Instructions and policies are on the board anyway. You have to read 'em all or I can't let you through." He takes a pen and two forms from the pile on the wooden counter and pushes them in our direction. "Fill out the forms, I'll brief you, and then you have one hour on the green. Targets are set up from section three to seven."

I nod. "Thanks."

As I steer Aisling over to the two armchairs, she whispers to me, "'Yes *sir*'? Lord, you really *are* a country boy."

I give her a little smirk as she looks up at me with curious eyes, squeezing her tighter against my side before depositing her in the comfiest looking chair of the two. I kneel down in front of her, setting the forms on her perfect golden knees.

I hold the pen out to her and she deliberates for a beat before quickly snatching it.

"Is this okay?" I ask her quietly as she glances nervously between me and the document. "We don't have to if you don't want to, but if you do I'll show you everything that you need to know."

She stares at me with those big unblinking eyes for a long deliberating beat and then she gives me a little nod, tucking a loose curl behind her ear as she begins filling in the paperwork.

When she finishes with her form, she places it carefully on the armrest. Then she begins to slowly fill out mine.

I watch in mildly amused silence as she frowns down at the boxes asking for personal information, and she hesitantly begins writing in the boxes that she knows the answers to. She slowly fills in the word 'Tanner' in the prettiest, loopiest handwriting that I've ever seen.

Warmth fills my chest and I give her another squeeze, loving everything about this moment.

She poises the pen over the next box, pretty eyes flicking up to meet mine.

"Surname?" she asks, blinking at me innocently.

I shake my head at her and smirk. "You're real funny."

Her brow quirks in curiosity, beautiful eyes still blinking at me expectantly.

I suddenly drop the smirk, glancing down at the form.

And then my eyes fly back up to hers.

"Aisling." I stare at her, and her pen-hand twitches expectantly.

Oh my God.

No way.

There is *no fucking way* that she doesn't know this.

I drag one of my palms down my face because, yeah – she doesn't fucking know.

"Aisling," I grind out. "Tanner *is* my surname."

We stare at each other in pin-drop silence, her eyes searching mine to see if I'm kidding.

Oh. My. Fucking. *God.*

"Aisling." I shove a hand through my hair, tugging at it roughly as I stare at her in fucking horror. "Tell me that you're joking."

She blinks at me quickly, her cheeks getting pinker by

the second.

I shove my tongue in my cheek, chest suddenly heaving.

"You didn't know that Tanner is my surname?" I rasp, mortified.

Another thought occurs to me and I grip hard at the back of my neck.

"Oh my God. You actually don't know my name, do you?"

Aisling bites nervously into her lower lip and whispers, "Tanner is your surname?"

I press my palms into my eyes, drop my forehead against her knees, and groan.

"Oh my *God*, Aisling. You don't know my fucking *name*?"

I have been head over heels for this girl for four fucking years... and she doesn't even know my *name*?!

"How was I supposed to know!" she whispers frantically, eyes wide as I lift my head from her warm lap. "The first time that we met you introduced yourself as Tanner, and it's the only name that people call you!"

"It's also the name on the *back of my jersey*. In other words Aisling, *it's my surname*."

She throws her hands up in the air and I drop my head back down to her thighs.

Which is actually really fucking nice. Like, it kind of sucks that the girl I spent my college career pining for doesn't know, as aforementioned, *my fucking name*, but the fact that she's allowing me to suffocate my face between her legs is pretty much balancing out the scales here.

I try not to groan in pleasure as she wiggles her little ass on the seat.

She places the paper form over my left shoulder and I feel the press of the pen nib as she positions it onto the page.

She swallows quietly. "So, uh... what is your name?"

I tip my head up an inch so that I can look up at her

from under my lashes while I keep my prime place right here between her thighs.

I clear my throat and feel my cheeks grow hot, suddenly self-conscious.

"Mason."

We look into each other's eyes for a good five seconds, before she finally mouths the word *Mason* and begins writing it onto the form. I drop my chin onto her thighs, my stubble making her squirm a little as she uses my shoulder like a writing table.

Knowing that she's going to need a hell of a lot more details that she doesn't know I slip my cell out of my jeans, type out the general details and turn the screen for her to look at.

"Thanks," she says quietly, eyes flicking between my phone and the paperwork. Then after a beat she looks me in the eyes and says, "Mason."

My quads clench tight and I quickly look away from her, pupils dilating.

"Don't mention it," I rumble, my voice gruff as hell, but I swear that there's a tiny smile playing around her lips as she drops her eyes and gets back to writing.

CHAPTER 20

Tanner

Present day

I keep Aisling tucked into my side as she frowns warily at the bipod stationed in front of us.

"Why's it so long for?" she whispers, fingers tentatively reaching out, but closing into a fist before she can touch it.

"It's a rifle, not a handgun. They look different on the outside but they have some internal similarities."

She gives me a suspicious little side-eye as if she's waiting for me to turn that into a metaphor. I huff out a laugh and shake my head, silently telling her that that is not gonna happen.

She increases the intensity of her scowl but then cuddles closer to me as she looks at the weapon again. I wrap both of my arms around her shoulders, a physical reminder that I'm here to help her through this.

"So what are the similarities?" she asks.

"Both of the barrels have rifling to put a spin on the

bullet, which helps to increase the accuracy of the shot. And they both have thick walls so that they can deal with high pressures."

I shrug, and my biceps brush snugly against her shoulders.

"Also, they're typically used for stationary targets, unlike a shotgun which is for a moving target." This range only offers rifle practice, but seeing as we aren't here to actually shoot – we're here so that Aisling can try to conquer her fear – that works fine.

"I can't believe that my fingerprints are on some cowboy's gun," she whispers, her fists clenching at the hem of my shirt.

I squeeze her tighter. "It's okay, mine are too."

"But what if, like, the gun was involved in something bad? And then the police came after me?"

"Aisling, if the police ever came looking, I would take the fall for you."

Her head whips around, staring up at me in surprise. I give her a half-smile before pressing a kiss against her temple.

"You don't mean that," she says when I pull back, enormous eyes going all sparkly when I look down into them.

"Yeah, I fucking do. Why do you think I told you to hand it to me in the first place?"

Her jaw drops open and warmth begins spreading through my cheeks. Uncomfortable with how fucking obvious my feelings for her are, I release her from my arms and look away.

"Okay. Before you touch that thing I need to grab a bullet-proof vest."

Aisling rolls her eyes. "I hardly think that I'll be so incompetent that I'll accidentally shoot myself."

I give her a smirk of my own. "I meant for *me*."

Her jaw hits her sandals and I snicker as I tug one of the

vests from the back of the booth.

"Kidding," I murmur, grinning as she flushes bright red. Then she turns her back to me, huffy as hell. I tuck my chin in the warm crook of her neck. "Lift your arms, baby."

"Asshole," she mumbles, before sulkily lifting her arms.

I grin and nuzzle into her as I slip her arms through the holes, pulling back when the suit is covering her front so that I can fasten her up at the back. It's not compulsory at the range, because it can affect a shooter's balance and stance, but it's available anyway as a ricochet precaution. Even though I have no intentions of us shooting anything, I want to keep Aisling as comfortable and protected as possible.

When I'm finished, I pull her back against my chest and walk us to the rifle.

I reach around her and gently adjust the positioning of the weapon on the bipod.

"You wanna touch it, or just have me point each part out to you?" I ask her quietly, wanting to keep this as calm as possible while giving her the information that could help keep her safe in the long-run.

"Um, I can… I can touch it," she whispers.

I nod and take her delicate hands in mine. Her golden nail polish sparkles in the early morning light, and I brush my thumb over hers, feeling her preen as I admire her.

"Pretty," I murmur, and she tries to hide her blush. Then, getting down to business I say, "Feather-light touches, okay? We're gonna use a gentle touch."

She nods again and I slowly position our hands, one at the butt of the rifle and one at the handguard.

My chest presses warm and firm against her back. I keep my body still and then begin carefully sliding our hands around the stock, matching the depth of our inhalations so that she can stay calm and focused.

"We're going bottom to top, okay?"

"Yeah," she whispers.

"Okay." I tap our thumbs against the back of the rifle. "This is the butt."

Aisling instantly explodes with laughter, head tipping back against my chest. "Shut the hell up, Tanner!"

"Jesus Christ!" I tighten my hold on her hands, temples throbbing as I hold her steady. "I don't mess around with this shit, Aisling. That's just… what it's called."

Her shoulders shake dangerously and she turns around to peek back at me, smiling naughtily over her shoulder before sinking her teeth into her lower lip.

At least I've distracted her from her fear. I jerk my chin at her, signalling for her to look back at the rifle, and then I tuck my chin back over her shoulder, exhaling as she relaxes into my hold.

"Stock, pistol grip." I remove our hands and point at the next couple of parts. "Safety, trigger guard, trigger. This is where the magazine will go." I squeeze one of her hands and say, "This is the handguard. Then up front we've got the barrel, flash suppressor, and muzzle. Okay so far?"

"Yeah," she says breathily, eyes unblinking as she takes it all in.

I pick up the magazine and then use our thumbs to gently test the spring.

"Feel that?" I ask.

She nods.

I press down on the first bullet and her breathing hitches, anxious at first and then a little more relaxed than before.

"Feels smooth, right?" I ask, and she nods again, her soft cheek rubbing against my stubble.

"Yeah, it feels smooth," she whispers.

"It's 'cause these bullets are polished real good," I tell her. What I don't tell her is the fact that these bullets are actually polished *way* too fucking good – like, these feel like goddamn sniper bullets.

"Want to hold it off the perch?" I ask her, and when she

nods her head I slowly lift the rifle up, watching her roll her lips into her mouth out of concentration as she takes the weight, feeling how heavy it is. I hold it up with her and press the magazine into place with a gentle push of my palm.

"Now what?" she asks quietly, totally still as her eyes flick between the weapon and the range. No sound to be heard except the subtle shift of my boots on the gravel and our slow, steady breathing.

"If I was going to shoot it, the next thing I'd do would be lay my cheek against the stock and look through the scope." I pause for a long, quiet moment before adding, "Then I'd ease my hand toward the trigger."

Slowly, Aisling presses her cheek against the stock, frowning a little as she tries to see through the tiny scope. I keep her hand clamped in mine, not allowing her to move her fingers toward the trigger.

"Are you a good shot?" she asks when she finally lifts her face from the viewpoint. She twists in my arms so that she can look up at me. Now I'm the only one of us holding the rifle, my whole body unmoving as she presses herself against me.

I look down at her and carefully search her curious eyes. Then I nod.

"Show me," she whispers.

I swallow hard.

"Aisling…" I'm shaking my head as my eyes move back and forth between her and the target at the bottom of the range. "I'm not sure if that's such a good idea."

"Why not?" she frowns, almost looking kind of hurt.

When my dad wasn't away on a mission, he'd spend our father-and-son time teaching me and my brothers all about this stuff. What each part of the weapon did. How the minutiae of geophysics affects each individual shot.

And above all else, the importance of waiting.

And waiting is something that I'm pretty fucking

amazing at.

I swipe my tongue over my lower lip, squinting at the target across the range. Then I glance back down at Aisling's beautiful face.

"It's loud," I warn her. "Louder than you'd maybe expect. We'll have to put on those ear protectors."

She shrugs her shoulders, blushing a little. "Sometimes I don't mind loud."

I clear my throat, quickly blinking away from her.

Yeah, I remember her not minding getting loud.

"Okay," I say hoarsely, lifting up one of my biceps so that she can slip behind me as I reposition myself to scope out the shot. We both slip on the headgear, and Aisling strokes at her ear covers. I watch her protectively over one of my shoulders and tip my chin, gesturing for her to stand a little further back.

"When I pull the trigger the stock's gonna ram against my shoulder and I don't want to knock you if my position budges."

Her hands move to the back of my shirt as she stares up at me but neither of us mention it. After a moment of hesitation she finally takes a few small steps backwards, but I've got control of the weapon so I nod, satisfied, and turn my full attention back to the target at the bottom of the range.

I lay my cheek against the stock and slow down my breathing, waiting for my heartbeat to drop as I keep my eye on the scope. Aisling doesn't say anything as she watches me hold my position, and I'm grateful for it because I wouldn't be able to say anything back to her. Every tiny vibration in my body is going to affect the bullet so I stay still and silent, my focus trained on the plus sign up ahead.

I slowly tighten the trigger, then hold still, waiting through one heartbeat, then two, then three.

In the next second I shoot the shot, grunting as the

stock jumps back against my shoulder. The blast is so instant that for a few seconds nothing can be made out, but I wait it out, keeping my breathing even.

When the vibrations settle I check my shot through the scope.

Barely a centimetre to the left of the plus sign, and slightly above, the smoothness of the bullet making the shot perfectly clean.

A dimple pops in my cheek, a secret smile trying to break free, but I stay still and refocus.

I shoot again. This time I'm a centimetre to the right of the target and slightly above, and I wait for the sound of the shot to quiet down before I pull the trigger for one final time.

Dead centre.

I lower the heavy rifle as I take in my handiwork, smirking quietly to myself as I take stock of what I just did.

Satisfied, I set the rifle down, stretch out my back, and turn around to face Aisling.

Her head is tilted to one side as she blinks at the target sheet.

Maybe it's for the best if she actually doesn't look at that too closely.

I clear my throat and move around her, positioning my body at her back so that I can undo the bullet proof vest.

"There," I rumble, easing the padding gently down her arms and then slinging it back over the post that I got it from. I remove our ear defenders, wrap my palm around her wrist, and begin dragging her away from our shooting booth.

"Did you–?" she sputters, blinking rapidly between the target board and then back to me.

I clear my throat, not saying anything.

"Did you just–?"

"No."

"But I can see–"

I shove my free hand through my hair and glance over at her.

"Tanner, did you" – she throws a disbelieving look back over to the target, the hand that I'm not hauling wrapped tight around my forearm – "did you just shoot the bullets... to make the shape of a heart?"

I pull us to a sharp stop in front of the ranger's door and I look down at her, eyes burning as they meet hers.

Her lashes flutter as she tilts her head back to look up at me.

"Tanner?" she asks warily, brows arching as if she's afraid of the answer.

But I don't need to give it to her. She already knows the truth.

I brush the pad of my thumb over her soft cheruby cheek and then wrap my hand back around her wrist. I open the door for her so that we can head back to my car.

"Come on," I say, my voice deeper than usual as I jerk my chin for her to walk through the door first, and then follow behind her. There's an almost-smile playing on my lips. "Let's share that muffin."

CHAPTER 21

Aisling

Present day

I pad out from the front door of the lake house and lean my hip against the porch railing, doing a brief wave to the delivery van as it slowly reverses beside my brother's 4x4.

It's the first time in four weeks that clouds have appeared in the sky – thick grey thunderclouds that blanket out every inch of light.

I peek up from under the canopy overhead, eyeing the weather warily as the driver jumps down from the van. Sandy dust kicks up around his boots, and he pulls the heavy door open at the back of his vehicle.

"You want help hauling this into a particular room?" he calls over to me, as he and his colleague begin mutually lifting and manoeuvring the first piece of the bed-frame down from the back.

"Please," I say, as they carefully make their way up the porch steps, turning the wood on its side as they breach their way through the front door. I follow in a couple of steps behind them, not wanting to get in their way when they'll be doing more than a few trips back and forth between the house and the van.

I point my finger above my head, gesturing to the guy who is walking backwards up the stairs that the master bedroom is at the front of the property.

He nods. "Gotcha."

After that I move back out to the porch, rolling my lips into my mouth as I look out towards the left, letting my eyes follow the trail of the silvery lake, rippling gently under the darkening sky.

Over the past week I have started to collate and order all of the pieces for the lake house's interior that will pull the property together and transform it from a house into a home. So now the open-plan downstairs living area has a multitude of still-wrapped sofas filling the space, as well as a number of made-to-order wooden tables and a few cosy décor pieces. All still untouched and in their cardboard boxes.

The delivery of the bed-frame for the master bedroom is the last essential item that I needed before I start unwrapping all of these pieces and finally turn this place into what it was always meant to be: rustic, rich, cosy. The perfect escape for when someone feels the call to come back to nature. With the glistening lake out the front and the emerald forest beyond the back the location couldn't be any more perfect, so it's my job to tie it all together by making the inside just as dreamy as the out.

It really is going to be the most beautiful home.

I hear the final piece of wooden bed-frame thump against the upstairs wall and I glance over my shoulder through the doorway, wondering how long it will take me to construct all of those pieces together.

Seeing as this is my first semi-official project for my family's company my parents had given me a two month timeframe to get the whole thing done, but I had obviously wanted to finish it ahead of schedule, to prove myself to them by showing them how capable I am.

The guys duck out of the front door and give me a quick nod and a smile as they trudge down the porch steps.

I turn my back to the gently shimmering water and gaze wistfully at the house before me, a small sparkle of satisfaction in my chest as I take in the fact that all of the hard work is now done. From this point on all I have left are the aesthetic finishing touches. I let out a tiny sigh of relief, proud of what I've achieved so far but not yet feeling complete. There's still work left to do.

The sound of a cabin door opening across the lake pulls me out of my daydream and I turn around, resting my palms back on the top of the porch railing. Connell had fitted a new working lock in the lake house's front door, so Tanner and I switched accommodations again last weekend.

Tanner walks slowly out of the front door of his cabin, his gait heavy with sleep as he rubs his palms into his eyes. He's wearing a cotton shirt stretched thin over his broad chest, and unbelted jeans sitting low on his strong hips.

I'm pretty sure that he spent yesterday in Carter Ridge with his mom – mainly because, when we were all having breakfast around the campfire yesterday morning, he said as much to Hunter, very loudly, all while looking me dead in the eyes.

Yeah, okay, it felt good to know where he was going. And even though I don't doubt that he's super interested in me, I was relieved to have the confirmation that he wasn't, like, hooking up or something.

Since taking me to the range last Saturday, Tanner has been cautiously optimistic with befriending me, which ironically enough has absolutely delighted Connell. Connell is such a freaking cinnamon roll that as soon as he watched Tanner knock at the lake house door on Sunday morning, so that he could walk me over to where everyone was eating breakfast, Connell got all excited and decided that Tanner is now his 'third best friend' – with me being his first, and Fallon and Logan being 'joint second'.

A small dot of rain hits my knuckle with a little *thump*, and I blink myself out of my thoughts before brushing the back of my hand against my baby pink sundress. I glance up at the heavens and watch as the deep slate clouds roll by faster, dark and thunderous.

The sound of rhythmic splashing causes me to glance toward the lake, and I blink at it in shock as I see Tanner effortlessly swimming my way.

He pauses midway so that he can pull himself to a standing position, raking one hand through his hair as we watch each other. His chest heaves deeply, causing the water to slosh over his large tan shoulders.

Suddenly nervous, I glance behind him to the other side of the shore, releasing a tiny gasp when I see that his shirt and jeans have both been discarded.

So the gorgeous guy who I don't want to fall for is wearing nothing but a pair of boxer briefs right now? Great.

Tanner's eyes travel reverently up and down my body before he resumes his stroke, slicing through the water with grace and precision.

And that's my cue.

I practically run down the porch steps and then begin speed-walking along the lake shore, cursing under my breath when another spot of rain splashes my forehead. I swipe it away quickly with my fingers and glance hastily behind myself, letting out a little squeak of fear when I see that Tanner is following behind me. He shakes some water from his hair before shoving it back off his tan forehead, heated eyes raking down my body as he squeezes some excess water from his shorts.

Well, at least he's wearing some.

I whip back around to continue my escape, only to let out a defeated *"aw man"* when I realise that the sandy lake shore has disappeared – it's totally swallowed up by the swollen lake, meaning that I've only walked about ten feet away from my starting point. I may as well have stayed up on the porch – at least then I would have been sheltered from the imminent downpour.

I release a shaky exhale and turn back around to face Tanner.

He glances briefly at the forest to his left, frowning slightly at how threatening it looks now that there's a storm overhead, and he instinctively moves a step closer to me before dropping his eyes to meet mine.

There's something kind and cautious in his sparkling irises.

"Morning," he murmurs, his voice still deep with sleep.

I blink up at him. "Tanner. It's two in the afternoon."

He blinks down at me in surprise before his face relaxes into a lazy grin, and he lifts and drops a shoulder as he breathes in another deep inhale.

"Sorry," he murmurs. "Got back real late last night."

Another raindrop gives me a tiny slap on the cheek and I frown as I bat it away. Tanner watches me swipe it in silence before lifting his eyes back to meet mine.

I fold my arms protectively over my chest and will myself to stay composed.

"What're you doing over here?" I ask him, feeling a little nervous and lightheaded.

A smirk tugs at the corner of his mouth. "I kept hearing these sad little sounds drifting over the lake."

I give him my stoniest glare as his handsome smile widens.

"I'm kidding. Just thought that the beautiful girl across the water might want some company. All the guys were going to the rink today because of the weather, so" – he shrugs lazily although there's a flame in his eyes – "it's just the two of us."

I swallow hard and look down at my sandals. I knew

that of course, but now that he's said the words out loud it suddenly feels all too real.

Just Tanner and me, with the whole place to ourselves.

The delivery van kicks to life beside us and Tanner glances at it over his shoulder.

"You get something delivered?" he asks, eyes flitting to the men at the front of the vehicle.

My cheeks burn crimson as I think about what is now upstairs in the lake house, ready to be assembled in the master bedroom.

"Nope," I lie, eyes unblinking as I stare up at him.

He narrows his eyes on me. "What'd you get?"

We are absolutely not going to find ourselves in the exact same position that we were in four years ago. There is no freaking way that he can find out that I have another bed to build.

"Nothing," I say quickly. Then I add, "Definitely not a bed."

The van's giant *BESPOKE ALL AMERICAN BEDFRAME COMPANY* slogan drives by painstakingly slowly in our peripheral vision.

Tanner's handsome lips fight a smirk as he watches the van crawl past us at one mile per hour.

"Right," he says dryly, grinning as he looks back down at me.

I drop my eyes and shake my head at myself, emotions bubbling up in my chest at all of the all-too-familiar full-circle feelings.

And Tanner can sense it.

"Aisling," he begins, his voice kind and deep.

"Please don't," I say immediately, stumbling back a step. "Please just... I know that it's only the two of us here but... I'll be leaving soon anyway, so let's not–"

"You're leaving?"

Tanner's eyes widen, frowning in shock and displeasure as he swiftly closes the small space between us.

"Tell me when. When are you leaving?"

I shake my head and look up at him, my right eye twitching when I catch another glimpse of the delivery van's sign.

I swallow hard.

"I'll probably be finished in two weeks, tops," I whisper. "Let's just not make this anymore… complicated than it already is."

"Aisling." Tanner's voice is husky, his eyes raging and stormy. "I've had four years of complicated with you. I want to put our past to bed."

I shudder dramatically at the b-word. "D-don't say the word *bed*," I whisper, tentatively pressing my wrist against my forehead.

He huffs out a humourless laugh. "Why? Because it reminds you of how good it was before you got all freaked out on me?"

I drop my arm, frowning up at him. "I only got freaked out because I realised how foolish I'd been. I only got freaked out because I realised I didn't know you *at all*."

Tanner steps right up against me, pushing his chest roughly against mine. "This is good. Get it all out, Ash."

I throw my arms in the air, releasing an exasperated growl. "Oh my *God*, Tanner! Let it *go* already, I don't want to think about it anymore!"

He nods down at me, eyes hard and unreadable. "So you admit that you have been thinking about it."

I smack one of my palms against his chest and he grunts, his position unmoving.

"Fine. You want to talk about it? Let's talk about it," I snap.

I breathe in a big shaky inhalation and then flick my eyes straight up to his, the fire in his irises licking dangerously against my own.

"I thought that you were exactly what I wanted to find at Carter Ridge, but the morning after I realised that you were the exact opposite. There was this whole other side to you that you decided to withhold from me. After all of the cute stuff you'd said the night before can you freaking blame me for cutting this thing short? For pushing you away? For not wanting to trust you?" I swallow down the acid climbing from my tummy as I stare up at him and choke out, "We met. We fucked–"

Tanner shakes his head, our bodies pressing closer.

"The goddamn *mouth* on you," he grits out, his palms shaking at his sides. "You wanna have it out like this? You wanna play dirty? Fine. We met and we *fucked*, over and over and over again."

His eyes scorch against mine and I quickly blink away from him, my cheeks absolutely on fire.

"But I already told you before any of that happened exactly how I felt about you." He exhales roughly. "I told you before we did it exactly how I wanted this thing to go."

"You couldn't possibly know how you felt about me, Tanner. No-one can make a decision that quickly."

"Uh, yes they can, Aisling – most people make their judgement of a person in the first seven seconds of laying their *goddamn eyes on them*. It's science, for fuck's sake."

He's right and I hate it.

"What we had was different and you know it."

I steel my jaw. "You were a player, Tanner. You played me like you did everyone else."

He shoves his tongue in his cheek, his broad chest pumping heavily. "Don't say that." He shakes his head at me, his rigid jaw ticking angrily. "Goddamn it, Aisling. That shit stings."

My voice is barely audible as I whisper, "Well, so did waking up and realising that I'd just fallen for the bad boy."

"Aisling." His stormy eyes are pleading. "How many times do I have to say it? It wasn't like that. It was *never* going to be like that with you. Even after you ghosted me I tried to prove myself to you."

"And why is that exactly?" I ask, cocking my head as I

play dumb with him. "How come guys magically decide to 'not mind' settling down when it comes to the heiress of a multi-million dollar fortune?"

He frowns down at me in confusion. Then he rumbles, "What the fuck are you talking about?"

"*Sure*," I drawl slowly, sarcastic as hell. "It was *totally* one-hundred-percent out of the love in your heart that you chose to pursue me out of every other girl you've ever slept with, right? I bet you just happen to 'not know' that we're staying in properties owned by *my parents*, on land bought up by *my family*." I breathe out a laugh as I roll my eyes. "What else? Did you also 'not know' that we own the condominium on campus at Carter Ridge?"

Tanner blinks down at me, mouth opening and closing as if he doesn't know what to say.

Oh.

Oh.

So… he actually *didn't* know that.

"Uh," I say, laughing slowly, "actually, maybe that's beside the point. I guess that that's totally not important–"

Tanner presses his palm against his forehead, squeezing his eyes shut.

"Tell me that you didn't think that part of the reason why I wanted to keep you was because of money. Money that – Jesus Christ – money that I didn't even know that you *had*. And, by the way, that makes no fucking difference to me whatsoever."

He frowns down at me, a flicker of hurt pride shimmering behind his striking eyes.

"Say what you want but you *know* me, Ash. I could have five dollars to my name and you could have five million, and if you ever gave me the time of day you *know* that I'd still pay for everything. Real men treat women the way that they deserve to be treated." He drops his eyes for a moment and mumbles, "You know I wanted to treat you like a princess."

I try to ignore how heart-warmingly perfect that sounds even though my defences are beginning to crumble.

"Okay, so you're a gentleman *in theory*. And, yeah, maybe your intentions were… honest. But that didn't stop you from being the biggest freaking player on campus, Tanner."

"I *hadn't* been a player since starting at Carter U! I had a shitty reputation that followed me to college. And you know it in your heart that I wouldn't have–"

"People don't change, Tanner! Once a player, always a player. Don't freaking lie to me – you're not going to change your ways for me."

"You're right. I'm not. Because I *already did*, four fucking years ago!"

I give him a vicious glare. "Tell that to the seven trillion girls you fucked."

He grips his hand around one of my biceps, hauling my body right against his. "I waited for you, Aisling. I waited for you for months. What the fuck was I supposed to do?"

When I lift my chin in defiance, refusing to respond, something dark flickers in his eyes.

"And that's another thing." He jerks his thumb across the lake and I glance briefly over to his discarded shirt and jeans. "Funny. You gave me your number the morning after and I've been hitting it up ever since. But when you pulled your phone out of your shorts the other day at the range, I know that it wasn't the same one."

The colour instantly drains from my face, eyes wide as I realise what he's realised, what he's about to say.

I swallow hastily. "Tanner," I begin.

"Thing is, I could swear that all of my messages have been delivered and read – you know, because it fucking *shows me* as much when you open up my goddamn texts. So tell me, *baby* – how am I texting a phone that you don't use anymore, when everyone else is texting you on another number?"

The silence that stretches between us, filled only by the

rapidly increasing fall of the rain and our quickening breathing, answers his question.

He shoves one of his hands into his hair, lake water spilling down his tan cheeks and over his swollen biceps.

"I knew it. I knew that you fucking liked me." He removes his hand from his hair so that he can cup it around my cheeks. The warmth of his touch makes me gasp, my eyelashes fluttering. "You kept a phone contract going for *four years*, just so that I could keep on texting you?"

I remain strategically silent but he already knows the truth.

Because how on earth can I ever rationalise having two phones, especially when one of them is only there so that Tanner can contact me?

He leans in closer so that we're pressed nose to nose. "No matter how hard you pretended not to care, I knew that you still felt it – still feel it." He pushes his forehead against mine and murmurs, "Scared little chicken."

I frown against him, making a smile tug faintly at his lips.

"I don't… I don't want you," I whisper, biting back a whimper as he brushes his forehead more firmly into mine.

"Yeah?" he rumbles deeply. "Whose hands are currently gripping into my pecs for dear life?"

I swallow hard.

Those would be mine.

I immediately try to pull them back but Tanner is quicker, and he grabs my wrists, keeping my hands in place as he closes his eyes.

"Just tell me, Aisling," he murmurs. "Tell me what happened."

"Tanner…" I say warily, shaking my head.

Because the truth of it is that I'm scared that he's right – that I'm a scared little chicken.

I've invested so much time in trying to convince myself to not want him that I don't know how to navigate *allowing* myself to want him.

"It's okay." His warm thumb brushes firmly against my jaw. "I'll fix it all, Aisling. All you've gotta do is tell me."

I nod my head, and recount my eighteen-year-old heartbreak.

CHAPTER 22

Aisling

Four years ago

There are two large forearms wrapped gently around my waist, soft hair tickling my cheek as he nuzzles his face into my neck. His chest expands against my back on a deep slow inhale, and it falls just as soothingly, content and fast asleep.

I tentatively lift my quilt cover, peeking down at the thick pair of arms – large, tan, and so wonderfully warm. What was it that he said he did again? I remember him saying that his family was military but I can't remember him saying what he did.

Did I even ask him?

I sink my teeth into my lower lip, frowning slightly as I stare down at his forearms.

The warm weight pressing into my back suddenly pulls me closer. His hands move to massage both sides of my waist as he slips his thick quad between my thighs.

"Aisling," he rumbles, groaning quietly as he pushes

himself against me. "Good morning."

I bite harder into my bottom lip as liquid heat pools in my belly, his quad rubbing back and forth beneath me making me feel hot and lightheaded.

But most of all I'm burning up because he actually remembered my name.

When it comes to a one night stand, I know the etiquette – I grew up with my brother's horny football friends who spent every summer hooking up with strangers. I know all of the cards they had up their sleeves when it came to the morning after.

One of the biggest ones being using a nickname to hide the fact that they'd already forgotten their partner's name.

As the reality of the situation sinks into me, I start to wonder about the other aspects of last night. I mean, in the moment it felt right – crazy soon, sure, but there was an honesty between us that was undeniable. I can't help but lie here and wonder if Tanner meant what he said.

And he said a *lot* of really nice things to me last night.

I look down at his hands on my waist, blushing as he presses a stubble-coated kiss to my cheek.

"Ash," he murmurs, one hand gently lifting up my chin. I can hear the warmth in his tone, the hint of a smile in his voice.

I twist to look up at him over my shoulder and my heart pounds uncontrollably in my chest.

A handsome dimple cuts into his cheek as he meets my eyes, smiling lazily.

"Hey Ash," he murmurs, cuddling me closer. "You good?"

With slightly shaking hands I push my hair back, breathing fast.

"Yeah," I whisper quietly, wondering when the other shoe is going to drop.

Like, no *way* can he actually be as sweet in the bright light of day as I had allowed myself to believe in the dark intimacy of last night.

"I'm just feeling, um… a little overwhelmed is all," I admit, my voice kind of breathless.

He watches me with an unreadable expression before subtly shifting his weight again, trying to prevent his erection from digging its way into my behind.

"Do, uh… do you want me to leave?" he asks gently.

He has the deepest voice that I've ever heard.

I gnaw anxiously at my bottom lip, feeling grateful that he hasn't removed his warm hands from me yet.

"Um," I whisper, my breathing picking up as I get even more shy. "No, it's not that. It's more like… you're free to go if you want. You don't have to, like… hang out, because of the stuff you said last night."

His eyes hold mine, heated and unblinking, before he gently eases my body around so that we're lying chest to chest.

He reaches up to brush a curl from my cheek, and he keeps his warm hand around my jaw.

"I meant what I said last night," he rumbles, watching me carefully as I twist my hands in front of my stomach. "If you don't feel the same, then okay. But what I said last night hasn't changed." He pauses for a moment, checking for my reaction before pulling me closer.

After what we did last night Tanner slipped back into his boxer briefs and then rummaged around for his shirt, easing it gently over my head so that I wasn't just wearing my lingerie. Then we had made out for a really long time, laughing and whispering intermittently before he finally cuddled me to sleep.

So now his hands stroke over the fabric of his own grey shirt, the cotton soft against my skin as he massages it against me.

"I wanna take you on a date," he continues. "Probably like a million dates, with loads of kissing."

I breathe out a laugh, flashing him a shy smile, and his

dimple deepens in his cheek as he presses his forehead against mine.

"What d'you say?" he murmurs, a warm flush staining his neck as he breathes deeply, awaiting my reply.

His hands stroke down my arms until he's caressing me just below my elbows, and my eyes flick down, catching on the tiny love heart freckle, just above where his thumb is rubbing me.

I've never actually worn my heart on my sleeve, I told him last night as the rain pounded gently against the windows.

But what if I did?

Because being at Carter U is my fresh start, right? No more acting like the bad girl when all I want is to be loved. To have something real and genuine – that once in a lifetime small town love.

I swallow hard, my eyes on my freckle.

Maybe it's time to finally wear my heart on my sleeve.

So instead of replying I wrap my arms around Tanner's neck and bring my lips softly to his.

He releases a low sound as he instantly kisses me back, his hands roaming up my waist and hauling me closer so that I can feel his heartbeat against mine.

"I'm taking that as a yes," he murmurs, which makes me pull away from him with a giggle. I have hearts in my eyes as he grins down at me.

I hear my phone vibrate on my bedside cabinet and Tanner drops his head to my neck, groaning as I reach over to glance at it. I don't pay any attention to the endless scroll of messages but I do check the time, my eyes widening as my jam-packed schedule comes crashing back to my mind.

I toss my phone and slap my hand over my forehead, moaning quietly as Tanner sucks a hickey into my skin.

"I have to go to class," I tell him breathlessly. He kisses my throat and slips two fingers down the front of my panties.

He grunts, rubbing me gently. "Want me to get you off

first?"

I gasp as he presses harder, his rough fingers making my eyes squeeze shut.

"I-I'll be late," I pant, although right now class is the last thing on my mind. I feel desire flood between my thighs and, when I squirm with need, Tanner feels it too.

"Jesus," he rasps, pulling back so that he can shove down his boxer briefs.

"N-no, we have to wait," I whisper, and he instantly stops, his eyes burning as they look deep into mine. But then he nods, dropping his eyes and cursing quietly as he eases his boxers back up his quads. His long thick erection is barely covered by the soft cotton, but he shoves at it for a good ten seconds until he finally manages to wrangle the length of it back underneath the waistband of his underwear.

"Sorry," he murmurs, cuddling me against his chest and kissing my forehead. "You're so beautiful, I was getting carried away." He rakes a hand through his hair and rumbles, "Didn't mean to."

A small smile plays at the corners of my lips as I cuddle him back, squishing my cheek against his chest and feeling my heart sparkle as he holds me tighter.

"I don't want you to go," I whisper. "I just need to get ready for class is all."

I look up at him and he jerks his chin at me, making me giggle loudly as he drags me up for a searing kiss.

"I understand," he murmurs, slowly sitting himself upright, looking around a little disoriented.

The black sheets pool around his knees, drawing my eyes to his tan quads, and he strokes himself over his underwear as he glances around the room in search of his clothes.

I point to his shirt on my body and he presses his palm against his forehead, releasing a quiet chuckle.

"Shit," he murmurs, grinning as he reaches down to kiss

me again. "Okay. You keep it," he adds as he gets to his feet, trudging around the bed as he goes to grab the rest of his clothes.

"No way!" I say, a laugh tinkling out of me as I pull off his shirt.

He watches me with a slack jaw, absently catching his shirt when I toss it to him without taking his eyes off my body.

"Fuck," he murmurs, the shirt dangling from his fist.

"Tanner," I giggle, rolling my eyes. I pull the sheets up over my bra to hide my lingerie from view and he scrubs his hand over his eyes, looking adorably distracted.

"Yeah, I know. Sorry. Again," he mumbles, pulling on the shirt before shucking up his shorts.

I mean, okay, I kind of wanted to keep his shirt – and I love it even more that he *wanted* me to – but I don't exactly love the idea of him rolling out of the condo shirtless, one, because he could inadvertently bump into my brother and, two, because I really don't want anyone else getting to see his gorgeous body.

That's just for me.

I tug on my newly-acquired Carter U Cheer sweatshirt as he pulls up the last of his clothes, and then he's entwining his fingers through mine as we walk through my living room to the front door.

He pulls my body against his and backs me up against the wall, leaning down so that he can kiss me and groaning quietly when he does. His fingers tangle up in my hair and his quad slips between my thighs, rubbing me gently as he caresses my lips with his.

"Give me your number," he murmurs, pulling away with eyes half-mast. He slips his cell from his pocket, unlocks it, and then pushes it into my palm. He rests his cheek against the top of my head as I type in my number.

"I'll text you later," he says as he pockets his phone, his hands moving back to my hips as he kisses me goodbye.

"You can let me know your schedule and I'll work our dates around that."

"What about your schedule?" I ask him.

His mouth lifts into a handsome smile. "My schedule is wide open for you, baby."

I laugh into his chest and he strokes my hair, chuckling with me.

"I mean it, Ash," he murmurs. "Any time you're free, so am I. Only for you," he whispers, before pressing a final kiss to my cheek.

"Okay," I whisper back to him, unlocking the door and leaning against the jamb.

He walks backwards down the hallway, eyes on mine as he waits for the elevator.

When it dings at our floor he shoves his hands through his hair, his eyes on mine as the doors slide open.

"Fuck it," he murmurs, and then he charges straight for me, making me squeal as he lifts me up off the floor and crushes his mouth against mine.

"Fuckin' miss you already," he pants, his palms all over my thighs.

"I miss you too," I giggle, yelping happily as he squeezes my ass.

He lowers me to the floor, kisses my mouth, and then races back to the elevator before it disappears.

"I'm gonna be blowing up your phone, so get ready!" he calls back to me, making me hug my arms over myself and laugh quietly as the doors slide closed.

And then I'm on my own, breathing heavily against the doorjamb, my heart pounding wildly in my chest as I try to bring myself back down to Earth.

I numbly move back into my condo and quietly close the door, locking it gently before padding over to the kitchen.

I drink a glass of water as I head back to my bedroom, and as soon as I'm through the door my heart stops in my chest.

Because there on the bedside cabinet is Tanner's khaki cap.

Almost as if he'd deliberately left it there for me.

I make my way over to it, one hand resting over my heart.

Too freaking cute, I think to myself as I brush my fingers over the brim.

Then the soft thrum of a vibration draws my attention to the object beside it; my phone screen blaring bright as text after text filters through.

I roll my eyes and pick it up, but then I'm smiling again as I see the message from an unknown number. I know for sure that it's Tanner and my heart cinches tight at his text.

Miss you already xxx

But before I can text him back my eyes drop to the stream of group chat messages below his. An already incessant influx from the star cheerleaders on Carter U's famous comp team.

I twist my lips as I scroll through their messages, not really paying attention until I see the small preview of a photo.

I blink at it – once, twice – trying to work out what I'm seeing. Then I tap on it quickly, my fingers shaking slightly at the prospect.

The image opens and my jaw drops.

No. Freaking. Way.

Because it's a photo of Tanner – *my* Tanner – surrounded by pretty much the whole cheer squad, taken from our first social the other night.

I wasn't there, but it looks like everyone else was.

I blink down at it, my heart thumping wildly, as I try to work out why the hell Tanner was there.

How is that even possible?

I scroll to the messages below it and suddenly I'm getting my answer loud and clear.

ARIA: *I'm sooooo jealous you girls met THE hockey heartthrob!*
WHITNEY: *The Carter Ridge Rangers have a BIG new player on their team!*
ARIA: *So when you say 'big'…?*
KASEY: *I've heard, like, nine inches.*
WHITNEY: *Girl, I heard ten – and from a LOT of different sources.*
KASEY: *look at his tagged photos though – he's been with, like, literally EVERY pretty girl in Carter Ridge*

I stare down in horror at the screen as more and more photos filter through, screenshots from one of his social media profiles and a million different selfies that he's been tagged in.

With, like, a million different girls.

I type out a message to the squad, fingers shaking as I tap the screen.

AISLING: *wait, who is this guy? what do you mean by 'hockey heartthrob'?*

Whitney, a fellow freshman, quickly answers my questions for me.

WHITNEY: *his name's Tanner and he's fucking FAMOUS in Carter Ridge – and not just because he's being predicted as a future star for the NHL, but because he's been AROUND if you get what I mean. The rumours about him are HUGE.*

I immediately message her back.

AISLING: *what rumours?*

The blood drains from my face as I hit the send button. It takes a minute before Whitney's message comes through and when it does, I wish that it hadn't.

> WHITNEY: *Aisling, what you are looking at right now is the biggest player on campus. There's genuinely a rumour that he fucked every single girl in his senior year class. From what we saw of him the other night, I'm pretty sure he's planning to continue his streak at college too. And like, thank God, because who wouldn't want a piece of that? Besides, there was a hockey social last night and he didn't show up, so it's freaking obvious what he was spending his evening doing instead. But seriously, get in line. Girl code doesn't exist when Tanner is involved.*

She follows up her message with a billion crying-laughing emojis and I slowly sit down on the edge of the bed, feeling my heart plummet in my chest.

"This was a huge mistake," I whisper to myself, fingers shaking as I hold my phone.

I was so caught up in how kind and handsome Tanner was last night that I didn't for one second think that it could have all been an act? That he might not be as sweet and wholesome as he'd let on?

I mean, come on, I didn't even know that he was a student at Carter U! And now I'm finding out that he's some big shot hockey heartthrob who's slept with the entire female population of the town that I'm about to spend *four years in?*

Tears sting at the back of my eyes as I tap back onto his message, a blank page except for the one text. My heart breaks a little bit in my chest.

I can't believe that I didn't even question him.

How the hell could I have been so naïve?

A million more messages fly through on the cheer chat – more photos screenshotted from his accounts with more pretty girls – and a sob rips through my chest as I realise what a fucking idiot I've been.

It's my first week at Carter U and I already fell for it – I fell for the exact type of shit that I specifically *didn't want to fall for.*

For a player.

For the guy who sweeps you off your feet and then immediately pulls the rug.

"Idiot, idiot, idiot," I whisper between my tears, swiping at them as they fall incessantly down my cheeks.

In what universe would Tanner be love-struck at first sight? Of course he was just trying to get into my panties – and that's literally exactly what he did.

I toss my phone across the room, grab my pillow and scream into it.

"Fuck – this – shit!" I yell, thumping my fist into the cushion after I drop it onto my sheets.

Fresh start my ass.

There's a good reason why I had my walls up all through high school, why I played the role of the heartless bad girl when guys were throwing themselves at my feet.

It was because of this, right here: because if you aren't the one breaking hearts, then you're the one getting your heart broken.

I rip off my sweater and storm into the condo's currently-spare bedroom, throwing open the wardrobe and staring in at the neat piles of clothes.

I pick up the cutest outfit that I own and then throw it down on the bathroom counter, ready to scrub that fucking big shot *jerk* off of my body before forcing myself to be the girl I always knew that I had to be.

The heartless player.

The bad girl with an attitude.

The type of girl who never gets to fall.

I stare down at my little freckle and feel my tears pour down my cheeks.

I was so naïve, I think to myself.

No more wearing my heart on my sleeve.

CHAPTER 23

Tanner

Present day

She won't meet my eyes. She keeps on looking out across the lake, then over to the house that she's staying in, but as soon as I duck down to try and capture her attention she's blinking down at those pretty sandals, bottom lip trembling dangerously.

But she hasn't walked away from me. I haven't lost her yet.

We breathe quietly in a deep unsteady silence, the fall of the rain the only constant as it pelts off the lake. The drops create small sparkling rivers as they trickle over Aisling's skin, the most beautiful shade of gold against the backdrop of the dark thunderous clouds.

I rake a hand through my hair and push it back off of my forehead, the action briefly capturing Aisling's attention before she quickly drops her eyes back to the water.

"Aisling," I begin, my voice low but softer than it usually is, because I want to comfort her in this moment of vulnerability in a way that I never comfort anyone.

I tentatively lift a hand so that I can position it beneath her chin, not touching her soft skin but feeling the warmth radiating out of her nonetheless. The action encourages her to lift her head and meet my eyes, and what I see in her wary gaze drives an arrow straight through my heart.

"I'm so sorry, Aisling," I tell her, my hand hovering over her shoulder before I wince and drop it completely, not sure where the line is right now. When it comes to breaking the touch barrier I need her to give me the green light first. "I… I can't imagine how that must have felt."

If I'd woken up next to Aisling that morning and found her phone littered with texts from guys, or if my teammates were talking about her like that in our group chat, I would have been pissed the hell off – the only difference is that I would have been pissed off with *them*, not her. But I can see it from her point of view and, in this instance, after having a whole squad of chicks talking smack about me to her, I understand why she shut me out.

They made me out to be the heartless player.

And it's not even a miscommunication. It's the truth. That *is* the guy that I was in high school – it's just not the guy who I wanted to be going into college.

It's not the guy I would have been with her.

Because if Aisling had given me a chance, the past four years would have been completely different.

Aisling's frown is quivering, making my own brow crease, hands dying to wrap themselves around her shoulders and comfort her.

"It was silly," she whispers, looking away from me when I shake my head. "It was… literally just a one night stand. I made it into this huge thing in my head but I think, at the end of the day, maybe it was just what we refused to call it the night before."

The cords in my throat tighten and I roll out my shoulders as they begin to swell.

"No." I swipe my tongue over my lower lip, refusing to let her lie to herself like this. "It was never like that. What your friends texted you the morning after... that's what everyone wanted me to be. It's not who I was."

She breathes out a quiet, sarcastic laugh, rolling her eyes to try and keep the mood light. "What, so it would have all been fine if I hadn't found out about your reputation?"

She gives me a sad, almost forgiving smile and it hurts in a way that no glare ever could.

She swallows and swipes at the rain hammering against her forehead, blinking away from me as her cheeks turn red.

"I was upset with what I saw, but I wasn't just sad about losing you, or the idea of who I thought you were," she says. "I was mad with myself because I was supposed to be turning a new leaf. I know about how hard it is to break a reputation and I thought that starting college would be my fresh start. I wouldn't have to be this icy heartbreaker anymore who only messed around with guys who were these big, brawny players. I didn't want to fall for the bad boy, because I didn't want to be the bad *girl* anymore. I didn't want a guy whose phone was blowing up every five seconds. I wanted the kind of small town sweetheart that a big city heiress never had the chance of meeting before." She takes a long shaky breath and adds on in a little whisper, "I wanted the guy that I thought you were before I knew who you really are."

My chest feels hard as steel, rigid and unmoving as she hits me with blow after blow.

She was sad about losing me before we had even had a chance to start.

I drag my palm down my jaw, scraping my stubble over my skin.

"Realising that I'd just made the same mistake that I

always did was kind of the wake up call that I needed – to put all of this, like, delusional 'hopeless romantic' stuff out of my mind and be the same girl who I've always been." She does this self-depreciating smile as she lifts her hands to make air-quotes, and a tiny dimple pops in her cheek. "The 'bad girl'," she says with a playful roll of her eyes, half-laughing, half-sighing as she drops her hands back to her sides.

I shake my head and step closer to her, begging her to touch me as I gently crowd her space.

"It doesn't have to be like that. Not anymore, Aisling."

I duck my head so that she has nowhere to look except straight in my eyes.

"You said it yourself – it's hard to break a reputation – and the reputation that I made for myself at high school followed me straight to Carter U."

I roll my shoulders uncomfortably, my chest feeling tight as I bare myself to her.

Wearing my heart on my sleeve.

"I fucked around a lot at high school. I didn't have relationships. It was just sex, nothing emotional. But that doesn't mean that I never intended to fall in love with someone. My parents had that instant-love type of thing and I just" – I shake more rain from my hair, then shove it back with my hand – "I knew that I'd be the same. Fall once, fall hard, and don't get back up. It's goddamn hereditary. And I knew the second that I saw you that I wouldn't want anyone else."

She shakes her head as she frowns down at her sandals but her twiddling fingers clutch tightly around the drawstring of my shorts.

Yes. I instantly wrap one of my forearms around her lower back, tugging her closer, and envelop my other hand around one of her biceps, caressing her gently as her eyes meet mine.

"Those texts?" I rumble, my voice hoarse and gruff.

"They were bullshit. We were – what? – one week into our freshman year? Those chicks didn't know me and I had no fuckin' interest in knowing them."

I breathe out a humourless laugh, still in disbelief over the story Aisling just enlightened me to.

"I really liked you, Aisling, and I thought that you liked me too. Liked me for something other than being a good fuck."

I frown at the thought and now I'm the one who can't meet her eyes, chest pumping rapidly as I stare at the rainfall slashing through the water's surface.

Aisling senses the sting in my chest.

"I did like you, Tanner. But you have to understand how bad it freaking *sucked* to have fallen asleep thinking that you were some, like, small town cutie, and woken up to realise that every girl on campus was lining up at your front door."

"I wouldn't have opened that door to them, Aisling. I only wanted you." My gaze collides with hers and a peal of thunder ripples threateningly beyond the mountain.

"I… get really nervous talking through my feelings like this," she whispers. "I hate the vulnerability that comes with putting my heart on my sleeve."

I slide my hand to that tiny heart-shaped freckle just beneath her elbow and give it a small caress with the large pad of my thumb.

"I know," I murmur. "But you never have to do it alone. I'm here with you, and I'm putting my heart on my sleeve too."

I offer her the briefest hint of a smile before swiping a hand down my chest to rid myself of the rain clinging to my pecs.

"Did you really wait for me?" she asks suddenly, brow arched as tears shimmer in her beautiful eyes.

I almost laugh as I tug her closer, the soft fabric of her dress rubbing up against the muscles of my abdomen.

"Check that secret cell phone you've got stashed away,"

I tell her, unable to resist towering over her as her palms scrunch the fabric of my soaked shorts in her fists. "How many goddamn months I spent trying to get you on dates that you never fucking turned up at. You remember those messages? You remember the fucking flowers I would leave outside the condo doors?"

She winces and shakes her head, and I stroke my fingers through her hair, stopping it from falling forward and hiding her beautiful face.

I did wait for Aisling, for most of my freshman year. But after all those months I knew that I had to take the hint. She wasn't interested, so I had to move on.

Didn't stop me from implementing a self-imposed no sex rule during my entire senior year though. Because even though she had a boyfriend at the time, I knew that Aisling and I had some seriously unfinished business.

"I was just... I was protecting myself," she says, her whisper frantic as she searches my eyes.

"I know."

I nod down at her and tangle my fingers in her soft, dark waves.

"I'm glad that you did. I'm glad that you put yourself first. And I can see it from your side and I know how fucking terrible it looked. But I would never do anything to hurt you, Aisling – that predestined lifestyle that the chicks at Carter U had set up for me was the goddamn opposite of what I wanted. I met you, and I wanted to keep you." I give the back of her neck a gentle squeeze. "End of story."

"Tanner…" she says warily, eyes wide as I hold her firmly against me in the rain.

"It was always you." I stroke her jaw. "That's something that you'll never need to question."

I move my hand from the back of her neck so that I can gently shield her face from the downpour with my palm, earning a wet little laugh from her as a stray tear streaks down her cheek.

"No crying," I tell her, leaning down to quickly kiss it away. Her chest shudders against mine as my lips meet her skin, and it takes every ounce of strength that I have to pull myself back from her. To resist finally claiming her mouth with mine.

"I didn't want to fall for you," she whispers, a concerned shimmer in her eyes.

"You didn't want to fall for the asshole that your friends were talking about. But you already fell for the real me, Aisling – the version that's there for you and only you. You want that quiet small town life? I can give you that. You know that, Aisling – that's what I've always wanted to do."

She gives me a dry look, pouting a little.

"You're about to become a famous hockey player. I hardly think that a quiet small town life is in the cards for you right now."

She is absolutely not finding another way to wiggle back out of my life again.

"Okay, look. Yeah, the NHL's a big deal, but how many players' private lives do you know about?"

I raise my eyebrows at her as she frowns and purses her lips. I hide my smirk. *Got her.*

"See? It's not one of those… showy sports, baby. Some of the guys might be like that, especially when they're crazy famous, but with guys like me – guys like Hunter and Caden and all of the other guys from Carter U who plan on going pro – we're just doing the sport. Playing the game, making some money, and then at the end of the day wanting nothing more than to get back to our girl."

I brush my thumb over her soft cheek and feel my chest swell with satisfaction as she relaxes against me.

My voice is low and quiet as I tease, "Now stop trying to make up obstacles and tell me that I can make you mine."

She scowls up at me from under the palm that I've got shielding her perfect face from the rain. My eyes drop down to her dress and I watch the downpour begin to turn the soft pink fabric wet and translucent.

My jaw muscles flex.

She's not wearing a bra.

She finally releases a shaky exhale and whispers, "I'm tired of fighting."

Rainwater slaps relentlessly against the muscles of my back as I nod my head and murmur, "I know."

Those tired little arms find the strength to pull me closer.

"I'm sorry," she whispers, eyes squeezed shut and her cheek pressed over my heart. She fits against me so perfectly that I can't help but squeeze her tighter in the cage of my biceps.

"Don't be sorry. You put yourself first and that will never be the wrong decision."

"But I hurt you. I pushed you away."

I stroke a knuckle over the tip of her nose as she peeks up at me, all sad and guilty. I shrug a shoulder.

"I came back, didn't I?" I offer her a genuine smile, dimples pulling taut as I look down at her. "So you couldn't have pushed me away that well."

Aisling gasps and then shoves me in the chest with her warm hands. "It's too soon to joke about," she mumbles, looking up at me with those enormous eyes, and I grin as I keep her in place, fucking obsessed with how adorable she is.

"Are we going to try and put the past behind us now?" I ask her gently, smiling as a raindrop bats against her collarbone because it gives me an excuse to caress it away with the pads of my fingers. "Are we going to try and move forward, and not let anyone get in our way?"

She swallows shallowly, her eyes wide and unsure as she sinks her teeth into her bottom lip. "But I was… really harsh on you. For a really long time."

I shake my head, smiling as I murmur, "Yeah, you were so mean. I still really liked you, though."

Her hands slide down over my pecs and the long muscle in my shorts begins thickening.

I steel my jaw as I force my eyes to not roll back into my head.

"I'm being serious, Tanner. Four years... that's, like, a really long time. How could you ever look past that? How could you ever forgive–?"

My lips meet hers and the whole world goes quiet.

I hunch low so that I can reach her and hold her firmly in place, my forearm around her lower back keeping her body pushed up against mine. The surprised flutter of her beautiful lashes touch softly against my skin before her whole body relaxes and she stands up on her tip-toes, helping me reach her.

I squeeze my palm gently around her shoulder before using my forearm to haul her up, a nervous gasp leaving her lips as I lift her off the ground. I can't help but smile against her mouth as her feet dangle above the darkening dirt and she tightens her arms around my neck, pulling herself up even higher so she can more easily reach my mouth.

The kiss is soft and chaste but neither of us can bring ourselves to end it, making it grow hungrier, deeper, my tongue sweeping against the soft seam of her lips. Her arms lock tighter around my shoulders and I tug her hips closer as she whimpers.

"Is this okay–?" I begin asking, my voice deep and rough, but Aisling shuts me up with another kiss, making me smirk as she silently answers my question.

I slide my fingers up into her hair, allowing my thumb to sweep low so that I can caress her perfect jaw, and I gently tilt her head backwards so that I can kiss her more intimately.

When I lick my tongue over the sweet curve of her lips she parts them with a shaky inhale, eyes fluttering open as she waits for me to kiss her deeper.

I roll my shoulders, eyes on her mouth as my breathing

gets heavier. "Can I–?"

She nods adamantly. "Yes."

"Okay."

And then I'm heaving her roughly up my chest and crushing my mouth back down on hers, groaning as I slant her open. She falls limp in my arms, her fingers squeezing desperately against the swollen muscles of my chest, and a satisfied rumble courses up my throat as I get that first gentle stroke of her tongue.

"I've missed you so much," I whisper, biting back another groan as she tentatively tries to lick my tongue with hers. I deepen my strokes, keeping them slow but firm, and then press a couple hard kisses against her lips before pulling back to look down at her.

I carefully rub my palm up her flushed cheek, swiping away the rain before sheltering her stunning eyes with my hand once more. I gently nudge her nose with the tip of mine before leaning in for another kiss.

My fingers push through the rich waves of her hair, rain droplets running down her curls and thumping against my face as I lift her above me. Her breathing is erratic and her eyes are wild, bright and sparkling with fresh-faced innocence even as her hands belie darker needs. Her right hand rubs a firm caress over my heart, while her other hand travels lower, slipping between our bodies until she can finally stroke–

"Ash, Ash, Ash," I choke out quickly, grabbing her left wrist and hauling it back around my shoulder. "We can't. Not yet. I rushed it with you once before and I'm not making that move again. I have to take my time with you – you have to know that you really want this before we… before you let me…"

She presses a kiss against my lips and I let the sentence end without finishing it.

The pelting rain slaps against our cheeks and down our shoulders, the repetitive whip of the downpour making our movements turn frantic and untamed. I hold her tighter against my body as I turn to trudge toward the lake house, knocking my quad against the hard porch railing as I try to manoeuvre us up the steps.

"Fuck," I grunt, reluctantly pulling away from her mouth so that I can briefly watch where I'm going. A soft laugh tinkles out of her and it's enough to fully recapture my attention, making me take her jaw in my palm and press another hungry kiss against her lips.

"You're so beautiful," I murmur as we finally make it to the sheltered landing, hauling one of her thighs up around my waist as I thrust her against the wood panelling.

"I'm wearing them," she whispers breathlessly as I press my forehead down against hers, my hands squeezing every inch of her as they roam over her body.

"Wearing what?" I rasp, dipping low so that I can kiss her throat.

"The panties," she whispers, "I'm wearing the panties that you bought for me."

My eyes flash to hers.

And my whole brain goes offline.

"You… you're wearing…" My voice becomes painfully deep, making Aisling suck in a shaky inhale. My eyes drop to where my groin is pushed right up against hers and I swipe my tongue over my lower lip, my pupils dialling out.

I clear my throat hard, my chest heaving in double time.

"Which…" I shake my head, trying to clear it, barely able to string a sentence together at the thought of what I'll see when I finally lift up the hem of Aisling's drenched sundress.

"Which ones?" I finally manage to rumble out, my palm hitching her thigh higher, desperate to see what she's hinting at. "Which panties?"

She strokes her thumb over my heart as she whispers, "Your favourite ones."

An exhale whooshes out of me in a rush and I drop my

forehead to hers, breathing hard.

"Khaki?" I ask hoarsely, my voice low and pleading.

She nods against me. I close my eyes and grunt.

"I bet you look so fuckin' beautiful in them," I rasp, bunching up the sides of her dress in my fists and scrunching the fabric, rainwater gushing between my fingers. Aisling arches her neck back and presses up onto her tiptoes, giving me access to claim her mouth again, a rough sound coursing through my chest as I slip my tongue back inside.

The downpour ricochets through the emerald canopy of trees surrounding the secluded side patio of the lake house, drowning out Aisling's delicate gasps as I slide my tongue in deeper.

Her palms squeeze desperately at the ridges of my rain-slicked chest, and I release my hold on one side of her sundress, roaming up towards the string strap slipping over her shoulder.

I stroke my tongue against hers, slow and firm, as I gently push the strap down her arm, sliding my hand back up so that I can feel the soft curve that I've just bared.

"Tanner," she gasps, making me drop my forehead to the curve of her throat. My hand massages her roughly as she rubs up against me.

I suck a kiss against the side of her neck as my hand begins squeezing her harder, and her hands get lost in my hair, tugging hard enough to make me grunt.

I nuzzle firmly in the warm curve of her neck, my other hand finally bunching her dress up to her hip so that two of my digits can slip their way beneath the side of her panties.

I shove two fingers under the band, grunting as her breathing hitches in her throat. I tug the fabric once, twice, testing how tight it is before slowly sliding the backs of my knuckles against her skin, rubbing her firmly as I make my way to her little heat.

Her fingers reach for my jaw and I open my eyes as she

grips at my stubble.

In less than a second my mouth dips back down to hers, caressing her lips with mine as my fingers finally meet her warmth.

"I wanna see you," I start to murmur, my voice like gravel as Aisling moans, but suddenly tires are crunching down the path behind us and I'm quickly shoving my body in front of Aisling's.

"Shit," I rasp, breathing heavily as I stare down into Aisling's eyes, before I finally glance at the dirt path leading to the cabins on the other side of the water.

I clench my fingers tightly around the fabric of Aisling's panties, knowing that we have to pause this for now.

I give her one more gentle nudge with my knuckles before reluctantly tearing my fist from her underwear, trying to get my breathing under control at the realisation that the guys are clearly coming back from their morning to afternoon session at the rink.

I swallow hard and keep my eyes averted as I tug Aisling's shoulder string back into place, and then I'm gripping my hands around her hips and shoving her quickly around to the back porch. Once I've got her out of view and up against the side of the wall I tuck my fingers into her hair, dipping down to kiss her again.

"Are the guys back?" she asks me, eyebrows arched in need and confusion.

I nod, kissing her again. "Yeah," I murmur, thumb rubbing up her jaw. Then I'm sighing and resting my forehead against hers, knowing that our private sanctuary is now temporarily interrupted. "Where does, uh... where does this leave us?" I ask her, my shoulders heaving with every breath.

I know exactly where I want this perfect moment to leave us – with Aisling letting me take her to the other side of the lake and telling all of those fuckers that she's officially my girlfriend – but I also know that Aisling has spent years trying to fight this feeling between us, not wanting to be with a guy who everyone knows fucks around. She's going to want to be a million percent sure about her own feelings before telling anyone that she's thinking of giving me the time of day.

She drops her eyes and pouts, a tiny crease forming between her perfect brows.

"You know where this leaves us," she mumbles, as I tuck my fingers under her chin.

"Enlighten me, baby," I rumble. I can hear the guys laughing and dismounting on the other side of the lake.

I slide my thick fingers through hers, locking our hands together.

"Okay," she breathes. "Well, we can't have anyone… you know… *know*. Yet."

I shove my tongue in my cheek, eyes burning down into hers. "Know what exactly?"

Say the words, baby. Say that we're a couple.

"We can't have anyone know that we're thinking of maybe… potentially… rekindling… something," she finishes raspily, eyes all big and earnest as she looks deep into mine.

I mean, they're not exactly the concrete fucking betrothal vows I was after, but it's a start.

I drop one of her hands so that I can quickly rub at the back of my neck, grinning at that affronted expression she pulls when she looks down at her now-empty hand.

I chuckle and leash my fingers back through hers, hunching low so that I can apologise for her one second of not having her hand held by giving her another gentle kiss.

"Kinda hurting my feelings, Ash," I murmur, a dimple popping in my cheek when she flashes me her vicious scowl. "Being treated like a dirty little secret."

Her eyes flicker to the drawstring of my shorts before she quickly blinks away.

She does a tiny cough.

"I wouldn't exactly say *little*," she whispers, and I'm instantly grinning, gripping her frowny little face in my palm and crushing rough kisses all over those cheruby cheeks.

"More compliments please," I rumble, chuckling quietly as she can't help but smile at my tease.

"Fine," I finally murmur as I reluctantly stand to my full height, smoothing my palms over her rain-drenched hair. "If you want, we can keep this thing a secret for now. Until you're sure" – *please God let her be sure* – "that this is the right decision."

That I'm the right decision.

I can hear the guys calling my name into the woods on the other side of the lake, thinking that I'm trekking through the forest like a werewolf or something.

I smirk at the thought and then look back down at Aisling.

"We're taking it slow," I reaffirm, cupping my hands around the nape of her neck.

She nods her head at me, eyes all pupil and unblinking.

I swipe my tongue over my lower lip before hunching down to kiss her again.

Now that we've started, I don't want to stop.

"Can I sneak around the lake when everyone heads to bed and cuddle up with you?" I murmur, leashing one of my forearms around her lower back so that I can press her right up against me.

"People will see," she whispers.

I shake my head, kissing her harder. "I'll go through the woods. No-one'll know."

"But Connell–"

Okay, I'll admit it, I kind of like Connell. Mainly because he's as easygoing as I am and, if I didn't have such a heartless reputation, I think that he wouldn't mind me dating Aisling. But as it is, he probably doesn't love the idea of my campus-renowned dick going anywhere near his baby sister.

229

Probably a good job that he doesn't know it already has.

I squeeze my palms gently down her throat.

"Okay. But if you change your mind you can text me back for the first time in four years, and I'll climb your fucking balcony just to get my arms around you."

She ducks her head and smiles, pretty as hell. I hunch lower so that I can take in the full force of it.

"You're the prettiest girl ever, you know that?" I tell her, pressing a kiss against her cheek as she preens and shimmers with happiness. "I gotta go see the guys, okay? Find out if they're planning on renting out the rink again for the rest of the weekend."

Aisling nods, fingers still toying tentatively with my drawstring. I smirk and shove a hand through my hair.

Go on, baby. Take a peek.

But she resists her feelings and places her hands back over my shoulders.

"I'll help you finish this place up," I tell her when she meets my eyes again. I mean, I'm pretty sure that she's just ordered another five-figure bed that she could use a helping hand with.

"No way," she breathes, but I just give her a knowing smile.

I'm going to be doing a hell of a lot of screwing inside those walls pretty soon.

"Sure," I laugh, giving her a final rough kiss, before pulling away from her and stepping back.

I glance over my shoulder, taking in the porch railing behind me. If I jump that thing then I can walk through the edge of the larch forest to make my way back to the cabins, meaning that the guys currently over there won't know that I was just over here – keeping what's happening between Aisling and me a secret for now.

I trudge to the railing and lay my hands flat over the wood, heaving my body upwards so that I can get my legs over the panel and jump the drop.

Aisling rushes forward with a squeak as I thud quietly to the forest floor.

"Jesus," I mumble, feeling about seven million twigs impale the soles of my feet. When I look up into her panicked eyes as she leans over the edge of the porch rim, I flash her an easy grin and reach up to squeeze her hands with mine.

"If I head to the rink with the guys tomorrow will you come?" I ask her, lacing our fingers together. Her brow arches, overwhelmed and unsure.

"Uh, maybe," she says, "but I still need to—"

"There's plenty time to get the interior job done, Ash," I assure her, before giving her another squeeze and finally letting go of her cool fingers. I run my palm over my hair, pushing it back off my forehead as the rain thumps heavily down on me from the deep green canopy.

"I'll come and get you in the morning," I tell her, smiling even as she sinks her teeth into her bottom lip. "And secret or not," I say as I walk backwards, away from the lake house and into the forest, "if I get you on the ice, there's no goddamn way that I'm not skating with you tomorrow."

She rests her chin on her palms and tries to hide her smile with her fingers.

"See you, big shot," she whispers, giggling when that name makes me smirk and raise my eyebrows.

I shake the rain from my hair and give her a once-over.

"See you, Ash."

CHAPTER 24

Aisling

Present day

I frown down at the ice shimmering one inch away from the tip of my rented skate. Connell muscles his way into the small space between my shoulder and the edge of the board, where the little gate has been pulled ajar.

"Hm," I mumble, tentatively lifting my toe so that I can prod at the ice, my frown furrowing.

Connell shoves a hand through his hair, whacking his elbow into the side of my head in the process, and I yelp as I topple off-balance, tearing at his shirt so that I don't actually fall over.

Large hands steady me from behind and I offer Logan, my brother's best friend, a grateful smile over my shoulder, before slapping my palm across Connell's stupid giant elbow.

My brother blinks down at me in surprise.

"What was that for?" he asks, rubbing his elbow

protectively.

I shake my head and laugh.

"Connell, you almost knocked me unconscious." I point one of my shimmery golden nails over my shoulder. "Logan can vouch for me."

I feel Logan's chuckle against my shoulders as Connell continues giving me that innocent wounded look. I give him another little shove and then he grins, strangling his forearms around my neck as he cuddles me into a headlock.

I claw at his arms and squeal as he begins carrying me onto the ice.

"Connell, no! I'm not ready, I'm not ready!"

My whole face turns crimson as the Carter U hockey boys – kitted out in actual sportswear after spending the past two hours training 'for fun' – glance around to watch. Tanner's eyes lock with mine and I practically whimper I'm so embarrassed. I cover my face with both of my palms and try not to die of mortification.

The hockey guys have been playing actual hockey, while I've been messing around in the stands with Fallon, Winter, and the football team; but since their hockey session seems to have concluded, Connell had the brilliant idea that we actually get on the ice with them.

His football team filters onto the ice around us, not exactly skating gracefully but managing to use their brute force to remain upright at least.

I swallow hard and peep through my fingertips, releasing a squeal when Connell finally lets go of me. He clomps around so that we're face to face.

He gives me his golden sunshine grin as he grips his palms over my shoulders, giving me a playful wobble.

My eyes are wide with panic and I do a close-mouthed squeak as I stare up at him.

"Come on, Ash, you're a cheerleader! You know that you can do this. If those guys can do it, you can definitely do it."

I try not to hyperventilate as he releases his hold on my shoulders, leaving me to hold my body on my own as he glides effortlessly back a couple inches.

"Connell," I wheeze, standing frozen in the centre of the rink. "Connell, please don't leave me."

"Ash," he says, tilting his head with a smile as if to say *come on, baby sis*. "Just kick off the ice. It's as easy as breathing."

I squeeze my eyes shut. "Funny that you say that, because I'm actually finding it really hard to breathe right now," I whisper, hands clenching into tiny fists as I roll my lips into my mouth, petrified.

"Aw, Ash," he says, his voice gentle and only slightly laughing. I peep one eye open and watch as he comes back to get me. "You're still scared shitless about this, huh?"

"I've only been skating once," I remind him, my voice a high-pitched whisper as he moves around me and starts gently shoving me forward. "It wasn't exactly a great experience."

Like a lot of people who don't come from a family of hockey lovers, my only skating experience took place during winter break of school, for a girl's sixteenth birthday. I spent my time on the ice white with fear, having had no-one to teach me what you're actually supposed to do. Needless to say, I haven't wanted to get back on the ice since.

"That's just because I wasn't there," Connell grins.

I breathe out a desperate laugh, gripping my fingers into his hands as he tries to push me.

"Ow," he laughs, trying to shake off my fingers as I cling to him. "Are you trying to draw blood? I won't be able to push you if you claw my hands off."

"Oh my God, just hurry up already," I wheeze, instantly screaming as my skates slip into a horizontal split, the guys' hockey puck hurtling towards one of my boots, making Connell lose his balance behind me.

"Shit, shit, shit!" he rasps.

"What do you mean 'shit, shit, shit'?!" I yell.

But then he's falling backwards and dragging me down with him, his whole body shaking with laughter as I thump down on top of him.

To his credit he does cup his hand around the back of my head to make sure that I don't hit it while we fall, but it's not enough to stop me from shoving off of him and whacking him relentlessly on his stupid biceps, making him laugh harder as he holds up his forearms trying to protect himself.

"You – big – freaking – klutz!" I shout, yelping when he manages to wrangle my wrists and stop my fight.

"Hey, you were the one who started breaking out into a cheer routine," he drawls, grinning when I give him a withering glare, and releasing one of my hands because he can tell that I want to give him another smack again.

I give him a nice little whack across the shoulder and he throws himself onto his side, grinning as he groans and pretends like I've maimed him.

I fight my smile for as long as I can but then I finally let my dimples pop, rolling my eyes. He instantly stops his injury routine and he gives me that special twin grin that telepathically lets me know that he's sorry, that he's glad that I'm okay, and that he wouldn't let anything bad actually happen to me, all without saying a single word.

He heaves himself up onto his blades with all the grace of a Mack truck, and then holds his palms down to me so that I can slap my hands in his and let him haul me up.

As soon as I'm back on my feet, feeling the slip of the ice beneath me, all of my fears come rushing back.

It's not that I don't want to be on the ice with everyone else – it's that I just can't skate.

I glance at the stands and see that the only two people who are currently off the ice are Caden, whose hair is dripping with sweat and cheeks are ruddy after so many hours of play, and Winter, who is sat on her boyfriend's lap, her back to his chest, as he squeezes her firmly with his forearms and murmurs something into her ear.

Winter is the only person who hasn't stepped foot on the ice yet but her little dimpled smile hasn't wavered for one single second.

I settle my blades on the ice, brow creased as I stare at the scuffed up rented boots, and I take a tiny swallow as I try to slide one of my feet towards Connell.

I shake my head, my cheeks burning red.

"It's no use," I whisper. "I think it would be better if you just, like, continue to push me toward the edge of the rink so that I can–"

"Hey man."

A deep voice sounds out behind me and I freeze on my already unmoving legs.

A big tan hand reaches around me to slap palms with Connell.

I blink at the thick tendons in the wrist, following it with my eyes as those fingers clamp down over my shoulder, the position casual but the grip firm. Possessive.

Connell gives Tanner a full-watt smile of his own before glancing down into my eyes and laughing gently at the look on my face. I look pointedly at the enormous hand currently holding me in place but Connell just smiles and shakes his head, giving me a little pinch on the chin for good measure.

I slap his hand away before looking down at my skates again, practically cracking the ice with how tensely I'm standing in them.

After the… *situation* that happened with Tanner yesterday – wherein he ended up kissing the sense out of me up against the lake house, and he told me that maybe I could join them at the rink today – I didn't really think that I would actually end up on the ice. I thought that *they* would be playing hockey and *I* would be watching hot guys bash into each other for a few hours. I didn't want him to see how bad I am at this, and the realisation that he already has makes me swallow thickly, blinking the stinging sensation away from my eyes.

Connell gives my free shoulder a squeeze of his own before looking over my head and asking, "Think you can teach her?"

Sparks sputter around my temples as I stare up at Connell, horrified.

"I'm sorry, what?" I croak out.

I smack my palm against my forehead because I'm so freaking embarrassed, only for Tanner's hand to quickly reach around me, clasp my wrist, and force it away from my face.

"Connell, you can't just ask guys on my behalf to teach me how to skate! I don't even want to learn how to skate," I tell him, really panicking now.

"Ash, you're going to be amazing," Connell says kindly, although I can barely focus on his words as Tanner's broad chest starts slowly pressing up behind me. "Just work through your fear. And Tanner's, like, half-alright at skating so I'm sure that he can teach you the basics."

I glance over my shoulder to see Tanner smirking at my brother.

"Thanks," he says dryly, although the smile on his face shows that they're both only teasing.

I look between them and narrow my eyes.

They're both being so friendly with each other.

It's very suspicious.

Before I can say anything else Tanner quietly clears his throat, looking into my eyes. Even though his expression is gentle and tentative, the directness of his gaze is so intense that it makes my breathing hitch.

With his helmet off his hair clings against his forehead, although he quickly shoves it back, making his striking gaze even clearer. His skin is ruddy beneath his tan, his breathing heavy and his shoulders hulking.

"If you, uh… if you really don't want to learn, I can just carry you over to the edge and get you back in the stands," Tanner murmurs to me. "But, uh…"

He glances back at Connell who gives him an encouraging nod, the damn traitor.

"If you want to learn I can… I can be the person who–"

"Put it this way," Connell says, recapturing my attention. "What if you were, like, stuck in Antarctica and the only way to… I don't know, reach the rescue plane was to cross a frozen lagoon, otherwise you're, you know, stranded there for life. Then you would be really glad that you could skate."

I blink up at my brother, unable to formulate words for a few seconds.

"Connell," I say, "what in the absolute *fuck* are you talking about?"

Tanner's chest shakes against my shoulders, a quiet laugh rumbling up his throat.

"How do you even think of this shit?!" I exclaim, groaning into my hands. "You are literally crazy. I'm never going to be stuck in Antarctica!"

Connell drops his hands to his sides and throws his head back, groaning.

"For fuck's sake, Ash – you know how karma works. Now you're *definitely* going to get stuck in Antarctica so I'm fucking insisting that you learn how to skate."

"You – are – *insane*," I laugh, shoving him in the chest, only to immediately lose my balance and squeak as Tanner's hands grip around my hips. He shoves me against his front, steadying me.

I stare at him with wide eyes over my shoulder, and after a long silent moment of having my ass up against his groin he pushes me a centimetre forwards and drops his eyes. The tips of his ears turn a deep shade of red.

"Just try and learn," Connell says kindly, giving me a

pinch on the cheek. "For me. And so you don't get eaten by any polar bears."

"Connell," I groan, grinning as he gives me a quick hug. "Fine," I say, shaking my head at him as I shove his bulky abdomen away from me.

Connell gives Tanner a flick of his chin and clomps over to his teammates, who are currently trying to score a puck in the net against Austin.

When my brother is finally out of earshot Tanner tightens his grip on my hips, turning me around and towering over me as he pushes his body flush against my chest.

"Hey," he rumbles, one of his hands gently squeezing my ass.

After two sweaty hours of playing hockey, Tanner looks *really* good.

"Why is my brother being so nice to you?" I whisper, becoming breathless when he wraps a hand around my throat.

He glances briefly over the top of my head so that he can ensure that everyone is out of earshot and then he murmurs against my cheek, "Because he doesn't know that I've fucked you."

I choke and stumble at his words but he keeps me firmly in place.

"You wanna learn how to skate?" he asks, as if he thinks he can change the course of this conversation after just saying *that*.

"Tanner, why are you and Connell–?"

He gives my throat a gentle squeeze before reluctantly releasing it. Both of his hands swoop down to take mine and he jerks his chin at me, silently commanding my attention.

"I'm gonna pull you, so just relax your feet and let yourself glide."

"Tanner," I say warily, instantly looking down at my

skates as he slowly begins moving backwards. I release a small squealing sound.

"Ash." His voice is so deep that I glance up at him without even meaning to. "That's it," he murmurs. "Eyes on me."

I sink my teeth into my bottom lip as he begins gently tugging me forwards, my Bambi-legs sliding dangerously outwards and making me squeeze my eyes shut as I whimper.

"Aisling."

One of his warm palms cups my cheek and I reluctantly squint one eye open so that I can peek up at him. When he sees that I'm still semi-functioning he relaxes a little and offers me a handsome smile.

"It'll be easier if you keep your eyes open, baby," he murmurs, making me hastily glance toward all of the guys that we're slowly skating closer to.

Well, Tanner is skating effortlessly closer to them – I'm just along for the ride.

"Tanner," I whisper frantically as he pulls me a little closer, "you can't call me that right now. We're supposed to be keeping this a secret. And here you are, holding my freaking hands."

I shake my head as I start to freak out about how obvious we're being.

"Everyone's going to know."

The look in Tanner's eyes is gentle, longing.

"Aisling, I swear, no-one is going to think that anything is going on between us." He caresses his thumbs firmly over my knuckles. "They all already know that I'm crazy about you, but no-one is going to think that you'd ever return those feelings."

I blink up at him in surprise, my body now stilling for a completely different reason.

"Why would… why would no-one think that?" I ask, my voice still light and breathless as I look him up and down.

Because, as much as I would have previously hated to admit it, me not liking Tanner just doesn't make sense.

Even though I have tried to ignore him since our freshman year, Tanner is undeniably the hottest guy that I've ever seen. His features are hard and beautiful, and his body is broad and strong. And then add on the fact that he's a hockey player? I can't believe that he's actually single.

A smile crease pulls taut beneath his sharp tan cheekbone.

"'Cause you're too good for me," he murmurs, locking my fingers tighter between his, "and you can have anyone you want, so why would you ever be with a guy like me."

The gentle chuckle that leaves his throat only makes my heart squeeze more painfully.

"But you can have anyone you want, too," I argue, searching his eyes with mine. I breathe out a humourless laugh as I mumble, "I mean, clearly. Seeing as you fucked your way around campus–"

This time he laughs loudly as he stops my skates from sliding out again, before he meets my eyes, something dark and dangerous in his irises.

Before I can even blink he's spinning me one-eighty, smothering my yelp with one of his palms before settling his other hand around my hip.

He stabs his chin into the curve of my neck, smiling against my skin when his rough stubble has me shivering.

"Who put me in that position, baby?" he taunts, a dark bite in his voice. One of his knees knocks into the back of mine, pushing me forwards.

I narrow my eyes at the empty half of the rink, glittering in front of us.

"Oh, so you screwed around at Carter U for *me*?" I breathe, my husky tone filled with mock-gratitude as I rest a hand over my heart. "How sweet," I whisper, "you shouldn't have."

He breathes out a laugh before hauling my hips up

against his groin.

"I told you, I only wanted you. You were the one who wouldn't let it happen."

Then he curses under his breath as my legs begin sliding apart into another deep split.

He kicks my boots back into place, huffing angrily.

"Damn it, Aisling. How the fuck are you so flexible?"

"I didn't hear you complaining about that four years ago," I mumble, my breath hitching in my throat as he presses his stubbled cheek against my pink one.

"We were alone in your bedroom, not on the ice with your brother," he rumbles. "I'm trying to not get turned on right now, Ash. And watching your legs slide open isn't helping with that."

Feeling a warm lick of mischief in my belly I deliberately let my skate slip sideways again and Tanner lets out a low growling sound, shoving it back into place.

He stands to his full height, removing the warm press of his cheek from mine, and I let out a sad whimper as I look up at him over my shoulder, earning me another gentle squeeze around the throat. He checks behind us when he hears his guys hollering because one of Connell's teammates must have finally got the puck in the net, and then he turns back to me, swiping a quick kiss against my temple as he murmurs, "You gonna let me teach you now or what?"

I try to push away the icy fear in my chest as I finally nod up at him.

He nods at me in turn, caressing his hands back down my body until he's holding my hips again.

"Might be easier if you try and squat a little," he says, leaning over me so that he can see my wobbly knees.

He reaches down with his hands so that he can gently push them equidistant apart.

"Now engage your core, hold the position, and then start rollin'."

I swallow nervously as I glance down at my legs.

"I don't know what that means," I whisper, "when you say, 'engage your core'. Isn't that, like, a sex thing?" I ask breathlessly.

"Your belly," he says, flattening a palm against my lower abdomen.

I gasp at the contact and he curses under his breath.

"Stop gettin' all horny," he murmurs warningly, "we're trying to keep this a secret, remember?"

I reach my arm across my body so that I can swat at his giant bicep.

"If you don't want me to be all horny then stop touching me like that," I whisper.

I feel him smirk against my temple before hunching lower so that he can suck my neck. His free hand smothers over my mouth before I can moan and then he's pulling back with a quiet laugh as my knees finally thump against the board at the opposite end of the rink.

I press my hands against the board to steady myself, and I blink up at our reflections in surprise.

I just skated a whole length.

The look on his handsome face is cocky and content.

"See?" he murmurs. "That wasn't so hard, was it?"

Shakily I lift my skates so that I can slowly turn to face him, my movements wobbly and nervous although he lets me grip his jersey for support. He casually wraps one of his forearms around my back, skating gracefully backwards so that I'm not pressed up against the board.

I look up at him with wide searching eyes.

"You distracted me," I whisper, hands clenching his shirt tightly as he smiles down at me.

"You needed to take your mind off the ice so that your blades could feel their way. Let your body do the work without your mind feeding it any fears."

He lifts the hand that isn't resting protectively against my lower back to lightly caress my jaw.

"You're skating even now, see?"

My eyes widen as I glance down, instantly stumbling over thin air and making Tanner chuckle as he rights my position.

"Well, you *were*," he murmurs, grinning and squeezing me against him tighter when I give him a little shove. "You're a natural, Aisling, I swear – you just gotta take your mind off the ice and then your body fuckin' owns it."

I look up at him from under my lashes, watching his broad chest steadily rise and fall.

I close my eyes momentarily and try to do what he just said – to let my body move naturally – even though I'm aware that Tanner is giving me a huge helping hand. I fumble clumsily on my boots and I feel my cheeks stain pink, but after taking a shaky little inhale I try to kick off with more precision than before.

My orientation isn't great but at least I'm moving forward.

I slowly open my eyes and find Tanner watching me, his pupils wide and his throat swallowing hard.

"That was good," he rasps, side-stepping some of the guys as he takes us around the back of their net, never taking his eyes off me. "So good, Aisling. I'm really fucking proud of you."

My heart squeezes tight, his rough words so surprisingly sweet. So unapologetically gruff but with the gentlest sentiment behind them.

The busy rink around us fades into the background, just a shimmering white canvas while I search his molten eyes.

His cheek lifts slightly as he watches me watch him.

"Maybe you're not the only one who wears their heart on their sleeve," he murmurs, one of his hands holding me just beneath my elbow so that he can squeeze over my tiny freckle.

I breathe out a small laugh, endlessly surprised by him.

"I can't believe that you even remembered that," I

whisper, as he pulls me in a gentle spin.

"How could I forget your freckle?" he murmurs, his voice so deep that it makes me giggle. Hearing that gruff voice say such cute words is doing crazy things to my heart.

Upon hearing me laugh his mouth lifts into a grin and he pulls me briefly against his chest as he hunches down to reach my ear. I shiver with pleasure as his stubble scrapes over my flushed cheek.

"I've been dreaming about your freckle for the past four years."

I laugh and shove at his chest, although I quickly yip as I lose balance and I yank him closer, which only makes me laugh harder as I stumble over my skates once again.

"Okay," I breathe, shaking my head at myself but still smiling. "So, I'm never going to be a professional figure skater," I admit.

Tanner pulls me into the centre of the rink, hands resting chastely around my waist as I cling to his jersey like a baby koala.

He glances over at Austin as he calls to us, saying something about heading out to grab dinner in five. Then Tanner settles his gaze back on mine, looking calm.

Looking happy.

"You didn't call me last night," he murmurs, and I give him a confused smile.

"Was I supposed to...?" I ask, laughing lightly.

He rubs roughly at the back of his neck before encasing my waist with his hand again.

"I mean, we didn't... like, I know if, uh..."

I lift my eyebrows slightly, kind of entranced by how nervous he seems.

"Yesterday, when the guys came back," he rasps, his cheeks staining crimson as he tries to choke some words together, "and I mentioned that... because if we're maybe... and I just, you know, really like you–"

"Oh my God, Tanner, just say what it is that you're

trying to say," I tell him, unable to stop myself from smiling up at him because he looks downright hopeless right now. I pry one of my hands from his jersey so that I can give him a brief caress over his heart.

The action seems to floor him, his pupils swallowing his sparkling irises.

"I wanted to come over," he murmurs. "When everyone had gone to bed, I wanted you to text me and tell me that you wanted me to come. I, uh…" His cheeks burn brighter as he swipes his tongue over his lower lip. "I slept outside last night, by the fire. In case you, uh, texted, so that Hunter and Fallon wouldn't know…"

I breathe out a shaky exhale, eyes on my hands as they twist into his jersey.

"Tanner…" I can't meet his eyes when his gaze is so dazzling and hopeful. "We have to take this slow, remember? We can't rush into this like we did last time."

He nods and tucks two fingers under my chin, making me meet his eyes as he looks fervently into mine.

"I know that, Aisling. And I wanna take it slow. But we can still, you know… cuddle and shit."

I thump my forehead against his jersey as I laugh out loud, and when I peek up at him again he's got this proud smile on his face. He rubs his palms into me harder, looking way too pleased with himself when I give him another giggle.

"Who knew that the biggest player on campus would be such a softie?" I say teasingly, tugging on his shirt so that he can help me do a final lap of the rink.

He checks over his shoulder to see that no-one is looking and then he grabs me by my jaw, crushing me into a rough hungry kiss. I laugh against his mouth until he pulls away, sparkly-eyed and grinning.

He gives me a little squeeze over my freckle and warmth surges through my heart.

Softie, I mouth at him, and he mouths back, *Only with you.*

CHAPTER 25

Tanner

Present day

I heave my body down onto my bed in the cabin, shoving my hands through my hair as I exhale deeply and close my eyes.

Hunter has had his girlfriend cuddled up under his sheets for the past half hour, so with the two of them asleep the only sounds are coming from outside – the gentle rhythmic lapping of the lake as it brushes up against the shore and retreats back into its moonlit swells.

A quiet vibrating sound comes from the small dresser next to my bed and I drop my hands from my face, eyes flashing over to it. As soon as I realise that the sound is coming from my phone, I practically fall off the bed in my haste to reach it.

I grab it and throw my shoulders back down against the mattress, chest pumping hard as my eyes race across the screen.

My heart pounds in my chest as more messages pop up, and I tap on the little bubble, taking me across to our message thread. A thread that, before this exact moment, had been entirely one-sided.

AISLING: *Hey.*
AISLING: *It's Aisling.*
AISLING: *Are you still awake?*

I shove my free hand through my hair as I prop my body up on one elbow, turning to face the wall so that I can give these messages the privacy that they deserve.

My thumb flies across the screen as I tug at my fringe, suddenly more wired than I've been all day.

TANNER: *Yeah, baby, still awake.*

I press send and watch the message go from Delivered to Read in the space of half a second.

"Oh my God, oh my God," I murmur, voice low and hoarse as I watch those three dots appear, vanish briefly, and then reappear again.

Unable to lie still I kick my legs off the bed, planting my feet on the floor and dropping my elbows to my knees. I hunch over my phone and wait to see what she's typing.

I swipe one of my palms down my thigh, knees bouncing at a thousand miles per minute, and when Aisling's message finally surfaces I'm instantly shoving my feet into my boots and grabbing my shit from the dresser.

AISLING: *Do you still want to come over?*

I rip the quilt and under-sheet from my bed, shoving them over one of my forearms as I quickly type back *Yyesxsd fucdk yes pleasxe.*

My thumbs are shaking so hard that I can't even fix my typos, so I hit send, tripping over the blankets as I quickly shoulder my way into the small bathroom. I give myself a brief check in the mirror, wanting to look the best that I can for when I break down Aisling's front door in one minute's time.

My hair's still damp from the shower, dripping down over my forehead instead of pushed back like I usually try and shove it, and my tan has darkened from the weeks of unfiltered mountain sunlight, not to mention ruddy as hell from my sudden surge of adrenaline. I'm wearing boots, sweatpants and no pyjama shirt, and hopefully that will work in my favour seeing as Aisling likes to palm her hands all over my muscles.

The little buzz in my hand recaptures my attention and my eyes fly across the screen as I read her message.

AISLING: *My door's unlocked.*

I stumble my way out of the cabin.

I haul the blankets higher up in my arms, and then gently close the cabin door as quietly as possible, not wanting to wake my roommate and his girl when I know that Aisling wants to keep this thing a secret. I stuff my phone in the front pocket of my pants and jog the distance around the head of the lake, mounting her porch steps two at a time before adjusting myself in my joggers and opening her front door.

I open it quietly, not wanting the sound to carry over the water, and then I ease it shut with the back of my shoulder.

Over the past week, Aisling has had all of the interior fixtures delivered to the lake house, meaning that the living area and kitchen are both packed with unwrapped appliances, as well as two long couches and a really comfortable looking armchair.

I give my stubble a swipe with my shoulder as my eyes

linger on the wood that I chopped for her, stacked into a neat pile beside the stone fireplace.

Something tight and protective flares in my chest.

I reluctantly tear my eyes away from the stack – the only area of the room that looks as if it's had some of her attention yet – and then I kick off my boots and begin walking up the stairs.

The door to the master bedroom is slightly ajar, a faint orange glow radiating through the gap from a small lamp or night-light. My heavy steps come to a stop on the threshold and I swallow quietly before rapping two knuckles against her door.

"Aisling?" I say, my voice quiet and rough. "It's me. It's Tanner."

The gentle sound of her clambering to her feet and then padding over to the door filters over to me through the wood.

I arch my neck as I close my eyes, gratitude surging through my chest.

I'm so fucking lucky that she actually wants me to be here. After so much time apart, a big part of me never expected us to get back into the situation that we originally lost ourselves in four years ago. So the fact that Aisling is dipping her toe back in the water here – giving me another shot – is making me really feel like I'm the luckiest guy in the world.

I can sense the moment where she presses the tips of her fingers against the other side of the door, making the dark wood sway slightly, both of us thrumming with tension and need.

I drop my chin to my chest and try to calm my breathing, eyes trained on her delicate shadow as she moves cautiously on the other side of the wood.

Then she pulls the door open and the air rushes out of my lungs.

"Hey," she says, light and casual, before stumbling back

with a squeak as I practically fall inside her room.

The lake house's master bedroom is set under a beautiful wooden A-frame, making it seem smaller than it is and cosy as hell. Right now it's got a deconstructed bed leaning heavily against the wall, a tiny night-light plugged in beside the balcony, a deflated blow-up mattress rolled up on the left, and a recently-vacated sleeping bag on the right.

But I barely register any of it.

I click the door closed with a shove of my shoulder, toss my two quilts over on top of her sleeping bag, and then take both sides of her hips in my hands, eyes raking her up and down as my blood rushes south.

"Why'd you bring your sheets?" she asks breathlessly, glancing hastily over to the thick quilts I've tossed down.

I can only think about one hot thing at a time and right now that hot thing is the captain of Carter U's cheer team wearing *my goddamn shirt.*

"This looks so fucking good on you," I rumble, dropping my forehead down to hers and hauling her body up against mine.

"The sheets?" she whispers again, trying fucking valiantly to keep my brain remotely working.

"There's only one sleeping bag," I reply, voice so deep that she sucks in a breath. And now that I see she hasn't put her blow-up mattress to use tonight, I'm extra glad that I brought the quilt over.

"Why didn't you blow up the mattress?" I ask quietly, as my palms grip into the sides of her waist. Her sleeping bag looks high quality but even a high quality one is no match for a mattress.

She shakes her head, inhaling shakily as her cheeks turn pink.

"I can't... I, uh... it's a big mattress, is all," she finally whispers. "It's hard to blow that much in one go."

I drop my head into the curve of her neck, groaning quietly.

"You've been trying to blow that thing up with your *mouth?*" I mumble into her skin, my hands tightening on her waist as my shoulder muscles flex.

No-one told this girl that airbed pumps exist? What the fuck?

"How else would I do it?" she whispers, hands tentatively moving to the back of my neck as I leash my arms around her and haul her up.

"Jesus Christ, baby," I whisper, too astounded and turned on by the image of her trying to blow up the mattress with her mouth to answer her question. "Don't tell me that you've just had that thing lying there and not being used this whole time."

She purses her lips together and stares guiltily at my chest.

I bounce her firmly against my body and she releases a sad guilty hum.

I duck my head so that I can reach her cheek with my mouth, pressing a couple of kisses against her as she cautiously lets her fingers trace over my shoulders, until she's fully massaging my pecs.

There's nowhere on Earth that I'd rather be right now.

I keep one arm leashed around her lower back and I use the other one to arrange the sheets, quickly tossing out both of the quilts before dragging her sleeping bag on top of them, and then folding the overhang over the top of it.

Aisling watches as I prepare the make-shift bed for us and, after spotting her small night-light again, I walk us over to it and push it a little closer to the sheets, hoping that it looks kind of rustic and cosy.

When I finally step back from the squishy pile of bedding, Aisling wraps her arms tighter around my shoulders and I press another kiss to one of her cheeks.

"Blanket fort," she whispers, her eyes sparkling.

I give her a playful squeeze on the ass before finally setting her down from her position on my waist. Then I turn her gently in my arms and hold her back up against my

252

front.

"Yeah," I murmur, as we walk over to it.

She lightly prods at the blankets with one of her sparkly toes. I huff a laugh against her neck, squeezing my arms around her tighter.

Then I press my mouth against her ear and growl, "Get in the fucking blanket fort."

She giggles loudly in my arms, making me grin and clutch her tighter, picking her back up off the floor so that I can lower her down on the sheets myself. I press her down on her belly and settle in behind her on my spread haunches, shoving her inside her plush sleeping bag and then swaddling her up with all of the blankets.

"Tanner," she laughs, shoving me playfully as she tries to wiggle back out of it.

I lean back on one of my elbows and let her, and as soon as she's free she climbs on top of me. The thick quilts envelop us in our own private world.

Aisling's sleeping bag and my quilt are cosy as fuck underneath me, and the weight of her perfect body on mine has my fingers squeezing roughly into the backs of her soft thighs.

"I wanna go to sleep like this every night," I murmur, one of my palms giving her a spank on the ass, before roaming up the curve of her waist and tangling its way into the back of her hair.

I wrap her waves around my fist before gently tugging backwards, making her lift her perfect face and look up at me from under her lashes.

There's something naughty about that shimmer in her eyes and it makes me lift myself back up onto my elbows, watching her warily as she tries to bite back her smile, trying to look innocent.

She slowly sits herself upright and presses her warm palms against my abdomen, her soft golden thighs straddling the thick ridge beneath my sweatpants.

"What is it?" I rasp, my gaze searching hers in the darkness.

Why's she looking at me so naughtily for?

"Um," she whispers, cheeks flushing pink as she smiles.

Slowly, she leans over me so that she can drag the night-light a little closer, her breasts almost scraping over my mouth as she pulls it into place. I turn my head away from her beautiful tits and grunt, my chest rapidly rising and falling.

"I, uh…" she begins as she sits back on my lap, sheets pooling behind her waist and letting me take her in unobstructed. The night-light is barely emitting a single watt of energy but the gentle stream of moonlight filtering in from the balcony makes Aisling glow warmly in the darkness.

I keep my body half-upright on my elbows, my palms roaming over the khaki shirt that she's wearing.

I've seen her wear it from across the lake, but it's different to see it while my hands are all over her.

She gently rubs her warmth over the long erection between my thighs and my gaze immediately snaps down to the hem of my shirt, covering her little heat.

I meet her eyes with mine as I tuck two fingers under the hem, silently asking her if I can lift the shirt and look at her underneath it. She swallows quietly and nods her head.

I gently lift up the shirt and practically swallow my tongue whole.

"Ash," I grunt, pupils dialling out as I take her in.

Because she's wearing the fucking khaki panties.

She's wearing my favourite khaki shirt with the panties that I bought for her.

I clench my jaw and stifle my groan as I reach behind her and grip my shaft.

"You put this on for me?" I ask her hoarsely, already knowing the answer. "You slip into these panties just for me to see?"

She shifts slightly on my lap and I choke on my grunt as my balls tighten.

"You didn't get to see me in them the other day because, like, we didn't want to get caught," she whispers, fingers trailing over my body and making me grow harder. "And, I don't know, it's probably really silly but I thought that you might, like, wanna see? So I–"

I grip both of my palms around her cheeks and kiss the goddamn fuck out of her.

She falls into me with a happy squeal and I lower myself onto my back, pulling Ash along for the ride and then rolling us onto our sides so that I can deepen the angle.

My tongue slides into her mouth and she tightens her arms around my neck as she whimpers, making me grunt low and deep as I shove my palm between her thighs.

"Dream girl," I rumble, loving the way that she goes all shy when she hears me say that word.

She drops her gaze and I gently nudge the tip of my nose against hers, before hunching back down to kiss her again.

"Tanner," she whispers against me, while I cup her roughly between her legs.

I grunt and pull back so that she can say whatever's on her beautiful mind.

"Yeah, what is it, baby?" I murmur when she keeps her eyes trained on my chest, nibbling on her lower lip and blinking fast as she builds up the courage to say what she wants to say.

"Do you, uh…" She looks up at me for a brief second and then quickly goes back to staring at my pecs.

Smirking, I flex them up and make them do a kind of dance, and she's instantly laughing, smacking my biceps as she rolls onto her back.

I grin and immediately roll on top of her, settling my hips between her legs before practically smothering her face with my chest.

She giggles up at me, enveloped in my muscles, and a happy rumble spreads through my chest at the sight of her so dazzlingly happy.

"You were saying?" I ask, lifting up about half a centimetre so that she can gasp in a couple of breaths before I get back to cuddling her again.

"I was gonna ask, um, if you... like, when I talk to you, if you have a preference about, you know…"

My mouth lifts up at the corner, a smile crease pulling taut in the centre of my cheek.

I can't believe that the prettiest girl in the world is almost as flustered around me as I am around her.

"Mm?" I ask, pressing a couple of kisses against her warm cheek. I let my hands roam down over her waist until I'm tangling my digits up in the sides of her panties.

"Do you prefer it if I call you Tanner?" she finally whispers and my hands pause, heart halting. The surge of warmth that explodes in my chest has me dropping my forehead into the curve of her neck and nuzzling hard as I try to tamper down the sudden swell of emotion.

Sweetest fucking girl.

After a good five seconds of fully inhaling her neck, I prop myself back up on one of my elbows and stare down at her, my eyes on fire.

I bracket her chin in my palm and press a rough kiss to her perfect lips.

My voice is low and rumbling when I finally pull away.

"Are you tryna work out if I prefer you calling me Mason or Tanner?" I ask her, downright in love with how nervous this conversation is making her. I don't know why she's so shy about saying my first name but it makes me breathe out a laugh as I slip my hand around her neck. "You can call me whatever you want, baby. Mason, Tanner – boyfriend also works."

She rolls her eyes and laughs before covering her blushing face with her hands. I'm grinning so hard that my cheeks are aching.

Then I grab her left hand and straight up suck her ring finger into my mouth.

Aisling gasps as I release her finger with a *pop*, pressing another stubble-coated kiss over where a big fat diamond needs to be.

She fans her face with her other hand before pulling me back down and letting me slow-kiss her.

She moans into my mouth when I get both of my hands around her butt cheeks, and I groan against her lips as I start palming them hard and firm.

"Missed your little ass," I murmur, and Aisling gasps quietly against my throat. She rubs the warm centre of her panties up against my flexing abdomen and I groan harder, delivering a firm spank.

She makes a little hissing sound and my cock instantly hardens as she tries to weakly keep her arms around my shoulders.

"Shit," I murmur, moving my mouth back to hers and slipping my tongue inside so that I can stroke her hungrily.

Warm fingers grip me over my sweatpants, and I grunt quietly.

"Not tonight," I choke out, swallowing hard.

But Aisling rolls over onto her stomach, spreads her legs for me, and moans.

"Fuck, fuck, fuck," I rasp, nuzzling my face in her beautiful hair, gripping my fingers around her hips, and thrusting against her as if we're naked. "No condoms," I manage to choke out as she turns her face around so that I can kiss her jaw. My temples pound as I rasp, "I didn't bring any fucking condoms."

She nods in understanding and rolls over so that she's on her back again, and then we're kissing like we're back in Carter Ridge, two love-struck freshmen who can't keep their hands off each other.

"Say my name," I murmur as I prop my elbows on

either side of her face, my shoulders bunching taut as I rub my hips purposefully between her thighs.

She looks up at me with those sparkling eyes, hands gripping as tight as they can around my biceps as I thrust her harder against the sheets.

"Tanner," she whispers, but she knows that isn't what I mean.

I huff out a laugh as I rub my cock against her faster.

"Other one," I grunt, removing one of my fists from above her head so that I can grab the back of her knee and shove it up over my shoulder.

"Oh my God!" she whimpers, squeezing her eyes shut as I wrap my forearm beneath her body, holding her against me as close as possible.

"Say it," I rasp, as she pants against my shoulder.

I pull back and stare down at her, my eyes burning as I wait for her to say it. But then we're laughing and groaning and I'm nudging her nose with mine before we kiss, the pace of my hips never relenting.

"Mason," she whispers and I release the deepest groan, rubbing my forehead against hers before slipping my hand between our bodies.

"Fuck, that's it," I murmur, "I fucking love hearing you say my name."

I push her panties an inch down her thighs and shove two digits against her little nub, sliding my tongue inside her mouth as her legs clench tight around my waist. Her brow arches high, telling me that she's there.

I rub her hard and fast, chest pumping as she moans against my throat, and when she finally falls back against the sheets I'm a grunting fucking mess, so close to my own release that I'm goddamn dizzy as I shove down my sweatpants.

"I'm done," I pant, my brow creased in pain as I grip the heavy muscle that's hanging between my thighs. I'm towering over her, one palm splayed flat beside her head, and the other tossing my cock as my eyes rake her up and down.

Her pretty khaki panties are twisted like a garter around her thighs.

I drop down on top of her, grunting like an animal as I finally snap, my release coming hard and fast as I pump roughly into my fist. Warm thick spurts release against her thighs and I hunch down to kiss her – trying to be soft and gentle despite the warm mess that I'm covering her in.

"Sorry, baby, I'm almost done," I whisper, groaning quietly against her neck as I toss out another spurt.

When I'm finally done I leash my arm around her waist so that I can haul her against me as tight as possible. Then I'm kissing her slow and gentle, my free hand cupping her jaw while the last of the tremors ripple through me.

I pull back so that I can rest my forehead against hers, breathing hard as I envelop her in my arms.

"I've missed holding you like this," I rasp quietly, pressing another kiss to her cheek when she nods breathlessly in response. I rub my thumb through the release on her thighs and have to take a few calming breaths before I finally speak again. "You got any towels in here, baby?"

Her pretty eyes flutter open and my heart pounds wildly when they meet mine.

It's always felt like this.

I'll never get over how beautiful she is.

My dream girl.

"Yeah," she whispers, glancing over to one of her luggage bags.

She releases one of her arms from around my neck so that she can point in the direction of her clean laundry, and I'm immediately distracted by her love heart freckle, gripping my fist around her elbow so that I can lift it gently and kiss it.

"This – fucking – freckle," I murmur against her soft

skin, groaning at how sugary-sweet she tastes as she strokes her free hand over the sharp stubble on my jaw.

My eyes close momentarily while the beautiful girl wrapped up in my arms gives me that gentle loving that I've always wanted.

I kiss her freckle again, then her wrist, and then I work my way across each of her knuckles.

"Gonna grab a towel, stay here," I murmur, reluctantly heaving myself up off of her and tucking the quilt back over her before I get to my feet. I pull my pants back up as I trudge over to Aisling's luggage, wincing hard when the fabric brushes against my shaft. I grab the first towel on the pile, giving it a quick squeeze to make sure that it's nice and soft, and then I'm settling in on my haunches between Aisling's thighs, pulling the hem of her shirt just over her belly button and giving it a little kiss before finally cleaning up the situation on her thighs.

"Tanner," she whispers, swallowing nervously as I stroke the towel over her skin.

I glance up at her from under my lashes, heart pounding as I take in the sight of her.

I give her a dimpled smile as she watches me nervously from the sleeping bag.

"Back to 'Tanner' again, huh?" I rumble quietly, hoping that she can't see the crimson stain beginning to spread its way up my neck to the tips of my ears.

I love when she calls me Tanner, probably because I'm so used to hearing her say it when she's giving me hell – and, yeah, okay, her attitude turns me the fuck on – but deep down I love it even more when she calls me Mason. I've never actually had a girl call me by my first name before. Unless they were to search it up when I was playing D1 college hockey with the Carter Ridge Rangers, I realise that none of the chicks that I was with at college would have even known my first name. So having Aisling whispering my name when I'm kissing her or we're being intimate… it feels like a sacred thing that's just for us, and I'm head over heels for it.

I'm head over heels for her.

I rub the towel over her skin, cleaning off my cum before gently sucking the soft curve of her waist.

She's so warm and sweet that a low growl spreads through my chest.

I toss the towel out of the blanket fort, tug the blankets back around us, and scrape my stubble over her soft skin, murmuring, "My fuckin' woman."

Aisling laughs quietly before tangling her fingers up in my hair and tugging hard, telling me to get my face up next to hers, right the fuck now.

I press another rough kiss against her belly button before heaving myself up beside her, easing her panties back into place.

As soon as I catch that amused sparkle in her eyes I immediately know exactly what she's trying not to laugh about.

I groan into my hands as I throw myself onto my back.

"Oh my *God*," I mumble, face-palming so freaking hard right now. "I'm an idiot," I laugh, my voice low as hell.

I drop my hands and look down at her, cupping her cheruby cheeks in my palms as I search her beautiful eyes.

"This was… way too soon again, wasn't it? I fucked up again, didn't I?" I rasp, but Aisling just laughs, cuddling her face between the large muscles of my chest. I wrap my biceps around her head, not wanting to ever let her go.

"It's okay," she says, her voice all muffled and giggly. "Maybe we just aren't meant to be conventional."

I pull one of my arms back from her head so that I can smack my palm straight down on my face.

"I literally fucking said that we were going to take it slow this time," I groan, and Aisling's whole body shakes with laughter, much to the interest of my suddenly very rigid cock.

I mean, it's not like we actually had sex. Fooling around counts as going slow, right? And my cum isn't even on her anymore, so it's technically like it never even happened.

I frown at that thought and glance down at her soft thighs. All cleaned up.

Huh.

Maybe we should… do it again?

Christ, what the hell is wrong with me? I steel my jaw and roll heavily on top of her, grunting against the quilt as I wrap her protectively in my arms.

"You're so beautiful," I murmur, kissing gently over her cheeks as she snuggles her face in the crook of my neck. "Just cuddling from now on," I mumble, heart squeezing in my chest as she does this tiny yawn that makes me chuckle. "So fucking cute."

"Are you sure you can do just cuddling?" she whispers, tilting her head back into the quilt so that she can look up at me.

I crush a kiss to her forehead. "Hell yeah," I murmur. "I love cuddling you."

She nods her head, looking away from me as she maps out her renovation itinerary in her mind.

"Okay," she whispers. "I mean, maybe that'll work until I've finally finished with the refurb. All I have left now is to set up all of the furniture and I think I can get that done by Friday – which means that I'll be, like, three weeks ahead of schedule anyway."

I try not to frown as I think about how hard she's been working, and how big this challenge was for a chick who has literally just graduated. I wonder what her parents are like and if they've always been so expectant of her. Or maybe they're just used to it – how determined Aisling is.

I roll onto my side, keeping her tucked up against my chest.

"I'll help you finish up," I tell her, digits getting tangled up in the side of her panties again.

She shakes her head. "I can do this. This one is all me."

I'm about to argue so she shuts me up with a kiss.

I grunt and hold her tighter. She smiles smug as hell against my lips.

"Trouble," I murmur, eliciting the prettiest laugh that I've ever heard.

"Big shot," she whispers back, and I smirk as I pull her closer, with no intentions of ever letting her go.

CHAPTER 26

Tanner

Present day

The tire thuds to the ground, a cloud of sand, dirt and dust rising around it as it hits the end of our makeshift workout area in front of the lakeshore. I shake out my palms as I trudge around to the other side of it, getting in position to start flipping it back to Austin.

I bend my legs as I grip my hands underneath it, swallowing a grunt as I push it vertical and then shove it back down.

Austin breathes out a laugh from where he's sat on the farthest of the three logs, knee bouncing up and down as he tosses his phone back inside his pocket and shakes his head at me.

"You can give yourself a second to recover, man," he laughs as he pushes one of his hands through his dripping wet hair.

I crack my neck from side to side, giving him an

emotionless glance before ignoring him. Water droplets trickle between my shoulder blades as I bend, heave, and flip the tire once again.

Yeah, Austin may be one of my best friends but that doesn't mean that I wasn't about to dunk that motherfucker for the shit he pulled in the bar the other week. I mean, I really like the guy and he's the best goalie that I've ever played with, but kissing on Aisling's ankles while she was dancing all giggly around that pole? Uh, absolutely the fuck not. Hence why when he came out here this morning to workout with the tire that Hunter decided to haul down from one of his dad's mechanic friends' garages in Larch Peak, I cracked out my knuckles and jerked my thumb toward the lake, not needing to explain why I wanted to trade a few punches with him seeing as he definitely fucking knows. So he just shrugged, ditched his cell, and then I wrestled that shit-eating grin off his stupid face.

When I'm two more flips away from where he's sitting he rises to his feet, getting ready for his turn. I glance down at the rolled-up brown bag with my breakfast in it and I steel my jaw, motivating myself to finish these reps.

Austin glances up at me with a smirk that has me shoving the tire a little more aggressively than I need to.

"What?" I grunt, feeling the thick muscles of my quads bulge as I get into my final squat.

His eyes slide over to the lake house and then back to me.

"You trying to impress someone or something?" he grins. I toss the tire to the ground, hitting him with a look.

Goading little shit.

"Watch it," I rumble. Then I clear my throat and add, "…yeah."

He drains the last of his take-out coffee, eyes fucking burning with glee because he may or may not have seen me push my way through the fringe of the forest this morning – rather than, you know, the *front door of my cabin*, so he quickly put two and two together about where I'd been trudging back from.

He doesn't know the details, like the fact that I've spent the past four nights sneaking over to Aisling's, wrapping her up in my arms, and tucking her into my chest as she falls asleep, but knowing part of my secret has made him suddenly extremely smug.

I wipe my hands on my drenched shorts and take his place on the log, inhaling half of a breakfast muffin before he's even got his hands on that tire. I shove in the other half and then hunch my shoulders, clenching my hands between my knees, as I allow myself a quick glance over to Ash's balcony.

She's talking quietly into her phone, eyes on her sparkly nails, as if she hasn't been stealing glances at our workout for the past thirty minutes.

I roll my shoulders, pop the top on a new coffee, and drink.

Austin puts on a real show of flexing his biceps when he reaches the end of his first lap, and I roll my eyes all the way to Alabama before begrudgingly checking to see if he actually caught Ash's attention. Warmth spreads through my chest as she fully turns her back to his performance and I quickly dip my head between my shoulders, trying to hide the smug smile of my own.

My loyal girl.

"Damn," Austin says, amusement tugging up the corners of his mouth as he starts flipping the tire my way again. "Maybe she actually likes you. Most chicks wouldn't be able to resist these guns."

"What guns?" I smirk, as if Austin isn't literally two-hundred-and-ten pounds.

He frowns at me before quickly peeking down to check on his 'guns'.

"Fully loaded," he mumbles to himself, before giving me another scowl and shoving the tire back into the dust.

Grinning, I lift my coffee back to my mouth, only to almost spill the whole thing as I hear the front door of the lake house click open. My eyes fly across the water, breath halting in my chest as Ash pads down the porch steps, hair swishing over her shoulders when she flicks it with the back of her hand.

"Fuck," I rumble, unable to tear my eyes off of her as she slowly makes her way around the head of the lake. She's wearing shortie overalls, like she has every day this week so far, plus a little white tank beneath it which makes her tan look extra golden.

I've kept my word with Aisling since the first time I snuck over there. Our secret nights have consisted of me making us our blanket fort, squishing her between my biceps, and then kissing the hell out of her before we finally go to sleep.

Strictly kissing and cuddling – no funny business – before she wakes up at the crack of dawn and tries to shove me off of her balcony. I managed to scale down it once, just because I knew that it would make her laugh, but that shit is high and I don't want to injure my ankle again, which means that I haven't attempted it again since the first time that I tried.

She did like it when I climbed it though so maybe I'll give it another go tomorrow morning.

At the same moment that Ash rounds the head of the lake, half of the cabin doors behind us creak open. Her brother and his teammates yawn as they thud down onto the logs, followed by Hughes, Tristan, and Shaw, because they all sensed the fact that there's food out here at the exact same time.

There's a whole load of grumbled "morning"'s which I completely ignore, eyes still locked onto Aisling as she pats her phone over the denim pocket of her overalls. Then she saunters over to our half circle of way too many fucking guys.

Her eyes slide down to mine as I stare up at her, and my quad is instantly bouncing up and down, pounding the dirt beneath my boot.

She's looking down at me with that aloof heiress nonchalance, even though we both know that I'll be sneaking into her bedroom later tonight.

I know it's just a front that she's putting on to keep us a secret from the guys, but my chest heaves anyway, not liking the fact that they don't know that she's taken.

I swipe my sweating palms down my quads and then shove my dripping hair back from my forehead, swallowing hard as she looks away from me. She laughs warmly as her brother crushes her into a hug and pulls her down next to him.

She's so beautiful it hurts.

I watch her from the other side of the logs as she digs around for her favourite flavour of muffin, barely able to believe that not two hours ago I was kissing my way down her throat, murmuring how much she means to me.

"We think we might know which site we wanna set up camp on tomorrow night," Connell announces, mostly to his sister who is back on her phone. He peeks over her shoulder as she taps at lightning speed, earning him a quick jab in the ribs with her elbow, making him grin.

"Can't come," Aisling mutters back, her voice so light and pretty that I genuinely have to readjust my shorts. "Got the lake house to finish off."

"Aw *man*," Connell mock-groans, before peeking down at her to see if his plight has earned him any sympathy from her. It hasn't, which makes me snicker. "Come on, Ash – you've been in there freakin' day and night this entire week working on the interior. You need a day off in the mountains – stretchin' those legs, getting some fresh air."

Austin tries and fails to smother a smirk, flicking his gaze between Aisling's legs and my *I'm gonna murder you, asshole* frown.

Aisling pockets her phone again, pursing her lips to the side in consideration as another strawberry muffin is magically outstretched to her.

"You can be the deciding factor about which site we choose," Connell offers, all wide puppy-dog eyes as he tries to tempt her with more breakfast foods.

Aisling watches the muffin with a wanting little scowl, before her eyes flick across the fire-pit to meet mine. That wary look on her face instantly sets me into motion.

I grab my phone from the dirt and immediately shoot my thumbs across the keys, glancing up at her with a meaningful look to let her know that her phone is about to vibrate at any second.

Her eyes widen in understanding and she shoots to her feet, quickly clutching her cell against her chest before swiping the muffin and excusing herself. I watch her half-run down the shore on our side of the lake, past the area where I was tire flipping this morning, until she's even past Connell's cabin. Then she looks down at her phone, the sunlight shimmering around her silhouette in a warm golden halo.

TANNER: *you're almost finished up in the lake house — you deserve a break.*

When my phone buzzes with her response my heart thumps into overdrive in my chest.

I'm never gonna get used to her actually replying to my texts.

AISLING: *I was just on the phone with my mom and she's stopping by, like, next week? I need to get everything finished before she actually arrives or I'm screwed.*

I've been in the lake house every night this week and I know damn well that it's almost finished. The entire

269

downstairs is furnished, plus she told me that she'd done the bathroom. The only thing that she's been putting off is building the master suite's giant bed, and I know that it's because she's too obstinate to admit that she can't lift the heavy wooden pieces.

I set my elbows on my bouncing knees, swallowing quickly when I see that she's glancing back at me.

TANNER: *you know that I'll help you finish it up, Ash.*
AISLING: *I would never ask that of you.*

I shove a hand through my hair.
Beautiful, stubborn woman.

TANNER: *I know you wouldn't, and you don't need to. You're ahead of schedule, and you've single-handedly almost finished this reno. You're so driven it's crazy – like, I am so fuckin' hot for you right now.*

Was that a risky text to send when her brother is sitting about three feet away from me? Maybe. But when I hit send and lift my head to glance up at her, she's swishing her hair over her shoulders, preening like a kitten.

I inhale hard and start typing my next text.

TANNER: *why don't you help them pick the campsite for tomorrow, baby. You've got so much time to finish up, I swear.*

I'm hoping that she can't see through my rouse because I know she'd fight me to the death if she did.

I watch her tap her finger on her chin in the distance, and a smirk tugs at my mouth when she hits me with her next message.

AISLING: *are you coming camping tomorrow too?*
TANNER: *anything for you, baby.*

AISLING: *are you gonna sneak into my tent?*
TANNER: *every freakin' night.*

She sends me an emoji of a smiley face all cuddled up in love hearts and I send her back as many 'x's as I can physically type. When she finally pads back to the campfire I catch her eyes and give her a wink.

She drops her gaze, cheeks turning pink, and a tiny dimple pops in her cheek.

Chest heaving with pride, I toss my cell to the dirt, and then I glance over the shimmering water toward Aisling's lake house.

I crack my knuckles and roll my neck.

I've got some work to do.

CHAPTER 27

Aisling

Present day

"What d'you think?"

I place my hands on my hips and purse my lips to hide my smile, turning in a slow circle with my head titled back, admiring the golden light streaming in through the emerald canopy. The rest of our group is scoping out the small sign-posted campsite.

Connell's football teammates are playing a 'no rules' version of football with the hockey guys, except for Hunter and Caden who are cosied up with their beautiful girlfriends.

Fallon and I are the only campers who actually brought a tent with us to Larch Peak, seeing as camping out was on our summer bucket list. But Hunter and Connell are going to head into town to buy a couple more, so that the whole group of us can spend a few nights here – so that we can all be together before Connell and the football guys who are just about to start their professional careers in the NFL leave, moving into their new places and starting their training.

"I think it's cool," I say, grinning as I turn to face my brother, and he gives me a grin of his own as he squeezes his arm around my shoulders.

"So we'll spend the rest of the week chillin' up here, then I'll head with the guys, unless you want me to be around for when Mom gets here?" he asks as he takes off his cap, scrubbing roughly at his messy golden hair before flipping the brim and placing it on his head backwards.

I shake my head at him, answering his question before the words even leave my mouth, and he gives me an understanding squeeze as he pre-empts my reply.

"You totally don't have to stay to make sure that everything's in place for when Mom comes down to see the lake house. I've basically finished it already so, fingers crossed, everything's pretty much in place for when she visits." Except for the bed, but I'll still have a couple of days to build that thing after we get back from our camping-in-the-mountains adventure.

Connell winces, breathing out a laugh.

"When you put it like that, it kind of makes me feel like I should stay even more." He shrugs the shoulder that isn't resting over mine and says, "But honestly Ash, I think that she'll be happy with whatever you do. I can tell that you're freaking out about her not liking it, but there isn't anything *not* to like."

I have to blink a couple of times before I fully understand what he's saying because his use of a double-negative is a little stretching for my early morning brain.

Sensing my confusion he shakes his head with a grin and prods my cheek with his big pointer finger.

"I mean that everything is going to be fine," he explains, his eyes kind and bright when I finally nod. "And even if it wasn't? There would be no point stressing out over it beforehand. If they honestly decide to knock the whole thing down, it would be out of our hands. But that's not going to happen because they're going to see how much you love this place and it's going to make them fall in love with it too. If things don't go to plan and they don't like your ideas for the company – which is *not going to happen*," he adds, head ducked down to mine when he sees a surge of fear in my wide eyes, "then I'll get my ass right back here, comfort the shit out of you, and then, like, probably buy you a place right next to mine."

I let out a shaky exhale, dropping my eyes to watch my twiddling hands.

"Ash, look at me," he says, prodding me gently in the ribs until I do. "You're my sister and I'll do anything for you. No matter how this thing goes, I'm going to always be on your side. I'm going to always be there to look after you, even though you're such a tough fuckin' cookie that I know you don't even need it."

I feel a dangerous stinging behind my eyes but don't blink away from him – trying to put up my tough cookie front.

He keeps his eyes locked on mine for a long, searching moment, and then he nods, standing back to his full height, before a smile starts tugging at the corner of his mouth.

There's a knowing glint in his dazzling irises.

"So, uh…" He looks away for a second, laughing as he plays with the brim of his cap. "Tanner seems pretty keen to help out."

"What?" I instantly blurt, eyes growing wider as I stumble over my words. "Tanner? The hockey guy? Help out? I d-don't know what you're… what you're talking about—"

"I am so glad that you aren't one of those chicks who wanted to get into acting," Connell says with a grin, swatting away my fist as I try to punch at his abdomen, and hunching low so that he can shove his shoulder into the back of my knees. I yelp loudly as he stands upright, bouncing his shoulder up and down so that I have to claw my fingers into his giant quarterback neck.

"Shoulder throne," he grins, and I squeak as he jerks me into the air, laughing as he easily catches me.

Okay, I admit, I do kind of enjoy that.

"You're so freaking *annoying!*" I yell, even though I can't hide my smile, knowing that he's just trying to distract me from my anxious thoughts about the lake house.

"So do you like him?" he asks, and I smother my face in my hands as colour rushes to my cheeks.

"Shut up, shut up, shut up," I whisper, peeking down at him through a gap in my fingers and then shoving my whole palm in his face when I see that he's still smirking up at me.

"Shouldn't you hate that?" I ask him as he grabs my wrist, shoving my hand off his face.

"Hate what?"

"*That,*" I say, giving him the *duh* eyebrow raise. "The idea of me *liking* someone like *him.*"

Connell drops the smile and inhales deeply, looking briefly away from me.

"Well, uh," he murmurs, his voice deeper than it was a moment ago, "maybe we don't need to think about it that deep right now. About his, uh" – he clears his throat hard, frowning as he tugs at the brim of his cap again – "reputation and shit."

I give him a sulky look, crossing my arms over my chest. "I thought you were just saying how you were always going to look out for me."

"And I am," he says immediately, deep and resolute. He blinks away from me, shaking his head as if he hates having to think about this – which is, admittedly, very understandable – before doing another chest-swelling inhale and flicking his eyes back to meet mine. "Look, I'm a guy, and my college experience was pretty similar to his."

"*Ewwwww!*" I start, even though I already know that Connell was a total player when we were at Carter U.

He snickers. "Yeah, yeah. My point is, I got to talkin' to him while we've been here and… you can tell when someone's being genuine. You'd know right off the bat if someone's intentions weren't good. Or maybe" – he looks away and laughs – "maybe Tanner wears his heart on his sleeve the same way that you do. But when we spoke, especially when we spoke about you, I could tell that he's–"

"You spoke about me?" I squeak, cheeks heating in alarm.

"Shit," Connell mumbles, ducking his head so that he doesn't have to look me in the eyes, avoiding our secret twin bond that lets me see exactly what he's thinking.

"Well, what were you saying about me?" I ask, brow arching at the horrifying thought.

My brother's eyes flash up to meet mine, to where I'm still sitting on his 'shoulder throne'.

"You think I'd talk smack about you?" he asks, genuinely offended. "As fucking if, Ash. Besides, we weren't really talking about you. Tanner asked some questions that he thought were subtle, but I could sense what he was trying to ask me loud and clear."

"Which was?" I ask, unblinking and alarmed.

Connell shrugs and I almost go flying.

"If he thinks that you'd give him a shot. And if I'd chop his dick off for even thinking about it."

I press my face into my hands, muffling my squeal of mortification.

Connell gives me a tap on the side of my leg, silently asking me to look at him. My face is almost as bright as the sunrays kissing my shoulders when I finally drop my palms and look down at him, so embarrassed that I'm almost in tears.

"I've never seen you be so shy about a guy before," Connell murmurs, head tilting slightly to the side as he looks deep into my eyes. "But you don't need to be embarrassed. Whatever happens, you know I'll support you. But in case you were wondering," he adds, giving me a vicious grin, "I *will* chop his dick off if he does *anything* to hurt you."

Wow. I don't really know what to say to that.

"…Thank you," I say, watching him warily.

He gives me another grin. "Anytime."

Okey-dokey then.

He carts me over to where Fallon and Hunter are messing around at the edge of the clearing, before leaning down so that I can slide off of his 'shoulder throne'. Fallon shoots me an excited smile as Hunter wraps his arms around her waist, stabbing his stubbled jaw into the curve of her neck as he gives Connell an easygoing *what up, man?* smile.

"I'm so excited!" Fallon exclaims, her eyes alight with happy sparkles. "I've never been camping before!"

"You're gonna have the best time," Hunter murmurs, his voice a deep country drawl. "Used to spend every summer here with Tanner and his brothers. Sleeping outside is fuckin' awesome."

At the mention of Tanner, Connell's eyes slide my way, and my cheeks instantly burn crimson.

"You guys used to spend every summer at Larch Peak?" Connell asks, and I roll my eyes at his not-so-subtle digging on my behalf, the lazy grin on his face obvious without my even glancing up at him.

I give him a swift elbow to the ribs but he just chuckles, pulling me into a side-hug.

Fallon's eyes flash to mine and she smiles mischievously, but she cuts in anyway because she can tell that I'm way embarrassed right now.

"So are we setting up camp tomorrow afternoon or in the morning?" she asks, deflecting for me like an angel. "We need to grab supplies in town so that we won't have to do any morning trips down the mountain, and that way we can just chill out and explore while we're up here."

Hunter and Connell exchange a look, both of them shrugging to indicate that it doesn't really matter.

"Early afternoon," Hunter decides, to which Fallon nods eagerly and unlocks her phone, tapping the information away into her neat digital planner.

Hunter jerks his chin at Connell and asks, "Y'all wanna see any of the other campsites, or are we set on this one?"

"This one's good – equidistant between the cabins and some of the vantage points overlooking the lake." Connell grips at the brim of his cap and winces a little as he adds, "Don't really wanna go *deep* into the mountain just in case there's any… animals, or whatever."

Hunter nods in understanding even as he rumbles, "The wildlife here isn't really like that." He gives Fallon a little squish with his bulging forearms and adds with a smile, "You think I'd bring my girl here if it was?"

Connell breathes out a laugh and drops his eyes, nodding down at his boots as a gentle blush spreads up his cheeks.

It's no secret that Connell adores Fallon, although now he sees her like a second sister rather than as a potential girlfriend. But I wonder if seeing Fallon and Hunter together, as well as Winter and Caden, has made him think about his own romantic status as I've been thinking about mine.

An exhilarated squeal snaps my attention to my right and I look toward the narrow break in the trees just in time to see Winter flying into the clearing, excitement sparkling in her eyes as she glances back over her shoulder. She lets out another happy scream before meeting my gaze and grinning, and then using my arm to propel herself so that she can whip around and hide behind Connell.

Connell glances down at her over his shoulder, an amused smile on his mouth as he gives her a wink, and then we turn back to the trees where Caden – her huge, tan, tattooed boyfriend – is trudging as quickly as he can down the slope without slipping, eyes on his boots because he's too large and muscular to race down the incline with the same lithe agility as Winter.

When his eyes flash to our small circle he instantly skids to a stop, his small smile immediately dropping as he takes in the fact that he's looking at Fallon, Hunter, Connell and me – rather than his girlfriend.

He blinks down at us and a hint of colour blooms on his cheeks.

But then he drops his eyes to our boots, spots his girlfriend's, and that almost-smile reappears again.

He restarts his trudge down the slope, not running this time, until he's walking slowly over to us. That is a *lot* of ink on his forearms. His palms smooth over his dark spiky hair so that he can push it back from where it's fallen over his tan forehead.

Hunter glances between where Winter is 'hiding' and where Caden's smirking, and he shares a brief grin with him, shaking his head in amusement. Caden being shy and love-struck is such a contradiction to his intimidating exterior.

Slowly Winter peeks out from behind the swell of Connell's biceps and Caden's arms immediately fly out to grab her, making her scream with giggles as he hauls her against his chest. He hides his quiet laughter in her hair before pressing a quick kiss to her flushed cheek.

"Found you," he murmurs.

Connell slaps his hand over his eyes and groans, "I am *soooooo* single."

I roll my eyes and laugh, shoving my elbow in his ribs.

Hunter snickers and tips his chin at Caden. "Y'all wanna hike, or d'you wanna head back down and we can grab some tents in town?"

Caden looks a question at his girlfriend, searching her

eyes to see if she has a preference, and they have a telepathic conversation filled with sparkly eyes and dimply smiles. Then Caden glances back up at Hunter and nods.

"Yeah," Caden rumbles quietly, his voice deep and gravelly. "We'll head down with y'all."

Winter looks up at me with raised eyebrows. "Are you not coming?" she asks gently, a little bit of her cute Kentucky twang slipping through.

I'm too nervous to head back to the lake right now, knowing that only one guy from our group is there doing who-knows-what.

Yeah. Tanner stayed back at the lake.

I swallow quickly and shake my head.

"I'm gonna hike a little with the guys," I tell her, looking nervously up at my brother. He gives me a reassuring smile and a nod of his head.

I nod back at him, grateful for our twin synergy right now.

A light whizzing sound filters through the air and in the next second Connell's head is whipping to our left. His arm slices through the air, grabbing the football in his large practiced grip before it can smack straight into my shoulder.

"The fuck?" he asks, tossing the ball in his hand as he shakes his head, glancing over to where his teammates are 'teaching' the hockey guys how to play.

Logan puts his hands in the air in surrender before pointing at Hughes, which makes Hughes drop his arms and groan *"aw man"*.

Connell snickers and hurls the ball straight at our attacker, who stealthily ducks it but then throws me a genuine apologetic smile.

Connell's teasing throw says, *try that shit again, I dare you.*

He glances back toward Hunter and jerks his thumb over to his former hockey teammates, an easygoing smile on his mouth but a glimmer of real threat behind his eyes.

"Tell me he wasn't actually aiming over here to get Ash's

attention," Connell says.

Hunter's eyes are playful as he glances between Connell, Hughes, and back again.

"What, you wanna give him a right hook?" he rumbles, a smirk playing on his mouth as he settles his chin comfortably on Fallon's shoulder.

I breathe out a laugh and shake my head.

"He was just being an idiot, let it slide," I tell my brother, casually admiring my twinkling nails as the sunlight catches and refracts against the golden sparkles.

Connell's jaw muscle flexes as he gives me a direct unblinking look. He seems to think about it for a long moment and then he breathes out a deep exhale, shooting another glance to the guys still throwing the ball across the clearing.

"Fine," he says curtly, dropping a heavy forearm over my shoulders. "But if he does that again his ass is grass, Aisling, I swear to God."

Hunter grins, clearly relating to those over-protective older brother genes, and then stands to his full height, enveloping Fallon's small hand in his large one. "Right, let's head."

Connell and Hunter do that secret dude hand-smacking thing while Fallon stares at me with her huge eyes and a mischievous smile that she's trying to rein in – even though, after being roommates pretty much all through college, I know exactly what she's thinking. She wants me to tell her every juicy Tanner-related thought in my head. I do a little sigh and give her a subtle nod.

Later, I mouth to her.

She looks fit to combust with excitement by the time that Hunter hauls her over his shoulder and begins carrying her back down the incline. I laugh and give her and Winter a little wave before turning back to my brother, who is using his arm over my shoulders to steer me toward the extremely testosterone-fuelled game of pass that's happening right now.

"Fucker's don't understand the basic rules of football," Logan says with an amused grin as we reach him, the ball hurtling through the air as he releases it from his large fist.

"Heard that," Austin calls back to him, throwing the ball with a little more vengeance than before, and smirking when Logan has to jump up to catch it.

Logan thumps back to the ground and turns to smile at me, bowing slightly as he holds out the football like an offering.

"M'lady," he rasps, before glancing up at me with a sexy wink.

"Alright, that's it." Connell swipes the football out of his hand, making his best friend grin as he confiscates the ball, and then he begins dragging me up the incline with him.

I offer Logan a quick grin over my shoulder, knowing that he's just messing around, and he smiles back at me as he falls into step with his teammates. The hockey boys jog ahead of the footballers so that they can walk beside me.

Connell glances down at me with a slightly wary expression, casually tossing the ball in the air with his free hand.

I give him a reassuring smile to let him know that I appreciate how he looks out for me, and that no harm has been done, so everything's fine.

He nods his head and then gently tips the ball into the air for me to catch. I laugh as I jump up and grab it, throwing it back to him as high as I can. He smirks as he drops his arm from my shoulders so that he can get into position, reach up and grab it.

"Tyrant," he grins, before running up ahead. He turns around and throws the ball lightly my way, his hands fiddling with his cap before he throws them back in the air, awaiting my next throw.

We laugh the whole way to the top.

CHAPTER 28

Aisling

Present day

By the time that we get back to the cabins it's late afternoon, meaning that we hop in a couple of the trucks and head into town for dinner. The two booths that we take up are filled with more food than I've ever seen.

When we return to the cabins the sun is still on the horizon, just about to set, and Fallon, Hunter, Winter and Caden are sat together around the lit campfire. Caden is holding two skewers over the flames, toasting two giant marshmallows as his girlfriend neatly prepares the cookies. Then she holds them out for his marshmallows so that they can make the world's most epic looking s'mores.

"S'mores? No way. Can we join?" Connell asks, jaw practically dislocating as he stares longingly at the marshmallow heaven happening in Winter's outstretched hands.

Caden glances up mid-marshmallow removal and suddenly lets out a surprised curse, his eyes flying back down to his thumb as he yanks it away from the molten marshmallow.

Winter lets out a sympathetic squeal before quickly placing down the cookies.

She takes Caden's big hockey player hand in her delicate palms.

"Are you okay?" she asks softly, a sympathetic dimple popping in her cheek when Caden swallows down the sting of the burn, clears his throat and nods.

"It's fine," he rumbles quietly.

Winter gives him a knowing smile before pressing a gentle kiss to his burnt thumb, then his palm, and then his stubble-coated cheek.

Caden drops his head so that no-one can see him blush.

Winter turns her attention back to us as she tugs at Caden's arm, silently asking him to stand, which he does instantaneously.

"Of course you can join," she says, smiling kindly. "We'll just be a minute."

Then she hauls Caden by his wrist to the smooth edge of the lake, tugging him so that he crouches down beside her. She eases his thumb just beneath the surface of the clear water, trying to ease the burn without even saying anything.

"They are so freaking cute," Connell murmurs to me as everyone starts settling around the fire, and I nod in agreement, in awe of how gentle their love is.

My eyes drift over the shimmering water until I'm looking at the lake house, and an excited warmth flutters in my belly as I catch the hint of a glow coming from the downstairs window. I'm unable to really see what's inside as the glass reflects the warm evening sunset.

But I can guess who will be inside there.

My phone has been vibrating with love notes from Tanner all afternoon, but I haven't been able to peek at most of them because I didn't want to draw any more suspicion than I already have from his teammates as we trekked to one of the beautiful lookout points in the nearest of the Larch Peak mountains.

Connell holds the bag of giant marshmallows in front of me, slapping away Austin's hand when he tries to take one before I do.

I scrunch my nose at them, laughing at how sweet and silly they are, before peeping into the bag and taking one of the pink ones.

Connell's eyes flick between my face and the lake house, a hint of a crease on his brow as he skewers his own marshmallow.

Then he pulls off his cap, roughly scrubbing at his hair.

"You calling it a night?" he asks, before glancing at the cabins behind us, undoubtedly wondering if Tanner is in there.

From the faint hint of a sconce glow radiating gently from beyond the lake house's porch, I am ninety-nine percent sure that I know exactly where Tanner is.

"Yeah," I breathe out, my voice quiet amongst the sounds of our friends. Connell nods at me and lifts his arm that isn't holding the skewer, silently requesting a hug.

I laugh quietly and give him a quick squish, squealing my way out of his arms when he tries to turn it into one of his bone-crushing bear hugs. I give him a playful punch on the shoulder and his expression relaxes, a laidback smile lighting up his face as he kicks off his boots and settles his backwards cap back onto his head.

And then I'm making my way over to the lake house.

I stuff the marshmallow into my mouth, the soft *thump* of my hiking boots pounding rhythmically against the dirt sounding in time with the loud beat of my heart. The talking and laughter coming from around the campfire becomes a faraway melody as I try to calm my breathing, holding up the hem of the sundress that I changed into as the lake laps tauntingly close to my boots.

The closer I get the more sure I am that the soft glow radiating onto the porch is coming from the inside of the cabin, rather than the sunset outside that's exuding its final burst of golden rays.

I jog lightly up the porch steps and then drop the skirt of my dress, staring at the front door as my heart thunders in my chest.

I quietly ease open the front door and step inside, eyes immediately moving over to the couch where Tanner is sleeping.

He's fast asleep even though he's sitting partially upright, with his quads spread wide apart and one hand tucked down the front of his unzipped jeans. He's wearing a light grey shirt that's stretched thin across his chest and there's a small metal toolbox on the floor beside the sofa.

My mind whirs as I contemplate exactly what it was that kept him from joining us on our hike today.

As I gently click the heavy front door closed Tanner's shoulders swell on a deep inhale and he rouses from his sleep, pressing the heel of his palm between his eyes.

When I slip my boots off my feet and they thud softly against the wooden floor his head turns in my direction and he immediately shoots to stand upright. He almost falls over the low coffee table as his big calves accidentally shove it across the rug.

"Fuck, sorry," he rasps out quietly, his deep voice hoarse with sleep. He quickly looks down at his pants, ears blazing red as he rips his hand from under the open zipper.

He shoots a quick look in my direction as he hastily tugs up his fly, and then he's rounding the side of the couch, meeting me in the middle just in front of the staircase. His palms immediately encase my waist as he looks reverently up and down.

"How was the campsite? Did you have a good day?" he asks, eyes searching mine before he reaches down to press a kiss to the heart freckle on my exposed arm.

I scrunch up my nose, laughing, and he grins up at me before standing back to his full height.

"It was beautiful, I can't wait to camp out there tomorrow night – I've never been camping before," I admit, my voice hushed and happy.

I tug gently at his thin grey shirt, fitted tight around his thick abdomen.

I look up at him from under my lashes as I think about what he said to me this morning, about me deserving a break from the reno as I'm already so close to the finish line.

You know that I'll help you finish it up, Ash.

My eyes subconsciously flick to the ceiling, toward the master bedroom, wondering if that subtle text meant what I thought it might.

He catches the movement and a smile touches his handsome mouth.

"What did you do today?" I ask carefully, my voice light and a little breathless as he pulls my body against his, the warmth of his broad chest pressing through my sundress.

His smile grows a little wider.

"Wanna see?"

I swallow hard, unable to prevent myself from smiling back, and then he gives me a full-on grin, a hint of a blush under his tan skin.

His big hand finds mine and then we're walking side by side up the staircase, Tanner only stopping when we reach the top so that I can step onto the landing before him.

Then he tugs me gently in the direction of the master bedroom.

"Tanner…" I say warily, laughing in disbelief before we even reach the closed door. "You didn't…" I say again as I shake my head, that blush on his cheeks spreading farther.

No way. No way did he do this for me again, even after the four years of disinterested hell that I put him through.

He breathes out a nervous chuckle, scratching at the back of his neck with his free hand, looking as nervous and shy and excited as I am.

"Do you, uh…" He breathes out a shaky laugh, pulling me closer against his side and weaving his strong fingers tighter through mine. "Do you still wanna see–?"

"Yes," I say immediately, breathlessly, and he nods his head, eyes burning as they flash against mine.

He twists the handle and pushes the door open.

My free hand flies up to my chest, trying to subdue the warm clench around my heart as I take in the sight of the room before me.

The small furniture fixtures, like the wooden bedside cabinets and the large lounge pouf, that I hadn't yet moved into place because I needed to construct the bed first have found their homes in the bedroom, framing the space and softening the angles of the A-frame with their natural placement. Their muted rustic colours make them seem as if they were here all along.

But most importantly? There resting against the centre of the side wall, at the perfect vantage point to watch the lake every morning and every night, is the fully-constructed master bed.

I don't know whether it's the fact that he built the bed on his own, the fact that he did it without me asking, or the fact that once he'd finished it, he'd taken it upon himself to dress the sheets in the deep emerald green bedding that I'd purchased, and carefully drape a long golden string of fairy lights that I *hadn't* purchased along the headboard, that makes my heart squeeze the tightest.

I press my knuckles against the love-struck smile on my lips and decide that it's all of those things combined.

"Tanner," I breathe, stepping into the room. He keeps his thick fingers locked around mine, still standing against the doorjamb with his large shoulder resting against the wall. "This is so…."

I turn around to look up at him and his expression is cautious, almost shy. His eyes bounce between my face and the bed, his cheeks heating up warmer and warmer as he steals quick glances at me every three seconds.

"Perfect," I finish at last, my voice light and soft. "This is so kind. You're the sweetest guy I've ever met."

He grins and meets my eyes, his gaze dazzling and direct, and then he uses our still-joined hands to tug me towards him, his large chest immediately pressing warm and hard against mine.

"You like it?" he asks, his other hand wrapping around my hip so that he can haul me against him even tighter.

"I love it," I admit, a little nervously, and his chest swells heavily as he squeezes my waist. I shudder against him and his eyelids drop, gaze flicking down to just below the high neckline of my sundress.

"Wasn't sure if I was overstepping," he murmurs, that large hand around my waist flattening against the curve of my lower back. I brush the knuckles of my free hand over his soft shirt, up his abdomen until I reach his chest. I caress his large pecs with my palm, before moving to his biceps, brushing my finger over his vein.

He's huge, and I love it.

"You didn't overstep," I reassure him, grinning teasingly as I add, "until now," pointing at the breached bedroom threshold and making him drop his head, laughing quietly. "No-one is this kind, Tanner, and I feel really grateful. This…"

I wave my hand in the direction of the bed and Tanner frowns and immediately grabs it, pressing it back against his muscles.

"This is the sweetest thing ever. You make me really happy."

Tanner grunts, turning his head as his chest pumps

faster, as if he can't handle the words that I'm saying to him.

It makes me laugh quietly, adoration in my eyes as I gently capture his hard jaw in my hand to draw his attention back to me.

His eyes drop to mine, hooded and smouldering, before he swipes his tongue over his lower lip, in preparation for whatever he's psyching himself up to say.

I swipe my thumb over his nipple and a deep laugh bellows out of him.

"Just say it," I whisper to him, as he gently nudges the tip of his nose against mine. "Whatever it is that's on your mind, you can say it."

He pulls back up and then wraps his arm around my shoulders, bringing our joined hands to his mouth so that he can press a warm kiss against the top of it.

"I'm glad that I make you happy," he rumbles finally, pressing our joined hands against his heart, looking at our locked fingers as he speaks. "Because making you happy is what makes me happy," he finishes quietly.

My heart squeezes so tight that for the briefest moment I think it's going to burst.

His striking eyes flick back to mine as he lifts up my hand to give it another kiss.

But that isn't where I want his mouth anymore.

So I push my body more firmly against his, making his chest swell as his pupils completely dial out, and I ask him huskily, "Can we, like, kiss properly now?"

Those sexy twin creases appear in his cheeks, eyes alight with desire and darkness as he clears his throat and nods his head.

"Yeah – I mean, yes," he rasps, deep and hoarse, so excited that he's struggling to get his words out. "Yeah, I want to. I mean–"

I breathe out a tiny laugh, stand onto my tip-toes, and kiss him.

CHAPTER 29

Tanner

Present day

A grunt rips through my chest as Aisling's lips meet mine and I stumble back against the wall, hauling her with me. I pull her body tighter against my chest as I hunch down to lessen the height difference, and then I reach out to the side, fumbling for the door handle so that I can close it.

I tear my mouth from hers with a groan, head snapping in the direction of the door so that I can finally grab it and shove it closed, making the room smaller, warmer, more intimate for just the two of us.

I grip her hand tighter in mine as I turn back to her, pressing kisses all over the smooth skin of her wrist before finally releasing it. She throws her arms around my shoulders and I grip my palms around her ass, leaning down and crushing her mouth with mine before I haul her up off the floor and start walking us toward the bed.

"You made me another bed," she breathes out, lashes

fluttering as I nudge my forehead against hers.

"I'm gonna make you every bed that you ever sleep in," I rasp, dropping her to the ground just before we reach the mattress. I bunch my fists in the sides of her long dress, scrunching the soft fabric up so that I can get a glimpse of her perfect legs.

My forearms flex the second that I see her smooth ankles, my cock growing heavier as I bunch the fabric higher and higher. The second that I see the first inch of her thighs I growl low and rough, and hunch down to take her lips with mine.

Her sweet moan fills my mouth until I pull away grunting, my fingers fumbling with my zipper so that I can get a little room to fucking breathe.

"Jesus Christ," I rasp, going lightheaded at the instant thickening of my cock, shoulders heaving faster by the second as I tower over Aisling. I tangle my fingers up in her hair. "I'm so fuckin' hard for you," I choke out, vision blurring when she bites me.

My hands drop the fabric of her dress, gripping her by her ass so that I can rub her against me, inhaling her scent before kissing my way back to her lips.

"We don't have to do anything," I say hoarsely, pulling back so that I can look down at her.

Even though I built the bed *for* Aisling I'm aware that she doesn't intend to keep this house. Whether her family is going to rent it or sell it I don't know, but she might not want to do anything on a bed that isn't for keeps.

"It's a tradition," she whispers breathlessly, mischief sparkling in her eyes.

I breathe out a laugh, squeezing my palms more roughly around her waist.

"What, me building you a bed?" I ask.

"Yeah," she whispers, "and then you showing me how to use it after."

I crush my mouth down on hers, grunting as I shove my

tongue inside, and she gasps as I slide in deeper, her nails digging hungrily into my biceps.

"You sure?" I rumble, hands rubbing up and down the back of her dress, searching for the fastening so that I can get her the fuck out of it.

She nods quickly, forehead pressing against mine, just as my fingers brush against a small button at the nape of her neck. *Fuck yes.* I flick it between my fingers and the tight neckline of the dress relaxes, making me drop my head against her shoulder as my chest expands with satisfaction.

I grip both of my fists around the thin straps but make no move to slide them down her shoulders, well aware that it's the only layer obstructing me from seeing Aisling in her bra and panties.

"You wearing a pair of the panties that I bought for you?" I ask gruffly, unable to lift my head as my breathing pumps faster and faster.

She makes a taunting noncommittal purr as she slides her delicate fingers down the neck of my shirt. My shoulder muscles flex, anticipating and hungry for the bite of her nails, wanting her to dig them in.

She gives me a gentle teasing scratch. "Guess you'll have to find out."

I stand upright on a deep inhale, searching her eyes before my mouth tugs into a grin, her little dimpled smile the prettiest thing that I've ever seen.

I tug the straps down gently – or at least I mean to. But the second that I've got them off her shoulders the whole dress drops to the floor, pooling in a soft pile of baby pink around her ankles.

"Fuck," I rasp, mind blanking as I stare at her bra. "Four years, baby. Four years since I saw you like this."

With those big innocent eyes she pushes her body right against my pecs and a rough sound rumbles through my chest as I stare down at those tempting curves.

"Fucking beautiful," I rumble, shoving my hands

through my hair, and raking my eyes over her perfect tits. "I shouldn't even… I shouldn't even be looking at them. Don't deserve to look at those things."

Aisling closes her eyes, arches her neck and shakes out her rich hair, making me choke on a growl as other parts start shaking too.

Done for. I'm fucking done for.

She peeks one sparkling eye open as I drop my shaking hands to my sides and she shows me one of her playful little dimples as she wraps her arms back around my neck.

"You don't think that you deserve to look at me?" she says, laughing quietly as she smiles.

"Hell no," I rasp, hands hovering around her hips, my whole body bathed in fucking fire. "They're… you're… they're just so…" I grit my teeth and tear my eyes away from her. "I'm… not gonna do it. I don't deserve–"

"You can touch them if you want," she whispers.

"Over the bra or under?"

Her eyes sparkle as she grins up at me, and I drop my forehead against hers, breathing roughly as I lift my hands to touch her.

"Definitely over the bra," I murmur, voice so deep that it's resonating in my balls.

Slowly, so slowly, my thumbs brush the lace cups of her bra, and the gentle peaks of her nipples make me grunt, rubbing harder.

"Tanner," she whispers.

I keep my eyes on her tits, lightheaded but nodding.

"You can touch me under–"

I slip two digits down the back of her bra and tug, yanking down the straps before tearing the whole thing off of her. I pull it hastily down her arms and shove it roughly in my back pocket.

She raises an eyebrow and breathes out a laugh.

"Uh, what exactly do you think that you're gonna do with that?" she asks, as if she doesn't fucking know.

I grip my hands around her jaw, hunch down and kiss the life out of her. I'm so damn overwhelmed by the knowledge that she's almost completely naked right now, only wearing her panties, that I have to try and calm down by licking my tongue gently against hers.

"Dream girl," I murmur, turning us around so that it's my back that's facing the bed. I lower my body down onto the thick sheets, hands immediately dropping to the backs of her thighs, easing her on top of me until she's straddling my lap. Then I press a couple of smaller kisses against her lips, take a deep breath, and pull back to look at her.

My cock jerks so hard beneath my jeans that Aisling jolts in my lap and yelps, before bursting into a fit of giggles. My neck flushes red as I give her an apologetic smile, palms roaming over her ass as I glance back down to her chest.

It's my first time ever seeing her bared to me.

Round, soft, perky. Everything that I ever dreamed they'd be.

And I've dreamt about them a *lot*.

"Beautiful," I say hoarsely, chest heaving as I rub her lap slowly up and back over my shaft. I meet her eyes, feeling dazed, and press a slow kiss against her lips. "Really gonna let me touch them?" I ask her, almost groaning when she nods her head.

I reach one hand behind my neck and rip my shirt over my head, tossing it across the room as Aisling's eyes grow wide, lips popping open.

"O-oh," she squeaks, making me smirk as she stares at my pecs.

"It's only fair," I rumble quietly. "If I'm allowed to touch your tits, then you're sure as shit allowed to get your hands on my pecs."

"I can… touch them?" she whispers, and I lean back, jerking my chin at her in the affirmative.

We both start breathlessly laughing as she giggles and squeezes at my chest, but it quickly turns into panting and grunts as she sinks her teeth into the meat of me, grazing her teeth dangerously over my nipple.

"Jesus," I rasp, chest heaving as I watch her mess around with me. "You are the hottest, weirdest, most fucking irresistible woman I've ever met."

I grip my hand around the nape of her neck and haul her upright, while keeping her hips shoved firmly down on my lap. She whimpers at the momentum and I grunt hard as those pretty curves bounce up and down.

Then I lift her up by her ass so that her breasts are at the perfect level for my mouth.

"My turn," I growl.

"W-what?" she whimpers. "You're gonna touch them with your... with your mouth–?"

The gasp that I pull from her throat is enough to turn me into an animal, and I look up into her wide eyes as I suck her hard and fast. Her fingers tug hard at my hair, more perfect sounds escaping her throat as she pushes her breast into me harder.

I smirk and let her go with a firm *pop*, massaging her ass as she digs her nails into the back of my neck.

"Like getting sucked?" I ask roughly.

She drops her voice to a husky whisper. "I like getting something-that-rhymes-with sucked."

In the next moment my pants are off and I'm hauling my bodyweight on top of her, stroking my tongue against hers as I grind my erection between her thighs.

"Your fuckin' mouth," I rasp, grunting when I shove my chest right down on hers, rubbing us together in a way that makes my mind explode.

"I've never seen you naked before," I rasp, well aware that her pretty panties are the only remaining thing keeping her covered from me.

She smiles naughtily as she bites her thumb and I push her hand away from her mouth, reclaiming it with mine.

She giggles excitedly as I kiss her, her body growing

softer as I work our lips together.

"I've seen you naked before," she whispers, a secret smile in her voice.

I grunt, reliving the memory of four years ago. Of how well she lay back and took me.

"Yeah," I rumble. "You wanna see it again?"

She nods and I roll us over, so that I'm laying on my back and she's tucked safely against my side, nestled protectively under my biceps.

I use my free hand to quickly shove down my boxer briefs, kicking them to the end of the bed when I get them unhooked from my ankles, and then I wrap my fist around the thick base of my cock and start pumping nice and slow, putting on a show for her.

Aisling releases a small sound that makes a smirk tug at the corner of my mouth, and my eyes search her face as she stares down at my cock.

"You like that?" I rumble, grinning at the expression on her face. I pause my strokes so that I can grab my balls and this time she fully squeals. She hides her face in the side of my chest, giggling uncontrollably and breathing hard.

I laugh quietly as I release my sac, rolling onto my side so that I can cuddle her into my chest. She peeks up at me with sparkling eyes, a nervous smile, and the most flushed cheeks that I've ever seen.

I hunch down so that I can kiss her and then I tug the sheets cosily around her body.

"You look terrified," I tease, smirking when she bites her bottom lip. "Forgot how big a hose from the holler was, huh?"

"Tanner!" she exclaims, burying her face in her hands.

I chuckle and wrestle her hands off of those cheeks, wrapping my palms around her waist so that I can haul her up the bed and bring her to my height.

"I'll go gentle," I drawl, brushing her nose with mine. As ego-boosting as it is to watch her pupils dial out at the size of my dick, I don't actually want her to be scared of taking it.

I gently squeeze my hands over her breasts, her little gasp making me groan.

"Prettiest tits I've ever seen," I murmur, pressing another kiss against her lips and slipping my tongue inside. I stroke my thumbs over her nipples and slide my tongue deeper as she moans for me.

"When we were together before," I rumble, pulling back so that I can look at her carefully, "when we did it in our freshman year, what did you think?"

Aisling blinks up at me and gives me the most beautiful smile.

"I thought you were *huge*," she laughs, pressing her body up against mine.

I smirk down at her, pleased with that lasting impression. "Yeah?"

"Like, you were so big that I thought you were gonna crush me."

I breathe out a laugh and slap a hand over my face, embarrassed.

"Great," I tease, "that's exactly what I was going for."

Aisling laughs and pries my hand from my eyes. "I mean it in a good way. I loved feeling you on top of me."

I suck in a sharp inhale as her palms squeeze their way over my muscles – over my biceps, down my heaving chest, and then lower, until she's–

"*Baby*," I growl, fingers gripping her waist as I thrust myself into her small fist. In the next second I'm rolling onto my back with Ash on top of me, grabbing one of her wrists and pushing it lower, begging for her to relieve that other ache.

"Tug 'em," I grunt, chest heaving fast as her fingers gently brush my sac. "Harder, baby. Harder. Yeah, *fuck*, just like that."

The brush of her chest against mine draws me back to

exactly what's happening, and I blink hard at the ceiling, trying to clear that red animal haze. I shove one hand through my hair and stare down at the beautiful girl straddling my quads, eyes alight with curiosity as the deep green bedding halos around her.

I pull her hands off of me, sit upright, and kiss her, the sheets falling to her waist as I massage my hands over her thighs.

"I didn't mean to crush you," I murmur, making her laugh as I kiss down her neck.

"I told you, I like it. You're the biggest guy I've ever been with."

I pull back, eyebrows raised, and Aisling instantly pauses, like she said too much.

I am very fucking intrigued with this new information.

"I'm sorry, what?" I ask, my voice so deep that Aisling's nipples pinch tighter.

"Uh, nothing," she mumbles, trying to scramble off my lap.

Not a fucking chance.

"I'm the biggest guy you've ever been with?" I ask, smirking like an asshole as I wrap my arms around her waist, keeping her in place. "Like, are we talkin' height, weight, or the size of my cock?"

She twists to claw at my forearms but I hold her tighter.

"None of those things," she huffs. "I take it back. You're the smallest."

I grin before giving her a quick bite to her throat.

"I can't tell you how good it feels to be the tallest, biggest guy that you've ever been with, baby. So, with regards to my cock, is it the longest *and* the thickest or–?"

She manages to wriggle off of my lap but I roll over on top of her ass, making her squeal and laugh until she remembers that she's angry with me and throws me a sulky glower.

I press a kiss to her shoulder, grinning wickedly as I

hold her eyes with mine.

"It's the longest *and* the thickest, isn't it?"

She twists her lips to one side, trying to hide her smile, before letting me roll her onto her back so that I'm not mounting her from behind.

I release a low contended rumble as I settle down on top of her, one hand toying with the side of her panties while the other gently strokes at her jaw.

My voice is teasing as I drawl, "Damn, it's tiring being this big."

Aisling throws her head back into the pillows with a giggle before saying, "Oh no, you're tired? We better get to sleep then."

"Did I say that I'm tired? I meant that I've never been more awake."

She laughs into my neck as I tangle one of my hands up in her hair.

"Seriously, I don't think I'll ever need to sleep again. Ever." She peeks up at me and I press a kiss to the warm apple of one of her cheeks, nuzzling into her hair as my digits tug more firmly at her panties. A silent question, looking for her instructions.

"I can't believe that you got me fairy lights," she whispers, and I pull back a couple of inches so that I can glance up at the headboard, the string of bulbs that I bought from the mom-and-pop home and electric store in town wrapped as neatly as I could get them around the ornate wood.

When I look down at her and see her pretty smile shimmering in the faint glow of the bulbs, my heart clenches tight, so in love with everything about her.

"Thought you might like 'em," I reply gruffly.

"I love them," she whispers back.

I avert my eyes, pumping myself a little, before resettling my palm around her hip and pressing my forehead down on hers.

"Do you still wanna…?" I rasp quietly, watching her hand as it roams over my chest, squeezing at the large muscles and getting me excited.

"I still wanna," she whispers back to me.

I hook two digits under the side of her panties, a pair of skimpy as fuck lace ones. A pair that was in her basket that day in the lingerie store.

I shove my tongue in my cheek as I give them an experimental tug.

One good yank will tear these things clean off her pussy.

My eyes meet hers, her pupils almost as wide as mine.

I clear my throat. "Can I take off your panties?"

She bites into her lower lip. "Do you have protection?"

"Yeah," I grunt immediately. My gaze rakes down to her belly, tongue swiping over my lower lip. "You're not on the pill?"

She hesitates for a beat before whispering, "I'm not on the pill."

I grunt and close my eyes.

Something about the fact that she's unprotected makes me fucking feral.

I nod my head and raise onto my haunches, quads splaying between her thighs. I caress her hips, scanning the room for wherever the fuck I threw my jeans.

"Condoms are in my wallet. I'll grab 'em."

She gently brushes her fingers over my cock, laying hard and heavy against her belly.

I clench the muscles in my jaw and start reciting the names of all the States.

"Okay," she whispers, "go and get them."

I lunge off the bed, sheets tangling around my feet as I grab my wallet, tear out the condoms, and half-sprint back to where Ash is giggling, fixing the sheets into place before climbing back on top of her.

I toss all but one of the condoms onto the bedside cabinet, ripping the foil packet in two before grabbing my dick with one hand and rolling the rubber into place. Aisling giggles and gets up onto her knees, letting me kiss her deep as my palms slip her panties down her thighs. By the time that I've tugged them off her ankles I'm so ready to see all of her, to be inside of her, that I'm almost growling.

I grip my palms into her bare behind, massaging her roughly as I pull away. "Can I look at you?" I rasp, eyes closed, waiting for the green light.

"Mm-hm," she whispers, and I exhale harshly.

My eyes are aflame as I take her hips and stare down at her.

I'm sat on my haunches while Aisling is on her knees, and she's still almost a full head shorter than me. My mouth goes dry as I take her in, loving every single curve and peak.

"I need you," I rumble, rubbing two digits between her thighs.

Her nails bite into my biceps, gasping gently as she squeezes my wrist.

"How do you want it?" I ask her, rubbing faster, pressing closer.

"I can't think straight right now," she admits on a whimper, and I nod once in understanding, trying to quickly decide which position will be the best for her, the most romantic.

"Wanna go on top?" I rasp, already knocking her thighs apart with the muscles of my quads, the hand wrapped around her hip roaming down to her ass. Hauling her up onto my lap. Getting ready to push inside of her.

"W-what?" she pants. "I thought that you liked—"

"Yeah," I grunt, "I like that. The position you're thinkin' about." Wow, it's really hard to remember the names of the States right now. "But, uh… for our first time in four years I shouldn't take you like that. I shouldn't take you from behind. Want it to be romantic."

Not that I didn't find it romantic the first and only time

that we did it in my favourite position but the angle is so deep, and it can get so rough, that I don't want to lose every fuckin' ounce of control when I'm trying to prove to her that I'm not a player.

"It was romantic," she whispers.

I nod gently before cupping my palms around her jaw and kissing her. I lay her back against the sheets and range my body over hers, my cock jerking eagerly against her heat as I try to nudge it carefully into place.

"I know," I murmur back to her, "but I don't wanna lose control with you tonight."

I only just got you back. I don't wanna scare you away again.

Aisling purses her lips and then purrs a disconcerting, "We'll see."

My mouth lifts into a half-grin and my eyes glance down between her thighs.

"Dream girl," I rumble, one hand gripping the nape of her neck while the other massages her soft behind.

She whimpers at the nickname and rakes her nails down my chest.

I hiss through bared teeth, slowly pushing at her entrance.

"That's it," I say gruffly. "Dig 'em in and hold on."

Her nails bite into me harder and then she's pushing her head into the pillow and whimpering, my balls scraping against the sheets as I ease in the first few inches.

I withdraw to the tip and then give her a few slow, languid strokes, getting her used to the size of half of me before I give her the whole thing.

She's breathless and panting as I pump her gently.

"Think you can take it all?" I ask, pulling back so that she can see what's left to go.

She glances down at it and squeals, her pussy clenching involuntarily.

I breathe out a laugh and she gives me a light slap across the chest.

"Mm, yeah. Get rough with me, baby," I tease, deep and gravelly.

She hides her smile in my neck and then nods, fingers gripping tight around my shoulder blades.

"You sure?" I murmur, cock flexing in anticipation.

"Yes, I'm sure," she whispers.

I pull back and take her jaw in my palm, holding her eyes with mine as I withdraw to the tip.

"Good," I rumble, rough and wanting. Then I shove it deep inside, shoulders heaving as she gasps.

"*Tanner*," she whimpers, thighs squeezing around my middle.

I grunt and thrust again, eyes on her beautiful face.

"My girl," I rumble, squeezing the nape of her neck as I start moving faster. There's still an inch at the base that I can't get inside but I'm more than satisfied at the amount she's taking.

My back muscles roll rhythmically as I pump my hips between her thighs.

"Big as you remember?" I grunt, dropping one of my forearms beside her head. My bicep crowds around her face, making her flush harder when she glances at it.

"Bigger," she whimpers, making me smirk like an asshole. She scowls at my expression and murmurs something that sounds a lot like *big shot*.

"What's that, now?" I grin, pumping her harder, making her drop that attitude real quick.

"N-nothing," she says quickly, before arching back and moaning hard. My eyes drop to her tits and my strokes instantly become faster, pushing myself deeper as I watch her whimper and bounce.

"You're so pretty," I rasp, groaning as a rope of pre-cum shoots out. "Ash, you're so pretty. I'm so into you, it's fuckin' crazy."

She makes a little gasp as she wheezes out, "You're telling me."

I breathe out a laugh, thrusting harder when she pulls my chest down to hers, cuddling me against her while I give her exactly what she's been needing.

Suddenly her gasps are getting louder, nails biting harder, and my balls are spanking against her ass as I thrust her straight to the finish line.

And as much as I want that, I want this to last longer for her even more.

Only problem is, her orgasm is no more than fifteen seconds away, and she's so goddamn tight that I'm not going to last once she starts squeezing me.

I pull back with a growl, tangling my fingers in her hair.

"Not yet, baby," I plead roughly. "Don't come. Not yet."

She blinks up at me quickly, swallowing hard as she watches me take her.

"W-what?" she whispers. "What d'you mean 'd-don't come'?"

"If you come, then I'm gonna come too," I rumble. "And I'm tryna make it last for you. Tryna make it last a little longer."

Her eyes stay on mine, wide and unblinking.

Looking guilty as hell, like she's about to do exactly what I just told her not to.

"Ash," I growl out. "Do not fucking come."

She digs her nails into my chest and moans, "Try and stop me."

"Ash," I grind out, groaning as she squeezes up tight. "Baby, for fuck's sake, I'm trying to make it last—"

I grunt and gasp as she suddenly grips my sac, massaging it so thoroughly that my vision turns hazy.

"Aisling," I rasp, "slow the fuck down."

She tugs them harder and I groan so loud that I have to bite my own goddamn tongue.

Keep it down, asshole. You want everyone across the lake to hear?
Ash wants to keep this thing private and you will not *fuck that*

up for her.

"You're holding back," she whimpers, brow arched upwards because she's so close to her release. "I need you with me and you're holding back."

I steel my jaw, eyes on fire as she glowers up at me.

"I'm being a gentleman," I growl. "Stop tryna make me get rough with you."

Something dangerous flashes in her eyes. "If you don't then someone else–"

I crush my mouth down over hers and shove my tongue straight inside, feeling her sparkle with satisfaction because she knows that she just pressed the right button.

"Dammit," I rumble, tearing my mouth away from hers, and giving her that deep relentless pounding that's going to ride her straight over the finish line. "Beautiful – stubborn – woman," I grunt out, forearm leashed tight beneath her back so that I can hold her flush against my chest.

Her head drops back against the pillow giving me clear access to her neck and I hunch down the second I see it, sucking hungrily at her throat.

"I'm almost there," she whispers, moaning loudly when I squeeze her tits.

"I fucking know," I growl, temples throbbing as she holds me tighter, burying her face in the crook of my neck as I alternate between rubbing two fingers against her clit and massaging her nipples.

"Tanner, I'm gonna, I'm gonna–"

I move both of my hands so that they're positioned behind her knees, grip them firmly, and then shove them back against the pillow. That extra inch of cock that was too thick to slip inside has me grunting like an animal when I thrust it right to the hilt.

"Tanner!" she screams, tight and soaked, and her orgasm explodes, chest heaving as I pump her through it.

"That's it," I say gruffly as I shove my shoulders beneath her calves, keeping her legs hitched up against the pillows while freeing my hands so that they're free to roam. They go straight for her breasts and I grunt hard as I squeeze them.

"Need to come," I tell her, growling when her nails bite into my shoulder blades. My back muscles bunch tight as I roll harder and faster, driving her through her orgasm while I hang on to my last shred of self-control. "Can you take it?" I ask gruffly. "Just a couple hard thrusts, then I'll be done."

Her answering nod, plus the soft hands that caress my biceps, are the last things that I see before I clench my fists in the pillow and come.

I power into her, barely seeing as I lick at her jaw and bite at her neck. I remove one fist from the pillow so that I can grab her ass and keep her flush against me, my movements rough and deep as I spurt my load into the condom.

"Almost done," I grunt, holding her tighter as she falls limp beneath me. I find her mouth with mine and slip my tongue inside, groaning with pleasure as her body instinctively tightens.

I thrust once, twice, three more times, and then I drop heavily on top of her as she lets out a breathless whimper. I wince as I tug off the condom and then roll onto my back, panting hard as I drag her on top of me.

I leash both of my hands in her hair and pull her face down to mine so that I can kiss her. She wraps her arms around my neck but she lets me take the lead, her body small and warm, her butt too soft and perky to resist. I untangle one of my hands from her hair so that I can squeeze lovingly at her butt and she giggles into my mouth, making me smile as I kiss her.

I don't let her out of my arms for the entire night.

CHAPTER 30

Aisling

Present day

I wake up warm and cosy, surrounded by thick green sheets.

I tentatively push the quilt below my eyes so that I can peek out from the bed and take in my surroundings.

I blink, suddenly realising where I am.

The bed.

The bed that Tanner made for me.

My breathing hitches in my throat and it all comes flooding back to me.

Sinking my teeth into my lower lip I pull the sheets back over my face and glance down beneath the dark green canopy to see two big hockey player arms wrapped around my waist, firmly leashing me flush against his warm abdomen.

I stare down at his forearms for a beat. Then, with twitching fingers, I give him a little prod in the meaty bit.

Tanner's body tenses and then his arms are strengthening their hold, his broad chest swelling behind my back as he wakes himself up.

I turn around in his arms just as he rolls himself onto his back, pushing his digits through his hair as he tries to calm his breathing back to normal. One of his arms is still wrapped tightly around my lower back, clutching me against his side, and the second that he realises what he's holding his eyes snap open, flashing down to my face.

His chest enlarges to twice its size and his large biceps flex, his arm still lifted in the air where he's paused it mid-tug.

He blinks down at me in wide-eyed wonder and then his hand is shooting down beneath the quilt cover, fisting his length.

"Jesus Christ," he rasps, his morning voice a billion octaves deeper than usual. The hand that was resting on my lower back slides down over my behind, and he uses his grip to shove me up his chest.

"Ash," he murmurs, giving me a tired but handsome smile. "I can't believe that last night happened. I can't believe that I have you in my arms again."

The hand on my ass palms me harder, and then he's groaning as he slips his thick quad between my thighs, breathing out a pained laugh as he tosses himself faster beneath the sheets.

With a rugged sound from deep in his chest he tears his arm away from his erection, immediately tangling his fingers up in my hair as he rolls me onto my back and drops down on top of me.

I choke on a gasp as his rigid dick impales my stomach.

"Sorry," he murmurs quickly, lifting himself up onto his elbows. His morning wood is so long that it's still dragging heavily over my stomach. He gives me a slightly embarrassed smile and says, "I can put some clothes on if you want."

My cheeks flush pink as I whisper, "Not on my account."

He immediately laughs and gives me the most gorgeous grin, smile creases taut in his cheeks as his gaze rakes down my body. There's a playful glint in his eyes when he shoves himself up onto his haunches, stepping heavily down from the bed and rolling his large shoulders.

I sit up on my elbows and frown.

"Where are you going?" I ask, my voice light and breathless.

He sees my expression, chuckles quietly, and leans down to kiss me.

When he lifts up from towering over me he gently pushes the sheet from under my chin, letting it rest gently just above my breasts. His eyes flare with heat but he doesn't push the quilt any further.

Then his gaze lifts back to mine and he swipes a condom from the bedside table.

"Gonna workout," he rumbles gruffly.

I blink up at him. First in shock, then in horror.

"You're gonna what?" I breathe, lifting an eyebrow and hoping that I misheard him.

Tanner fists his thick cock with one hand and I go a little lightheaded as I glance down at it.

"Correction: *we're* gonna workout." He drops his erection, letting it hang hard and heavy between his thighs. "You're joining."

I gasp and place one of my hands over my heart.

"Tanner, that is the worst thing that you have ever said to me."

He smirks and gently eases the sheets from my body, keeping his eyes on mine as he leashes our fingers together.

"Not the kind of workout that you're thinking, baby," he murmurs, tugging me to my feet and then hunching down so that he can kiss my cheek.

I try not to flush too hard when he pulls away, his

mouth leaving a sparkling tingle in its wake.

"What kind of workout?" I mumble, looking up at him from under my lashes.

"You wanna know what kind of workout we're gonna do this morning?" he asks, his voice all deep morning gravel. He walks backwards so that I follow him out of the room, fingers warm and strong as he squeezes my hands with his.

I frown up at him in reply, not dignifying that stupid question with an answer.

He laughs quietly and in the next second I'm squealing, as he hauls me against his chest, pressing kisses all over my cheeks.

"Weights," he grunts, grinning as he bounces me in his arms. He gives my body an approving once-over before adding with a smirk, "A pretty tiny weight today though."

It takes me a moment to realise what he's really saying and when I do I'm giggling and trying to hide my smile.

Okay, that was cute.

I'm the workout.

Tanner's deep chuckle reverberates through my body and I cling onto him harder as he tries to find the room that he's looking for.

"Where are you taking me?" I ask him, looking over my shoulder.

"To Heaven, hopefully," he drawls, smirking as I roll my eyes. "Bathroom," he says finally, and I point my finger toward the correct door.

"Didn't you snoop around while I was trekking yesterday?" I ask him.

He sets me gently down on my feet as we reach the threshold.

"Hell no. Wouldn't have felt right. Had to keep goin' back and forth to the cabins when I needed to take a leak."

I breathe out a surprised laugh because that's… really thoughtful. In a kind of country boy way.

He herds me through the door but stops short the second that we're inside.

I feel heat rise to my cheeks because this is the first time that anyone has seen the bathroom's renovation.

"Jesus," Tanner rumbles, shoving his hand through his hair. I peek up at him as he takes in the room, nerves twisting in my gut.

His eyes instantly drop to mine and I almost look away from the intensity of his stare.

"You did all this?" he asks, his voice deep as he gestures to the wall behind me. "You did all of this on your own? In, what, a matter of weeks?"

I search his eyes warily before glancing over my shoulder at my handiwork.

There was a lot of plumbing and electrical work that had to be checked out when I hired in the contractors, but after that it was a matter of working the room into my own design. The whole lake house is walled with rich medium-brown wood, bar the shower right in front of us which I spent days turning into black-tiled perfection. It's sexy and intimate and exactly how I wanted it to be, and when I glance back up at Tanner I think that he might like it too.

I shake my hair out of my face and put on my most emotionless, business-like expression.

"What do you think?" I ask, my voice a little husky.

Tanner's palms settle on my waist, drawing me against him as he walks me backwards, further into the room.

"It's fucking beautiful, just like you." He grips my chin in his palm, tilts my head back and kisses me. His free hand slides down to my behind, massaging me roughly as his tongue caresses mine.

When he pulls away his big chest is heaving.

"Your parents are gonna be so fuckin' impressed."

I breathe out a nervous laugh and press my hands against his abdomen.

"Maybe," I laugh, "but this isn't really their thing. Small

towns, lake houses… that isn't where the money is."

Tanner strokes his thumb up my jaw, eyes too striking, too penetrative.

"But it's your thing," he rumbles. "And there is some money in it."

"Not the kind of money that they're after," I explain.

"But it's a market that they may as well be involved in, because if they aren't providing the properties then someone else will."

It's a good point, even though I can't be sure my parents will care.

I hum quietly down at my sparkly toes.

Tanner's fingers push gently beneath my chin, tilting my face up to his as he presses his body against mine.

"It's perfect," he tells me. "You did so fuckin' good."

I swallow and force myself to maintain his intimidating eye-contact.

"Thank you," I breathe shakily.

"You're welcome," he replies, his voice confident and hard.

A thought flashes through his eyes and he glances back at the shower before looking down at me again. His palms squeeze around my waist as I caress my hands over his chest.

"Did I tell you that, uh… did I tell you that the hockey team that I signed to is this one? The one in Larch Peak?"

I blink up at him in surprise. "No, I don't think that you told me that," I whisper.

He links his fingers through mine, eyes on our hands as he nods his head.

"Well, this is where I'm gonna be. In Larch Peak. Playing hockey."

"Okay," I whisper, my thoughts so loud that I swear he'll be able to hear them. "So, have you… bought a place here yet, or are you still looking around?"

"Still looking around," he answers immediately, eyes

shooting back to mine. "What about you? Do you know where you're gonna move to?"

I shake my head, the tension in the room almost too much to handle.

Maybe I'll move back home to where my parents are, or maybe I could move to be close to Connell. But the fact of the matter is that there's nowhere I need to be.

If my parents let me take up my dream role in their company then the majority of the job is going to be in individual small towns, my home base permanently in flux.

But it would be pretty nice to have a place to call home.

Tanner looks down at me, eyes burning, and then nods once – silently letting me know that he'll drop the subject… for now.

Suddenly we catch movement over to the side and Tanner quickly turns to his left, brow lifting in surprise. When he sees our reflections looking back at us in the vanity mirror above the sink, his handsome smile meets mine, mouth lifting into a smirk.

I breathe out a giggle when he pushes his broad chest against my face and I shove at his pecs, the height difference giving me butterflies.

He quickly wraps his forearms around my middle and hauls me even closer, growling when my pinch-happy fingers hover dangerously close to his nipple.

"Do it, I fucking dare you," he rumbles, a barely veiled threat, and then he's stumbling forward, groaning as I pinch him hard and tight.

"*Aisling*," he rasps, heaving me up by my ass, and kissing me long and deep before turning us back to face the mirror.

"Look at how pretty you are," he murmurs deeply, as I stroke gently over his stubble. "Way too pretty to take pipe from a brute like me."

"Tanner!" I exclaim in surprise, giggling as he presses a rough kiss against my lips.

"Am I wrong?" he rumbles, chest heaving as he stares

315

down at me. "Look at yourself, Ash. You're so beautiful it's crazy."

I glance over my shoulder to look at us in the mirror and the physical contradictions only make me love him more. He looks every bit the bad boy hockey player that I spent four years knowing him to be, only now I also know that he's a secret sweetheart.

"You know that you're the hottest guy I've ever seen, right?" I ask, arching an eyebrow because I'm genuinely curious. "You're all muscles and smile creases, and your neck's so thick that I wanna, like… sink my teeth into it."

Tanner swipes his tongue over his lower lip, grinning lazily down at me.

Okay, someone definitely did *not* need to have their ego stroked.

I'm still mid eye-roll as he drawls, "God, baby, you're right. Former junior year hockey captain and former senior year cheer captain? You're fuckin' made for me, Ash. Sink your teeth into my neck, right now."

I huff out a laugh, shoving him off of me as he squeezes my ass.

"You're also way too cocky for your own good," I add, squealing when he herds me into the shower, slapping on the spray and shielding me from the instant downpour.

He presses my back against the wall, steam haloing his shoulders as he smirks down at me.

"One of the perils of having such a giant cock."

I burst into a fit of laughter as he crushes his mouth down on mine, his tongue sliding deep as the water begins pelting hard against his skin.

He cages me in with one of his forearms, resting his fist just above my head, and he rubs his tongue faster against mine, grunting as he shoves his other hand between my legs.

I gasp in shock as he rubs my clit, my fingers digging into his shoulders as heat floods my body. He rubs me fast and thorough, tearing his mouth from mine so that he can watch himself touch me.

"So hot," he rasps, rubbing faster as he kisses his way down to my breasts. He licks over each of my nipples, ripping hungry growls from deep in his chest.

When he starts scraping over me with his stubble I can't take it anymore.

"Tanner," I gasp, "if you're trying to get me wet, you r-really don't have to. I don't know if you can tell but I... I'm already—"

"I can tell," he grunts. "Trust me, I can tell."

My cheeks flush crimson as Tanner kisses me again, his arm pumping relentlessly between my unsteady thighs.

I arch my back against the tiled wall, my fingers digging into Tanner's shoulders, and he drops his forehead to the curve of my neck, breathing heavily.

"Tanner," I pant, my voice a whisper beneath the spray, "you d-don't have to do that... we can... we can just—"

And suddenly I'm whimpering as he shoves his entire palm against my clit, rubbing it roughly as he hunches down and sucks hard on one of my nipples.

"Tanner!" I gasp. "I'm going to... to, like, *explode*," I squeak, fingers yanking at his hair and making him growl as he stands upright to tower over me.

He jerks his chin at me and if I was wearing panties right now it's safe to say that they would have melted right off of me.

"Good," he rumbles. "That's what I was going for."

I rake my nails down his chest and his shoulders swell, his abdomen clenching. My vision blurs into a haze of black tiles, silver steam, and Tanner's perfect sun-kissed body as he shoves his palm against me harder, his jaw muscles bunched tight as he drives me over the edge.

"Don't stop, don't stop," I whisper quickly, and Tanner all but comes with me, gripping the base of his erection on a loud guttural groan, tossing himself roughly as he watches me come undone.

"Fuck," he rasps as soon as I'm done, slipping his tongue inside my mouth while simultaneously hitching my hips around his. "Condom," he murmurs as he pushes the shower door open, quickly snatching the black foil square from the sink and tearing it open with his teeth.

"Ohhhhh my God," I whisper as he spits out the wrapper, and he flashes me that cocky smirk as he carries me back inside the shower. He shoulders the door shut, drops me to the floor, and keeps his eyes on mine as he starts fisting the muscle between his thighs.

His eyes slowly rake their way down my body and then work their way back up, stopping when he reaches my chest and using that point to start rolling on the condom.

"Last night meant so much to me," he murmurs when he finishes rolling it on, pulling me flush against his chest and then walking me backward so that I'm up against the wall. "You mean so much to me."

I press the back of my hand against my cheeks, feeling dizzy and lightheaded.

"It's way too hot in here," I whisper breathlessly, "for, like, a couple of different reasons."

Tanner shakes his head and gives me that handsome grin, before easily scooping me up in his arms so that we're chest to chest, and positioning his hips exactly how he wants between my thighs.

"Can I make it hotter?" he asks gruffly, fisting his cock and rubbing it against me.

I press my palm to my forehead. "I don't know if I can take it," I wheeze.

His breathing is turning heavy, chest pumping hard in the increasing steam. "Want me to stop?" he murmurs, his erection flexing against my heat.

Cocky façade aside, Tanner's the most considerate man that I've ever met.

I arch my body up against his and he grits his teeth, his

self-control rippling.

"I don't want you to stop," I whisper and he's instantly groaning, kissing me hard while he nudges his hard muscle between my thighs. He pushes my legs a little farther back and then he's dropping his forehead to mine, meeting my gaze in a hot and heavy silent question.

I nod my head quickly and he grunts as he thrusts inside.

"*Aisling,*" he growls, and he pulls out long and slow, wrapping one of his palms around the side of my throat as he shoves it back in.

"Tanner," I gasp, my back sliding against the hot wall, condensation slipping over my nipples as he thrusts in harder and harder.

"Is this alright?" he rasps, his voice hoarse and eyes heavy. "I'm not... not crushing you, am I?"

I choke out a little laugh and he laughs quietly with me, brow arched in pleasure-pain as he takes my mouth with his.

"You mean everything to me," he pants as he presses his forehead down on mine. "I can't wait to get you in my tent tonight. Can't wait to slow-fuck you in the middle of the forest."

I suck in a sharp inhalation and my head drops back against the dark tiles. Tanner clutches his forearm tighter around my lower back, his other hand gripping firmly at my nape. He pumps me harder and faster against the shower wall.

"Just gonna say it," he rumbles, shoulder muscles bunching as he thrusts deeper. "I've fantasised about us doing this so many times. After every training session, every game — always had this fantasy that I'd sneak you into the locker room with me and take you right there in the shower stall, our little secret."

He presses a kiss against my lips, warm and gentle as his palm grips my jaw.

When he pulls back to stare down at me I look up at

him from under my lashes, my fingers tight at the back of his neck and he rolls into me harder.

"I'm sorry for fighting this for so long," I whisper.

He shakes his head. "Don't be. You were real good at it."

I breathe out a laugh but still feel my cheeks grow warmer, my eyes stinging with tears.

"I'm serious," he rumbles, his voice deep and slurring. "Don't apologise, baby."

"We spent four years apart," I whisper. "That was all my fault."

"Four years is nothing. You're the rest of my life."

I squeeze my eyes shut, heart fluttering when he meets my lips with his. He kisses me so sweetly, so unlike how he's moving between my thighs. Rough, rugged thrusts that have him moving both palms to grip my behind, his hands squeezing gruffly as he kisses me soft and warm.

"You done feeling sorry for yourself now?" he murmurs, hips driving faster.

I gasp and scowl up at him, a teasing smirk tugging at his lips.

"Jerk," I whisper, but I can't stop my little smile, and when his chest swells contentedly I realise how much he means to me too. I arch my neck, wanting to kiss him, and seeing my little struggle he grins and leans down.

He licks his tongue against mine, one hand roaming up to my breasts as I begin squirming.

"You're gonna come," he rumbles, voice low and matter-of-fact. He looks down at my breasts, squeezes one, and grunts quietly.

"Y-yeah," I whisper, nodding my head as he caresses me.

"I still wanna fuck you in the locker room," he says, eyes burning as he thrusts harder. "When I start playing pro this fall, you're gonna come to my games. I'm gonna take you like this."

"Th-that's definitely not going to be allowed," I whisper, "but, like, okay."

Tanner grins before growling roughly against my throat, sinking his teeth into my neck as he bounces me hard on his hockey player thighs.

"Tanner!" I squeal, and then it's all happening at once, my toes curling and my abdomen tightening as my body explodes in unending pleasure.

Tanner releases his teeth from my throat, licking the area while he continues pounding me.

"I'm there, baby," he murmurs, pinning one forearm above my head, hips thrusting frantically. "Right behind you."

I choke out a tiny laugh. "W-well, technically you're not *behind* me—"

The sound that rips from Tanner's throat is so rough that my nipples pinch, and I squeal as he thrusts me straight into another orgasm.

His big palm grips into my behind, massages it gruffly, and then gives it a spank.

I squeeze the large muscles of his chest, gasping and sighing as he ejaculates.

"I can't wait to take you like that," he rasps, biceps flexing as he shudders. "Layin' you down on your belly and makin' love to you from the back."

"Oh my God," I whimper, biting my teeth into my lower lip. "You have got to stop with the dirty talk or I'm going to be on, like, orgasm number four."

Tanner huffs out a pained laugh as he thrusts slowly inside of me, jerking rougher every few seconds when he releases another long spurt.

When he finally stops shuddering he pushes my back against the wall, holding me tight against his chest as the water cascades around us, warm and never-ending.

CHAPTER 31

Tanner

Present day

After spending all of last night and this morning giving orgasms to the hottest girl that I've ever seen, I can't deny that I'm feeling pretty fucking incredible.

Aisling's currently sashaying up the mountain's incline at about ten feet ahead of me, occasionally throwing impassive little glances over her shoulder as the guys and I trail behind her.

As if I don't have her nail marks all over my chest.

She flashes those dismissive vixen eyes in my direction while Fallon and Winter talk on either side of her, and I give her a quick jerk of my chin, forearms flexing as I give her a once-over. I've got four bags in each fist slung back over my shoulders, six carrying either tents or camping equipment and the others belonging to Miss Two-Hundred-Dollar Panties in front of me.

Seeing as most of Aisling's belongings are extremely expensive, the group collectively decided to help her bring most of her stuff with us while we're camping up the mountain – just in case any shit was to happen down at the lake while we aren't there. It's unlikely that it would but it's better to be safe than sorry.

And I don't mind carrying half of Aisling's possessions, especially when some of them are of the lacy-variety.

Aisling lifts a hand above her eyes, shielding them from the bright morning rays, and then turns back to face the make-shift trail, a wooden post that the girls just walked past signalling the opening of the campsite just ahead.

It only takes another two minutes and then we're breaching the clearing.

There's a large National Parks bathroom situated inconspicuously to the camp's edge in deep brown wood, but the remainder of the space is a bright open expanse.

The clearing is so large that the trees can't eclipse the canopy overhead, meaning that there's plenty of sunlight pouring through to make the area a perfect suntrap.

We start dropping our gear into the centre of the clearing, where previous campers' make-shift seating logs are still hauled into the middle. There's a medium-sized circle of rocks beside them that they must have used to set a small controlled campfire inside. It's cute.

Then we itinerate who's sleeping where and start hauling the tents into a large circle, although the area of it is quickly swallowed up by the size of the gear.

Because the clearing may be big but our tents are damn massive.

Ash and Fallon would have been sharing the tent that they brought to Larch Peak, but seeing as Hunter bought the store's worth of camping gear, Fallon is now going to be bunking with her boyfriend. Meaning that I'm going to have a tent to myself and, even more importantly, so is Aisling.

I catch her eyes across the clearing while I'm crouched down unzipping the tent and I can't help but flash her a small smile, my chest expanding at the sight of her. She's sat in the centre of the campsite soaking up the sun with Fallon, long legs stretched out across the length of the log while she rests her palms behind her back. The golden summer rays make heat flood to her cheeks, so she's flushed a pretty shade of pink while she smiles back at me.

I glance to the other guys setting up their sticks around the campsite, and then I'm getting to my feet, rolling my shoulders, and just thinking *fuck it*. Aisling's tent is rolled up right beside her and there is no way that I'm setting mine up before I've done hers. Doesn't matter who's watching.

I should be the one to do it for her.

And if that secretive smile on her lips is anything to go by she can tell exactly what I'm thinking, her eyes sparkling wildly as she arches her neck in the sun, her body golden and glowing.

I keep my eyes locked on hers without needing to say anything, a satisfied feeling in my chest as she watches me grab her tent and haul it over my shoulder.

"Hey," I rumble as I grip one hand over the tent bag, re-shifting it on my shoulder as I flick a wary glance across to Fallon. I'm not sure how much Aisling has told her – if anything – so I'm not sure of how I'm supposed to play this. Although from the way that Fallon currently looks as if she's about to explode with excitement, I'm pretty sure that she may be in the know.

Aisling drapes one leg over the other and I try not to get hard as I look down at her thighs.

"Hey," Aisling replies, all husky and casual, swishing her hair out over her shoulders and drawing my attention back to her neck.

I shove my free hand through my hair and take another step closer.

"Where'd you want your tent?" I ask, unable to stop

myself from smiling as Aisling lifts up and stands to her feet in front of me. I might be the one towering over her but it's pretty obvious who's really in control here.

Aisling gives me a little smile and says, "As far away from yours as possible, I suppose."

I huff out a laugh, tongue in my cheek as her pretty eyes sparkle up at me.

Yeah, yeah. I want Aisling's tent right next to mine so that I can sneak over tonight without drawing anyone's attention.

I lower my voice so that Fallon can't hear us, assuming that maybe that's why Ash is putting on her little *we're still enemies* pretence.

"Real funny," I murmur. "But seriously. Where should we set this up?"

"Seriously," she replies. "I want it opposite yours."

I blink down at her beautiful face, no longer sure if she's kidding. And then when she gives me that taunting raise of her eyebrow I know for sure that she *isn't* kidding.

"Baby," I rasp quickly, eyes widening as I search her face. "I meant what I said this morning. I want you in my tent tonight," I whisper quietly.

"Ooh, what happened this morning?" Fallon asks, grinning.

I shoot her a look before returning my attention back to my beautiful soon-to-be girlfriend.

"I know," Aisling whispers back to me, "but I'm not ready for people to know yet. I'm still not, you know…"

I lift my eyebrows, my heart subtly tearing at the seams.

"You're still not what?" I rasp. "You're still not sure?"

"I'm sure about *you*," Aisling whispers quickly, and I sigh quietly with relief. No longer caring if anyone's watching, I entwine my free hand with hers. "But I'm still not sure about what I'm doing, or where I'm going to live for what I'm doing. So I need to be sure about all of that before we do anything… official."

I take a deep breath and swallow, my chest still pumping hard after that moment of uncertainty.

"No-one'll see, baby," I murmur, shooting Fallon another look when she perks up on her log. "And anyone who does see will be *sworn to secrecy*," I add pointedly, making Fallon smile up at me, smug as hell.

I look back down to Aisling and squeeze her beautiful hand in mine.

"If I put your tent next to mine then it'll be easier to sneak over tonight with no-one seeing. And I wanna hold you, Ash. All night."

Please don't make me go without you again.

She smiles up at me all confident and beautiful, making me feel exactly the way that she did when we met four years ago.

Speechless. Love-struck. Willing to do anything for her.

She squeezes her fingers around mine and I grunt, tugging her closer.

"Fine," I rumble. "I'll set your tent opposite mine. But don't think for one second that I'm happy about it."

I drop her hand so that I can give her perfect waist a subtle squeeze, and then I'm trudging my way to the opposite side of the camp. I haul Aisling's tent down in the space between Connell's and Logan's, and then I glance at her over my shoulder while I start unzipping the carrier.

The smile that she's biting back is naughty as hell, but knowing that her eyes are on me has me working like a machine.

When I've finally set the whole tent up I start un-bagging quilts and sheets, padding out her tent to make sure that it's soft enough for her to sleep on.

Then, after checking that the guys are too busy either throwing around Logan's football or watching game footage on their phones to notice, I slip her new battery-operated fairy lights from the bottom of one of the bags, twining the string through the pole-loops in the fabric so that later tonight she can switch them on before she goes to sleep. I flip the switch to check that the batteries are still working and, seeing that they are, I turn them back off. I set the power-pack on one of her cushions, and then hunch out of the tent, re-zipping the door before I stretch in the sunlight.

The guys have finished setting up their tents when I get back to mine, although Hunter and Austin are currently half-building it for me.

The other half of their concentration is going on murdering Logan at his own sport.

"Career change?" I suggest to Logan with a smirk, grinning when he launches the football right at me. I grab it with one hand and send it flying back in his direction.

He grins back at me, eyes sliding down to my precariously half-formulated tent. The football twitches tauntingly in his fists.

I splay one hand in front of the tent poles and laugh, "Leave my tent alone, man."

But before he can launch into a full attack the four of us instantly go silent as Aisling – my beautiful secret girlfriend – walks my way.

Like, she's walking right over to me. In front of everyone.

She flicks a smile over at Austin that has the fucker turning to mush and then she's right in front of me, pushing a hand through her hair before shielding her eyes from the sun.

A sliver of a ray manages to slip through her fingers, setting her irises aflame and shimmering like diamonds.

"Thanks for setting up my tent," she says, that husky voice making my biceps flex.

I grip a hand at the back of my neck and rasp, "Thank you – I mean, you're welcome." *Oh God.* "I mean, it's no problem. Like, thank you for, uh, thanking me."

Hunter lets out a low whistle.

Austin mumbles, "Oh boy."

Aisling breathes out a laugh, that perfect smile sparkling in the sunshine.

"You're welcome," she says, teasing the shit out of me, but it still makes me grin like that love-struck freshman, the hand that isn't at the back of my neck gripping firmly around my belt.

I shoot a quick glance at the guys behind her, who are looking at literally anywhere other than us, and I take a careful step forward, not wanting to breach the distance between kind-of-friendly and we're-fucking when we're not disclosing that publically yet.

She arches her eyebrow at me under the shield of her hand and suddenly a thought flashes through my mind, making me smirk down at her.

"You need a cap?" I ask, and her breathing halts.

Her eyes momentarily widen. *Yeah, I thought so.*

She tries to shake it off by rasping, "Um, I didn't bring one."

My smirk widens as I deadpan, "Didn't you now."

She blinks up at me, unsure, assessing, and then in the next second her cheeks are burning scarlet.

She glances hastily over her shoulder – checking that the guys aren't looking – and then she spins back around to give me a rough slap across the pecs.

I grunt quietly, grinning like an idiot.

"Knew it," I rumble.

"How the *hell* did you know?"

"Caught a glance of something khaki in your bags two months ago," I smile.

I knew it the second that I saw it. When I was helping Aisling carry her bags into the lake house, I could have sworn that I saw the khaki cap I used to wear religiously. Then, after we hooked up, it never made its way back to me.

No way did I imagine that she'd keep it but it feels really

fucking good knowing that she did.

I lower my voice. "And until recently," I murmur, looking pointedly at her panty-region, "I'm pretty sure you didn't have anything khaki of your own."

She gasps, indignant, and scowls up at me.

"You weren't supposed to know that I'd kept it," she whispers, glowering straight into the centre of my pecs. Then she shoots me a look and says, "You shouldn't have been snooping. Snooper."

"Hey, I wasn't snoopin'," I drawl, laughing quietly at her expression. "You didn't zip your bags up and something familiar caught my eye."

I check that no-one is looking and hunch down to whisper against her ear.

"Little thief," I rumble quietly.

A shiver ripples through her body and she gasps, shoving me back.

"Am I wrong?" I ask roughly, moving so close that her chin is almost resting against my chest. "Or did you save a little souvenir even though you supposedly 'hated' me?"

"What was I supposed to do?" she whispers. "Throw it out?"

I grin down at her because, if you hated someone, that's exactly what you would do.

She reads my thoughts as we look into each other's eyes and then she folds her arms over her chest, breathing out a huff.

"I just... I liked it, okay? Your cap, I mean. When you left it I... I tried it on. It fits me just right."

I rub my palm over my smirk and murmur, "I know something else of mine that fits you just right."

Aisling's knees give way and I laugh quietly as I wrap my palms around her biceps, stabilising her.

When she risks another glance up at me my heart clenches, warm and tight.

"You can deny it all you want, but I love the fact that

you kept it, Aisling. That you wanted to use it." I lower my voice and murmur, "And honestly? I like it because you keeping that cap tells me everything that I need to know. That despite all the shit that happened, deep down, you liked me. Through it all."

She looks up at me with those big beautiful eyes and doesn't deny a thing.

It's all the confirmation that I need.

She's always been mine.

"Do I get to keep it?" she asks, less frowny now but still unsure.

I nod down at her and my heart clenches.

"Yeah," I smile. "It's yours. Always has been."

CHAPTER 32

Tanner

Present day

Ash has been wearing that khaki cap all night.

No-one knows that it's mine except for Hunter, and the second that she put it on this morning he was grinning at me from across the fire-pit. I held my palms in the air and smirked right back.

Now it's nightfall, we just finished eating a batch of team-made tacos, and the guys – buzzed off a couple of sixers – are getting loud as hell. But I've tuned out of the conversation, only paying it the briefest attention when one of the guys talks to me directly, because I'm way too preoccupied with taking in the sight of my cap set low over Aisling's pretty eyes.

Even though she said it fit her just right, I can tell that it's too big for her – I mean, what else is new. But I'm obsessed with the sight of it. The shadow that it casts over her sultry vixen eyes makes those glances that she keeps throwing me look even darker, more dangerous. I've barely been able to look away from her for pretty much the past four hours.

I roll the can in my hands between my palms, setting my elbows on my knees while I give her another once-over across the fire.

Ash has got hiking boots on her feet, socks rolled down to her ankles, exposing her flawless golden legs. She changed out of her long pink sundress just before we ate, which means that she's now wearing a matching soft grey lounge set – a fitted cami wrapped over her chest and a pair of shorts barely hitting her mid-thigh. And I am not fucking complaining. Add on the khaki cap sitting low over her eyes and I've had to restrain the hard-on in my jeans roughly every five minutes.

Now her fingers are twiddling with the small bag in her lap while she laughs at something Tristan just whispered to her. Because, yeah, that fucker is sat right next to her.

Her brother's teammate Logan is on one side and Tristan is on the other, which I'll admit is making my jaw twitch because they have no business breathing air with her. But I just let my quads hammer it out, my knees bouncing like crazy as I steal glances at Ash and wish that it was me making her laugh right now.

I crack the top off the can and drain half of it in one long pull. Then I get back to rolling the metal between my palms, unable to stop looking at her for longer than half a minute.

When she catches me looking I feel my chest lock and tighten, and I give her a quick jerk of my chin before dropping my eyes back to the dirt.

It's only when Hunter shoves his elbow into my side that I glance up again, heat twisting in my abdomen when I see that there's now an empty space beside her.

I flick my eyes over to Tristan who is currently

scratching the back of his neck, eyes on his boots. It's only when he glances up and offers me a cautious half-smile that I realise that he left Ash's side so that *I* could take that place instead.

Tristan is a great guy. Like, one of my favourite teammates.

I'm on my feet in less than a second.

I practically break his wrist when we smack our hands together, a gratitude handshake that turns into a rough half-hug.

"You are so fuckin' whipped," he chuckles when we shove away from each other.

"Yeah," I admit, raking a hand back through my hair, eyes on Aisling as she watches us from under the brim of my cap.

I clear my throat and give him a departing nod before making my way over to Aisling.

With the exception of the crackling orange fire, the night is pitch black, and filled with the loud laughter of our friends, everyone warm and beer-drunk.

After sparing a glance to the guys currently hollering at some game footage on Connell's phone, I drop down next to Aisling, nestling my boot right up against hers. She squeezes her thighs together and I press my quad against her harder.

She looks up at me from under the cap, her head barely reaching the swell of my shoulder, and I hold the heated stare of her eyes while I splay my palm on her lower back.

"You tryna make me jealous?" I murmur gruffly. I jerk my chin in the direction that my new best friend Tristan just walked away in.

She flutters her lashes at me and teases, "Why, is it working?"

"Yeah," I grunt immediately, pressing my palm against her more firmly. "Haven't been able to take my eyes off of you all night. Especially when you're wearing…" I trail off and let my eyes roam to the cap pulled low over her eyes. I give the brim a gentle nudge with my beer and feel my heart-rate pick up when she laughs quietly, a dimple popping in her cheek.

I drain another pull from my can and glance down at the baby pink bag that she's still fiddling with in her lap.

It's one of those small travel bags that chicks store miniature soap bottles and shit in, and for some reason I find myself really adamant to know what she's got in there.

I clear my throat and jab my finger at the bag.

"What's in your… bathroom purse?" I ask roughly, narrowing my eyes when she immediately zips it up.

She gives me a naughty little smile that has me shifting my body on the log. There's no way I can readjust what's happening in my jeans while her brother is barely five feet away from us so I just send up a prayer that I won't die from this hard-on and let my eyes continue raking her up and down.

"Just girly things," she whispers, teasing and coy as hell.

I slide my palm lower down her back, check that the guys are too busy laughing to notice us, and then I dip my fingers below her waistband, breathing hard when they snag her panties.

I'm thinking about kissing the soft lobe of her ear when a sudden thought occurs to me.

"Baby," I whisper, "where'd your earrings go?"

Aisling has been wearing this pair of diamond earrings for pretty much the whole summer – hell, I'm pretty sure she wore them during most of our senior year, too. But a little over a week ago she suddenly stopped wearing them.

Aisling makes a small squeaking sound.

I glance down at her, arching my brow in a gentle question.

"Um," she whispers, her eyes fucking gigantic as she peeks up at me.

I breathe out a laugh. "What is it?" I murmur, not

understanding that reaction.

"Are you sure that you wanna know?" she asks quietly, which instantly has my heart rate kicking up a notch.

"…Yeah," I rumble, even though now I'm a little nervous.

She pushes her hair back from her shoulder, looking almost as nervous as I am.

"Fine," she breathes out. "They were a gift from Brennan, my ex. I guess that I thought it was time to stop wearing them."

I blink down at her for a moment in total fucking silence.

Because… that's a good thing. She stopped wearing a gift from her ex boyfriend, meaning that he's no longer of importance to her.

And maybe that's partially because of me. Maybe it's because she wants the two of us to get serious. Maybe she–

"Hold up." I pull back, heart thundering. "What did you say that his name was again?"

Aisling peers up at me, a tiny frown on her nervous brow.

"…Brennan," she says, because she's probably wondering why the hell that's of interest to me.

Oh my God.

I'll tell you why it's of interest to me.

Because when I almost got my ankle broken this year, before the Frozen Four final?

The player who did it was fucking called *Brennan*.

I'm so damn shocked that my jaw practically hits my boots.

"Are you fuckin' kidding me?" I ask, my voice deep and hushed.

"…No?" she says, looking confused. Can't blame her.

"Did he play hockey?" I ask, already knowing the answer.

Her cheeks instantly flame, and she drops her eyes,

mumbling, "Um, maybe."

"Holy shit." I genuinely cannot believe this. "That motherfucker almost broke my damn ankle."

Aisling peeks up at me, blushes harder, then looks back down.

A million thoughts crash into me at once.

Aisling broke up with her boyfriend before my ankle got sprained.

And I never knew who Aisling was dating because she has no social media.

But that doesn't mean that they didn't know about me.

Jesus Christ. Did her ex try to break my ankle because Aisling had broken up with him?

Was *I* part of the reason *why* she broke up with him?

I don't even have to say it out loud. Aisling can sense every thought whipping through my mind right now.

"He knew about me." I say it like a fact, because it is one. "He knew about *us*. Like" – I lick my bottom lip – "the fact that we'd been together, and that we had unfinished business."

Aisling breathes out a shaky exhale. "Maybe," she whispers.

Holy shit.

Holy shit.

Maybe I should be mad about it, but honestly I'm kind of stoked.

Because Aisling's ex knowing about me? It means that she hadn't gotten over us.

It means that Aisling liked me *this whole time.*

She watches me nervously, like she thinks I might be pissed about this.

I'm shocked, sure. But this is actually great for me.

"I'm not mad," I murmur, and she instantly relaxes.

I brush her panties with my fingers again, getting hard as she moves a little closer.

"I'm sorry, anyway," she whispers back to me. "I didn't

mean for anything bad to happen to you."

I grunt and spread my quads wider. I kind of like it when she's concerned about me.

"Don't worry about it," I murmur, feeling the air between us grow warmer.

Between Aisling's panties brushing my fingers and me learning that she's been into me this whole time? I'm well and truly turned the hell on right now.

"I'm turning in for the night," she says suddenly, eyes sliding up to mine with a dangerous glint in them.

My brow lifts in disappointment, hand hungrily fisting the back of her panties.

"Already?" I ask quietly, my voice rough as my eyes search hers. "Baby, I want more time with you," I murmur, well aware that she already told me that we won't be sharing a tent tonight. If that means that the only time I'm going to get with her tonight is by the campfire when we're surrounded by our friends then so be it – but it can't be over already when I haven't even had five minutes with her yet.

"I just think I should get to bed," she explains, eyes flicking over to where her brother, the star quarterback, is currently shaking with laughter over something that Austin just shouted to him. She lifts her big eyes back to mine and says, "I'll see you in the morning."

Before I can argue with her she swiftly reaches up to press a tiny heart-stopping kiss on my cheek, her breasts rubbing over my chest when she leans in to give it to me. I bunch my fist in her panties tighter, giving her a quick squeeze over her shorts before letting her go completely, and then I stare after her, fully-erect and dying, while she takes her sweet time walking that ass over to the wooden bathroom hut.

I shove my free hand through my hair while I stare at the wooden structure, wondering if she's being fucking serious, or if this is some kind of game that I don't know how to play. I'm no good at games when it comes to women – I've always been candid from the outset, what you see is what you get. There's no room for miscommunication because I will have already stated my intentions loud and clear.

Like when I first met Aisling and I told her that I wanted to date the fuck out of her – that I wanted to earn that pussy – I meant it. Same applies to when I was a senior in high school and everyone was just experimenting with hook-ups: we knew it from the outset, that it was just going to be a hook-up.

But now I'm confused. Does she want me to, like… follow her into the bathroom so that we can have a part two from this morning? 'Cause that sounds really fucking good to me. Or does she actually just want to go to bed? I mean, she said *I'll see you in the morning*, so that must be what she wanted, right?

I rub my hand down my jaw, knees bouncing as I decipher what she said.

There's no way that she meant for me to follow her to the bathroom – it's way too obvious, especially in front of her brother. But, at the same time, she did give me a kiss on the cheek, and she would obviously know that rubbing her tits on me would get me hungry for more.

Does she want me to go to her tent? Did she want me to sneak in there while no-one was looking?

It's been around fifteen minutes by the time that I push up to my feet, having been unable to see her leave the bathroom because it's so damn dark. Instead I clap my fist with Logan's, grab my can, and then take another sip while I pull my phone out of my jeans.

I type out a quick text to Aisling saying: *baby, I'm heading to my tent right now. Let me know if you want me to sneak over to yours – everyone's buzzed, they won't see a thing.*

Then I push it back in my pocket and make my way to my edge of the site.

I kick off my boots as I reach my tent, draining the rest of my beer as I hunch low and unzip the door.

I pull back the fabric and immediately stumble forward.

"Holy fuck," I rasp hoarsely, eyes wide as I take her in.

Because Aisling didn't go to her tent. She came into *mine*. And she's currently getting cosy on my sleeping bag wearing nothing but hiking socks, black lingerie, and *my fucking cap*.

She drops the book that she had in her hands – *my* book, for fuck's sake – and sets herself up onto her elbows while scraping her tip-toes down my heaving chest.

I don't even question it. Not wanting to draw any attention from the guys laughing loudly around the fire-pit I just crush the can in my fist, toss it, and then muscle my shoulders through the small unzipped door.

As soon as I'm inside I quickly yank the zipper shut and then Aisling is climbing up onto her knees, wrapping her arms around my shoulders when I duck down to kiss her.

I make a deep pleasured sound before pulling away and looking down at her. I pull my shirt off over my head, throwing it to the side before I grab her waist and pull her closer. Then I take the cap off her head and set it down on mine, twisting it backwards so that I can kiss her easier.

I cup both of my palms around her jaw, searching her eyes wildly before taking her mouth with mine.

"You planned this," I rumble, hands roaming down to her ass and squeezing tight. "This morning, when I told you that I wanted you in my tent with me and you said no."

I kiss her again, harder, and then give her a firm spank on the ass.

"Had me stressin' all day, baby," I rasp. "Had me pining for you across the damn fire-pit."

"I'm an evil mastermind," she teases breathlessly, one of her hands tugging roughly at my belt buckle.

I make a rough sound as I help her fumble that shit open.

"You're fuckin' beautiful is what you are," I murmur, hissing through my teeth when she works my jeans and boxer-briefs down my quads. My cock hangs long and hard between my thighs and I wrap my fist around the base, tossing quickly.

The campfire outside is the only source of light in the area and it lights up the orange tent way more brightly than I was expecting. Not wanting the guys to see our shadows in the firelight I wrap her thighs around my lap and push her firmly onto her back.

"Why'd you have a book on constellations?" she whispers, breathless and sparkly-eyed.

My cheeks heat the fuck up because obviously there's only one reason why a guy who's camping with a girl that he's into would have bought a book on constellations.

I grunt quietly as I rub my shoulder against my jaw, willing away some of the heat rushing up my neck. She smiles up at me, gorgeous and pleased, and I growl roughly as I slip my tongue into her mouth.

"You know why," I rumble, squeezing her ass when she giggles prettily.

"You wanted to woo me with your encyclopaedic knowledge of the constellations," she whispers, chest heaving almost as fast as mine as I pull away to look down at her.

"Yeah," I admit, questioning the hell out of my logic. It was meant to be romantic but now I'm thinking it was stupid.

But she just smiles brighter, both her dimples popping, and I can't stop myself from dropping down on top of her and working her tongue with mine.

"You're a romantic," she whispers, and I grunt as I kiss my way down her neck.

"For you, yeah." I drop my forehead to her shoulder and wrap those skimpy bra straps around my fists. "How'd you even get in here?" I ask, panting against her throat as I give the lace another twist.

"I half-crawled through the edge of the trees," she whispers, giggling wildly at my horrified expression. I pull back to inspect her knees and shove a hand through my hair when I realise that she wasn't kidding. She obviously didn't go on her hands and knees around the whole way but there's small scuffs of dirt here and there that have me thinking that she was pretty close to the ground.

I brush away a small scuff of dirt with my thumb while kissing gently at her inner thigh. "You didn't have to do that for me," I murmur.

"I thought you liked me on my hands and knees."

I splay my palms on either side of her head and look her hard in the eyes. She flutters her lashes innocently up at me, only swallowing nervously when she feels my shaft flex against her belly.

I search her flaming eyes for a few long moments before wrapping one of my hands through the back of her hair, gently lowering my mouth to hers. I kiss her slow and deep, growling when she wraps her arms around the breadth of my shoulders.

"I do like you on your hands and knees," I rasp, sliding my other hand beneath her back and gripping my fist around the fastening of her bra. "Did, uh…" I swallow hard. "Did you like that? When we did it before?"

"Yeah," she whispers breathlessly and my shoulders swell on instinct, my digits twitching in the lace and accidentally yanking the closure open.

"Sorry," I grunt quickly, as her bra slips slightly, now that it's no longer strapped in place.

"It's okay," she whispers, gentle fingers holding my wrist when I try to push it back into place. "You don't need to refasten it. You can take it off."

"You sure?" I ask gruffly, and the second that she nods that shit is on the other side of the tent, exposing her breasts to me while I massage my palms around her waist.

"Jesus," I murmur, hunching down so that I can taste them.

Her hands fly up to my nape, nails digging in as she pants shakily.

"Can't believe that you snuck into my tent," I rumble, tongue lapping faster against her nipples. "You snuck into my tent so that I'd fuck you, didn't you?"

She arches her neck back and teases, "What are you, a mind reader?"

I huff a laugh against her chest, sucking her roughly when she meets my eyes. Then I shove both of my palms underneath her breasts, pushing them up as I tower over her.

"God, you're funny," I murmur, smirking as I brush my thumbs over her nipples. "You drive me crazy, you know that? I get so hard when you give me that attitude."

She tries to smother her pleased smile but after a couple of seconds she bursts into quiet laughter.

"There's that beautiful smile," I murmur, grinning as I take her lips with mine.

"You look like such a big shot when you're wearing this cap," she whispers, and I drop my face into her hair, shoulders shaking with laughter.

"Thanks," I deadpan, trying to keep the volume of my laughter down when I reach up to take the cap off.

"No, no," she whispers quickly. "I didn't mean that I didn't like it. You look like a cocky hockey player but it's, you know, not a bad thing."

I blink down at her, unsure, hand still hovering at the brim.

"It's *hot*," she whispers finally, cheeks flushing almost as dark as mine.

I frown slightly as I lower my hand, not sure if it's disrespectful to fuck her when I've got a backwards baseball cap on my head. Then again, I've also got my jeans halfway down my thighs, so if she's into the way it looks then I'm not about to deprive her of it.

I clear my throat quietly, eyes dropping to her breasts as I squeeze them.

"You sure you like that, baby?" I ask.

"You know what I like, Tanner," she whispers back to me.

My eyes flick to hers, our irises aflame.

Yeah, I do know what she likes, and she knows what I like too. She likes rough small-towners who can't help but fuck on the first date. And I like pretty cheerleaders who can take it on their hands and knees.

Without saying another word I wrap my digits in the sides of her panties, twisting them tight before tugging them down. Then I gently roll down her hiking socks, kissing her ankles as I bare them to me.

And then she's fully naked, in my tent, cast in the soft glow of the crackling campfire outside.

I slide my wallet out of my back pocket, tossing it behind me after I slip out a condom. Then I'm tearing it open with my teeth and spitting out the foil as I roll it on, eyes burning into that place between her thighs while I give my balls a warning squeeze.

The kind that says, *do not fuck this up for me, and just wait your fucking turn.*

I settle my elbows on either side of her beautiful face, caging her in with the thick muscles of my biceps, and then I hunch down to take her lips with mine. I roll my back muscles slowly while I deepen the kiss, letting my cock drag heavily over her heat while I lick her tongue with mine.

"We don't have to fuck," I murmur, panting hard when I pull away. "We can just mess around, if you want. Cuddle and shit."

Aisling nuzzles into my neck, laughing quietly against the heat of my skin. "You already put your condom on," she reminds me, smiling prettily when she peeks up at me from the centre of my chest.

I grip at the back of my neck. "That was… a precaution, baby. Kinda need to get that shit on as soon as I've got your pussy in sight."

She smiles wider, fingers squeezing over my pecs. "Oh?"

I grunt really fucking hard. My voice is like gravel when I manage to rumble out the words.

"Otherwise I'll get too excited and just wanna, you know… slam that thing home."

"Is that what you want to do now?" she whispers, still amused, I can fucking tell. "You want to slam–"

I wrap my palm over her mouth, giving her cheeks a playful squish as she giggles against my hand. Then I let it slide down her neck, squeezing gently as I fill her mouth with my tongue.

"Let's cuddle and shit," she whispers teasingly, making me drop my forehead against hers as I try not to laugh too loudly, so goddamn in love with her that I can't stop grinning even as she pulls me back down so that I can kiss her again.

I groan loudly as I stroke her tongue with mine, hands roaming down to her tits so that I can give them the attention that they deserve.

"More," she whispers quickly, eyes wide and fluttering up at me.

I rub her breasts faster, searching her eyes to see if she's into it. "More of that?" I rumble. "More of me working these pretty tits?"

Her eyes squeeze shut but then she opens them, nodding frantically.

"Or," she pants out, eyes dangerously taunting as they lock with mine, "we could just read about the constellations–"

I growl and kiss her hard, massaging her roughly as she giggles into my mouth.

"Goddamn," I grunt, rolling her body underneath me, so that her belly and breasts are pressed down on the

344

sleeping bag. I knock her thighs apart with the hard muscles of my quads, sliding one hand around her neck so that I can arch it back and kiss her from behind.

"This okay?" I ask her quietly, my chest heavy on her back.

"Yeah," she whispers, eyes all big and nervous and beautiful.

I search her expression cautiously, making sure that what she's feeling is nervous excitement rather than nervous fear, and then I hunch back down to kiss her slow and deep, as I position the dome of my cock against her heat.

I slide her knees a little higher, getting her into a better position for a deeper fuck, and then I'm resting the stubble of my jaw against her flushed cheek, breathing heavily as I notch the tip against her entrance.

The guys are laughing loud and drunk about twenty feet away from us, unaware of the fire currently blazing in our tent. I wait a few long moments before I ask for Ash's consent again.

"Want me to take you like this?" I rasp, holding my cock in place.

She leans backwards to let me kiss her and she nods gently when I slip my tongue inside.

I grunt into her mouth, grab her waist, and thrust it home.

"*Tanner*," she whimpers, squealing and breathless.

I curse gruffly against her temple. "Yeah, baby. I know."

I wrap my palm around her jaw and stroke my tongue into her mouth, filling her with it as I withdraw my shaft and push it back inside.

She gasps, pulling her mouth from mine, and I grunt against the back of her neck. I shove her breasts down on the sleeping bag as I take both sides of her hips and begin to thrust.

"Four years," I grunt, pumping her pussy nice and

rough. "Four years since I had you like this. Four years of wanting you."

I slide my hands up to her breasts, palming her roughly as I increase my tempo. She grips her fists around the soft pillow, knees slipping farther apart as I take her faster.

"You're so pretty," I murmur, pressing hard kisses against her jaw. "Want me to keep rubbing on your tits like this?" I ask quickly, tugging on her nipples as I drive into her harder.

She tilts her head back to me and whispers, "Yeah, p-please."

My biceps flex to twice their size as I wrap a palm around her throat and start kissing her neck.

"Yeah?" I ask, using one hand to massage her tits more gruffly, rubbing my coarse palm over those soft pretty peaks.

My sac swings heavily against her heat and suddenly I'm growling into her hair, the muscles swelling in my chest as I shove a hand between her thighs.

"Wider," I order roughly, shoulders heaving as I knock her knees farther apart. Then I drop my weight onto my right elbow and envelop both of her fists with my right hand. Something warm twists in my abdomen when our fingers entwine. She grips her other hand over my wrist and tilts her head back, like she's looking for approval.

I rub two digits between her thighs and jerk my chin at her, pumping as hard as I can from the back.

A shaky whimper escapes her throat and I steel my jaw. I'm trying to keep my volume down so that we don't get caught tonight, but it's easier said than done when fucking her feels this good. The feel of her soft ass against my groin is driving me insane.

Her nails start biting into my hand and I watch as she digs them in, my mind instantly blacking out as soon as I see our size difference.

Aisling isn't the shortest chick in the world but

compared to me she's fucking tiny, and I drop my head between my shoulders on a growl, eyes raking down her waist as I shove her harder and harder against the sleeping bag.

"I'm close," I growl, teeth grazing her shoulder.

"No, no, don't stop," she whispers quickly, and I bite into her harder, my palm sliding up from her pussy to her tits.

"God, you're beautiful," I rumble, caressing her breasts from left to right, and then starting to grip them more roughly as I begin to pump her over the finish line.

"You're there, aren't you, baby?" I pant, tugging on her breasts as she buries her beautiful face in my pillow. I suck gently at the curve of her neck, then grunt like an animal as she tightens beneath me.

"Jesus Christ," I rasp, temples throbbing as her orgasm explodes, squeezing her breasts for dear life while her pussy tightens around me. As soon as she collapses onto the pillow, her whole body wracked with after-shocks, I grip her jaw in my hand and tilt her face up so that I can kiss her.

"Tanner," she whispers, her voice faint and shaking.

"You're so beautiful," I murmur back to her, crushing a kiss against her cheek when she can't hold her head up any longer.

Her lashes flutter sleepily as I tower over her and I suddenly get the recollection of what I'm wearing – dirty jeans halfway down my quads and the backwards baseball cap, all while having my girl on her hands and knees.

I clench my jaw at the thought of what this must look like and hold her gaze as I pull off the cap. I rake my hand through my hair before settling heavily back down on top of her.

"I need to come," I rumble, gently kissing at her jaw.

She nods her head in consent. I squeeze her breasts and withdraw my cock.

"You took it so good," I murmur, rebuilding my momentum. Slipping it in and out lazily at first, and then beginning to pump her rougher and faster. I bury my face in her warm neck as she tentatively reaches one hand beneath our bodies, and then I'm grunting like a beast as those soft hands roll my balls.

"Harder," I growl, gripping at her breasts as I shove it back inside. "Grip that shit, baby. Squeeze as hard as you can."

She whimpers against the pillow, turning her gorgeous face so that she can look at me. "Are you sure–?"

"Yes," I grunt, releasing one of her breasts so that I can fist her hair. I wind it tight over my knuckles and then pull it taut, arching her back. "Hard. Please."

Her fist turns into a vise around my balls and my vision goes blind.

"Oh yeah. Good girl," I pant, pumping frantically. "Keep squeezing like that and I'm gonna give you my–"

The first spurt of my release shoots into the condom and I sink my teeth into her neck, grunting as I come.

I pull her hair tighter, my other palm caressing her breasts, as my cock jerks inside her, long and thick and solid.

"You're doing so well," I rasp, my chest pumping hard against her shoulders. "Just a couple more pumps, baby. Just a couple more."

I groan as I stroke her nipples before spanking my palm against her behind.

"*Oh my God, oh my God,*" she whimpers, one of her hands gripping into the back of my neck. She keeps her other fist tight around my sac, helping me shoot out my release.

I nuzzle into her neck and grunt roughly with every thrust, hauling her tight against my chest the second that my release finally empties.

I slip the length of myself slowly out of her, and kiss her gently as I tug off the condom.

"You're perfect," I murmur, hissing as my cock nudges against her ass. I lean up so that she can settle onto her back and then I carefully position myself on top of her. "That was... fucking perfect."

"Yeah," she whispers, breasts heaving quickly up and down.

I smirk lazily down at her and then hunch low so that I can smell her neck.

"Mmm," I murmur, eyes closing as she runs her fingers through my hair.

I roll us onto our sides, kiss her gently, and hold her closer. She buries her face between the muscles of my chest. I restrain my cock when it starts nudging its way back to her pussy.

"Can I...?" she starts, not meeting my gaze as I pull back to look at her.

"Anything you want, the answer's yes," I murmur, massaging my fingers through her hair. "What is it?"

"Um." She twists her lips to the side, frowning angrily at one of my nipples. "Can I stay in your tent tonight?" she asks my pecs, making me chuckle quietly and squeeze her tighter.

She looks up at me, nervous and wary, but I just grin and crush my mouth down on hers. A small laugh tinkles out of her as I rub our foreheads together.

"Of course you're staying in my tent, baby," I murmur. "I wouldn't have it any other way."

CHAPTER 33

Aisling

Present day

I wake up to the sounds of birds chirping, the tent glowing orange in the morning light. I lift my head from Tanner's broad chest and he groans quietly, immediately slapping his hand down over his eyes.

He repositions us gently, my back meeting the soft sheet that we slept on as Tanner nudges his large quads between my thighs.

"Not ready to sneak you back over to your tent yet," he rumbles in his deep morning voice, stubble scraping over my breasts as he laps gently at my nipples.

"Don't make me go," I plead teasingly, giggling into my hand when he smirks up at me, sucking harder.

He leans up and cages a thick forearm above my head, grinning cockily down at me as he rubs his length between my thighs. Then he dips down to kiss me gently, a growl in his throat as he pushes my knees wide.

He buries his face in my hair, biceps flexing as he fists his length.

"Let me put it inside of you," he rasps, his voice so gravelly that my nipples pinch.

He nudges the thick head against my heat and my hands clutch desperately to his broad shoulders.

Just as he begins groaning, licking warm stripes up my neck, he immediately halts his hips as we both think the same thing at the same time.

"Condom," he rumbles gruffly, panting like crazy.

He gives himself a few long seconds before dropping his rigid cock onto my belly.

"Sorry," he rasps quietly, kissing my cheek before he rises onto his elbow, squinting around for his wallet so that he can find a condom. "I'm so turned on that I can't even see," he admits, an anguished laugh leaving his throat.

He pulls up a couple of sheets and pieces of clothing, before dropping himself back on top of me, bunching his fists in the pillow.

"Just gimme one minute," he drawls, voice muffled against my throat. "Then I'll find the rubbers and take that pussy nice and slow."

"But I want you now," I whisper, smothering my giggles when he immediately throws himself upright. He whacks the back of his head against one of the poles and mouths the word *ow* as he fights his own laughter.

"Fuck," he whispers, grinning down at me as he rubs his head. Then he scans the area for his wallet, tossing his shaft while he looks around for it.

He spots his wallet at the edge of the tent and practically tears the thing in two, grabbing the three remaining foil squares and smiling down at me when he sees me giggling excitedly.

He's just about to tear into one when his phone suddenly buzzes beneath his discarded shirt.

He's still holding the edge of the square in his teeth, one second away from ripping it open as his eyes flash to mine. Then they flicker down between my thighs and I see his irises flash and darken.

I ease the packet from his teeth and rise up onto my knees, kissing the centre of his heaving chest.

"Take the call," I whisper, kissing his mouth when he frowns warily, torn.

After a long beat he exhales deeply, glancing down at his shirt and to the rectangle glowing beneath it. He grabs his phone from beneath the cotton, blinks down at the screen, and hits *answer*.

"Hey," he rumbles quietly, laying back down and hauling me on top of him. I have to stifle a yelp as he hauls me onto his chest and he grunts against my throat when he accidentally slips an inch inside of me.

His eyes are practically watering as he withdraws his cock from between my thighs, his shaft flexing violently as he tucks me firmly against his side.

"Yeah," he rasps into the phone, clearing his throat before whispering, "yeah, that's great."

I keep my eyes on his heaving chest, not wanting to draw his attention when he's taking a call.

The large warm hand wrapped around my shoulder reaches up to brush my cheek. I peek up at him from under my lashes and he turns his phone screen so that I can read it.

Mom.

A little disturbing considering the fact that he was almost inside of me a second ago but I nod up at him anyway, realising that he's showing me the screen so that I know that he isn't hiding anything – or anyone – from me.

"Okay, yeah," he murmurs, his voice a hoarse scrape. "On it, Mom. Okay, love y'all, bye."

His thumb taps the *end call* button on the screen and he tosses his phone to the bottom of the tent, broad chest lifting heavily as he rakes his free hand roughly through his hair.

"I need to go," he rasps, his palm scrubbing over his tan forehead. "Have to head back to Carter Ridge for a few days. Important stuff."

When he drops his hand and looks down at me I know that he sees the flash of fear in my eyes, the sudden worry that this is his way of leaving me after getting what he really wanted.

He instantly presses his mouth down on mine, grunting quietly as his hand squeezes my throat.

"Let me rephrase that," he murmurs, panting hard as he pulls away. "Don't know if I mentioned it before, the other reason why I came to spend the summer in Larch Peak, but if I didn't... okay, so one reason why I came here is because it's where Hunter and I are going pro this fall. But I also wanted to spend the summer somewhere close to Carter Ridge, because I wanted to be able to head there ASAP when my dad got back from deployment."

Tanner holds me closer, gazing toward the warm orange tent canopied above us.

"He's home," he says simply, "so I need to head over there and see him."

My eyes flick between his strong handsome face and the large muscles of his chest.

"Okay," I whisper, even though I wish that I could keep him here with me until my own journey at Larch Peak is over – until my mom has seen my first renovation and decided whether or not I can start working on a small-town house-flipping branch of their business. I listen to the powerful thump of his heartbeat. "I hope that you have a lovely time."

His large muscles shift beneath me and when I look up he's lifted himself onto one elbow. His brow is slightly raised and he's giving me an amused lazy smirk.

"Ash, are you fuckin' kidding?" He laughs quietly as he

grips my ass, dragging me back on top of him. "You're obviously coming with me. I'm not about to leave you here."

I blink down at him in surprise and let him push my chest roughly down onto his.

"I can't meet your parents," I whisper, gasping when his palms cup my breasts. "Especially when your dad has just got back from d-deployment."

Tanner rolls me onto my back and takes my mouth with his.

"Good a time as any," he rumbles. "He's away so much you gotta take every opportunity you can get."

My heart squeezes in my chest at the thought of Tanner, younger than he is now, waiting for months at a time and wondering if he would ever see his dad again.

"Tanner…" I argue, not wanting to intrude. "That's a really big deal. It's, like, family time."

"Exactly," he rumbles. "That's why you should be there."

I try to smooth away the little crease in my brow. "But we aren't even together yet. It's way too soon."

A hint of a smile crease flexes in the strong hollow of Tanner's cheek.

"If it was up to me we would have already done this four years ago. Trust me baby, it's not too soon."

He hunches down to kiss me slowly and then he rolls onto his back, pulling me along with him so that I'm laying on his large chest.

"Everyone here is going to know," I whisper as he pulls back slightly, cupping my face in his big warm palms.

"What d'you mean?" he murmurs, kissing my cheeks as I frown at my own thoughts.

"Like, no-one knows about us yet," I whisper, "and if we suddenly both leave the campsite–"

"We don't have to stay in Carter Ridge," he murmurs quickly, voice rasping as he kisses my neck. "We'll come back as soon as you need. Your mom's gonna check out the lake house next week right?"

I kind of can't believe that he remembered me telling him that.

"Yeah," I say warily, "but–"

"We'll be back before that, by at least four days. And fuck the guys here knowing where we are – as long as we tell your brother, it's no-one else's damn business."

"You think we should tell Connell?" I gasp, swallowing nervously as Tanner shifts us again and ranges his large body on top of me.

"I don't wanna lie to him," he rumbles, his stunning eyes looking sincere as they carefully search mine. "Do you... not want him to know? I'd just rather be honest, let him know where you are."

I nibble nervously on my lower lip, eyes on Tanner's chest as I try to calm down.

"I know you're right," I admit quietly, "it's just hard for me to be so open about... feelings and stuff is all. Putting my heart back on my sleeve," I whisper, glancing down at my little freckle.

Tanner flashes me a handsome grin and lifts my arm up so that he can kiss the tiny love-heart. He grins as I smother my laughter with my free hand, and he starts licking at it like an animal, groaning obscenely when I try to kick him away.

"You're such a caveman," I pant, giggling into the pillow as he rolls me over.

"And you're in my cave, baby," he rumbles, smothering me with kisses.

He rolls on a condom and positions himself behind me, giving me that handsome grin when I can't stop laughing.

Then he presses a kiss to my dimpled cheek and murmurs, "Again."

CHAPTER 34

Aisling

Present day

I tug the brim of Tanner's khaki cap a little lower over my eyes, glancing out of the G-wagon's passenger window at the emerald larch trees towering over us, enveloping the long stretch of lower-mountain road.

I rub my palms down my thighs, over the baby pink cotton of my long sundress. I didn't have a huge array of meet-the-parents clothes options with me, but seeing as this dress covers me from neck to ankle I'm hoping that it'll suffice.

Tanner takes one of his hands off the wheel, eyes remaining on the road as he stills my twiddling fingers and gives them a loving squeeze.

I take a deep breath and shake out my hair, trying to psych myself up as we approach the edge of Larch Peak.

"Maybe you should, like, tell me what to expect," I say

to him, my voice breathless and a little more high pitched than usual.

I shoot my eyes up to Tanner and there's a hint of a smirk on his handsome face. His hair is pushed back from his tan forehead, the sides buzzed in that neat military-fade cut, and he's wearing a cotton pull-over with sleeves for probably the first time ever – most likely some attempt at male modesty, to hide the thick biceps and forearms beneath.

I keep one hand entwined with his and use the other to gently squeeze his pumped muscles.

He grunts quietly and flashes me a smirk.

"Why the sleeves?" I ask him, because, sure it's a little cloudy and overcast, but it's still crazy summer degrees out here.

He grins down at me. "Can't go into a military household with guns blazing, baby."

I cover my eyes with one of my hands, laughing out loud. Tanner squeezes my hand tighter with his, a smile crease in his cheek when I peek back up at him.

"So what are they like?" I ask him, a tiny bit more at ease than I was a second ago.

"My mom and dad?" he asks me, his voice still low with morning gravel. "Probably exactly what you're imagining when you picture the people who raised me."

"All I've imagined so far is, like, a total DILF."

Tanner breathes out a laugh, releasing my hand from his so that he can playfully squish my cheeks.

"Okay, naughty girl. What d'you wanna know?"

I purse my lips, considering. "Maybe, like… how they met?"

Tanner nods his head, quiet for a moment as he manoeuvres his giant SUV through a tight exit.

"Yeah, okay," he rumbles. "So my dad's military – a higher-up – and maybe a couple of years after he was fully enlisted there was some kind of… dinner, I guess. Black tie.

You know just before we graduated and Carter U had that sports gala? I guess it was something like that, but more serious. More intense.

"My dad's always been a quiet guy – straight-laced, no nonsense. And uh… he also didn't… date around," Tanner continues, putting a little more emphasis on the word *date* so that I can catch his meaning without him having to say it. "But then he's at this dinner celebrating all of these incredible military men and women, and it's winter so they decided to have… winter entertainment."

He rolls his shoulders and takes my hand with his again.

"That's, uh… where my mom comes in."

I wrap my free hand around his wrist, massaging his flexing forearm and silently asking him to continue.

"The main reason why I play hockey?" he says quietly, his voice rasping as if he's nervous. "It's because of my mom. She was an Olympic figure skater. And with a house full of military guys, doing all of these dangerous missions, I wanted to continue her legacy, while also giving her one less person to ever have to worry about."

My eyebrows lift in surprise, because I *definitely* hadn't expected that.

I squeeze Tanner's hand tighter.

What an amazing man.

"That's really beautiful," I breathe out.

"Uh, thank you," he rumbles shyly, lifting my hand so that he can brush a kiss to it. Then he swipes his tongue over his lower lip and says, "Always wondered which path was the right one for me."

I swallow quietly and ask, "Like, hockey or the army?"

"Yeah."

"And do you… think that you picked the right one?" I say, feeling a little breathless.

A smile crease appears in Tanner's cheek. "Yeah," he says simply.

"How do you know?" I ask.

359

"Because I met you."

I press my palm over my chest, feeling my heart thunder as I look up at him.

He gives me a loving squeeze, laughing quietly when I squish up against his biceps.

Then he gets back to telling me his parents' story.

"So at this military dinner they set up a rink for her to recreate her gold-medal-winning performance on, and as soon as my dad saw her he was like... he just knew. And bear in mind, at this point my dad barely spoke to his co-workers, let alone total strangers. But after her performance when everyone was free to mill around, he just walked straight up to her. Asked her if she wanted to dance."

Tanner casts a glance at me, a secretive smirk tugging up the corner of his lips.

"I should also probably mention the fact that she didn't speak a word of English."

A surprised laugh leaves my throat and I ask, "Then how did they talk?"

He clears his throat. Hard. "They found other ways to communicate."

My jaw instantly drops. And from the set of Tanner's jaw, I can tell that he's a little less comfortable with this part of the story.

"So... *did* they dance?" I ask, feeling Tanner's hand tighten around my own.

He rolls his shoulders, glances down at me, and simply says, "Yeah."

"...And?" I ask, biting back a smile at how rigid he's suddenly sitting.

He shifts uncomfortably on his seat, his wrist flexing as he grips the wheel.

"They, uh... they danced. All night. He didn't let her out of his sight after that."

I watch him carefully. "Didn't she need to... go home?"

Tanner cracks his knuckles, eyes refusing to meet mine.

"Yeah," he murmurs. "But, uh… she didn't."

I can't take it anymore. Uncontrollable laughter bubbles out of me and Tanner breathes out a nervous laugh of his own.

"Sorry," he laughs. "I know this is awkward as hell to talk about."

"Oh no, don't stop now," I tease, and he half-laughs half-groans, his cheeks turning ruddy. "So if she didn't go home then–?"

"She went home with him," he finishes quickly, gruff and matter-of-fact. "They moved in together that night. That's the end of the story."

"I bet," I say dryly, smiling up at his embarrassed expression. "So did they–?"

"Yeah," he grunts. "I'm one of three boys. My oldest brother Morgan… yeah, that was his night."

"Oh my God," I laugh, burying my face against his biceps to smother my giggles. "Okay, that was so mean of me. I shouldn't have made you finish that story Tanner, I'm sorry."

Tanner keeps his eyes on the road but a brief smile touches his lips.

"It's okay," he rumbles, even though his dark red cheeks say otherwise.

I lean up to press a kiss against his cheekbone and his smile grows a little wider, his chest expanding contentedly.

"What's your other brother called?" I ask, resettling on my seat.

"Wyatt. Morgan's the oldest, then Wyatt, then me. And by the way," he says, amusement glinting in his eyes, "when you hear my parents say the name 'Mason', they're talking about me."

"Oh my God!" I exclaim, shooting him a glare. "Very funny," I mumble dryly, folding my arms over my chest.

His grin widens as he wrestles one of my hands back into his.

I stare sulkily at our entwined fingers.

Am I ever going to live down not knowing his first name?

"Not if I have anything to do with it," Tanner drawls, grinning wider when I gasp.

"Oh great, now I'm saying my private thoughts out loud," I whimper. I look down at my love-heart freckle and say, "This is all your fault."

Tanner breathes out a laugh, bringing my hand to his mouth so that he can kiss it.

"While we're on the subject of shit I probably should have mentioned before I brought you here, you're not afraid of dogs are you?" he asks, using our joined hands to move the shift.

I blink up at him, eyes wide.

"…Only big ones," I say slowly. I swallow hard and squeak, "Why?"

He swipes his tongue over his bottom lip, staring hard at the road.

"Tanner!" I exclaim. "What the hell?! Fine, just tell me. How big is it?"

He presses an apologetic kiss firmly against my wrist.

"He's… normal size, baby. Totally normal."

"Define normal," I say dryly, well aware that six-foot-four Tanner's perspective of size is not the same as mine.

He grunts quietly, clearing his throat. "Uh…"

"Tanner," I warn.

"He's regular size," he rumbles cautiously, "…for a fully grown Alsatian."

"Tanner!" I shout, horrified.

"Look, baby, if it makes you feel any better we also have a Pekinese."

I slap my free hand over my forehead and squeal, "What kind of owners get an Alsatian *and then also get a Pekinese?*"

He breathes out a laugh and bites playfully at my wrist.

"I'm going to be eaten alive," I whimper, soaking in my last ever look at the larch trees that Tanner is gunning past.

"By me maybe," Tanner smirks, flashing me a cocky grin when I peek up at him. Then he has the grace to look a little guilty and he squeezes my thighs over my dress as he returns his attention to the road. "They're both rescue dogs," he says. "And Cookie's only got three legs."

"Oh my God," I whisper, closing my eyes. "You have a three-legged Pekinese, and you freaking named it Cookie."

Tanner snickers, rubbing his thumb more firmly into my thigh.

"The Alsatian's called Cobie."

"Great," I deadpan. "A name for my killer."

"Baby," Tanner says, laughing kindly. "Please don't believe those stereotypes about big dogs. He's a total sweetheart, my mom trained him so good."

I purse my lips, unconvinced. "Dogs don't like outsiders," I say, worrying my bottom lip between my teeth.

"He's fine with everyone, and he's even better with family."

I look up at him. "I'm not family, Tanner."

Something like a smirk tugs at the corner of his mouth. "Baby, he's a dog. He's going to know that you're mine."

I arch a petulant eyebrow. "And why's that? Is he also a mind-reader?"

Tanner tries to bite back his grin. "Ash." He flicks a glance my way. "What I meant is that his senses are stronger than a human's. He's going to know that you're family because he's going to smell my scent all over you."

I blush so hard that my cheeks turn darker than my dress.

Twenty minutes later we're driving through Carter Ridge, and Tanner is pulling up outside a small local florist's to get something for his parents.

"Wanna come in? I'll be two minutes, tops," he says. He clicks open his seatbelt and wraps his forearm around the headrest of my seat.

I blink at his biceps straining through the dark cotton of

his shirt, before looking up at him with love-struck eyes and shaking my head.

He smirks down at me, grabs my chin, and kisses me hard.

"Two minutes," he murmurs, before hunching beneath the roof of the G-wagon and trudging heavily into the shop.

A little bell tinkles about a minute and a half later, and Tanner leaves the florist's holding the largest bouquet of sunflowers that I've ever seen.

He grins when he sees my surprised expression and he muscles his way into the driver's seat.

"Wanna smell them?" he asks, gently tilting the bouquet my way when I lean forward. I pull back after a second and offer him a little smile.

"Your parents are super lucky," I tell him, and he smiles even harder, shifting the bouquet to his other side so that he can kiss me again.

"Close your eyes," he murmurs as he pulls back a little.

"My eyes are already closed," I giggle, but I swallow nervously in anticipation anyway.

I hear a lot of shifting around, the rustle of bouquet cellophane, and then there's only stillness in the cabin of the car as he waits for me to open my eyes.

"Open them," he says and my heart thunders in my chest.

Because in Tanner's hand is a single red rose.

I squeal and practically throw myself on top of him, making a chuckle rumble in his chest as he splays his free hand over my back, hunching down to meet my kiss.

"Like it?" he asks gruffly, pulling back so that he can pass it to me.

"Cinnamon roll," I whisper up at him, totally entranced.

He shakes his head as he laughs before dipping down to kiss me again.

"You know that I have no idea what you mean when you say stuff like that, right?" he asks, helping me climb back over to the passenger seat. The sunflowers are now sitting in the back and my rose is laid carefully on my lap.

"You're the most thoughtful person ever," I say, staring up at him as he backs out of the parking spot. "Why'd you even get it for me?"

He squeezes my thigh with his right hand. "A beautiful rose for a beautiful rose."

CHAPTER 35

Aisling

Present day

Fifteen minutes later Tanner is easing his G-wagon to a stop outside of a large white house with two giant garages and a wrap-around porch. I blink up at it in confusion before flicking my eyes back to Tanner.

He puts the car in park, unbuckles our seatbelts, and spreads his quads, waiting for me to say something.

"Is that…" I breathe out a shaky exhale, eyes flickering between him and the house. It literally has a white picket fence, unironically.

With the exception of the lake house that I've spent the summer working on, I've never seen a home so perfect before.

He jerks his thumb toward the porch, knees bouncing as he grunts, "That's us."

I stare at him for a long moment before turning my eyes

back toward the house.

"Oh my God," I whisper. "You're not just six-foot-four and gorgeous. You're *rich* six-foot-four and gorgeous."

Tanner breathes out a laugh and grips firmly at the back of his neck. Then he reaches over to me and gently sets my rose on the dash, before removing my khaki cap, wrapping his hands beneath my jaw, and leaning down to chastely kiss me.

"That's my parents' cash, baby," he murmurs. "That's nothing to do with me."

I pull back and shake my head up at him, my arms tight around his neck.

"That's not what I meant," I whisper. "I didn't mean, like, 'yay, he's rich'. I meant more like... I can't believe that you're rich... while also being so kind and sweet and humble."

When he just smiles and shakes his head I say, "Seriously, Tanner, that's super rare."

I grew up around people who had a lot of money, and absolutely none of those guys behaved the way that Tanner does.

He lifts my face up to his, shoulders swelling as he kisses me deeply.

"Maybe it's 'cause this is still the holler," he murmurs.

"What d'you mean?" I ask.

"We're raised a different way."

I wrap my arms tighter around his neck, urging him closer as he grips my waist. He strokes his tongue into my mouth and grunts quietly, squeezing harder.

Suddenly the sound of a door opening behind us punctuates our haze, and Tanner reluctantly removes his mouth from mine, blocking me from view as he scopes out the scene over his shoulder.

"Shit," he grunts.

I hear a loud excited bark and immediately understand why.

I lean up to peek over his shoulder and yelp with fear. A giant caramel brown Alsatian is hurtling towards us at a billion miles per hour.

Tanner turns back to face me and brackets my chin with his large palm. Then he leans down and presses a hungry kiss to my lips.

"Just stay beside me," he rumbles when he pulls back. "I've got this under control."

In the next second Tanner dips out of the vehicle, closes his door and orders, "Cobe! Heel!"

The dog skids to an immediate stop.

It chases circles around itself a few times before letting out a happy *woof* and settling quickly into a sitting position. It's large round eyes flick between the palm of Tanner's hand and *me*.

"Oh my God," I squeal, shoving a hand over my mouth.

Tanner glances at me through the driver's window, palm still outstretched toward the dog.

"I'm coming to get you out now, okay?" he says gently. "Cobie's not going to do anything, I promise."

I glance back toward the Alsatian and it's set its chin on its front paws, its giant tail thumping frantically up and down against the grass. It catches me looking and suddenly the tail is thumping harder.

I let out a little whimper as Tanner rounds the SUV and opens my door.

He grips one hand over the roof and murmurs, "He's not gonna touch you."

"Tanner," I whisper nervously, fists gripping into the material of my dress.

He leans in to kiss me gently and then pulls back and jerks his chin. "Look at him, baby."

I reluctantly turn back to look out of the windshield, breathing out a small laugh of surprise when I see the dog belly-up on the lawn. It wiggles around on its back before rolling those big round eyes our way again.

"He's excited to meet you," Tanner says, but I don't miss the way that his whole body is blocking me in right now, keeping me away from his dog in case I suddenly decide that I'm too scared to approach it.

I pick up my rose and the cap, and then I finally nod up at him.

"You're coming in?" he asks, smile creases appearing in his cheeks.

"Yeah," I swallow, although I'm nervous as hell.

I take his hand when he offers it, feeling unsteady as I step down from the SUV.

Once I'm out Tanner grabs the sunflowers from the backseat, pockets his keys, and pushes his fingers firmly through mine.

"You got this, baby," he says quietly, squeezing my hand as we make our way up the driveway.

The dog is instantly on its belly, eyes bouncing between us.

"Cobe," Tanner warns, jerking his chin toward the front door. The dog glances over toward the house, seemingly weighing up its options. Then it rolls over again and lets out another happy *woof.*

"I think that must mean 'no'," I whisper. Tanner breathes out a laugh, rubbing his thumb over mine.

"He probably... really wants to smell you," he murmurs, his eyes unblinking, trained on the dog.

"Would that be a good thing?" I ask, swallowing when Cobie's ears prick up at the sound of my voice.

"If you're okay with it, yeah," Tanner murmurs, only looking away from the dog when it finally blinks away from him.

When we finally reach Cobie on the grass, Tanner looks down at me, his expression confident and reassuring.

"It's up to you, baby," he rumbles. "D'you want him to take your scent?"

And in this moment, I realise how many fears Tanner

has helped me conquer this summer – being the strong hand to guide me through it when no-one else has ever noticed, let alone tried.

That's probably why I reach up on my tip-toes and give him a gentle grateful kiss. He immediately compresses me against his chest with his forearms, grunting quietly as he licks his tongue against mine.

A small yipping breaks through the moment and we both turn to face the white porch steps. A tiny three-legged pom-pom hurtles towards us, yapping happily before yelping and tumbling over itself. When it gets back to its feet it starts running laps around our legs.

Tanner presses his forearm against his eyes, laughing quietly and looking embarrassed.

"Okay," he chuckles, flashing me an apologetic smile as he tucks the sunflowers he bought for his parents under his biceps. Then he tucks two digits under Cobie's collar and gently tugs him into a sitting position.

Tanner gives my hand another squeeze.

"Okay, baby. If you're ready we can hold our hands out for him now."

I look down at our joined hands and Tanner presses a reassuring kiss against my temple. Cookie runs a figure of eight between Tanner's strong legs, squeaking in delight when he glances down at her with a smile.

Me and you both, Cookie.

"Okay," I whisper, tentatively holding our joined hands in front of Cobie's nose.

The Alsatian glances quickly at Tanner before cautiously getting to its feet, tail wagging furiously as it finally looks up into my eyes.

It shoves its nose against my hand, stumbles backwards, and instantly pees.

"Cobe!" Tanner exclaims. "What the fuck, man?!"

I can't help but laugh as he tugs the dog's collar, immediately ceasing its excited trickle.

"Calm that shit, man," Tanner orders, before jerking his chin at the front door again. "For real, go in there and think about what you just did," he says, laughing with me as I giggle into his shoulder.

Tanner presses another kiss to my cheek and murmurs, "You smell so good that my dog pissed himself."

My chest shakes with laughter, smiling uncontrollably as Tanner squishes me closer.

Because that's what being with Tanner is like.

It's like all of my fears are forgotten, and I immediately feel at home.

Cobie shoots me a longing glance before dipping his head and racing back inside. Cookie immediately attempts to follow him but she's stuck bouncing at the bottom step.

Tanner holds my hand tighter, looking a little embarrassed as he picks Cookie up by the belly.

"She's, uh… she's good for running down the steps, but she kinda struggles to get back up," Tanner says, carrying her with us like a little football.

When she starts wriggling in his grip, he places her gently on the top of the porch, allowing her to bolt through the front door and chase after the easygoing Alsatian.

As soon as we're about four steps away from the front door a gorgeous blonde woman steps out onto the porch, her skin tan and rosy, her hair a soft blown-out pouf.

The second that she sees Tanner she squeals and raises her arms.

"There's my boy!" she exclaims, her voice a gentle husky American, barely accented by her original European roots.

She spots the explosion of sunflowers and *ooh*s excitedly.

"Mace, they're gorgeous!" she giggles. "Are those for us?"

I pause on an inhale, suddenly too stunned to breathe.

Mace.

They call him Mace.

My heart clenches, feeling so unbearably lucky to have

this inside look into Tanner's private life.

Tanner glances down at me, his eyes bright, trying to gauge my reaction before smiling back at his mom.

"Yeah, Mom, they're for you and Dad," he says, before adding teasingly, "if you grab them from me I'll have an arm to hug you with."

Tanner and his mom both laugh as she takes the flowers, and he presses a sweet kiss to my cheek when she turns momentarily away. Then he steps back so that I can head through the front door first.

I send him a slightly nervous look over my shoulder and he dips down to nuzzle into my neck.

"Don't worry, baby," he murmurs. "They're gonna love you, I swear."

His mom comes back into the hallway, brushing her palms over her hips before reaching up to give her youngest son a big happy hug.

When she pulls away she turns her attention to me, offering me a dimple-popping smile as she says, "And you must be Aisling."

My heart stutters in my chest.

She knows my name.

I feel Tanner's shoulders swell, brushing firmly against my own, and I nod my head at her, almost too nervous to speak.

I've done the 'meet the parents' thing before but it has honest to God never felt like this – like this isn't the last time that I'll ever see them.

"Yeah, I'm Aisling," I squeak, feeling a little dazed.

She offers me a comforting squeeze of my shoulder, trying to help me relieve my nerves.

"We're making food in the kitchen, if you want to say hello before Mace gives you the tour? Oh, and *also*," she adds, giving a pointed look to Tanner, "I would love to know why my lovely dog is urinating all over the hardwood flooring?"

Tanner breathes out a nervous laugh, gripping the back of his neck with his hand as his mom turns around and heads down to their kitchen.

When she's out of sight he grabs my waist and hauls me against him, swallowing my happy squeak as he crushes his mouth down on mine.

"Feelin' okay so far?" he asks, pulling back to search my eyes.

I nod. "Yeah," I breathe, "but I didn't know that they knew I was coming."

Tanner looks me straight in the eyes before saying, "They didn't."

He drops his gaze as he kicks off his boots and then instantly kneels down so that he can un-lace mine.

"But…" I swallow hard. "Your mom knows my name."

Tanner eases off both of my shoes, neck heating up as he gets to his feet.

"Yeah," he says, entwining our fingers and avoiding my eyes. He tugs me gently after him as we begin making our way down the hall.

He doesn't say anything else.

My lips fall open as understanding truly dawns.

His mom knew exactly who Tanner would be bringing home without him having to even mention it.

Tanner has talked to his mom about me.

Before I can say anything to him about it we're crossing the threshold of the large cream and white ranch-style kitchen, and the room is erupting into deep male laughter as Tanner slaps his palm roughly against his dad's back.

The two are laughing and grinning as they share a gruff father-son embrace, and when his dad pulls back he flicks his eyes over to me.

He has dark hair and the beginnings of a beard that I presume he doesn't have when he's on base. He's at least two-hundred-and-sixty pounds of pure muscle, standing at around the same height as his son but with a number of

battle scars on his neck and arms, as well as deeper marks over his large tan hands.

"Dad, this is Aisling," Tanner says, his voice deep and proud. He drops his forearm heavily over my shoulders, hauling me in firmly against his side. He lowers his voice and murmurs, "Ash, baby, this is my dad, Linc."

The volume of testosterone radiating from the large male bodies around me has my breathing turning shaky as I tentatively offer him my hand.

"Hi," I say, a little breathlessly. "Thank you both for, um... letting me come inside your home."

Tanner's dad takes my hand and gives it a hard warm squeeze, which is surprisingly more comforting than I would have been expecting.

Also, I'm not going to deny it. Tanner's dad is freaking *hot*.

"Welcome," he grunts, before looking behind me through the doorway. His mouth lifts into a smirk and, confused, Tanner glances behind us.

"No fuckin' way!" Tanner suddenly shouts, clutching me tighter as another guy steps into the room. He grabs him with his free arm and chuckles in disbelief.

The other guy pounds his palm down on his back, still dressed in army fatigues.

"Are you fuckin' kidding me?" Tanner laughs, shoving his hand through his hair. He turns to face his mom and grins, "You hid this from me on purpose, huh? I can't believe you didn't tell me that Wyatt was back."

"I thought it would be a lovely surprise," she rasps, smiling all cute and smug. Her husband grunts in agreement as he pulls her into his side.

Tanner looks down at me, eyes alight, and says, "Baby, this is my brother Wyatt."

I glance up at Wyatt as he runs both palms over his dark buzz-cut, smirking down at me before hitting me with a wink.

I think I wheeze a little. "Hey," I whisper, as Tanner rubs his palm lovingly down my arm.

Wyatt gives me a once-over that has his brother clearing his throat. Then Wyatt smirks at his dad and says, "Well that explains why Cobe's pissing all over the furniture."

"Alright, enough swearing for one afternoon, don't you think, boys?" Tanner's mom says lightly, with a pointed look at her middle son. Then she gives me a happy smile and asks, "Aisling, will you be staying for lunch? Dinner? Mason's room is obviously available if you would both like to stay over tonight?"

"Jeez, Mom," Wyatt laughs. "You tryna scare her away or something? Although," he adds, flashing me a grin, "my room is right next door to Mason's."

"Wyatt!" their mom exclaims.

Linc leans back against the kitchen counter and tugs her more tightly into his side.

Tanner smirks at his brother. "Man, I would love to punch you in that mouth you're always running, but my hands are too preoccupied loving on my beautiful girlfriend right now."

"Mason!" their mom shouts again, this time shooting me a flushed *I am so sorry about my boys* kind of look.

I'm too stunned to react, completely hung up on one detail in particular.

The fact that Tanner just referred to me in front of his family as his *girlfriend*.

Tanner grins at her over his shoulder and rumbles, "Sorry, Mom."

Then he presses a kiss to my temple and murmurs, "Sorry, baby."

Wyatt grins, leaning a large shoulder against the archway. "And what about a 'sorry, Wyatt'?"

Tanner smirks, wrapping his arms around my shoulders from behind. "In your dreams, man."

CHAPTER 36

Aisling

Present day

Half an hour later we're all setting up on the back porch, Wyatt finally changed out of his military gear and their parents heading both ends of the table.

It's a bright and sparkly summer afternoon, with the sunrays turning the garden into the perfect suntrap.

Tanner pulls my chair out before I reach it, leaning down to kiss my cheek before sitting himself beside me. His dad seems to be the head chef in the house when he's not away on deployment, being responsible for not only most of the cooking but the plating up too. His striking eyes flash to mine every time he goes to add something to my plate, waiting for me to accept or refuse whatever it is that he's offering.

It's so heart-squeezingly endearing that I say yes to every single thing.

Cookie is sprawled on her belly beside Wyatt's big boots, glittery eyes peeking up at him every time he lifts his fork to his mouth, and Cobie's chin rests on her tiny back, gaze flitting keenly from plate to plate.

When he glances up at me his tongue happily lolls out of his mouth.

"How long now until the season starts?" Tanner's dad asks.

He's holding his beer bottle under the table and he wrenches off the top with a quick grunt. His eyes meet his son's as he takes a long pull.

Tanner's eyes flick between his food and his dad's unwavering gaze.

"You mean 'til I start training for the NHL as an official player on Larch Peak's team?" he asks.

His dad says, "Yeah."

Tanner shovels in another mouthful.

I watch him in awe. The man can *eat.*

"The official start is in two months, but there's some preliminary stuff before then. And" – Tanner glances down at me, squeezing my thigh – "we might head to the rink prior to that anyway."

"Thought you couldn't do unofficial training once you're signed," Wyatt says, biting off the cap of his own beer and then spitting it out like a trucker.

"*Wyatt,*" his dad barks, which makes Tanner chuckle quietly.

Wyatt holds up his palms and goes to retrieve the rogue beer cap.

Like Tanner's, Wyatt's plate is also more than half empty. I look down at my own, spear some green beans, and try to catch up.

They're caramelised green beans. Tanner's dad is freaking incredible.

"We won't be training," Tanner says, squeezing his palm over my thigh. "Just need some ice-time with Ash before game season begins."

"Oh, can you skate?" Tanner's mom asks me, smiling excitedly.

"Um," I say, well aware that she's a gold-medal-winning Olympic figure skater. "I'm not sure that you can call what I do 'skating'," I admit, laughing nervously.

Tanner's palm roams to my knee, warm and reassuring.

"She's only skated twice before, Mom," he tells her. "But I'm gonna try and teach her a little before I'm on the road."

"Adorable," Wyatt smirks.

Tanner flicks a cherry tomato at him.

Wyatt catches it in his mouth.

"*Boys*," their mom groans, dropping her face into her palms.

"Have you bought a place yet?" Tanner's dad asks, his eyes flicking my way briefly in a silent *extra* question.

Namely: are you two going to be living *together*?

Tanner rolls his shoulders, setting his cutlery neatly on his plate. His *empty* plate. The man is simply unstoppable. I shovel in another forkful of potato salad, borderline swallowing it whole in order to speed up.

"Haven't bought a place yet," Tanner admits, his voice deep as he drops his gaze to mine. He moves his hand from my knee so that he can splay it over my lower back. "We haven't… spoken about it yet. Ash's plans are still up in the air."

"Oh?" his mom asks, eyes kind as she leans forward, paying me her full attention.

Tanner nods down at me, encouraging me to open up a little.

"Well," I rasp, looking down at my lap to refold my napkin, "I'm going to be working for my family's business – they're in real estate. But I want to be part of a division that they don't really have yet. So, careerwise, I'm up in the air."

My cheeks heat up and Tanner's hand strokes me

harder.

"The job is partially remote," Tanner rumbles, his eyes on mine when I look up at him from my napkin. "And Ash knows that if she chooses to she can move in with me when I get my place."

My heart stumbles in my chest because we haven't talked about this before.

But I tuck a curl behind my ear and nod before returning to the green beans, not sure yet how to respond to such an obvious offer of commitment. Of generosity.

Exclusivity.

A sudden knock at the front door has the two dogs immediately jumping to their feet, Cookie bolting in through the open patio and Cobie shooting a look to Linc. When he gets the nod of approval Cobie instantly chases in after her, the sunlight streaking across his fur like a bright flash of caramel.

Tanner's eyes flick to his mom's, his irises sparkling as she smiles back at him.

"Is that…?" he asks, laughing as she nods her head.

"Christ," Wyatt says, shaking his head and grinning. He jerks his thumb toward his brother and says, "This guy and his love for cobbler. You'd never guess it from looking at him, would you?"

Tanner gives my waist a squeeze as he moves to stand, eyes on mine after a gentle kiss to the cheek.

"They ordered in dessert," he murmurs. "I'm gonna grab the door, okay?"

I nod up at him and he leans down to press a kiss to my forehead, not a hint of embarrassment on his face as his parents and brother stare at us in awe-struck silence.

Which is fine, because I've turned red enough for the both of us.

When we hear Tanner opening the front door, accompanied by the happy yips of his dogs, Wyatt tips his chin at me and says, "Wait until you try this cobbler."

I can't help but drop my chin into my palms, eyes on my empty plate as I laugh.

"He's actually already had me try it," I admit, scrunching my nose in happiness.

Wyatt shoves his chair away from the table, eyes crinkling as he chuckles.

"You're shitting me," he grins.

"*Wyatt*," his mom laughs, slapping one of his biceps to try and prevent further swearing.

Ten seconds later Tanner steps out of the patio doors, holding the tray of piping hot cobbler in one hand while the dogs jump around his legs, making him place his steps carefully so as not to step on them.

He runs his other hand over the khaki cap sat backwards on his head, which he must have picked up during his trek through the kitchen. He looks laidback and way too hot to handle.

When he catches me staring he smiles at me and winks.

His dad glances up at him as he swaps the cute gold-trimmed dinner plates for dessert ones.

"Hat," Linc orders. "Off."

Tanner places the cobbler in the centre of the table before settling heavily into the seat beside me. Then he gently moves the cap from his head to mine.

"Tanner!" I hiss, which makes him smirk handsomely down at me.

My eyes fly over to his dad and I quickly reach up to take it off but after a long look at his son Linc glances down at me, subtly gesturing that I can leave it on.

"Where'd you find it anyway?" Wyatt asks, his voice rough. He flicks a glance at his brother as he helps him remove the foil covering from the cobbler.

"What?" Tanner asks.

"The cap."

Tanner's eyes flash to mine, our secret heating the air between us.

I didn't know any significance to Tanner's cap when I kept it as my Carter U hostage, but what I do know is that it was never lost – Tanner let me keep it.

Before Tanner can answer his mom leans toward me.

"Oh Aisling, he used to wear that thing all of the time. Military green, like army fatigues – it's always been his favourite colour. It was too big for him at first but he's a big guy now, so he grew into it."

Wyatt smirks and says callously, "He does have a pretty big head now."

Tanner flashes his eyes to his brother, smirking back at him as he slides his forearm over the back of my chair.

"You see who I brought to the dinner table? Of course I've got a big head," Tanner replies, before turning his gaze back to me and giving me a handsome smile. He leans down to my cheek, brushing a gentle kiss over it before whispering, "You can see my other big head later."

My eyes grow wide, cheeks heating, as I bite back my laughter and shove him off of me. It only encourages him to envelop his palm around my hip, clutching me tighter as his dad stands up to dish out dessert.

Tanner's mom watches us in silence for a few beats before saying to Tanner with a curious lilt in her tone, "You know, I thought that maybe you had given it away."

Tanner runs his fingers through his hair, knee bouncing up and down as he rumbles, "I kinda did."

Linc scoops out large servings of cobbler while his wife grabs ice cream from the kitchen, setting it in the centre of the table before sitting back down into her seat.

Wyatt laughs at the serving size, borderline overflowing from the small lilac dessert plate.

"You tryna put me in a food coma?" he asks his dad.

Linc glances at him as he takes his seat. "You complaining?"

"No, sir," Wyatt grins. "I plan on sleeping this whole week through anyway."

Tanner looks up at his brother across the table. Half of Tanner's cobbler has already magically disappeared. "Did you really just get back today?" he asks him.

Wyatt nods, shovelling in another mouthful, before gesturing toward his dad with his fork and looking up at Tanner. "We both did. But dad got changed and shit as soon as we came home, whereas I napped on the sofa for, like, two hours straight. Then Cobe almost pissed on my feet and I realised that you must've arrived. Although now," he adds, flashing me a handsome grin, "I realise that your woman here is what all the excitement was about."

Tanner pauses his chewing for a brief moment, scoping out whether or not he wants to retaliate to his brother's comment. Then he feels my hand caress gently against his quad and he resumes his chewing, squeezing me back.

"We're all going to have an early night tonight," Linc rumbles quietly, slapping another scoop of ice cream on his plate before passing the tub back to Wyatt. "Like your mother said, y'all are welcome to stay over, for as long as you'd like."

Tanner looks at me for confirmation and I nod up at him, wanting him to spend as much time with his family as possible.

He wraps his arm around me tighter and says, "Yeah, we'd love to stay over. Thought you guys would want to head out tonight though, celebrate with friends in town or something."

Linc shakes his head. "Maybe in a couple days' time. In the meantime, we've got about seven months worth of sleep to catch up on."

"When are you seeing Jason?" his wife asks him, leaning down for a moment so that she can scoop Cookie up off the floor. The dog cuddles up to her in contentment, eyes closing as she smoothes down her fur.

"He's heading up tomorrow," Linc replies.

Sensing my lack of understanding, Wyatt supplies for

me, "Jason Coleson, one of his former military buddies. Stopping over for a few nights from Phoenix Falls."

Linc scoops in a mouthful of cobbler and says quietly, "He's a good man."

"What about you?" I ask Wyatt, playing with my little spoon.

I appreciate that Tanner's brother has also been trying to make me feel at home, and so I think that I should take the olive branch he's extending by starting to actively get to know him.

He leans back in his chair, smiling down at me lazily. "What about me?"

"Are you going to celebrate your homecoming in town?" I ask. "What you guys do for this country is incredible. Everyone in Carter Ridge will see you as a hero."

Wyatt grins at me from across the table, the smile creases in his cheeks so similar to his brother's.

"That's sweet," he smiles, his voice low and gruff. "You're real sweet."

Then he glances over to Tanner and says, "How the hell did you land this chick?"

Tanner squeezes my knee beneath the table and flashes a grin to his brother.

"God delivered. I signed."

I burst out laughing at that one, shoving him playfully as he smirks down at me.

"That's got to be the most country thing that you've ever said. Like, literally ever," I say through my giggles as he squeezes his arms around my shoulders, hauling me against him so that he can kiss my cheeks.

"That's the most country thing that *anyone* has ever said," Linc agrees quietly, his expression still stoic although I see the hint of a smile on his handsome mouth.

"Mason, why don't you show Aisling your room, and your father and I will clear up this table?" his mom suggests, giving us that *aw, young love* kind of smile.

383

Tanner pulls back an inch, eyes sliding down to the table.

"Can't," he says. "She's still eating her cobbler."

I've eaten about half of the mountain that Linc scooped out for me and, honestly, I currently have no more room for it.

But you know who probably does?

"Tanner." I squeeze his forearm. "Would you like to finish my cobbler?"

Tanner's eyes flash down to mine, his irises sparkling before he glances at the cobbler.

He swipes his tongue over his lower lip, shaking his head.

"You should... you should have it," he rasps. "It's yours. I've already had my share."

I try not to laugh.

"I'm offering it to you because I know how much you like it," I say quietly, grateful that his parents are currently talking too, so that I'm not a focal point.

Tanner rubs a hand down his jaw, stubble scratching over his palm as he flicks his eyes between me and the cobbler.

"You sure?" he rumbles hoarsely.

I feel my dimples deepen in my cheeks. *My adorable country boy.*

"Of course," I tell him, laughing when he hunches down to crush a kiss to my cheek.

He takes the dessert spoon from my hand and uses it to scoop up half the serving in one go. Then he drops his forehead to my shoulder as he swallows it down, groaning quietly against my neck and making me giggle.

I fiddle with the khaki cap set low over my eyes before wrapping my arms around his large shoulders, feeling so contentedly at home.

"This is, like, the best moment of my life," he rumbles. I giggle quietly as he purposefully scrapes my skin with his stubble.

Then he pulls back so that he can make the final scoop, his large palm massaging the nape of my neck as he finishes swallowing it down.

"'Kay," he murmurs. "We're gonna go to my room." He glances between his parents and says, "Leave this stuff and I'll come back down to clear it later."

His dad grunts.

"No you damn won't." He jerks his chin in my direction. "Not when you've got company."

Tanner rises to his feet, tugging me up with him. Cobie sits up to attention, tail thumping as he looks between us.

"I can do it tonight, when everyone's in bed," Tanner offers. Then he laughs incredulously, saying, "No way am I gonna let you do the dishes. Y'all just got back from deployment. Let me."

Linc steeples his fingers, watching his son with sharp but thoughtful eyes.

"Mace," he says finally, quiet and deep. "We can handle a few dishes. Trust me." He gestures calmly with his large battle-scarred hand. "Now go and give your girl a tour of our home."

I can see the argument warring in Tanner's eyes but after a moment he thinks better of it and he wraps my hand in his.

"Thank you for the lovely meal," I say over my shoulder as Tanner tugs me quickly through the porch door, his hand thrumming with adrenaline as he weaves us through the rustic kitchen.

I yelp as something hard shoves against my butt and we both turn around to see Cobie shooting me his guiltiest expression.

"Jesus," Tanner murmurs, half-laughing as he positions himself behind me, away from further nose-butting. "Cobe's crazy for your scent," he says, his hands sliding down to my hips. "Not that I blame him," he adds, chest swelling as he squeezes me.

When we reach the stairs he turns to the Alsatian. "Back to the porch, man."

Cobie sits down on his back legs, tongue lolling innocently, even as his eyes glance up at the top landing.

"Cobe," Tanner laughs. "Come on, man. Outside."

He jerks his chin to where we just came from and waits it out until Cobie finally does a reluctant howl and then trudges back down the hallway.

Tanner takes my hand in his and leads me up the beautiful white staircase.

"How was that?" he asks me, his deep voice a little nervous. "What'd you think of everyone? Hope it was, uh, okay for a first meeting."

We reach the top step and I nod up at him as he looks down at me.

"Everyone was so lovely. Your family is amazing."

"Yeah?" he asks, his gorgeous eyes searching mine. "It was okay?"

"It was better than okay," I laugh. "They were... so thoughtful. And considerate and kind." I move to wrap my arms around his neck as his fingers start gripping at my waist. "Just like you."

His mouth tugs into a half-smirk.

"Coming from the girl who let me finish her goddamn cobbler," he rumbles, making me laugh delightedly as he ducks down to take my lips with his. He groans deeply as he hauls my body against his chest, his grip tightening on my waist as he shoves a door shut behind us.

I gasp as his mouth moves slowly down to my throat, sucking rough kisses into my skin as one of his palms roams up to squeeze my breasts.

"Are we in your bedroom?" I whisper, clutching him tighter as he caresses me.

"I fuckin' hope so," he rumbles, making my chest shake as I laugh.

He pulls back with hazy eyes, his shoulders heaving quickly up and down. Then he flicks his eyes across the room and nods, one of his hands tugging the cap off my head and tossing it gently on a pretty wooden dresser.

I allow myself to do a three-sixty in the room, more than a little surprised by the choice in décor. It's all rustic and cosy, with low-beam ceilings that Tanner literally has to duck under. The only hint that this room once belonged to a teenage boy is the large TV and game console in the corner behind the door, with a cosy brown recliner set in front of it, where presumably he did those multi-player video games with his friends.

"I never had a games console," I admit, running a hand through my curls as I shake them back over my shoulders.

"No?" he asks, gently brushing his fingers through my hair. "We can use it if you want. Haven't touched that thing since I was about seventeen, though."

We walk slowly around his room, him watching my expressions as I peek inside drawers and flick through a small pile of DVDs. When I move to the long wooden desk in front of the window I pause for a beat as my eyes land on a flyer.

I blink down at it before reaching over tentatively.

"Is that–?" I begin, just as Tanner shoves it off of the table, cheeks burning red as he moves in front of me, blocking the view.

I look up at his face, gorgeously rugged and flushed with embarrassment.

"Was that a cheer flyer?" I ask him incredulously, fighting the pull of my dimples. "Was that a flyer for one of my competitions?"

I already know the answer seeing as I helped *design that flyer*. Not to mention the fact that there's a *photo of me on it*.

Tanner shoves a hand through his hair, chest pumping hard as he glances down at me.

The long-sleeved shirt really does nothing but

accentuate his enormous biceps and pecs.

"Tanner?" I ask again, really smiling now.

"Yeah?" he rasps, dropping his eyes as he takes my hips.

"Did you… keep one of my Carter U cheer flyers?" I ask him, rubbing my palms over his chest as he drops his forehead to mine.

"What'd, uh… what'd make you say that?" he asks, his hands bunching the fabric of my dress, twisting it in his fists.

I squeeze his pecs and giggle. "Because that flyer on your desk had a photo of me on it."

And it was also folded over multiple times so that I was the only girl he could see. My heart squeezes in pleasure but I refrain from mentioning that.

"Would that… bother you? If I did?" he says, panting slightly.

"Well, it's a bit too late to ask that now seeing as I've already seen it, stalker," I laugh teasingly.

He swallows hard, eyes molten when they meet mine.

"Is that weird?" he rumbles, walking me backwards until my thighs hit the soft cushioning of his bed. "That I kept it?"

I shake my head at him, eyes sparkling. Then I whisper, "What did you use it for?"

He pokes his tongue in his cheek, gaze raking down my front and then back up.

"You don't have any social media," he says gruffly, by way of explanation. Then he moves his mouth to my ear and murmurs, "You know exactly what I used it for."

I breathe out a shaky exhale, hands moving to his biceps to squeeze him harder. "No way did you use it for that," I whisper, and now it's his turn to breathe out a laugh.

"Yeah way I used it for that," he rumbles, hitting me with one of his belly-flipping smirks before dipping his mouth down to mine.

Sunlight streams in through the window as he helps me

wrap my arms up around his broad shoulders, hunching low so that he can kiss me while we stand.

I jump up onto my tip-toes to lessen the distance between us and I feel him smile against my lips, chuckling quietly.

"Shortie," he murmurs, smirking.

"I'm normal sized," I whisper back. "You're just a man mountain."

"Yeah," he murmurs, still smiling as he kisses me again.

One of his hands roams down my back until he's gripping my behind, and he gives it a rough knead with his palm before swatting it with a firm spank.

"You sure that you're okay staying here for a few days, before we head back to Larch Peak?" he asks quietly.

He turns us around so that he can sit at the edge of the bed. Then he splays his large quads, the denim of his jeans pulling tight, and he pulls me between his legs so that he can look up at me from under those long dark lashes.

I nod down at him, stroking my fingers through his hair, then down his stubble. He closes his eyes momentarily, practically growling at my touch, and his fingers grip harder into my behind as he shifts his quads wider.

"I don't have to stay," I offer quietly, "if you'd prefer to have some real family time with your dad and your brother while they're home."

Tanner's beautiful eyes flash up to mine, bright and burning as he massages his palms over my hips.

"Why would I not want you here?" he asks, his voice painfully deep. "Having you here is what made today perfect. Getting to spend my time with all of the people who I love the most." He pulls me closer by my hips. "Most of all, you."

My eyes blink wide, my breathing stuttering in my throat.

Because when I think back to what he just said, I realise that Tanner said the L-word.

"What?" he asks gruffly. "What's that scared little expression for?"

I press a palm against my burning cheeks and his mouth tilts up into a lazy grin.

"You serious?" he asks incredulously. "You seriously didn't know how I feel about you?"

"Tanner," I breathe, "you don't have to say what you just said—"

He stands to his feet, making me stumble back a step until he catches me. He crushes my chest against his, breathing heavily as I swallow and look up at him.

"I'm gonna say it, Aisling. So I'm going to give you a second to prepare yourself first."

I shake my head. "It's too soon, right? Surely it's too soon."

"Baby, I've been feeling these feelings for you for four goddamn years. It's not too soon. It's coming four years too late."

My heart squeezes in my chest and, sensing my emotions, Tanner holds me tighter.

"It's been a long time coming," he rumbles, stroking his palm around the nape of my neck. "We could've made four babies in the time that I've been head over heels for you, Aisling. Eight, given your genetics."

A happy laugh bubbles out of me, quickly followed by alarm – *eight babies?* – but Tanner's handsome grin brings me back to the present. To where I'm standing in his cosy childhood bedroom, a soft bed behind him, low beams that he has to duck under overhead. A cheer flyer from Carter U currently hiding at the side of his desk, even though I have no doubt that he'll retrieve it later tonight when I'm not looking.

To his warm hands holding me firmly, his heart pumping steadily over mine.

"You ready for me to say it?" he asks roughly.

"No," I whimper.

He breathes out a laugh, those perfect creases pulling taut in his cheeks.

"Can't hold it in any longer, baby."

I bury my face in his neck but he gently tugs my hair, pulling me back so that I can look up at him as he says it.

"I love you, Aisling. I love you so goddamn much."

I jump up onto my tip-toes, making him laugh quietly as I yank him down by his stupid sexy long-sleeved shirt.

I press a kiss against his mouth and Tanner keeps it chaste and gentle, or at least he tries to until his body won't let him anymore. He pulls back with a groan, gaze dropping to the thick tent in his jeans.

"Fuck," he pants, quickly gripping it and urging it to go down. "Sorry," he rasps at me, hunching down once more so that he can kiss me again.

"I know we're not gonna, uh… be doing anything physical while we're here," he murmurs, eyes still on his enormous erection as he rakes a hand through his hair, "but I'm gonna apologise in advance for how hard I'm gonna get when we're trying to sleep tonight. And when we wake up tomorrow. And probably just every couple of minutes throughout the day when we're alone together."

"Will it make it even harder if I say that I love you too?" I breathe.

Tanner's mouth crashes down to mine and suddenly I'm squealing as we tumble to his bed.

"Say that again," he rasps, pulling back to look down at me. His eyes are hazy and heated and filled with so much love.

"I love you," I tell him, feeling my cheeks flush under the directness of his gaze.

"Again," he demands, licking his lips as he watches me giggle.

"I love you," I whisper, hands stroking over the swollen muscles of his chest.

"I love you too," he rumbles, his eyes unblinking as they

burn into mine. Heat pools in my stomach as his gaze slow-rakes me up and down. "I love you so much that I wish that I was inside of you right now," he murmurs, one fist bunching the side of my dress so that he can scrunch it up to the top of my hip. He settles his lap between my legs, thrusting roughly over my panties.

"You'll have to wait," I whisper, eyes rolling back as he squeezes my ass.

He thrusts harder, his back muscles rolling, until his bed slams against the wall and I'm instantly yelping, laughing as I shove him off of me.

He laughs, covering his face with his palms, before pulling me against his chest and pressing kisses all over my forehead.

"Maybe they're still outside and didn't hear that," he murmurs, making me giggle as he squeezes my butt.

"We aren't, and we did!" Wyatt yells through the wall, making my eyes grow wide before I groan into my hands.

Tanner rolls on top of me and shouts a quick, "Mind your goddamn business!"

And then we're laughing, Tanner holding me tight in his arms.

I fall asleep to the sound of his steadily beating heart.

CHAPTER 37

Tanner

Present day

"How long's it gonna be until y'all come back?" Wyatt asks, gravelly as hell because he slept until 2pm today.

We both look up as Aisling makes her way down the stairs. She's holding her rose in one hand and wearing the only change of clothes that she brought with her for our stop here in Carter Ridge. Denim jeans and a grey fitted long-sleeve shirt, which has me folding my arms over my chest as I watch my brother grin up at her.

Wyatt holds out an arm for her as she reaches the last step so that he can give her a parting side-hug and I stare him out as he gives her a squeeze. I'm not much caring for the smug wink he gives me as he squishes her.

"If you hold my girl any longer, we won't be coming back, period," I tell him, only half joking, but he breathes out a laugh and releases Aisling anyway.

Cobe's tail pounds the hardwood like a jackhammer and he all but purrs when Ash leans down to gently stroke him behind his ears.

She's still a little anxious about being around such a massive dog but Cobe has been on his best behaviour with her, initial excited pissing aside.

He's been following her around, giving her his most innocent eyes, and settling down beside her anywhere that she happens to sit. If anything, I think that he can tell that she's been a little scared, so being gentle while keeping her close is his way of putting her at ease.

And I feel pretty fucking proud of Aisling *and* Cobe, because it's ninety-nine percent worked.

Not one to miss out on a little loving, Cookie shoots down the hallway and flies straight into the calf of my jeans before putting herself right and then trotting over to sniff Aisling goodbye.

"Uh, earth to Mace," Wyatt says, shoving his hard elbow in my side.

I jab the fucker right back before raking a hand through my hair.

"We're going back to Larch Peak for around a week. We've got friends camping up the mountain so, unless they head back down tomorrow, we'll join them. Otherwise, we'll be staying at the lake house while Ash waits for her mom to give it its official surveying. And once that's been dealt with…" I shrug, my chest expanding contentedly. "Then we're free. Ash'll be ready to start looking into her next project, God willing, and I'll be almost about to start NHL training."

"So as soon as the lake house has been" – Wyatt scratches his stubble, searching for a word – "approved, then y'all will come back here for a bit?" he asks.

I look over at him and smirk. "Why? You missing me already?"

"Not you, asshole," he grins. "I wanna see Aisling

again."

I humour him with a smile before socking him in the gut.

When Aisling turns around to look at us Wyatt is keeled over and choking, and she flashes me a concerned look which I wave away with a satisfied expression.

"Don't worry about him," I tell her, which has Wyatt laughing as he stands back to his full height.

"Yeah, yeah," he rumbles. Then he gives Ash a wink as I pull her into my side and says, "Good meeting you, *Aisling*."

I jerk my chin at him and, joking aside, we clasp our palms together, re-solidifying our brother's bond.

"We'll be back soon," I tell him, those four words laced with so many others: like, *I'm glad that you got on so well with Aisling* and *I'm so proud to call a hero like you my brother*.

He nods at me, smile creases crinkling the corners of his eyes, and then I turn to the kitchen doorway to see my mom and my dad.

It's been good to spend time with them – even better to have Aisling here with me – and as soon as Ash is finished up with her first project it'll feel good to come back here and make the most of seeing my dad and Wyatt before they go out and deploy again.

"Thank you for having me," Aisling says, laughing lightly when my mom pulls her in for a hug.

The two most important women in my life, smiling happily and laughing with each other.

It's a beautiful sight.

"Anytime, Aisling," my mom says, and even my dad gives her a nod from the doorway, arms folded over his chest as he watches my mom.

His eyes flick over to mine and he tips his chin at me.

"Don't be gone too long," he rumbles, and hell if I don't feel my whole heart fucking burn.

I gently move around Aisling, giving her a squeeze on her waist, before meeting my dad in the middle and embracing him in a hard hug. He slaps his fist on my back and I huff out a laugh, wondering what he just punctured.

"Love you, dad," I tell him.

He grunts, nods, and says, "Love you too, son."

＊

The drive back to Larch Peak is quiet but fast, with Aisling curled up on the passenger seat and both of her hands wrapped around one of mine. We were blessed with two days of heat but the sky has finally turned overcast, with thick grey clouds blanketing low over the dark tops of the trees.

Doesn't matter. The SUV is pounding with heat.

We didn't do anything physical while staying at my parents' house – one, because everyone would hear everything, and two, because that would be really fucking weird – but now my balls are so heavy that I have to shift on my seat every five seconds.

Aisling glances over, notices, and removes one of her hands from mine so that she can gently caress my quad.

I grunt, shaking my head, silently asking her to stop before I literally come.

"We're almost at the lake house," she says in her beautiful husky voice.

"Yeah," I rasp. I take the right turn that leads to the lake and rumble quietly, "Thank God."

The cabins come into view and I'm relieved to see that everyone must still be camping up the mountain. I steer us carefully around the head of the lake and then put the car in park the second that we're beside the lake house porch.

I drop back in my seat, gripping myself before I've even released the seatbelt. I hear the sound of Ash unbuckling hers beside me and I release my death-grip from the front of my jeans, smacking open the belt mechanism and yanking the strap from over my chest. Then I'm shifting my quads uncomfortably on my seat as I turn around to face her, immediately hunching low as she pushes up onto her knees, leaning over and reaching for me.

My warm palms encase her waist as I dip low to take her mouth, groaning loudly as she sighs with relief. One of her hands caresses over the muscles of my chest while the other grips at the back of my neck, pulling me down so that she can reach me better.

I try and slip my digits down the waistband of her jeans but my fingers are literally too damn big to shove in.

I grunt and pull back, chest heaving as I look down at her.

"Haven't been inside of you since I told you that I love you," I rumble. "I need to fix that, right the fuck now."

"In your car?" she asks, suddenly gasping as I suck her neck.

"Anywhere you want it," I tell her. "Probably not enough room in the car."

I kiss my way back to her mouth, releasing a rough grunt when she parts her lips for my tongue. I lick it gently against hers, my hands fumbling with her zipper, then mine, and then I'm reaching behind my neck so that I can rip my shirt over my head.

I toss my shirt in the back, palms cupping Aisling's cheeks as she massages my chest.

Can't deny it, that feels really fucking good.

"You gonna bite 'em again?" I ask her, thinking back to that night in the cabin when she sunk her teeth into my nipple.

She smiles up at me, all taunting dimples and beautiful long lashes.

"Why, did you like it?" she purrs, her hands massaging my abdomen now. My muscles flex under her attention, swelling and thickening as she strokes me gently.

"You know I liked it. I loved it."

I hunch down and crush a gruff kiss to her smart

mouth.

"I love you," I murmur, groaning through my teeth when she helps ease my jeans down my quads.

Or at least she tries to. They get stuck before they're even down an inch and I'm wincing with every tug as I try to drag them slowly over my throbbing cock.

"Your thighs are huge," she rasps, pupils dialled the hell out as she watches me.

I breathe out a nervous laugh.

"That a good thing?" I pant, sighing in relief when the denim is finally just above my knees. The muscles of my quads are thick and swollen, flexing hard with adrenaline and the knowledge of what we're about to do.

She nods up at me, looking flushed and lightheaded.

"Yeah," she breathes out. "You have hockey player thighs."

A half-smile tugs up the corner of my mouth as I pull her up for another kiss. I shove my other hand down the waistband of my boxer briefs, grunting hard as I give myself that first rough pump.

She digs her nails into the sides of my neck, pulling back to watch my hand. Seeing the lust and innocence and need on her face, I quickly fumble down my underwear and grip my shaft in my hand, wanting her to see what I've got for her as I stroke myself up and down.

"Take off your shirt," I rumble. "Let me see you."

I wrap one hand around her hip and work the other over my cock, chest heaving up and down as Aisling pulls off her shirt. She tosses it in the back with mine and then leans over the stick shift, making me groan as she rubs herself up against me. I steel my jaw and toss my cock harder, looking down at her with heated eyes, groaning as she presses those soft tits right up against the large muscles of my chest.

"This bra," I rasp, glancing down at the baby pink cups. I clear my throat and rumble out, "It's… pretty. I like it."

Then I'm removing my hand from my cock and arching my neck as I try to calm my heavy breathing.

"Shouldn't be jerking off," I rasp, wincing as the broad head smacks against Aisling's jeans. "Just got too hard when I looked at you. Needed some relief."

I cup her face in my palms and start kissing her long and slow.

"I need to be inside of you," I murmur, jaw hardening as her fingers trail up my shaft.

I open my eyes and look down at her, my palms caressing her denim-clad ass.

"I'm gonna need you to put that hand away unless you want me to come all over it," I warn her.

She presses her breasts against me harder and I spank her ass, grunting loudly.

"Aisling," I rasp, as her hand slides down to cup my sac. "I'm too excited right now. Tug them once more and I'm gonna come on your belly."

To both my relief and fucking agony Aisling releases her hands from my balls, sliding her fingers slowly up my chest as I splay my palms over her behind.

I meet her in the middle of the SUV so that she doesn't have to crawl over the centre console and slowly stroke my tongue inside her mouth, winding her dark curls around my fist.

A light pattering of rain thumps gently against the windshield and I pull away breathing heavily. I squint as I glance out of the window, peering up at the silver sky.

"This is my favourite kind of weather," Aisling whispers, and I look back down at her, pushing her hair back from her cheeks.

"Yeah?" I ask. Though now that I think about it, that makes perfect sense.

Of course Aisling is a summer storm kind of girl.

"It's romantic," she whispers softly, "and I find it really grounding. It's harder to over-think about things when you're listening to the rain."

She shrugs gently and I hold her closer.

"And because of that, because it makes me remember that nothing is that deep… it shows me that it's okay to wear my heart on my sleeve after all. Like, why not? Why not be exactly who I really am?"

She glances down at her heart-shaped freckle and murmurs, "I don't know. I just think that it's beautiful."

I press a gentle kiss against her lips, lost in the warmth of her touch, her softness, her sweet sighs and the thrum of the rain.

"Wanna stay out here?" I murmur, inhaling deeply as she squeezes my biceps.

She shakes her head, a little smile tugging at her mouth.

"You said that there isn't enough room for what you want to do," she whispers.

"Yeah, but that was before you told me how much you love the rain," I rumble, feeling a dimple crease in my cheek as I pull back to smile down at her.

"I do love the rain," she whispers, "but I love you even more."

That confession has my heart stumbling in my chest, my shoulders heaving as I stare down at her.

Then I'm winding her hair tighter around my fist and hunching low so that I can take her mouth with mine.

"Get on top of me," I grunt, grabbing one of her hands and wrapping it around my cock. "Get that pretty pussy on top of me so that I can show you how much I love you."

But now she's pulling backwards, her eyes sparkling, and pushing me off of her while I try to pull her closer.

"You'll have to come and get me," she whispers, giggling when I groan against her neck.

"The fuck does that mean?" I murmur, desperately trying to shove my digits beneath the zipper of her jeans, the warm feel of her panties enough to make me pre-come halfway up my abs.

I grunt and wipe away the warm moisture with my palm, dead-set on pulling her jeans down her thighs even as she giggles and arches against me.

"What do you think it means?" she whispers, fingers tugging at my hair as I slide my tongue down the cup of her bra. I groan like an animal, gently licking at her peak. I grip my sac with my free hand and get lost in the feel of her as I suck her lovingly into my mouth.

You'll have to come and get me.

I murmur her words back to myself, trying to make sense of them, trying to figure out what she could possibly mean—

My head snaps up, eyes burning as they shoot straight to hers.

Oh Jesus. I know exactly what she's saying.

"No," I order, eyes flicking to her hand on the door handle. "Ash, baby, I'm way too turned on for games right now."

Eyes on mine, she clicks the door open, biting back her smile. I glance out of the door and pull myself upright so that I'm towering over her.

The rain sounds like a downpour, hammering relentlessly against the silver surface of the lake. I drop my gaze back down to Aisling, catching her adorable baby dimples as she giggles. I let myself take in her sun-kissed skin, her baby pink bra, her fitted denim jeans that are going to look even more sexy when they're speckled with rain.

Then I flick my eyes back to hers as I push my hair off my forehead.

I clear my throat, my voice like gravel.

"You want me to chase you?" I ask gruffly, already knowing the answer as she scooches another inch backwards.

She gives me a naughty smile. "Only if you think that you can catch me."

I huff out a pained laugh, watching as she slides one leg

out onto the passenger-side step.

"Baby," I rasp, gripping my cock in my fist. "I'm barely gonna be able to walk, let alone run with this thing."

She slips her other sandal onto the step, slow-sliding off her seat until she suddenly jumps down onto the dirt. And yeah, I was right: she looks hot as fuck getting showered in rain while she's half naked.

"Sounds like an excuse to me," she purrs, palms flat on her seat as she leans inside. Squeezing her tits together to drive me wild. Little fucking tease.

"Ash," I pant, releasing my cock with a choked sound. "No games right now, baby. Get back in the car."

She slips her fingers into the tight front pocket of her jeans and my chest heaves up and down as I watch her. After a moment of rubbing she finally frees her hand, holding up a key.

The key to the lake house.

And then she's off.

My head smacks loudly off the roof of my car as I pull back from over the centre console and I curse like a trucker as I watch her sprint alongside the lake. She tosses a grin at me over her shoulder as I try to wrangle my boxer briefs back over my cock.

I'm groaning in fucking agony as I finally shove my jeans up my quads, eyes on the vixen trying to ram her key in the lock as I grab our shirts from the back of the G-wagon.

I lean over the shift to slam her door closed before swinging mine open, and I hear her squeal with excitement as she manages to push the front of the lake house open.

"*Ash*," I bark, smacking my door shut as I watch her kick off her sandals and run into the house. I keep our shirts under one of my biceps and grip my other fist over my groin, steeling my jaw as I jog up the porch steps because I've never been this hard in my life.

I yank off my boots and socks, and then kick the door

open, storming into the rich lake house foyer as rainwater streams down my chest.

I swipe at the water with one of my palms and use the other to toss our shirts into the kitchen.

The second that I lock my eyes on her – standing very fucking precariously on the back of one of the couches – she shot-puts her rolled-up jeans straight at my chest. I grunt as I catch them, the rain-heavy denim smacking hard against my jaw and my pecs, and I throw them in the same direction as our shirts, eyes raking her up and down.

Now she's left in nothing but her baby pink bra and a pair of matching panties – panties that look way too familiar – and she's smiling at me all cute and coy as she pushes her curls from her face, sparkling raindrops cascading down her shoulders.

"Get down from there, Ash, right the fuck now."

"From here?" she asks, sweet and taunting. She does a little twirl that has my heart lurching up my throat.

"Not funny," I warn her, grabbing my wallet from my pants. I flick it open, not taking my eyes off of her as I slip out two condoms, and then I toss that to the floor too, before shoving my jeans down my quads.

I kick them to the side as I lock the front door.

When I turn back to face her she's still doing her little dance on the back of the sofa, giggling as I scrape a hand down my jaw.

"Get over here," I rumble.

"Come and get me," she teases.

My mouth tugs up at the corner and I thunder right for her.

She yelps with excitement, jumping off the back of the sofa as I move to grab her from the front, and then she's sprinting up the stairs, screaming as she hears me pounding the wood behind her.

My eyes are locked in on her beautiful behind until she spins around to face me, a low sound rumbling through my chest as I realise what she's wearing.

"Crotchless?" I growl, eyes flashing up to hers as she fluffs up her dark hair.

"Maybe," she taunts, giving me another twirl before racing down the corridor.

I hit the top step and put my foot on the accelerator, charging for her as she reaches the bathroom and making her squeal in pleasure as I rush her from behind.

"This what you wanted?" I rumble, stubble scraping against her cheek as I haul her against my chest, forearms wrapped tight around her belly.

She giggles and squirms, gasping when I sink my teeth into the curve of her neck.

"*Yes,*" she gasps, moaning loudly when I grip my palm around her heat. I clutch it tight, over her panties, and inhale deeply against her throat.

"I love that you make me work for it," I murmur, holding her tighter as I walk us to the master bedroom. She giggles as I roam one palm over her breast, massaging it firmly as I rumble, "My fuckin' woman."

Half falling over each other, we manage to get over the bedroom doorway, but then I'm picking her up around the middle, kicking the door closed, and settling us down beside the jamb on the floor. There's a thick furry rug placed over the hardwood, nestled intimately under the lowest part of the A-frame roof. I pin her carefully underneath me, rolling her onto her back as I position myself between her thighs, and tossing the condoms to the floor so that I can quickly grab one before I push inside of her.

She giggles up at me, cheruby cheeks flushed pink and big eyes sparkling bright. I cage one forearm above her head and squeeze my other palm over her bra.

"You're the prettiest girl that I've ever seen," I rasp, slipping my digits underneath the sexy cup. "Can we do it here?" I ask, rubbing my hips against hers.

She arches her neck backwards, moaning as I push our

bodies together.

"On the floor?" she whispers, laughing quietly as I kiss her neck. "You're such a caveman," she whimpers, thighs squeezing around me as I caress her nipple.

"Yeah," I rumble, sliding my hand around to the back of her bra for the fastening.

Reading my mind she says, "It's at the front," and I nod, heaving my body up onto one elbow so that I can get a better look at her bra.

A dent creases between my brow as I fumble between the pretty cups, temples pounding harder and harder as my gaze keeps straying to her tits. They're pushed up beneath the fabric and their plumpness is driving me insane. I have to pause my fingers for half a minute just so that I can hunch down and press my face between them, hand slipping into my boxers so that I can tug my aching sac.

"Ash," I rasp, licking relentlessly above her nipple. "Can't find the clasp."

She scrapes her fingers through my fade, rough enough to make me buck against her, before tangling them in my rain-slicked fringe, tugging at it to recapture my attention.

"That's because you were right the first time," she whispers, "and the clasp actually is at the back."

A laugh rumbles out of me as I shake my head and grin down at her. Then Aisling sinks her teeth into her gorgeous smile as I grip the back of her bra and yank it backwards.

The bra opens, the straps instantly slip down her shoulders, and then I push them even farther, baring her to me. I cup both of my palms around her breasts, squeezing them together as I hunch down to suck her.

Her back arches off the furry rug and I palm her more roughly, sucking her harder. I release one nipple and move over to the other, working it in my mouth with deep long pulls.

When I finally lift my face back to hers her lashes are fluttering wildly, her breathing uneven. Her nipples are sucked pink and sensitive, making her gasp when they rub against me.

I grab one of the condoms from beside us, bite it open, and spit out the foil.

She watches me in a heated daze, lids heavy, irises on fire.

I free myself of my boxer briefs and hover over her as I roll down the condom. Sheathed to the hilt, I smack my cock against her pussy, her thighs spread wide, baring the crotchless area to me.

"Prettiest chick I've ever seen," I rumble, gripping one hand behind her head and keeping the other tight around my cock. She wraps both of her arms around my shoulders, tugging me closer so that we're chest to chest.

I nudge my shaft between the lace, grunting roughly as she gasps.

"Can I have you?" I rumble, looking down at her beautiful face.

She nods up at me from beneath my chest, making my shoulders swell as I push myself inside.

I drop my forehead to her neck, a growl tearing up my throat.

"So tight," I tell her, my hand tightening around the nape of her neck. My other hand roams up to her breasts, squeezing roughly as I withdraw.

She lets out a ball-cinching moan and I roll into her again, vision blurring.

"It's so thick," she whimpers, thighs slipping higher up my sides.

I grunt and thrust faster, gripping at her breasts as I up the pace.

"These past few days," she pants, nails biting into the muscles of my back as I pump my cock between her thighs, "you, uh – at the house – y-you called me your... your girlfriend."

Satisfaction throbs through my abdomen, making me

smirk as I suck her neck. "Yeah."

Her nails dig into me harder as she whimpers, "We haven't talked about that yet."

I lap gently at her throat before moving my mouth back to hers. I press a kiss against her lips, her chest bouncing as I pump her harder.

"Nothing to talk about," I tell her. "I said what I said. Simple as that."

When those pretty eyes take on a darker shade, her vixen side coming out, I roll into her deeper, sensing that she's about to give me some of that attitude.

Her eyes roll into the back of her head as she moans, but even when I grip her chin she refuses to meet my gaze.

Is she serious right now? She's going to start a fight with me while I'm inside of her?

If anything, that makes me harder, amused disbelief turning into lust.

I jerk my chin at her, gripping her cheeks. "You got a problem with that?" I ask her.

She turns her head to the side, hands tightening on my shoulders as I thrust deeper.

I huff out a laugh, jaw clenching as I groan.

"Ash," I grunt.

This damn woman.

"We gonna argue about this?" I ask her, lifting my eyebrows when she finally shoots me a little glare.

She whimpers something that I can't quite catch so I massage her more gently, loosening her up as I slow-thrust between her thighs.

"Didn't hear you, baby. Talk to me."

I nudge her nose with mine as she mumbles, "You coulda asked me about it first."

I mean, she's got a point. But we did everything else in this relationship out of order, so why start breaking that chain now?

"Shoulda asked you," I admit.

She cuddles into my neck as she mumbles, "Yeah, you should've."

I laugh and kiss at her cheek.

"You someone else's girlfriend or something?" I ask teasingly.

She gives me a frosty look before mumbling, "No."

I grunt and pump harder.

"Wanna be my girlfriend?" I ask, lifting up slightly so that I can gauge her reaction.

I roll my shoulders, waiting for her answer.

"Taking your sweet time there, Ash."

She looks up at me and whispers, "Ask me nicely."

You have got to be fucking kidding me right now.

"Aisling," I rumble, breathing out a laugh as she blinks up at me. "I love you so much, and I'll do anything for you. Will you do me the honour of being my girlfriend?"

She clutches me closer as she whispers, "Say please."

I wet my lower lip, voice deep as I say, "Please."

She involuntarily squeezes tighter and I drop my forehead to hers, groaning loudly.

"Yes," she pants, "Tanner, yes, I'll be your girlfriend."

"Yeah?" I rasp, letting out a pained laugh.

She nods up at me and I grip her cheeks, kissing her hard.

"You love me?" I ask, chest heaving as she nods again.

"Say it," I demand.

She shoves playfully at my chest, giggling as she whispers, "*You* say it."

I press a kiss to her cheek and rumble, "Aisling, I love you."

"How much?" she teases and we both start laughing, brows arched in pleasure-pain.

"Too much," I pant. "I love you so goddamn much."

"I love you too," she whispers, squealing as I change the position. Heaving myself up onto my haunches, spreading my quads, and settling her across my thighs. Pushing her back up against the dark wall beside the door, one hand wrapped protectively around her head and the other keeping her lap positioned firmly over mine. Like missionary but on my knees, with my girl's soft thighs wrapped around my hips.

I give an experimental upward thrust, pumping her roughly against the wall, and when she gasps against my throat I know that she'll be able to finish in this position.

I squeeze my palm over her thigh, hold her hips, and thrust again.

"Tanner!" she gasps, arms tightening around my neck.

"I love you so much," I rasp, my digits tangling in her crotchless panties.

"I'm there," she whimpers, thighs searching for purchase against me.

I push her harder against the wall, spreading my quads wider so that I can hit it as deep as possible. I grip her hair tighter, arch her neck, and suck her throat as I drive her over the edge.

"My girlfriend," I grunt, slamming my free palm against the wall as she comes.

She whimpers breathlessly, arms tightening around my shoulders, and I shove myself inside of her as hard as I can.

"I love you so much," I groan, head feeling heavy as she finishes, my own release shooting upwards and blanking every thought from my mind.

"I l-love you too," she whispers, and suddenly I can't take it anymore. I grunt against her throat, hips driving in and out, and then I'm punching my fist against the drywall, biceps rippling as I break through it.

"*God, yeah*," I grind out, not registering what just happened. I grip my right hand around her hip and ride her hard as I come.

"Tanner!" she whimpers. "Oh my God, did you just–?"

Aisling lets out a squeal and, reading it as pleasure, I spank her ass.

I bury my face in her throat, temples throbbing as I slip it out of her. I press a kiss against her jaw, massaging her hips as I pull back to reach her mouth.

And then I see it.

Next to her flushed, surprised, kind of impressed expression is a fucking hole in the wall that I just punched my fist through.

I blink at it for a moment before looking down at my hand. My bleeding hand. Which I just punched through the wall.

The wall in the lake house that Aisling's mom is coming to visit in two day's time.

The lake house that her entire small-town-flipping career is riding on.

My eyes drop back down to hers and she blinks up at me, her shock mirroring mine.

"Oh fuck," I whisper, watching every emotion possible flash through her irises.

Luckily, the main emotion there is the relief of her orgasm, but I can see that just behind the pink haze of love a kindling of anger is flickering dangerously.

"Ash," I rumble, my voice hoarse.

Her eyes shoot over to the wall and I slap my palm over the break, making those dazzling irises flash straight back to mine.

"Tanner," she whimpers nervously.

I shut her up with a kiss.

"Baby, I'm so fuckin' sorry," I rasp quickly, cuddling her tightly against my pecs. "I'm so sorry, baby. I swear I'm going to fix this."

"Tanner! You broke the *wall!*" she exclaims, but relief instantly surges through my chest as I realise that she's burst into a fit of laughter. She peeks up at me through her fingers and then slaps her palm playfully against my chest.

"Caveman," she says, scolding and teasing at the same time.

I'm so fucking grateful that she's not livid with me right now but I need her to know that I'm still taking this seriously.

"I'm so sorry," I tell her again, pressing her chest against mine as I look down at her. "That was – I didn't mean to – I was just…" I shake my head, trying to force myself to think straight. "You felt so good. I couldn't take it."

I cup a palm around her cheek, my irises burning apologetically as I search her eyes.

"You're an idiot," she mumbles, but she is still smiling, even as she drops her eyes to my chest.

"I am," I growl, "and I'm going to fix this."

She shakes her head.

"You can't," she whispers. "There's a hole in the wall. Now I'm screwed."

I squeeze her cheeks gently, silently asking her to meet my eyes.

"I'm going to fix it," I tell her. "I know someone who works in construction. By the time that your mom comes here, you'll never know that I just…" I glance at the hole in the wall and clear my throat. "…did that."

Aisling's gentle hands stroke up my pecs, nervousness creasing her brow.

This is one thing that she's been unsure about this whole summer – disappointing her parents, and therefore not getting the role that she's after in their business – and I've just goddamn added to that.

"Aisling." I drop my forehead to hers. "I love you. And I'm going to fix this."

She waits a moment before finally nodding her head.

I wrap her waist up with my arms and pick her up, carrying her to the bed.

After I drop her down on the sheets, I move over to the small pile of her fancy luggage bags and start stacking them in front of the hole.

She giggles from the bed, shaking her head at me as I

look over my shoulder at her.

Once I've covered up the little incident I heave myself down beside her on the sheets. The mattress groans loudly as I settle down, which only makes Aisling cover her face with her palms and laugh even louder.

I wrap my fists around her wrists, tugging them away from her face so that I can watch her giggle.

"Caveman," she whispers, making me flush as I smile, embarrassed.

"I'm sorry," I murmur back to her. "And I'll fix this, baby. I promise."

CHAPTER 38

Tanner

Present day

My eyes flick across to the other side of the lake, to where our friends are currently on their second haul-down from the campsite that we made part way up the mountain. We're all going to be disbanding tomorrow – with the guys who have graduated starting up training with their respective sports teams, and the guys who will be back to college in the fall heading home before school starts again – so we're having one final day soaking up the Larch Peak lakeside summer.

I keep my gaze on Aisling as her brother drops his camping gear and scoops her up, giving her a big brotherly bear hug as she laughs and shoves him off of her.

My heart swells in my chest.

My beautiful girlfriend.

I would be over there right now if I didn't have

something damn important to do here at the lake house, but I'll join them later in the afternoon, or as soon as Jace and I can get the drywall fixed.

I turn my attention back to the black truck that's just pulled up beside the porch railing, and I give Jason Coleson a jerk of my chin as he heaves himself out of the driver's side, shaking his head at me in amusement.

He's one of my dad's closest friends from the start of his military career, and even though Jace is no longer in the army he still stops by when my dad returns home from deployment.

Now he runs his own company, Coleson Construction, and seeing as he was heading to Carter Ridge today, I asked him if he could lend a hand.

"What the hell did you do, Mason?" he says as he starts making his way up the porch steps. He's got a toolbox in one hand and a decent sized piece of drywall in the other. The smirk tugging at his mouth makes me grin back at him, feeling like a kid again.

I rub my palm over the back of my head, neck burning red as I lead him inside.

"Uh, nothing," I rumble, sharing a grin with him as he chuckles. "Could use a little of your expertise though."

He huffs out a laugh and squints at me as we mount the stairs.

"You tryna flatter me?" he asks, and I hold my palms up in surrender.

"I'm being dead serious," I tell him. "I'll pay anything to get this fixed today."

We trudge across the landing, Jason following behind as I lead him down the corridor.

"One, I'm not asking for compensation," he says gruffly, stepping over the threshold as I jerk my thumb toward the affected drywall, "and two…"

He blinks down at the area a few feet away from the door, slowly tilting his head to the side as he frowns down at it.

After a long moment he glances back to me and repeats, "Uh... what'd you do?"

I breathe out a nervous laugh as he crouches in front of the dent. His eyes slide to the soft faux-fur rug beside his boot – as in, the rug which I made love to Ash on the second that we got back to Larch Peak – and after a slightly amused, slightly pained glimpse in my direction, he jokingly moves a few inches farther away from it.

I rub awkwardly at the back of my neck. Yeah, I should have thought to move that before he got here.

"Jesus, Mace," he mumbles, setting down the piece of drywall and his toolbox. He gets a measuring tape from his pocket, takes a mental note, and then finds his utility knife.

He turns to look at me over his shoulder, gesturing for me to take a look at what he's doing.

I crouch down next to him, nodding as he explains the procedure, and grateful as hell that a damage this small doesn't require a full wall upheaval.

"We're gonna replace the damaged area with a new piece of drywall," he says, "putting in a little wooden support before we slot in the new square. After we've screwed the support in, we'll use some joint compound to fill in the edges and scrape away the excess with a putty knife."

I nod. "Got it."

"Tomorrow morning you're gonna use this sanding block" – he holds it up to me – "and brush it over the area so that you're left with a smooth surface. You might need to add some more joint compound and repeat the sanding process, but it just depends. Then all that's left to do is paint the area to match the rest of the wall. You got the paint that was used in this project?"

"Yeah, Ash has it."

He glances over at me. "Who's Ash?"

"The chick who owns this house."

He stares at me for a beat. "And you put a hole through her wall?"

I wince and grip the back of my neck. "It was an accident."

Jace gives me an amused, kind of pitying look.

"She mad at you?" he asks, while he places a ruler beside the dent. He pencils a faint line to create one side of a square.

I shake my head, looking down at my locked fingers.

"Not even," I admit. "She was, like, real sweet about it. As long as I get this fixed for her I think everything'll be okay."

"Sounds like a very understanding girl," he says quietly, brow low in concentration as he finishes marking up the area.

"She's the best," I murmur, clearing my throat as I duck my head.

Jace gives my shoulder a fatherly shove and I glance up at him, pulling myself from my thoughts. Thoughts about how much Ash has grown this summer, how much trust she's put in me – and how, for the first time in four years, she's started wearing her heart on her sleeve.

Jace holds the utility knife between us and raises his brow in a question.

"You wanna do the fixing?" he offers. "I'll make sure you don't mess it up."

I breathe out a laugh and take the knife. "Trust me, I won't be doing that again."

He laughs, quiet and kind, and then we get to work on fixing the wall.

*

It's late in the afternoon by the time that Jason packs up to leave, having shown me how to fix up the wall and then offering to survey the rest of the house for before Aisling's mom comes by tomorrow.

I quickly sent off a text to Aisling to see if she'd like him to check out the house, and she immediately came over, looking beautifully sun-kissed and super shy. She settled down on one of the couches with Jace for around ten minutes before saying that, if he was happy to, she'd really appreciate him looking over her first ever renovation.

And to say that Jason was impressed, given what I told him the original state of the lake house was in when we first arrived, would be a damn understatement.

I'm so freaking proud of everything that Aisling's achieved this summer.

Afterwards, seeing as Jason runs a construction company of his own, Aisling asked for his business details so that maybe she could link up her family's company with his for her upcoming ventures.

When they finished talking, I caught a glimpse of our group heading down into the lake for one final get-together before we all leave, so I gave Aisling a gentle kiss on the temple and suggested that she head out there with everyone else, and that I'd join them as soon as Jason and I had finished up here.

We went back to check on the drywall and Jace reiterated what he'd already told me this morning – that I need to wait until tomorrow morning to paint it, and then hopefully it'll at least look dry in time for Aisling's mom's visit.

Jason drops his toolbox on the floor in front of the backseat of his truck, closing the door and then pulling open the drivers' side.

"Can't tell you how grateful I am right now," I tell him, not sure how to fully convey my gratitude. "Seriously. Thank you so fuckin' much."

"No problem," he replies, clasping my hand, and then hunching down to settle inside of his truck.

Before he closes the door he jerks his chin in the

direction of the lake, where the sounds of my teammates and my girl are filtering through the air.

"She did real good, especially for a first project. She should be proud."

I nod in agreement as he closes his door, before stepping back as his tires begin crunching over the gravel.

He rolls down his window as he slowly manoeuvres over the rocky terrain.

"Will I see you in Carter Ridge after you've finished up here?" he calls out.

A smile pulls at the corner of my mouth and I nod my head in case he can see me in his mirrors.

"Yeah, fingers crossed Ash and I will be over to see y'all in a few days," I call back to him, breathing out a laugh when he sticks his giant hand out of his window and gives me a quick thumbs-up.

I raise my hand in a saluting wave until his truck reaches the tall larch tree canopy, and then I turn around, eyes on the lake as I begin heading down the shore.

The late afternoon sun is bright and golden, reflecting off the warm water as my friends splash around in the lake. They're bellowing with laughter as they throw around a football – hockey guys on one side and football guys on another.

Hunter has Fallon on his back with her long legs wrapped around his middle, his hands holding her firmly as she reaches overhead for the ball.

And Caden has Winter's back plastered to his front, his face nuzzling into her neck, making her scream with laughter as they mess around in the middle of the fray.

Ash is the only chick splashing on her own for the ball, and I pause on the shoreline as I watch her fucking go for it.

She jumps up onto Austin's back as he tries to hide the football from her and she claws the ball into the water, jumping down from him so that she can grab it. Then she throws her arm backwards, laughing and shouting for Logan to go long before she hurtles the ball through the air, slapping her hand against the water in excitement when he catches her shot.

Regardless of the fact that they're playing football without any fucking rules, my chest swells with warmth as I watch Aisling howl with laughter.

My eyes trail down her body – semi-submerged in the water but exposed from the waist up – and I tug a hand through my hair as I take in her soaked khaki bathing suit and sparkling golden skin. Her hair is down and drenched, covering her entire back, and she grins widely as she catches the ball again, readjusting the cap that she's wearing before hauling the ball over to her brother.

It's that khaki cap that I was wearing when we first met, and watching her play with the brim that she's got on backwards as she splashes around with all of our friends is doing crazy things to my heart.

I kick off my boots and socks, dropping the pair of swim shorts in my hand down onto the dirt beside them.

Aisling's back suddenly straightens. As if she senses me, she slowly glances back at me over her shoulder.

We get lost in each other's eyes for a long, beautiful moment.

Aisling's eyes are sparkling and rimmed with the longest black lashes – even from here I can see the unbelievable contrast between the golden shade of her skin and the stunning hue of her irises.

With her eyes on mine, I rip my shirt off over my head.

She blinks quickly up at me, suddenly a little less interested in the game of football than she was ten seconds ago, and I flick open the button on my jeans before shoving the denim down my quads.

Her eyes go wide as she watches me stand on the shoreline in nothing but my boxer briefs, and I almost smirk at how nervous she looks, obviously forgetting the fact that all of the guys here are accustomed to getting naked in a locker room.

Standing out here in my underwear comes pretty natural to me.

She blinks fast, fiddling with her cap, and I hit her with a wink before grabbing my shorts and tugging them on.

I'm trudging into the lake before she's taken her eyes off my crotch.

"Hey," I say, smirking as she wades backwards, enticing me closer. I give her a once-over and murmur, "I fuckin' love this colour on you."

She turns around slightly, glancing over her shoulder and then back to me. Her teeth are biting into her bottom lip as she tries to tell me with her eyes *stop flirting with me, asshole, or everyone will see.*

My chest heaves impatiently, not exactly pleased at having to hold back with her on the most beautiful evening that's ever existed – especially when she's soaking wet and wearing an outfit that I'm pretty sure she chose for me.

I shove both of my hands through my hair, pushing it backwards, letting the clear lake water stream down my neck and chest.

I give her a subtle shake of my head, telling her that I don't want to hold back with her in front of everyone anymore – but, if that's what she wants, I'll continue going along with it.

Even if I'm not damn pleased about it.

Austin tosses the ball to Caden, who holds Winter higher in his arms so that she can reach for it, and then Winter hurls it over to Fallon, who jumps as high as she can on Hunter's back, squeals, and then screams her lungs out as the momentum of the ball tips her backwards.

Hunter's forearm whips around behind him, steadying Fallon from a fall, before re-locking his palms around her thighs and hauling her back into place.

"You good?" he pants gruffly, turning his head slightly

to check on her. She wraps her arms around his throat, practically burying his face in her rack, and Hunter grunts quietly, his neck turning crimson.

"I'm good," Fallon whispers back to him, pressing a grateful kiss to his cheekbone.

Hunter's chest starts pumping up and down, and he just nods, no longer capable of speech.

Fallon scopes out the positions of the guys in the water and hauls the ball back to Austin, who is immediately laughing as he grabs it and shoves his elbow into Logan's gut.

I drop my eyes back down to Aisling as we wade closer to our friends. When the water finally reaches the bottom of her ribcage she lifts her chin and turns around, pulling her hair down over her shoulder.

I stumble over a rocky patch, lurching forward an extra inch as my gaze locks in on what Aisling is showing me.

Not only is her swimsuit khaki. It's also fucking *backless.*

So with her dripping hair now pulled around to her front, her entire flawless back is exposed to me. Every inch of golden skin, every dip and curve – it's all right there, wet and ready to be touched.

"Ash," I rumble quietly, hands finding her perfect waist beneath the lake's sparkling surface and squeezing her roughly as I press myself up behind her.

She slaps at one of my hands, light enough that I know she doesn't really want me to pull away.

"You're not allowed to touch me in front of everyone," she whispers, and I can't help but grin, hunching low so that my chin presses into her shoulder.

"I'm not allowed to touch my girlfriend in front of everyone?" I ask her, my voice deep and amused. "You wore a goddamn backless swimsuit for me, baby. How in the hell am I supposed to keep my hands off of you?"

She stomps on my foot and I try to restrain my smirk.

"Try."

"I am trying," I laugh.

"Try harder," she hisses, her eyes frantic as she glances over at her brother.

I give her waist another squeeze, my thumbs rubbing firmly into her lower back.

She fucking melts against me.

"Everyone here knows that I love you," I murmur to her, gently scraping my stubble back and forth over her warm, water-speckled skin.

She pouts nervously, a little frown between those perfect eyebrows.

"But they all think that I hate you," she whispers back to me. "How's it gonna look when I go back on everything that they thought they knew about me? It'll look disingenuous. They're not gonna know what to think."

I press a kiss to her cheek, keeping it chaste but pressing it hard.

"Listen to me, baby," I tell her, wrapping my arms around her waist as she shoots worried looks toward her brother and my teammates. "One, it doesn't matter what anyone thinks about you. Your opinion on your life is the only one that matters. Two, showing your real feelings is the least disingenuous thing in the world. People's thoughts and feelings change, and that's damn well okay. It's more than okay – it's growth. It's maturity. It's being true to yourself in a world where everyone is trying to impress everyone else. It's being kind to yourself – making yourself happy. And that's the most important thing of all."

I press another kiss to her cheek, loving the way that she turns in closer, wanting my touch.

"That's my priority," I murmur. "Making sure that you're happy." I rub my thumb over her gorgeous little love-heart freckle and say, "You can wear your heart on your sleeve, baby. And I'll always be here to look after it."

She looks up at me over her shoulder, meeting my eyes, and hers are so full of fear of the unknown that I almost drop my forehead to hers, wanting to show her that everything will be alright. But while she doesn't want me to be so obvious about our relationship, I just press another kiss to her shoulder, palm her hips, and then move back a step.

Like, a really fucking small step, because I don't actually want to hide this thing from anyone. But, you know – compromise.

Aisling looks down at her freckle, frowning slightly, before glancing up and suddenly meeting her brother's eyes.

Her brother's kind, knowing, smiling eyes.

He's holding the football in front of his chest and he tosses it easily over into the fray before wading over to us.

We're still next to everybody but closer to the edge. It's a little more private over here.

The sunlight pours over the lake right behind him and his smile is as warm as the rays on the water.

"Ash," he says, his eyes flicking between hers and mine. He gives her chin a little rub and says, "Ash, everybody knows."

She stares up at her brother, unblinking, and then fiddles with the brim of her cap again.

"Everybody knows what?" she breathes out, her voice sounding husky as hell, the way that it does when she's getting nervous.

I can't lie, I find it really hot, but I just bite back my smirk as her brother shoots me a knowing smile.

"Everybody knows about you and Tanner," he continues, laughing gently as Aisling's jaw drops to her chest. "It's obvious, Ash. You two are clearly crazy about each other."

I share a half-grin with Connell that has warmth spreading through my chest. Having gotten his growing seal of approval over our summer by the lake has been a blessing that I wasn't expecting but that I'm unbelievably grateful for. Has he been teasing me senseless about how down I am for Aisling over the past couple of weeks? Yeah. But I wouldn't change that for anything, knowing that we've built a solid brother's bond based on mutual trust and understanding as a result of it.

Smile creases appear beside his eyes as he grins back at me, satisfied by the fact that I'd do anything for his sister.

Aisling on the other hand? Yeah, she still hasn't grasped the fact that Connell knowing about us is a good thing.

She brings her palms to her chest, cheeks flushing as she pants.

"You heard us?" she gasps, looking absolutely mortified, and this is the part where I have to stifle a groan.

Because Connell is simply telling Ash that everyone can tell that we're into each other. That they've seen us playing around and they know that we're head over heels.

But does Aisling understand that? Nope. In fact, Aisling has immediately jumped to the worst conclusion possible.

That they must have heard us in the forest when she was on her knees in my tent.

Which, seeing as no-one mentioned it, they definitely fucking didn't.

I pinch the bridge of my nose.

God save us both.

Connell squints, laughing and looking a little confused.

I mentally face-palm the shit out of myself while trying to simultaneously transmit to Aisling: *baby, I love you, but you need to shut the fuck up, right now.*

"Heard what?" Connell chuckles, but then he blinks a couple of times and his smile drops.

His wide eyes flash to mine, jaw steeled as his irises flicker.

"Heard *what?*" he repeats darkly, biceps flexing as he cracks his knuckles.

He looks about five seconds away from breaking my jaw, so that's fucking awesome.

Because Connell may be cool with me dating his sister

but he won't be so cool with me banging her when he's barely twenty feet away from us.

I wrap both of my palms over Ash's sun-kissed shoulders, making Connell's glower flare, and I breathe out the most convincing over-confident laugh that I can muster, trying to diffuse her slip-up.

"She's kidding," I tell him, casual as fuck, even though this is probably the most tense moment that I've had all goddamn year. My dimples are fucking twitching as I try to keep my easygoing smile in place.

Ash turns around to face me, eyes still wide, because she hasn't yet realised that her brother had not, in fact, heard us fucking in the forest.

"Tanner," she breathes out, panicking like crazy. "If they know," she whispers, "then they must have heard–"

I pull my dimples tighter and grip the side of her neck. Hard.

"She's kidding," I reiterate, eyes staring pointedly into hers. I see the exact moment that she comes to her senses, her lips popping open as she breathes out a tiny *ohhhh*.

If her brother wasn't standing right behind her I would probably be chuckling right now, but seeing as he is *right fucking there* I just press a small kiss to Ash's cheek, a simple display of *yeah, this is how PG we've been keeping things, man*.

I doubt that Connell buys it but, seeing as the alternative is to realise that I've been making love to his sister while we've all been staying at Larch Peak, Connell breathes out a deep sigh, rolling his shoulders back as he gives Aisling a nod.

His eyes slide to mine, not exactly pleased, but he gives me a nod too before clasping a hand over my shoulder.

I try not to wince as I meet his eyes, feeling a little guilty but hoping that he won't hold it against me.

"We good?" I ask him, my voice deep and gravelly.

He nods. Thank fuck. "We're good," he says in agreement. Then he gives me a brief half smile, before squishing one of Aisling's cheeks to make her giggle.

Then he rejoins the game and I breathe out a shaky exhale.

That wasn't so bad.

Could've gone worse.

When he's just out of earshot Winter, Caden's pink-haired girlfriend, sidles up beside Aisling.

She whispers in her soft Kentucky twang, "Yikes, girl. That was close."

A burst of laughter ripples out of both of them and then Aisling is burying her face in her hands, giggling her little tush off.

She peeks at me over her shoulder with her big bright eyes and I shake my head at her, amusement tugging at my mouth.

"Not funny," I tell her, even though now I'm smiling too. And the second that she wraps her arms around my neck, in front of fucking everyone, I'm full-on grinning because she's just made me the happiest guy in the world.

Showing everyone who's close to us that we're officially together.

Showing them that she's moved past our history – and that her future is all mine.

Heat and happiness spreads through my chest, making it swell in size as I bend to nuzzle my face in her neck.

"My beautiful girlfriend," I murmur to her, making her giggle harder, her water-slicked chest shaking against mine.

I keep my hands just above her waist and over the lake's surface for her brother's sake, but Ash doesn't follow the same rules, leaving only one hand wrapped around the back of my neck. Her other hand reaches down between our bodies and grips the thick ridge of my cock, making me grunt like an animal as my shaft grows harder and heavier.

Even worse than that, I'm really goddamn tall, meaning that I have to drag us deeper into the lake otherwise everyone is going to see what she just did to me.

From the wolf-whistles and cheering going on over to our right, I can tell that the guys must have all noticed that Aisling and I are finally officially making this thing public.

But whether I'm in a lake full of our friends or not, I only have eyes for Aisling.

She's everything to me.

I walk backwards, the scorching early-evening sun beating down on the breadth of my shoulders, and I drag Ash in front of me, hauling her deeper into the lake, all of our friends far off behind her now.

Aisling's not a total shortie but she's petite compared to me, so once we reach a spot that's deep enough to cover the large tent of my erection I haul her up by her thighs, not wanting her to struggle if the water gets any deeper for her.

I continue walking backwards, enjoying the way that the sunlight behind my back is bringing out all of the sugary sparkles in her stunning irises. I turn three-sixty, giving her a little spin, and she laughs gently as I stroke my palms over her thighs.

"Mmm," I murmur against her neck, "you smell so sweet. You're like my own personal little cobbler."

She squeezes her arms tighter around my shoulders, giggling quietly.

"Alright, that's enough!" Connell calls over to us, his tone tough but I can tell that there's no real malice in it. "Get your asses over here! Ash, we're losing without you."

Aisling glances over her shoulder, shooting her brother her perfect smile.

"Shock," she calls out to him, flicking her hair over her back.

Connell jabs his thick pointer finger in my direction and I nod at him in understanding, giving him an easy smile because I've definitely pushed my luck with him enough today.

Aisling turns back around to me and before I can smile down at her she's grabbing my face and kissing the life out of me.

My chest swells on a deep inhale, and I grunt into her mouth, almost stumbling. My hands grip tighter around her thighs and I groan in anguish as she parts her lips for me.

"You tryna get me murdered?" I rasp against her, before moving back in and taking her lips once more. And yeah, crowd or not, I can't help but slide my tongue inside, my cock suddenly so long and heavy that it's practically scraping against the floor of the lake.

"Goddamn," I pant, flicking her tongue with the tip of mine. "Ash, baby – we need to fucking stop."

Devious as hell, Ash pulls back with an innocent smile. She slips her thighs from around my middle and splashes down into the water, giggling as she pulls me back toward our friends.

My brain is so fried that I don't register one thing that the guys say to me.

It takes around ten minutes before I'm fully conscious again and, as soon as I am, I'm pulling Aisling more firmly into my arms, not caring that I'm stealing her from the game.

"So this hasn't been, like, a total disaster," she laughs, smiling up at me as I press hard kisses against her forehead.

"What hasn't?" I ask her.

"Like, letting everyone know," she says. "Wearing my heart on my sleeve," she adds quietly.

"Yeah?" I ask, grinning at her realisation, and grateful that our friends have been so solid about our relationship's hard-launch.

She nods, eyes on the large muscles of my chest, before they suddenly slide over to my right, to where Caden is loving on his girlfriend.

She makes a thoughtful hum, her eyes trailing over his body.

"He has so much ink," she whispers, taking in the tattoos on his forearms and thigh.

I glance over at Caden, those inked arms wrapped tight around Winter's waist.

"Yeah," I say, absentmindedly wrapping Aisling's hair around my fist. "He gets them for her."

Aisling's eyes shoot up to mine, her eyebrows raised in intrigue.

"He gets them *for* her?" she asks huskily, her breathing suddenly a little shallow.

I look down and meet her eyes, a half-grin tugging at the corner of my mouth.

"Yeah," I tell her. "You like that?"

She looks quickly away from me, one hand reaching up to play with her cap.

"I mean... well... I hadn't really thought about it before," she whispers quickly, eyes flicking to my arms and my chest – big, tan, and with a fuck-tonne of surface area to ink.

I smirk and yank her hips against mine, dropping my forehead to hers so that no-one else can see her turned-the-hell-on expression.

"Want me to get some ink for you?" I murmur, but she frantically shakes her head, cheeks getting warmer and more pink by the second.

"I love your body," she whispers. "You don't need to do that for me. I mean, if... if *you* want to... because with or without it I would, you know... I love everything about your body so..."

I don't think that my ego has ever been this goddamn big. I smirk like a motherfucker as I dip my hand beneath the lake's surface, groping her ass.

"I can get some ink for you," I tell her and she does a full-body shiver. Grinning, I add, "This year we had to talk Caden down from getting his nipple pierced."

Aisling's eyes flash to mine before she lifts her palms to my pecs, giving them a gentle massage, and breathing out a little *oooh*.

A chuckle rumbles through my chest as I rub her hips.

"Obviously, that'd be a fucking terrible idea with the amount of full-body clashing hockey players do," I tell her, but, with the innocent, intrigued look that she's now giving me, I suddenly understand how hell-for-leather Caden was about wanting one when he was thinking that maybe Winter would be into it.

I mean, if Aisling asked me to get it done then maybe…?

"But if you had a barbell then I would only be able to lick it, not bite it," she whispers suddenly, "so maybe… maybe yes to a tattoo, but no to a piercing."

I cup my palms around her face, bringing us nose to nose.

"You are a very smart woman," I rumble, crushing my mouth straight down on hers.

She giggles against my mouth and I hold her tighter, my heart fit to burst.

CHAPTER 39

Aisling

Present day

I scoop my hair up in the palms of my hands, tying it tightly into a high ponytail. Tanner stands behind me, leaning against the bathroom wall in the lake house with his large forearms folded across his chest. His eyes are on mine even when mine aren't on his.

I give my hair another tug, tightening it in the band, and then I turn to face him, resting my palms on the counter behind me.

He immediately closes the small space between us, resting one hand on my hip and using the other to entwine his fingers with mine.

"You've got this," he tells me, his voice a quiet rumble.

I stroke my free palm over the broad muscles of his chest, closing my fingers around the unbuttoned collar of his shirt and giving him a little tug, wanting him closer.

431

"Yeah," I breathe out, even though I can't deny that I'm a little nervous.

And Tanner can tell.

Tanner releases my hand from his so that he can cup both of his palms around my cheeks, tilting my face upwards before pressing a slow kiss to my lips.

I woke up this morning to the sound of quiet brushstrokes. I wrapped the thick emerald quilt over my chest as I sat up on one elbow, fluffing my hair as I peeked down from the bed.

Tanner had gotten up at the crack of dawn to paint over the area that he had fixed with his dad's friend Jason Coleson yesterday – and to the delight of the happy butterflies in my chest Tanner was wearing nothing but his jeans. He heard the hitch in my breathing and turned to look at me over his shoulder, his tan back muscles flexing as he grinned, and then hunched back down to finish painting the drywall.

Now, with my mom less than five minutes away, Tanner is no longer shirtless or wearing his country boy jeans.

He was almost shy when he had told me this morning that he'd brought some of his clothes back with us from when we left his parents' house the other day, and then he went on to cautiously show me that he'd taken one of his white shirts and a pair of navy suit pants that he had often had to wear when the Carter Ridge Rangers played hockey games at other Division I colleges.

He also reiterated that he would give me and my mom some space if I wasn't ready to introduce him yet, but I could tell from the frantic bounce in his knees as he sat on the edge of the bed that he really wanted me to have him with me.

So now he's towering over me at the bathroom counter, wearing a pristine white shirt that can barely contain his giant biceps, and deep navy suit pants that accentuate the thick muscles of his thighs.

His hair is pushed back to expose the perfect golden skin of his forehead, and his large palms are sliding down my throat, squeezing me gently as his gaze rakes me up and down.

Today I've opted to wear my long baby pink sundress with the halter neck and flirty skirt – partially because it's the kind of pretty and demure outfit that I think is appropriate to wear in front of my mom after two months of not seeing her, and partially because it drives Tanner wild.

I tilt my head to the side, making my ponytail swish back and forth behind me, as Tanner pushes his hard body up against mine. His chest rises and falls rapidly as his fingers toy with the little button at the back of my neck.

"You look beautiful," he says quietly, his eyes meeting mine.

"Thank you," I whisper back to him. "You look so hot my mom is probably going to have a crush on you."

He presses our foreheads together, chuckling quietly as his palms move down to massage my waist.

We stay like that for a few moments, the only sounds Tanner's handsome laughter and my light quick-paced breathing, the rustle of the larch tree leaves filtering in through the small window on this quiet overcast day.

In the darkness of the intimate bathroom – just Tanner and me and the beautiful black tiles shining on the walls around us – I let my breathing slow, feeling his calmness radiate into me, and I soak up this quiet secret moment as I wait for the sound of my mom's tires to appear outside.

He presses another kiss to my cheek and says in his deep voice, "Baby, let's go downstairs."

I nod up at him and let him take my hand, leading the way.

My mom has been slowly making her way over to Larch Peak over the past two months, checking in on all of the family's properties on route, like a sort of multimillionaire road trip because she prefers to travel by car rather than plane. Not because she's afraid of flying, which she isn't, but because she hates how detrimental air travel is for the welfare of the Earth.

So she prefers to drive her two-hundred-thousand dollar eco sedan instead.

I glance around the open-plan areas of the lake house's bottom floor, checking that everything looks perfect for before she arrives. Tanner wraps me up in his arms when I finally hop down from the last step, crushing kisses over my cheeks and making me giggle into distraction.

"I love you," he murmurs, taking my wrist in his fist, and tugging me behind him over to the front door.

He opens it up, letting me step out onto the porch first, and then he places his hands over my hips, his large chest rising and falling steadily behind my ponytail as I nervously twiddle with my fingers, eyes on the dirt road between the trees.

The sleek front of my mom's car gleams into view and, even though it wasn't built for off-roading, it glides effortlessly along the head of the lake. It has as much grace and speed as a multi-million dollar race car.

I quickly smooth a hand down my swishing ponytail, feeling my nerves spike as the car pulls up right in front of the porch.

Tanner breathes out a quiet laugh.

"Jesus, baby," he murmurs, the hint of a grin tugging at his mouth. "Is your mom in the F1 or something?"

I give him a scowly little look and he smiles wider, palms caressing my hips.

"You've got this," he reiterates quietly, just as the drivers' side of my mom's car opens.

In a way, my mom looks very much like me, only she's a little taller and with brighter hair – hers taking on a more auburn and traditionally Irish colouring.

She closes the door of her car with a little pat and then

she brings both of her hands to her chest, letting out a happy burst of laughter as she sees me offer her an excited but nervous wave.

"Aisling!" she exclaims, her bright green eyes roaming all across the newly reconstructed porch – Tanner's incredible handiwork.

I set up two matching wooden lounge chairs out the front and there's a soft garden couch in the back, under the weather-protecting safety of the overhanging roof, which means that it now looks so cosy and homely – the perfect place to sit back and watch the lake.

My mom half-jogs up the porch steps, her delicate fingers trailing over the railing as she ascends, and then as soon as she's in front of us she's opening up her arms for me, squealing with laughter as we embrace.

"Oh, Aisling, this already looks incredible!" she says, and I breathe out a quick relieved exhale, the anxiety in my stomach halving as her mood tells me everything that I needed to know: that this project isn't a disaster, and there is every chance that she might decide that the business can expand into small town house-flipping, rather than being solely focused on million-dollar residential construction.

I pull back from her arms, admiring her long green skirt and matching long-sleeved shirt. Subtle rather than ostentatious – an admirable rarity for someone who's earned more money than they could ever need.

"Mom," I say, moving back a step so that I can stand beside Tanner. I peek up at him under my lashes and his cheeks are burning the most adorable shade of red. His jaw muscle rolls as he glances quickly between my mom and me.

His hand settles on my lower back, his nerves evident from the subtle shake in his forearm.

My heart clenches tight.

He is absolutely adorable.

"Mom, this is Tanner," I say, my husky voice even

lighter than usual, lifted by my gentle laughter as I squeeze my body against Tanner's muscular side.

"He's my boyfriend," I breathe out, my eyes sparkling as Tanner pushes a hand through his hair.

His broad chest swells with pride.

"And Tanner, this is my mom, Aoife," I tell him, unable to look away from him as his eyes move to hers, his biceps flexing as he extends his hand.

"Ma'am," he says, his voice gravelly and deep. His large shoulders are set steel-straight, the effect of his military upbringing, but he gives her a tiny hint of his handsome smile and those gorgeous dimples. "It's a pleasure to meet you," he rasps, his hand all but swallowing hers as he gives her a firm but deliberately-trying-to-be-gentle handshake.

My mom slides a slightly wry glance my way, the smile she can't fight back telling me, *Aisling, you did good.*

I roll my eyes, smiling back at her.

"No, no," she says, eyes lifting back to Tanner's. "The pleasure's all mine."

I laugh out loud at that one, and Tanner flashes me a nervous look, not getting her little joke.

I place my hand over his warm abdomen, comforting and reassuring him as I return my attention back to my mom.

"So I've done a full reno – inside and outside," I tell her, deciding to just rip the Band-Aid when it comes to bringing up business.

There's no point being tentative about it. I'm wearing my heart on my sleeve from now on.

"I can give you, like, a whole tour of the place if you want, or – if you'd rather – you're totally free to look around on your own."

I bite my lip as she peeks over my shoulder, glancing inside.

"It's fully repaired and fully furnished," I add, stepping out of her way as she lingers on the threshold.

She turns her confident gaze back to mine and, with a kind smile, she says, "It looks beautiful, Aisling. Want to give me the tour?"

So that's what we do for almost a full hour – me taking her from room to room, explaining the changes that I made and how I've utilised the space to turn a rundown lake house into something so gorgeous and cosy.

From the way that she keeps on smiling at me I can tell that she knows I've fallen in love with the place – meaning that, if she thinks that it *is* up to standard and they can sell or rent it out, I guess I might be, like, a little bit heartbroken when I have to say goodbye to it.

By the time that we're back downstairs we take up a seat on the plush dark sofa, my eyes flicking out of the front window to where Tanner is sat on the top porch step, eyes on his palms as he patiently waits for me to finish my pitch. His large shoulders are slightly hunched, his breathing steady as he keeps his head down, although I can still see the slight bounce to his right leg, his biggest tell when it comes to him being excited and full of anticipation.

Well, maybe his second biggest tell.

The huge bouquet that he bought for my mom is sat in a glass vase in the centre of the coffee table – the rarest lilac roses interspersed with tiny Irish clovers.

I swallow quietly and blink back to my mom, my palms face-up on my lap as I pour my business heart out to her.

Telling her why house-flipping, especially with hidden gems like this inconspicuous small town lake house, will be beneficial to the business alongside their larger scale builds. How renovating a place like this completely aligns with their eco ethos, as well as bringing life back to these beautiful places, without in any way changing their original small town charm. New condos can look so out of place in the country, whereas house-flipping reinstates the true rustic beauty in a place like this.

By the time that I'm finished, Tanner is glancing at me

over his shoulder, watching me through the large lake house window. His fingers are leashed together and he gives me a confident nod of his head – telling me that, no matter what, this dream was worth going for.

My eyes meet my mom's and as soon as I see her gorgeous smile happy tears are immediately flowing down my cheeks.

I bury my face in my hands, shoulders shaking with emotion as she laughs gently and places a reassuring palm on my shoulder.

"It's perfect, Aisling," she tells me. "Of course you've got the job."

CHAPTER 40

Tanner

One week later

I grip my fist tighter around the wheel as the Polaris lurches up the incline, mud shooting up on either side of the cage as I push the vehicle harder, getting us to the top of the mound.

The tall forest trees around the mud trail are dense and emerald green, canopying over the UTV as I get us into position for a messy slide down.

And for an off-road track that's thick with wet dirt and slippery as hell, we're going *fast*.

"Tanner!" Aisling squeals, laughing as she squeezes her hands around one of my biceps.

She's wearing a mudding wetsuit that I bought just after we picked the UTV from the rental, meaning that she's in a dirt-covered black thermal, topped with a pair of khaki waterproof overalls. Her rain boots are packed with fresh brown mud, because the vehicle is open-sided and the track couldn't be more slick if we'd wanted it to be.

I flash her a grin as I begin tipping the front of the UTV over the mud mound, removing one hand from the wheel so that I can give her mud-splattered thigh a rough squeeze.

"You ready?" I ask her, knowing that her answer is going to be simultaneously a yes and a no.

Regardless of how I felt about the contents of Aisling's summer bucket list, I hadn't forgotten about the final point on her checklist.

One of the first things that she said to me at the start of this summer was the fact that, once she and Fallon had finished up on her lake house renovation, she wanted to go mudding – an adrenaline rush that would also work to blow off some steam.

But I know that it was also on her list for a few other reasons.

One, because being raised as a city girl means that Aisling never had these country experiences, and her heart has been beating for the small town life for as long as she knew it existed.

And two, I'm pretty sure that this summer was secretly Aisling's way of ripping off the Band-Aid and facing a fuck-tonne of her fears.

She might not be scared of driving but as soon as she scooched into the UTV I could tell that she was feeling tentative. I mean, who the hell wouldn't be? Mudding is goddamn reckless, not to mention dangerous. But from the resolute set to her pretty brow I knew that this experience was about conquering a fear, exposing herself to a situation and then coming out of the other side better for it.

That being said, we were less than three minutes into her tearing up the dirt before she was half-laughing, half-whimpering, and begging for me to take over. Which, I can't deny, was probably the biggest honour of my life – Ash trusting me so fucking much that she was happy to put her life in my hands during something like this.

So now I'm handling the wheel and Ash is free to take in the thrill of the ride, feeling the heavy pull of the tires through the wet dirt as we race up and down over every slope of the dense terrain.

She nods her head at me, her bright eyes sparkling behind the headgear, and I grin as I nudge the top of my helmet against hers, closing my eyes for a moment and soaking up the feeling of how grateful I am.

She giggles and gives my biceps a rough squeeze, and after flashing her another grin I get us racing down the mud mound.

The dirt flies past the cage, wheels going hard as we jerk over the terrain, and I keep my eyes focused on the steering as Aisling squeals with laughter and delight. We hit the bottom of the slope, the UTV bouncing as I propel us forward even faster, and the air – scented like a downpour waiting to happen – lashes like a whip through the open windshield, wheels ploughing the dirt as we race toward a turn.

I keep the pace fast and the moves smooth, laser focused on the turn because I want to impress Aisling's sexy little panties off. We whip the turn with barely any over-steering and Ash giggles with happiness as we hit a long stretch of straight forest – just us, the dirt track, and the thick trees canopying us overhead.

Since there are no more turns on this stretch, I move my right hand down to her thigh, squeezing her hungrily over the overalls. In the next second she's leaning over to cuddle up to me, breasts pressed against my biceps as I keep us flying down the track.

"You good?" I ask gruffly, my hand inching higher.

It's only us on the dirt track right now and it would take at least ten minutes for anyone else to reach us, so we're safe to get handsy under the dark shelter of the green trees.

"So good," she sighs, one of her own palms caressing

over my abdomen.

I steel my jaw and try not to get too excited as I keep the vehicle bouncing fast over the undulating peaks and valleys.

We gun the trail until we reach another turn, and then I pull up the UTV, wanting a moment to just be with my girl.

I unfasten my helmet and pull off my gloves, dropping them down to the dirt-soaked interior. Then I get my hands on the headgear that Aisling is wearing and ease it carefully over her beautiful face.

She blinks fast when she's free of the helmet, those long black lashes so dark and intense against the incredible brightness of her stunning irises.

She pulls out her hair-tie to free her bouncy ponytail and I immediately scoop it back up, winding it around my fist.

I wrap it until it's tight and then I give it a little tug, helping her climb up over onto my lap and settling back in my seat as she straddles me. I palm my free hand over her behind, massaging it gently as I dip down to kiss her.

"Hey, baby," I murmur, my heart warm and full as she digs her fingers into the sides of my neck.

"Hey," she whispers back to me, the little mud flecks on her cheeks making me grin because they remind me of her love-heart freckle.

I fist her hair tighter around my hand and kiss her again, longer and deeper. Her hands slide over the large swells of my chest and she grinds her lap against mine, whimpering in gratitude.

Gratitude because she knows that I'm kind of distracting her right now.

Because even though she's so excited to officially have the green-light from her parents when it comes to starting up the beginning of a house-flipping section of the company, she's been more than a little sad about the prospect of letting the lake house go.

Maybe it's because she's had her sights set on the house ever since she first saw it in her parents' folder of acquisitions.

Maybe it's because it's the first flip that she ever did.

Or maybe it's because it's the place where she allowed herself to fall in love, and the thought of having someone else living there, whether it's as a rental or as a permanent thing, feels like letting someone take a little piece of her heart.

Whatever the reason, she's had mixed feelings about her mom saying that the lake house is so perfect that they can immediately put it up on the market. Even more so seeing as this morning her mom told her that a buyer put an offer in, matching their asking price.

And with that information she knows that it's about to sell.

With a sum like that, it's an offer that they won't refuse.

So I'm distracting her. First with the mudding, now with my mouth on hers. I keep her hips grinding back and forth with my palm enveloping her ass, quickening her momentum as I deepen the kiss.

"I love you," I rumble, gripping her hair harder as she rides me.

She drops her forehead against my heaving chest, arms around my neck as we move our bodies together.

We've been staying at the lake house this whole past week and, even though it was bittersweet seeing all of our friends leave on the morning that her mom was arriving, it's been the best part of the summer so far. Just Aisling and me, taking it slow for once.

Making out while I hold her in the lake, with the sun warming the muscles of my back and my shoulders. Slow-hiking through the forest beyond the back porch, and then piggy-backing her down the hill, just to make her laugh. Having my hands massaging her waist as we stand on her balcony after midnight, murmuring the names of the constellations in her ear while she giggles and pretends not to care.

Fucking her in every room of the house, and having no-one in those cabins to stop me.

And fucking her outside of the house too, because the couch on the back porch – enveloped by the larch forest beyond – has turned out to be the perfect place to run to when the summer rain hits and we can't fumble fast enough for the house keys.

So instead we jump the steps, race to the back, and then I'm bunching her dress around her waist, shoving down my pants, and pushing slowly inside of her. Murmuring how much I love her with every rough thrust.

She'll be officially starting work for her parents – partially remotely – in the next couple of weeks. I'll be beginning my official training for Larch Peak's NHL season.

The only thing left is for us to find a place to live.

After we take the UTV back to the rental point and change back into our jeans and shirts, I grab her by the hips before she can get onto the passenger seat, crushing my mouth down on hers as I shove her up against the side of my car.

She giggles and slaps at my chest, pulling back with flushed cheeks as she quickly checks that the guys who own the UTVs aren't looking.

"They can't see you behind my shoulders," I tell her, hunching back down so that I can kiss her again.

I rub my palms over her muddy cheeks and she laughs uncontrollably as I move one hand down so that I can grip and spank her ass.

"Tanner," she laughs, hiding her face in the warm crook of my neck.

"I need you," I murmur back to her, laughing with her as she play-fights me off of her.

She turns around in my arms and I all but shove her under the roof and into the passenger seat, not releasing her from my arms until she's squealing with giddy fear.

When she's finally sitting upright in her seat I grip her chin and meet her big sparkling eyes with mine.

"You had a good time?" I ask her, wanting her to have had a fucking amazing time on the mud tracks with me.

She nods up at me, her cheeks dimpling as I rub my thumb up her jaw.

"Yeah," she whispers, grinning happily as I nudge our foreheads together.

"Think you might want us to come back here? Come mudding again?" I ask.

She nods again, whispers another, "Yeah."

I slide my hand down to her throat, giving her a gentle squeeze.

"Good girl," I rumble. "Now I've got something to show you."

I close up her door and make my way to the drivers' side, hunching in and punching the G-wagon to life, the wheels gliding on the road like my hockey blades on the ice, the feeling so damn smooth after our session on the dirt track.

"What are you going to show me?" she asks, eyes flicking between my face and the road ahead.

I swipe my tongue over my lower lip, trying to gauge the best way to say this.

"I, uh…" I clear my throat and gently squeeze her thigh. "I found a house," I tell her.

The air leaves her lungs in a quiet rush and I feel her gaze on my face as I keep my eyes on the road.

"Here?" she asks gently. Her voice is a little nervous. To Aisling, there's no property that could compare to the one she just renovated. "Here in Larch Peak?"

"Yeah, here in Larch Peak," I reply, giving her knee a firm rub before replacing my hand on the wheel. We cruise around the bend, Aisling's eyes on me the whole time.

I feel my cheeks heat up, nervous for her reaction.

"Have you… have you bought it already?" she asks

breathlessly, her voice a little surprised.

"No," I rasp, my shoulders swelling as I shift on the seat. "No way. You know I want your seal of approval before I buy it."

"I'll obviously pay half–" she begins to say, but I grip my right hand around her cheeks, making her laugh as I shut her up.

She might be a multi-million dollar heiress but that doesn't mean that I'm not about to spoil the shit out of her.

"Baby, you know what my entry level contract salary is," I rumble, moving my hand to the nape of her neck before resettling it on her thigh. "You won't be paying for shit. It's the rules."

"The rules of what?" she says, smiling despite her little eye roll.

"The rules of being a guy who is head-over-heels in love."

Her breathing catches in her throat and I lock my fingers through hers, squeezing tight.

"You're my dream girl, Ash," I tell her, "and I want to treat you right. Please let me."

She releases a shaky exhale. After a quiet moment she whispers, "Okay."

A smile tugs at the corner of my mouth and, seeing as the road is pretty much empty, I glance down to meet her eyes.

"I love you so much," I tell her, chuckling quietly as she reaches up to press a cute kiss to the smile crease in my cheek. "Now I need you to close your eyes so that you can have the full impact of seeing this house for the first time. Hands over your eyes, baby – no peeking."

I can tell that she's still feeling a little sad but she nods her head as she places her hands over her eyes.

I glance down at her a few times to check that she really isn't peeking, and then I do a U-turn on the road, heading back from the climb we were just making on the mountain.

I'm not sure if she feels it but, if she does, she doesn't say anything. She just breathes gently in and out, like she's calming herself down from her inner turmoil.

It takes barely ten minutes until we're where we need to be, and then the G-wagon is crunching slowly over the gravel, undulating gently side to side.

She swallows quietly beside me, a tinkle of nervous laughter rising up her throat.

"You're not taking me back to the UTV place are you?" she says teasingly. "Like, I enjoyed mudding – sure – but I don't want to live in the Polaris."

I breathe out a laugh, rounding the gentle curve and then pulling to a stop.

"Open your eyes, baby," I tell her.

With slightly shaking fingers she moves her hands to her lap.

It takes all but one second for her to burst into tears.

Needles prick at the back of my eyes as I take in the depth of her emotion, her shoulders shaking violently as she tries to swipe her cascading tears from her cheeks, and I immediately yank the seatbelt from over my lap so that I can move closer to her, tucking her under my arm.

She buries her face in my neck and I stroke my palms down her hair, pressing hard kisses against her forehead as her body shakes with the intensity of her tears.

She pulls back after a moment, her eyes sparkling as she looks up into mine.

"You bought the lake house?" she whispers, her voice cracking and full of hope.

I brush my thumb over her cheruby cheek, stroking away her tears as I hold her against me.

"Yeah, baby," I tell her. "If you're okay with it, I'm buying the lake house."

She drops her forehead against my chest, sobbing uncontrollably as I try to console her. I laugh gently as she shakes her head, mumbling embarrassed apologies over her crying.

I just hold her tighter, letting her get it all out.

We listen to the lake lapping against the shore, soft and peaceful, as her tears subside.

Then she's wrapping her arms around my neck and kissing me, and a smile tugs at my mouth as I bring her over the centre console, settling her down over my lap.

"You're the buyer who matched the asking price?" she whispers, her chest pumping quickly against my own.

I glance down at her body, held flush against mine, and I shove a hand through my hair as my cock grows heavier under her lap.

"Yeah," I rumble. "I matched the asking price."

"That's a lot of money," she breathes out.

I press a rough kiss against her lips. "I would have paid triple that for you. I'll do anything to make you happy."

She wheezes out a laugh, looking all loved-up and lightheaded as I hold her more firmly against my abdomen.

"Is this okay?" I ask, jerking my chin at her. "Us living here? Us living in the lake house?"

"Yeah," she breathes out. Then she gives me a naughty smile and says, "*Our* lake house."

I grin down at her, laughing as she lunges up to kiss me.

"I love you so much," she whispers, arms around my neck as I nudge our foreheads together.

"I love you so much, too," I rumble, kissing at her cheeks as she starts squeezing at my biceps. They flex and swell under her touch, making her giggle as I tug my shirt off over my head.

"Never believed I could be this lucky in my life – this blessed," I rasp, ducking down to kiss her again, and smirking when she *ooooh*s over how big all of my muscles are.

She clutches herself tighter against me, all signs of her tears officially gone.

She's beaming. My happy, sparkling, beautiful girl.

"Is it everything that you ever imagined?" she whispers, smiling contentedly up at me.

I grin back down at her and cup her perfect face in the palms of my hands.

"It's better, baby," I murmur back to her. "It's better than my wildest dreams."

EPILOGUE

Tanner

Four months later

I keep my eyes on the off-road path that leads from the trees' canopy to the head of the lake, waiting in the quiet winter afternoon for Aisling's car to appear. My knee bounces up and down, navy suit pants stretching tight over my quads, as my fingers clutch the wrapper around the base of the bouquet.

I glance down at the pretty arrangement – the flowers all silver, white, and a soft shade of lilac – and my knee bounces a little harder when I see the label tucked in between the stems.

"Winter Dream".

As soon as the florist told me the name, I knew that I had to get them for Aisling.

Because Aisling is my dream girl, in every season.

We've had just over two weeks away from each other,

with Aisling finishing up her second official house-flip and me playing a bunch of away games that were too far for Aisling to get to while she was on the home-stretch of her project. So I'm more than a little excited to finally get her home again and wrapped up in my arms.

There was also something that I'd been meaning to do for Aisling since we first got together this summer, but I had to wait a little longer than I wanted to. I couldn't do it once I'd started training, let alone when I started actually playing official games, but now I have a decent number of days off over the Christmas to New Year's stretch so it's the perfect time to do that thing that I'd been secretly planning in the summer.

The sound of tires crunching over snow makes my head snap straight to the clearing, and then I'm shooting up to my feet, chest swelling as my heart pumps wildly.

I can only just see her through her windshield as she rounds the head of the lake, but even that hint of her through the glass is enough to make the air whoosh out of my lungs.

Mine.

Finally mine.

Aisling and I both decided to head back to our Larch Peak lake house today, so that we could spend a few days as just the two of us before heading over to see my family and then hers for the holidays.

And yeah, I can't deny it – we turned our drives home into a race. I mean, I was way closer so she didn't stand a chance, and I also set off way before she did, specifically so that I could get everything perfect for when she arrived. I got dinner prepared and cooked, set some romantic candles on the table, and even managed to wrap up all of her Christmas gifts without fear of her peeking.

My wrapping skills are a little rough around the edges but I tried damn hard to make everything as pretty for her as possible.

I keep hold of the bouquet with one hand and shove the other one through my hair, grinning with untamed relief as her car pulls up next to the porch, right beside mine.

I'm racing down the steps two at a time before she's even put her car in park, pulling open her door at the same moment that she unleashes her seatbelt.

She practically squeals as she smiles up at me, her eyes all sparkly because she loves it when I wear a suit.

I grin right back at her, holding out my free hand to help her down from the vehicle, and then I'm heaving her up by her little ass, chuckling against her neck as she squeezes her arms around my shoulders.

"Hi," she squeaks, giggling like crazy as I kiss her cheeks.

"Hi, baby," I murmur back to her, before leaning down to kiss her lips.

She yelps excitedly as I give her a spank, and then I help her shut the car door and begin walking us up the porch steps.

"For you," I tell her, handing her the large bouquet.

Her cheeks flush a soft pink and she smiles shyly before taking them, cuddling the flowers against her chest.

"Thank you," she whispers, her voice sugary-sweet.

I brush a kiss against her temple, carrying her over the threshold and then locking up behind us.

Because right now, there's nowhere else that we need to be.

I set her gently down to her feet, both of us kicking off our shoes, before I lead her to the kitchen and I water a vase for her to set her flowers in.

She eyes the foil-topped dessert tray resting in the centre of the table and slides her gaze up to mine, a smug smile playing on her lips.

"I wonder what that could be," she says teasingly, squealing when I yank her into my arms.

"Yeah, yeah," I mumble, smiling back at her but still

flushing crimson.

She wriggles out of my arms enough to lean over the table, flicking the edge of the foil so that she can take a peek underneath it.

Her eyebrows lift in surprise.

"Wait," she breathes out, compassion colouring her tone. She raises her eyes back to mine, biting into the beautiful smile on her lips. "That isn't... that isn't the cobbler that you order in. That's..."

I swallow hard and nod my head. My neck is warm as fuck.

"Tanner!" she squeals. "Did you... make us a cobbler? Like, from scratch?"

I tug at the collar of my shirt, eyes searching hers to gauge her reaction.

After a long moment of blushing the hardest I ever have in my whole life I manage to quietly rumble out a, "...Yeah."

"Oh my God, you're the sweetest ever!" she exclaims, her eyes alight with happiness. And then I'm grinning right back at her, relieved as hell over her reaction, because I like doing cute stuff for her even though I'm always a little nervous in the build up.

"Your first homemade cobbler," she whispers, a teasing smile on her beautiful mouth.

But as soon as my eyes flick down to her lips I'm no longer thinking about the homemade cobbler. I'm thinking about how I've had two weeks without my girlfriend sleeping in my arms. I'm thinking about the way her hands are gripping my shirt and the way my quad is slipping between her thighs.

I'm thinking about how there are lots of other things that I can do for Aisling to show her how much I love her.

And she's thinking the same thing too.

She yanks me forward by my tie, I grip firmly at the back of her neck, and then I'm groaning loudly into her mouth as I kiss the goddamn life out of her.

She giggles excitedly as I walk her backward to the couch, my mouth only leaving hers while I get to work on ripping off her shirt. Soon she's left in nothing but her underwear, kneeling up on the sofa while I tower over her.

"I missed you so much," I rumble, tugging off my tie as she pushes her body up against me. I toss it to the side and rip open a couple of my shirt buttons, needing the expansion room as my chest begins heaving in anticipation.

Then I'm easing her onto her back and settling down between her thighs, one hand rummaging in my pocket for a condom as she drags her nails through the sides of my hair – freshly faded, just the way she likes it.

"I missed you too. I've been watching every game," she whispers up to me.

My heart feels as though it could fucking burst.

I breathe out a laugh and rumble quietly, "I know, baby. We've been FaceTiming after each one of them."

"But you've been so busy," she counters breathlessly, little palms squeezing my biceps. "I wasn't sure if you'd, like, remember."

I press a firm kiss to her lips.

"Of course I remember. You're the highlight of every game."

Her gorgeous smile turns into a full-on grin and she laughs with nervous excitement as we both shuck my pants down my quads. I grab the condom, roll it on, and then I'm pushing myself inside of her, massaging the nape of her neck as she arches back and moans.

"I needed this so much," she whispers, her arms wrapped tight around my broad shoulders.

I grunt and thrust deeper, too turned on to speak.

I roll my hips between her thighs, harder and faster until she's whimpering, and then I shove my suit jacket off my back, my biceps too swollen to be contained any longer.

"I love you," I rasp, as I grip a hold of her hips,

pumping her quick and rough so that I can get her over the finish line.

She smothers another whimper in my neck, clutching me as tight as she can as she finishes.

The second that she's done I push her thighs backwards, thrusting deeper.

"I'll never get enough of you," I rumble, grunting breathlessly against the curve of her neck.

I hold her protectively against my chest, hips jerking roughly as I finish, and then I'm hunching down to kiss her mouth, murmuring how much I love her.

We eat our homemade dinner and dessert – my first attempt at making Aisling a cobbler from scratch earning me a crazy sexy make-out session at the table – and then we move back to the couch, unable to take our hands off of each other.

And that target sheet from the summer, from when I took Aisling to the range? The sheet that I shot three times to make the perfect shape of a love heart?

Yeah, Aisling retrieved it for us, and it's now in pride of place on our living room wall.

I have the most thoughtful girlfriend in the world.

Aisling's palms lovingly squeeze my biceps and I pull back to cup her face in my hands.

"I've got something to show you," I tell her, grinning down at her as she starts to giggle.

"No! No presents until Christmas!" she squeals, her little dimples twinkling up at me as I tickle her into the cushions.

"This one has to be before Christmas, baby," I say, smirking as she wiggles around.

She bites her perfect white teeth into her lower lip, smiling up at me curiously as I tower over her.

"Okay," she whispers, eyes sparkling as I pull us into a sitting position.

I spread my quads wide as Aisling settles herself on top of me, her beautiful smile enough to make me almost forget what I was about to show her.

I swallow hard, suddenly nervous about what she'll think – but I quickly drop my eyes to my shirt, bringing up my shaking hands to begin unbuttoning it.

"Let me," she says, those gorgeous eyes burning into mine.

I glance down at her, still cautious, but then I nod and drop my hands down to caress her soft thighs. I massage her gently as her fingers work their way down the buttons.

I grunt quietly when she finishes unbuttoning it, and she tentatively begins pushing the cotton off of my shoulders.

Breathing hard, I take her wrists, and I keep my eyes on hers as I kiss her knuckles. Then I settle her hands in my lap, taking over so that she can have the full effect.

She bites into her little smile, eyes wild as she watches me.

"What did you do?" she whispers, giggling when I can't resist giving her another kiss.

I swipe my tongue over my bottom lip, shucking the shirt down my biceps as I watch her reaction. I'm so nervous that my chest is pumping like crazy, but I try not to blush too hard as I finally toss the shirt to the side of the couch.

My shaking hands encase her hips and I wait for her to see it.

Her eyes find it immediately and then they're straight back up to mine.

In the next moment her arms are wrapped like a vise around my neck, as she squeals and reaches up to cover my face in kisses.

I grunt, squeezing her thighs, and I kiss her back, trying to gauge her reaction.

"You like it?" I ask her gruffly, hoping to God that she does.

Tears cascade down her cheeks as she strokes her palms up my jaw.

I clear my throat, overcome by her sudden show of emotion. "Ash, baby, you're crying."

"Happy tears," she whispers up to me.

"Happy tears or not – don't want you crying over me."

She reaches up to kiss me again and I hunch down to meet her in the middle, practically growling in relief as her hands caress gently down my forearms.

After a moment she pulls back and I watch her in wonder as she holds her arm out next to mine.

Her little love-heart freckle that I love so much sits tiny and perfect, just below her elbow.

And now, in the same place on mine, is a small dark piece of script – the only tattoo that I'll ever need.

Her name.

Aisling.

She drops her forehead to my chest for a moment, her shoulders shaking as she tries to compose herself.

The heat pumping out of my chest is enough to make us both get a little lightheaded, so I leash a hand through her hair, tugging her head back so that I can look at her.

"You got a tattoo for me," she whispers, holding still as I brush the tears off her pink cheeks.

"Yeah," I murmur, laughing quietly when she gives me her little smile. "So we match."

She shakes her head, tears still falling even as she giggles, and she strokes her fingers reverently beneath the tattoo wrap banded over the ink.

"I love it," she whispers.

"I love you," I whisper back to her.

"I was… always so scared of wearing my heart on my sleeve," she says, eyes wide and sparkling as they look up into mine. My own eyes sting with tears but I blink them back, my hands wrapped tight around her waist as I hold her preciously against me. "Tanner, I love you so much," she whispers. "I'm so grateful that you never gave up on me."

I nudge my forehead against hers and clutch her tighter.

"I would've waited for you forever," I tell her, and she suddenly giggles, snuggling up closer to me.

"And now everyone knows that you're mine," she teases, biting into her smile as I grin back at her.

"Hell yeah," I breathe out, loving that she's branded on me forever.

"So is that why you got my name instead of a heart?" she asks, her voice happy as she strokes my forearm. Looking at her name on my skin. A name I'll be in love with forever. "So that everyone knows that you belong to me?"

I smirk down at her, gently brushing my thumb over her dimple.

Prettiest girl.

"That's one reason," I murmur.

"So what's the other?"

I cup her beautiful face in my palms, leaning down so that I can kiss her. Moving my lips gently over hers. Another way of telling her that I love her.

I nudge her little nose with the tip of mine, holding her closer as she smiles up at me.

"Because you *are* my heart, Aisling," I murmur, laughing gently as we kiss. "And now I'll always have my heart on my sleeve, too."

ABOUT THE AUTHOR

Sapphire is a writer who specializes in New Adult and contemporary romance stories. She has a First Class Honours Bachelor of Arts degree from Durham University and a Master of Philosophy degree from Cambridge University.

She loves love.

You can find out more about the author on her website: www.sapphireauthor.com

For more updates, Sapphire can be found on TikTok and Instagram: @sapphiresbookshelf

P.S…

Thank you to every reader who has ever sent me a wonderful message, comment, bookish edit, review and DM! Your kind words mean more to me than you will ever know.
Love always,
Sapphire

Printed in Great Britain
by Amazon